# Two for Holding

## Minor Penalties, Book One

### S.B. Barnes

NineStar Press

A NineStar Press Publication

www.ninestarpress.com

# Two for Holding

eBook ISBN: 978-1-64890-901-6

Print, ISBN: 978-1-64890-923-8

Cover Art © 2025 Tuisku Hiltunen

Edited by Elizabetta McKay

Published in October 2025 by NineStar Press, New Mexico, USA.

CONTENT WARNING: This book contains sexually explicit content, which may only be suitable for mature readers. Depictions of homophobia and transphobia, including internalized homophobia; strong language; POV character struggling with low self-esteem and anxiety.

# Contents

# Prologue

Kayleigh: Hi everyone, I'm Kayleigh, your San Francisco Sea Lions media gal, and I'm here in the Sea Lions' home base, Cyberian Arena, with the team's newest addition, Jaxon Grant! Jax, how does it feel to be on the West Coast?

Jaxon: Um, good, yeah. Different. Less humid than in Philly.

Kayleigh: [leans in toward the camera] So, Jax—I can call you Jax, right?

Jaxon: Yeah, of course.

Kayleigh: Your trade came as a bit of a surprise, and so close to preseason. Can you tell us what brought you here?

Jaxon: [laughs] Uh. Good question. Honestly, if I could answer it, I might not be here.

## Top comments:

sealions4lyfe: I know we had an offensive gap but…this guy? Really? He's good, but does that make up for his personality?

Jefferson Howard: In my day, hockey players played hockey instead of dyeing their hair and buying designer watches.

(Video posted in The Rookery, the direct-to-consumer streaming service of the San Francisco Sea Lions and all associated teams, on 09/18/2024)

Joining a new team was always nerve-wracking.

The last time Jax had to do it, he'd been drafted third overall by the Philadelphia Magpies and had already gone through development and rookie camps. He'd earned his place. At the time, he was also eighteen and making more money playing hockey than his parents' house had cost. He might have been slightly overconfident.

Now, Jax knew he was exactly the right amount of confident. He had six years in the NHL under his belt as well as the Calder his rookie year and an Art Ross two years ago. Any team would be lucky to have him.

As he walked into the San Francisco Sea Lions' locker room for the first time at the tail end of training camp, he kept his shoulders back and his chin up, projecting all the confidence he could muster. No one had seen his trade coming, least of all Jax, and he'd missed all the team bonding events to start the season, but he was used to coming in as the underdog. He could make this work for him. He *would* make this work for him.

With that in mind, he strolled up to Tom Crowler, team captain, absolute beast on the ice and averaging comfortably over a point per game for the last decade. "Hi. Nice to meet you. Tom, right? I'm Jax, I'll be—"

"I know who you are," Crowler said.

"Um. Okay. So—"

"They're probably going to give you an *A*. Phil can tell you what you need to know about your responsibilities." Crowler waved vaguely in the direction of Phil "East" Easton, the only other person who'd been on the team as long as him.

Then, Crowler got up and walked out of the locker room.

Jax stared at his retreating back. Had he said something wrong? Accidentally worn a Magpies jersey out of habit? He looked down at himself. No, there was the stupid Sea Lions logo, a stylized swirl of lines only vaguely reminiscent of a real animal.

"Don't worry about it." A man roughly twice as broad as most humans came up to Jax and slapped him on the back, hard enough he had to brace for impact. "Captain's always like that."

"Seriously?"

"I'd been on the team for a month before he talked to me. I wasn't even sure he knew my name." The man smiled toothily. "Chris, by the way. Chris Calabrese. But everyone calls me Breezy."

Right, a junior defenseman who'd gotten more and more minutes toward the end of last season and a lot of buzz in the press.

"Nice to meet you," Jax said.

"You too, man. Excited to have you. We need some more young guys around here, you know? It's just me and the rookies." Breezy nodded over at two other guys in his corner of the locker room, both staring down at their phones.

Did no one in this locker room talk to one another? Chat?

"Sounds awesome," Jax said weakly. Then he rallied. He'd make it work here. He would make himself integral to the team so he wouldn't have the rug pulled out from under him with another goddamn trade. "What do y'all do for fun?"

Breezy made an odd face as if no one had ever spoken the word "fun" in the locker room before. "We don't really do much as a team. But, hey, we should totally change it up!"

They absolutely should. They would be spending the next seven to ten months sharing a locker room and a charter plane and a team bus. What did they do, sit quietly next to one another, not talking? Jax wouldn't survive for ten minutes, let alone eighty-two hockey games.

Breezy could definitely see his trepidation. "Here, come meet East. He'll tell you everything you need to know."

Twice now, someone had referred him to Easton for guidance, though he wasn't the captain of this team. As Breezy led him across the locker room, Jax peeked out through the door. On the fresh, empty ice, Crowler drew circles around and around, all by himself, skating faster and faster as he went.

He was so good. Why was he so alone?

# One

Tom: Person on the team most likely to be in bed by nine? Oh, that's, uh, probably me, to be honest. Not much of a partier. What's next? Person on the team who's worst at video games. I'm gonna have to say me again. Person on the team with the least-cool ride— Kayleigh, are these all just me?

**Top comments:**

bethanyjones: I went to high school with Tom Crowler. Yes, he is exactly that boring.

SFCLions: watching Tom talk about how he goes to bed at nine makes me want to lick him all over and then tuck him in.

(From "San Francisco Sea Lions Call Each Other Out For Fun," posted to YouTube 10/15/2024)

It was four in the morning, and Tom was awake.

His hip twinged again. It wouldn't stop no matter how many stretches he did and arnica compresses he used. He had a fool's hope that rotating it the right way for long enough would make everything click into place the way it ought to, so he hadn't brought the issue up with the trainers yet. As he lay awake in bed examining the play of shadows across the ceiling as lone cars passed through Edmonton's otherwise dead nightlife, Tom had to admit that he was, in fact, a fool, and the hope was probably for nothing.

With a groan, he leveraged himself out of the too-soft hotel bed and down the hall to the ice machine. He probably wouldn't get back to sleep anytime soon, but he might as well do something productive about the hip. He'd be spending hours cramped in an airplane seat to San Francisco soon enough.

He was limping back up the corridor when he heard it: the telltale sound of a door clicking open and the whoosh of someone leaving their room.

Assigned as captain ten years ago at all of twenty-two years old, Tom had been touted as one of the most promising players the NHL had seen in years. With three ninety-point-plus seasons behind him and no history of significant injury, everyone thought he'd be the one to take the Bay Area's brand-new expansion team all the way when they drafted him. It was a lot of pressure for a guy whose most pressing worries included helmet acne and whether he'd be able to grow a playoff beard.

One of the first lessons Tom learned as captain was to keep his nose firmly out of his teammates' business when it came to extracurricular activities. He did not need to know who had cheated on their wife, who had crossed the very shaky line between acceptable and unacceptable drug use, and who had a penchant for waifish, potentially underage prostitutes. When the inevitable press conference about the divorce or the lawsuit came, he wanted to be able to say, as honestly as possible, that he'd had no idea and was as shocked as everyone else.

What compelled him to turn and look this time was anyone's guess.

In a series of events not unlike bearing witness to a particularly heinous traffic accident, Tom noticed three things in quick succession.

First, the room number. He'd handed the keycard for 2247 to Jaxon Grant some twelve hours prior.

Second, the person exiting. A dark-haired, dark-eyed man in his mid-to-late twenties in gray sweatpants and a rumpled number 16 Grant jersey (not even a navy-and-sage San Francisco Sea Lions jersey, but one of the old, hideously orange Philadelphia ones) slipped through the door. He wore the shirt knotted at the waist the way Tom had seen some guys' girlfriends wear them.

Third, Jaxon Grant. He stood in the doorway, shirtless, his blond hair tousled, with his hand on the other man's bare hip.

Tom turned tail and explicitly did not run back to his hotel room. He did walk fast enough to make his hip twinge more than it already did.

He didn't think about what he'd seen while he lay in bed with ice slowly melting on his hip through a fluffy white hotel towel, concentrating instead on going over last night's penalty kill. Maybe they could experiment with switching out Phil Easton for Chris Calabrese. Calabrese might have been younger and less experienced, but Phil had been struggling with his knees this season.

Tom didn't think about it while he did a half hour of stretching on the scratchy carpet to the dulcet sound of CNN. He had a policy of not watching any sports broadcasting before 6:00 a.m. to establish some sort of work-life balance.

He definitely didn't think about it when he read the text from his mom.

Mom: *Good game last night, sweetheart! I hope you keep winning!*

*It was a little too close for comfort,* he typed in response and then deleted it. She wouldn't care that Edmonton almost had them when they'd equalized in the third, and only Jax Grant on a breakaway had saved them from overtime. No wonder Jax had gone out to celebrate, leading to— But no, Tom wasn't thinking about it.

*We can't win every game,* he tried next. On consideration, it seemed unnecessarily defeatist for the third game of the season.

Finally, he settled on *Thanks, Mom.*

Tom kept up his streak of not thinking about it during breakfast. At seven sharp, none of his teammates joined him, because he'd been one of the only ones who hadn't gone out last night. Tom debated sitting with the coaching staff, but he wasn't *that* old yet. Although he supposed the new head coach, Morris, had barely ten years on Tom. He carried an air of exhaustion about him that spoke of having been around the block which made him seem older. And he brought his own homemade salads to work like a real adult. Tom still lived in the high-rise apartment right by the practice rink he'd bought with his first big contract, and while technically capable of cooking, he was in no way organized enough to do meal prep. He had no idea what he'd talk to Morris about over breakfast. Morris had a wildly different life than Tom's despite seeing him every day; up until this season, Morris had worked in the Utah college hockey circuit, which was why no one in the show had ever heard of him until the GM gave him the head coach gig. Tom didn't know anything about life outside the NHL and couldn't make small talk about much else. He doubted the man would appreciate his thoughts on the penalty kill before having his morning coffee.

Instead, Tom loitered around the buffet, pretending to decide between turkey sausage and turkey bacon for a good five minutes before Phil showed up.

"Up at dawn again, old man?" Phil asked jovially, reaching for the sausages and drowning them in maple syrup.

"You're one to talk." Tom loaded up on bacon and reconstituted egg scramble, which was both soggy and crumbly and tasted of wet cardboard. Protein-laden cardboard.

They both stopped by the cereal station for bowls piled high with Greek yogurt, oats, and raisins before finding a table close, but not too close, to the coaches.

"Have fun with the rookies last night?" Tom asked.

Phil groaned. "I went to bed at ten. Left them out there to experience the bright lights of Edmonton all by themselves."

"Phil."

"I know, I know."

"The *A* is for alt—"

"Fuck's sake, Tom." Phil thrust out his stupidly expensive watch. "It is 7:08 a.m. Do not tell me about the responsibility of being an alternate captain. So the rookies might have gotten a little wasted. We're in fucking Alberta. What's the worst they could do here?"

"I don't know, crystal meth?"

Phil gave him an unimpressed look. "Breezy seem like the kind of guy who could get a dealer at the drop of a hat?"

Chris Calabrese, a twenty-two-year-old defenseman, absolutely didn't seem like that kind of guy, and the rookies tended to follow his lead.

"You know they always let loose in Canada," Tom said. "They're all legal to drink here."

"Jax was there. It's fine."

"Jax was there," Tom repeated to himself darkly. As if his presence meant anything.

Sure, Jax had an *A* as well, but more as a PR move than a statement about his role in the team dynamics. Tom had to admit Jax could make the team look good; Kayleigh Williams from the media staff practically salivated the minute the call came in from the general manager about Jax joining the team. Having a personable, friendly guy would be a blessing for postgame media segments, even if he spoke a little too openly with reporters if you asked Tom (which no one had).

Tom was awful at media.

Kayleigh, the bubbly, friendly sort of person who actually enjoyed making phone calls and using social media, never told him so. But the longer she worked with them, the less well she hid her beleaguered sighs every time Tom clammed up when someone pointed a camera in his direction.

But PR gold or not, the *A* hadn't only been given to Jax for the team's sake. He wasn't a responsible senior member of the leadership group, and based on his media personality and the way he always seemed to be wearing the most expensive designer clothes he could get his hands on, Tom doubted he ever would be. Breezy might worship the ground Jax walked on, but who knew what Jax might talk the rookies into? Rumor had it Philly dropped him like a hot potato because of all his partying. San Francisco's general manager invited Tom to a special meeting to explain that a shiny new letter on Jax's chest would "rehabilitate his image," as if at some point on the six-hour flight from one coast to another, he'd turned over a new leaf and become responsible, making him fit to wear the letter.

No one needed the rookies to get into whatever he did in his wild, crazy parties.

Unbidden, the image of Jax standing in the doorway of his hotel room, with his sweats slung low on his hips and his hair a mess, paraded across the forefront of Tom's mind.

Phil flicked at Tom's forehead, drawing him back to the here and now. "You've got to get over your problem with him."

Tom coughed up half his orange juice. "I don't have a problem with him."

"Uh-huh. You just never talk to him outside of practice, and you only hang out with the other guys when he won't be there. Not super captain-y of you, man."

Wincing internally, Tom admitted, "I didn't think anyone noticed."

"He definitely did."

Great. Now, Tom had to start spending time with Jax *and* make it seem as if he'd never seen what he'd seen last night. What a nightmare.

"I promise he's a nice guy."

Tom rolled his eyes. "Phil, you think everyone is nice. You think *journalists* are nice."

Phil shrugged, unrepentant, digging into his yogurt. "Most people are nice."

"To you, maybe."

The glare Phil shot his way cowed Tom, and he ate his own yogurt in silence. Journalists, especially, were frequently not very nice to Phil, and it had nothing to do with his defending.

"I'll talk to him," Tom allowed when they'd both finished eating.

As it transpired, Tom was saved from having to interact with Jax by virtue of him not showing up to breakfast. That tracked. Based on what Tom saw, he hadn't gotten to sleep until after four, and the team bus left for the airport at nine. Kilian Howard and Diego Lunes, the two youngest players on the team at nineteen and twenty, respectively, made it by eight thirty. Breezy stumbled in at eight forty-five, bleary-eyed and wearing a backward baseball cap (the universal uniform of the hockey player too vain to cut his hair close and too hungover to put any effort into it). Tom, who had already been to his room to grab his luggage and check he hadn't forgotten anything, waited patiently in the lobby for the rest of the team and watched Breezy shovel down whole wheat toast and eggs like a man on a mission. At least he was sticking to the diet plan. One could only hope he wouldn't be regurgitating it all over the bus.

When the clock ticked over to eight fifty and then eight fifty-five with no sign of Jax, Tom grabbed a banana and a bran muffin for the road from the buffet table and got on the team bus. Everyone else was accounted for, and it was time to go. Jax could grab a commercial flight home if he couldn't respect the team's time.

Jax lurched onto the bus at eight fifty-nine and thirty-two seconds. He'd clearly rolled out of bed and straight into track pants and a backward T-shirt. Parts of his hair stood straight up, making the platinum strands dyed into it even more obvious than usual.

Breezy wolf-whistled and started a slow clap, which got Howard and Lunes going immediately.

Jax shot Breezy a lazy salute. "Breezy, my man."

Thinking himself safely out of sight line, Tom rolled his eyes.

"Something funny?" Jax slid into the seat next to Tom.

It took effort, but Tom didn't flinch. "I don't tend to think of Breezy as a man. More like an overgrown puppy."

"Mm. He does give good dog eyes."

Tom shivered. Jax's voice was pitched low and easy, seductive. "Sounds dirty."

"I'm not fucking him."

Tom whipped around so fast he smacked his hand on the window. "What?!" he hissed.

"I'm not. I know what you saw last night and what you must think, but I'm not slutting it up all over the league."

Slutting it up all over the league. Slutting it up. All over the league. Slutting it up. Slutting. Tom hadn't known that could be a verb. "I never said I—"

"Look, bro. I know you don't like me or whatever, but—"

"Again, I never said I didn't like you."

"Well, I guess now you have a reason not to. But if you tell anyone, if you go to the press or management or whatever, I am not fucking afraid to stand up for my rights. There's a nondiscrimination clause in—"

"Banana?"

Jax ground to a halt, staring at him, his heavy, dark eyebrows down-turned enough to show his confusion, his wide, wide mouth still open. "Um."

"Do you want a banana? Or a muffin? You missed breakfast." Tom didn't know why he offered. He'd have to eat plane food for lunch, and he hated plane food. Being an athlete with access to a charter plane hadn't miraculously fixed all the annoying parts of flying besides lack of leg room. But Jax kept talking and talking, and the words "press" and "management" in conjunction with "slutting it up all over the league" made every hair on Tom's body stand on end, and he had to make it stop.

As Jax studied him, Tom tried not to squirm under his intense, critical gaze. He was seven years older than this guy.

"I guess I'll have the muffin?"

"Great." Tom dug it out of his backpack, unwrapped the napkin around it, and handed it over.

Jax ate in silence, but every time Tom dared glance over at him, Jax's eyes remained on him. Even when he'd finished, he kept watching, so intently Tom didn't dare point out the crumb hovering at the corner of his pink lips.

Later, on the plane, Tom slid into a four-way seat next to Phil and across from Jimmy Hayes and Mike Vanderbilt, the only other two players over thirty. They played cards for half the flight, which mostly meant Tom threw whatever was at the top of his hand into the middle while trying his best not to focus on Jax, four rows down on the left, staring out the window with his big, clunky designer headphones on. With a gun to his head, Tom couldn't have said what game they were playing.

The match against Florida would take place tomorrow evening, and the only scheduled workout beforehand was a weight routine. Tom could use his home gym. He'd have more than twenty-four hours to get his head on straight, to act normal about all of this. He only had to get through the flight, the landing, the team bus, and then walk home. He could handle this. He'd learned how to wait out the minutes of a losing game without showing emotion during Juniors.

Management. The press. Slutting it up all over the league. *Management.* Why would— That didn't make any sense. Why on earth would Tom talk to management about—

As the plane dipped over the San Francisco Bay, looping around to reach the runway from the right angle, Tom's stomach sank all the way past his twingy hip into his knees and to his feet. Jax thought he'd tell people because he had a problem with it. Jax thought Tom didn't like him because he'd slept with a man. Jax thought he was a homophobe.

A panicked laugh tore its way out of his throat before he could stop it.

Phil tore his eyes away from Candy Crush to shoot a questioning raised eyebrow Tom's way.

"Just remembered something funny." Even to himself, Tom's voice sounded strange, high and tight. It must have been a tricky level though. Phil seemed satisfied.

Tom got through the remaining trip on autopilot. He could barely remember the walk home; luckily, he lived right by the rink and didn't have to drive. The minute the door closed behind him in his swanky, four-bedroom, empty apartment, Tom sank onto the floor and tried to remember how to breathe.

# Two

Kayleigh [off-screen]: Can you explain your hockey nicknames?

Breezy: Sure! So, usually it's, like, your last name and then someone adds a letter or makes it shorter. Like, we call Phil Easton "East." And my name's Calabrese, but that's pretty long, so people call me Breezy.

Jax: Also, he keeps it light and breezy! [laughs]

Kayleigh: And what about you, Jax?

Breezy: He doesn't have one. He's just Jax.

Jax: Nothing "just" about it, bro!

Breezy: Damn straight!

[Jax and Breezy fist-bump]

## Top comments:

grant16rules: guess I'm a sea lions fan now. No one keeps it real like just Jax!

clions2010: @grant16rules—You've gotta be kidding me. Keeping it real? The man is as fake as they get. Not even his hair is real. Can't believe we traded THREE draft picks for a self-impressed pretty boy

(Video posted in The Rookery, the direct-to-consumer streaming service of the San Francisco Sea Lions and all associated teams, on 10/29/2024)

Something was wrong with the captain.

Not that Jax would claim there had ever been anything especially right about Tom Crowler. Except for his hockey. His hockey was fucking beautiful.

In general, Jax thought hockey nicknames were dumb as shit, as evidenced by his being "Granite" up to his rookie year in the NHL because the last name "Grant" didn't offer up a lot of nicknames. Rock-based puns were for defensemen's nicknames, not two-way forwards. Thankfully, he'd been able to make "Jax" stick in the big leagues.

But the captain's nickname was "the Crow." And damn, if it didn't make a weird sort of sense when Jax watched him swoop in out of nowhere, all six foot three of him suddenly appearing right on top of the puck in the middle of a tricky play, snatching it out from the opposition. For such a big guy, he could skate stupidly fast, and the way he worked his angles made his footwork seem light.

If you asked Jax, Crowler had been robbed of the Calder his rookie year. No one ever had asked though; everyone who asked Jax about the Calder only wanted to know if he thought he deserved it, to which the answer was, "Yeah, actually, I did."

He'd gotten eighty-three points his rookie year. Damn good showing.

Crowler barely lost out to some Russian goalie wunderkind in 2011. Similarly, he spent the last seven or so years in the league making the top five but never quite winning the Art Ross. Two years ago, Jax beat him by three points with a sweet-as-hell hat trick in his last regular season game.

Come to think of it, maybe he did know why Crowler hated him so much.

Hate, Jax could deal with. Hate was an acceptable emotion to have toward Jax Grant, hockey superstar. Sometimes Jax hated himself too.

But whatever was wrong with Crowler became less straightforward than hatred after Edmonton. Jax knew, because he was being *nice*. Looking Jax in the eye, saying good morning. Offering fucking bananas and disappointing bran muffins.

Alarming behavior to say the least.

That night after Crowler saw his hookup, Jax hadn't slept, tossing and turning, terrified his new captain had caught him out after only a few weeks on the team. It was stupid of him to invite a guy to his hotel room; he knew as much before he did it. He'd known since the day he got traded in the first place, after his agent told him management in Philly wasn't interested in the sustained PR risk his behavior courted after Jax had gone to them about a potential scandal.

*It's one thing to have the first out player*, Matt had said on the phone.

Jax had corrected him, as always, but it didn't matter.

*Sorry, out NHL player. You know no one cares about some kid in the minor leagues though. Anyway, it's another thing to have a player who's banging a different guy in every city. Family values, you know?*

Family values—the first thing Jax associated with a league full of homophobes and racists who regularly sent one another hurtling into the boards headfirst for the entertainment of the masses. Somehow, he doubted Philly would have been thrilled to keep him even if he had managed to scrounge up a cute, family-appropriate boyfriend. The kind of guy they pointed the kiss cam at during Pride Nights. Some dude who wore a lot of plaid and parted his hair to the side and passed as straight except for when he pressed a single chaste kiss to his boyfriend's cheek.

Just imagining their fictitious relationship bored Jax to tears.

Maybe if he'd found a girlfriend, Philly would have kept him. Some girl who wouldn't mind pretending for the money. He knew there were women out there who did that kind of thing, but the thought soured his stomach too much.

So did the heavy-handed hint from his agent about toning it down on the new team. Jax had never toned down a single thing, not his style, not his sense of humor, not any aspect of being Jaxon Grant, and the league lapped it up. Sure, he wasn't out. No one was. But to be told unmistakably, albeit obliquely, to hide his sexuality made him want to throw things.

It also made him realize he'd never expected to stay *not* out forever. Jax wasn't meant for subterfuge. He was meant to be himself, loudly and unapologetically.

For the same reason, Captain Tom Crowler treating him with kid gloves instead of telling Jax what his problem was made Jax want to scream.

When the third game day of their homestead after Edmonton dawned, and Crowler smiled and nodded at him when he arrived for morning skate, Jax decided he'd had enough.

"You don't have to be nice to me," he said.

They weren't alone. Easton and Breezy ran drills with the defensive coach on the far side of the ice, but Jax *had* checked whether he'd be heard by anyone but Crowler before he spoke.

Not trusting Jax's judgment as per usual, Crowler yanked his head around to check for listeners so fast he almost tripped over his own skates. "I'm not—it's not—"

"Seriously. You don't like me; you don't like what I do in my spare time; it's fine. As long as you're not ratting me out, I can deal with it. Whatever you're trying to do now is freaking me out though."

"I'm not trying to do anything, and I'm not a homophobe. And keep your voice down."

Jax stared at him. Did he realize how ridiculous those two sentences sounded one after the other?

"If you don't want me to rat you out," Tom said, "don't rat yourself out by mentioning it in team spaces all the time."

"All right, fine." Jax could concede the point at least. "But stop with the good mornings and the—the banana shit. It's freaking me out."

"It's been brought to my attention that it's not very captainly of me to ignore you."

"You ignore everyone who hasn't been on this team a million years."

"I do not!"

Jax raised his eyebrows. "Really. When's the last time you talked to Howie? Or Mooney?"

"Mooney?"

Jax couldn't have stopped the smug smile if he tried. He loved being right. "Diego. You know, Lunes? Moon? Mooney."

"I didn't know he had a nickname yet."

"If you talked to him, you would."

Crowler gave him a long, assessing look. "Okay," he said. "So what have I missed?"

"Huh?"

"You're right. I don't talk to the rookies enough. They gave me the *C* because I get a lot of points, not because I'm great with people. You have an *A*. You're supposed to help me not fuck up."

"You saying I don't get a lot of points?"

"You don't need me to stroke your ego. You know how good you are."

A man could always stand to hear more about how good he was, but this conversation was weird enough already. "Fine. Well, Howie—that's Kilian Howard, in case you missed another nickname—he's struggling 'cause he hasn't scored a goal yet."

Ignoring Jax's potshot, Crowler frowned. "It's not even November. He has all the time in the world, and four assists."

"That's what *I* said, but what do I know. I'm just an *A*."

Crowler sighed, exasperated. "I get it, okay? I'm a shit captain. Let it go."

Jax hadn't meant to imply anything of the sort. He'd meant to make Crowler feel shitty about his treatment toward him, not about Crowler's own performance. "I don't think you're a shit captain."

"You think I hate you, I'm a homophobe, and I don't talk to rookies. Clearly, I am a shit captain."

"I *don't* think you're a ship captain—shit captain— Can we stop saying that?"

Crowler gave him another one of those coolly assessing once-overs. "All right. What *do* you think?"

"I think," Jax began, and then paused to actually think about it. "I think you're good at talking to the refs."

"What?"

"Yeah, when there's a bullshit penalty call, you're really good at keeping your temper and calling it into question. You always stand up for our guys."

"My job is to—"

"Yeah, yeah, but some captains get all angry about it. And you're great at the whole leading-by-example deal. You know, first on the ice, last off it, sticking to the meal plan, all the stuff everyone knows they should do but no one manages. Half the reason Howie's so worried is because he doesn't want to disappoint you."

Crowler's demeanor softened. The change to his face alarmed Jax in its intensity. His dark, wavy hair and blue-gray eyes, along with his long, straight nose and heavy eyebrows, could make him appear so severe and untouchable. But when he let himself smile, he became unfairly handsome. Hockey players weren't supposed to be handsome, Jax excepted.

"I'll talk to him," Crowler said. "So what about, uh, Mooney?"

By the time Jax had finished discussing Mooney's homesickness for Southern California—a little ridiculous if you asked Jax, he lived in the same damn state—they'd gotten cold standing on the ice, gabbing, and had to start running laps, which turned into racing. Going against the Crow proved a challenge, but one Jax welcomed. He loved the burn in his thighs and the pounding of his pulse more than anything. If he didn't, he'd never have been stupid enough to pursue this career path.

The rest of the team trickled in slowly. Mooney joined them for a while, but he struggled to keep up. The solid third-line winger had been promoted to second line a bit too early in Jax's opinion. He had to slow down when he centered Mooney, and it was messing with his game. He held out hope Coach Morris would see it and promote Jax to first line before he had to say something himself.

Practice went well, at least for the forwards. The offensive coach, Edwards, was pretty laid back as far as Jax could tell. Maybe he benefited from comparison; Jax's offensive coach in Philly had been a fucking psychopath who yelled "BAG SKATE" if you so much as breathed wrong. Edwards liked to do finicky passing drills and give speeches about teamwork. They only really started to sweat when Morris rotated through their section of the ice, asking for sprints and footwork drills, seemingly at random.

Even better than a solid morning on the ice, Crowler kept his word. In the locker room afterward, he sought out Howie and spoke to him, ending with a clap on the shoulder. Jax watched the interaction like a hawk, including the way Howie's eyes lit up afterward and how he held his shoulders a little straighter on the way to his stall.

But Crowler wasn't finished yet. Next, he got up on his bench and whistled for attention.

"Team barbecue," he announced. "Phil's place, Saturday before the next roadie. Bring a side. I'll get the drinks."

Breezy whistled and clapped because Breezy was a bro at heart and bros loved nothing more than a barbecue in fucking November. At least a California November was significantly more livable than a Philadelphia winter.

Jax grinned wide, thrilled at the invitation. Not because it sounded fun—it sounded excruciatingly awkward—but because he would be granted another opportunity to understand Crowler's deal. After showering and changing, he returned to the sad, pathetic hotel room the team arranged for him while he slowly considered getting his ass in gear to sell his place in Philly and buy an actual apartment.

He tossed his bag into a corner and his phone onto the scratchy, olive-green bedspread, where his lock screen (his baby sisters pulling identical faces) blinked up at him. Jax expected Breezy to make good on his threat to invite him over for video games or maybe his agent sending some new interview to make Jax seem like a totally respectable, upstanding citizen. Instead, he found the Sea Lions leadership group chat packed with messages. It had been dead silent since he'd joined the team.

*East: I did not ask to host a barbecue.*
*The Crow: I don't have the space*
*East: So move out of your bachelor pad, that place is depressing anyway*
*The Crow: Not by Saturday*
*Hayesie: why is it so important we do this saturday?*
*The Crow: Apparently I've been slacking on my captain duties*
*Hayesie: ???*
*East: bbq is a captain duty?*
*The Crow: Social stuff. Team bonding.*
*Hayesie: I have been on this team for five years bro. this is the first time you wanted to bond*

No responses followed Hayes's last message.

Jax typed out half a dozen answers, from "he's trying to prove he doesn't hate me" to "I think he's been replaced by a pod person". In the end, he sent an offer to help with drinks, which Crowler turned down immediately.

It still felt wrong. So, all Crowler needed to completely change his attitude about how he ran the team was to catch Jax sleeping with another dude? Unlikely. Or had he actually paid attention at one of those nondiscrimination seminars the NHL sometimes held as lip service to all the people who rightly called the whole sport a classist, racist, sexist, homophobic clusterfuck? He did seem to be the kind of Goody Two-shoes who would.

Which Jax wouldn't disagree with. He could fuck with a good seminar more than the next hockey player for obvious reasons. He'd met a lot of people who could do with having that brand of kool-aid poured directly into their ears and noses and mouths, like some sort of super-PC waterboarding. But Crowler hadn't given an inkling he cared about inclusivity in the month or so Jax had been here. His sudden heel-face turn the instant he found out about Jax being gay had to be fake and covering for something, and Jax planned to figure out what.

# Three

Phil [reading from a notecard]: Favorite things to do on your downtime. Oh, this should be good.

Tom: What's that supposed to mean?

Phil: Name one hobby you have that isn't hockey-related.

Tom: I, um…I…watch the news sometimes?

Phil: [looks pointedly at the camera]

Tom: Okay, at least I don't have old man hobbies.

Phil: Who are you calling old?

Tom: He goes fishing. For hours. Every couple days in the summer. It's the most boring thing I have ever done on an off day, and I don't even have hobbies.

Phil: Fishing is a sport! It's a question of endurance and patience, and it clears your mind. You should try it some time. Maybe you'd find space in there for something besides hockey plays—

Kayleigh: Okay, maybe we should move on to the next question.

**Top comments:**

sealions4lyfe: bros being bros

stickstickpuck: does anyone else get old married vibes?

magpiesmolt16: This just in: Sea Lions continue to be the NHL team most
devoid of charisma. Jax Grant must be going insane in their locker room.

(From "Get to Know the Sea Lions Leadership Team," posted on Instagram on
11/03/2024)

On the last free day before a weeklong road trip to the East Coast, Tom found
himself standing in Phil Easton's kitchen chopping bell peppers.

"You want a barbecue, you make a barbecue," Phil had said when he
left Tom with the cutting board and the peppers. Shamefully, Tom had been
banking on Phil's wife to help him pick up the slack, but according to Phil,
Camille was "in Paris or maybe New York, I don't know."

Tom did not understand their marriage.

This had been an extremely stupid idea.

As a general rule, Tom tried not to let his ego get in the way. Hard to do
when you made nine million dollars a year chasing a piece of rubber across ice
with a big stick, but he did try. In this concrete instance, he failed miserably.
Something about the way Jax had so easily slotted himself into the team, giving
out nicknames and listening to personal problems, rubbed Tom the wrong way
by highlighting all his own failings.

Tom wasn't mad about Jax doing a good job as an alternate.

He wasn't mad Jax had called him out on falling short of his responsibilities.

He was furious Jax had gotten such an accurate read on Tom after knowing
him for so short a time, and, worse, that he could do nothing but accept it and
try to do better. Which led him here, chopping peppers while Phil went out to
buy lighter fluid.

Jax arrived before Phil returned, which was the poop icing on a shit cake.

Tom pasted on a smile. "Hi, you're early. We're just getting set up."

"I know. I'm here to help."

Tom had been afraid of that. After Tom issued the invitation on Wednesday, Jax had asked several times if he could do anything or bring anything, and it brought Tom a small sliver of pleasure to turn him down each time.

Jax picked up a massive plastic container from the stoop and pushed his way inside. "I brought brownies."

"Brownies." Why did proximity to Jax turn him into an idiot who repeated things? It'd been more than a week at this point, and the words "slutting it up" still rolled around Tom's mind when his hip kept him up at night.

"Yeah, I bake. Promise they're gluten-free and low sugar."

"Sounds delicious."

"Excuse you. I am good at what I do."

"I know."

Therein lay the crux of the problem. Jax insisted on being good at everything, and he was also— Well. He had strange men coming out of his room in the middle of the night, and he thought Tom hated him because of it, not because of the stark reminder of his own inadequacy. All of it was terrible, but the worst part was Jax legitimately being good at everything, from hockey to making friends to, apparently, baking. As much as Tom wanted to hate him, he made it kind of impossible.

With no other alternatives, Tom turned tail and returned to the kitchen and his bell peppers.

Jax followed, set his brownies on the table, and leaned casually against the counter. "Really? Me being good at stuff?"

"Huh?"

"You don't like me because I'm good at baking?"

"I never said I didn't like you."

"You didn't have to. So, the baking?"

"No," Tom lied through gritted teeth.

"Is it the Calder? You definitely should have won it too."

"Ivan Abramov is the best goalie in the Atlantic Division. He deserved it."

"You're the best left wing in the Pacific *and* Central."

Tom stopped mid-cut. "I am not."

"Crow. You are. Don't bullshit me."

"It's not bullshit. I didn't win the Calder for a reason. I haven't won the Art Ross for a reason. This team hasn't won a Cup for a reason." Tom had never said as much out loud, but he found it a relief to put words to the disappointment of it all. The disappointment he had turned out to be. He rubbed his hip absentmindedly; remembering all the things he had yet to achieve in his career worsened the ache.

Jax stared at him as if he was insane. "Tom, the reason isn't you."

Tom couldn't help the disbelieving sound that scratched its way out of his throat.

"Seriously?" Jax shook his head. "You're only one player. San Francisco hasn't won a Cup because it took ten years for management to build a decent team."

"This team has been around for thirteen years." Tom would know. He'd been there for every unlucky second, barring the four weeks in February 2016 when he'd sprained his wrist and the team hadn't made the playoffs for the fourth year running. He'd stuck it out through every other strain and tear, relying on anti-inflammatories and ice baths and his own lack of a life outside of work.

"Yeah, and your offensive coach is shit, your defensive coach is a maniac, and the special teams are a mess."

"Our."

"What?"

"It's *our* offensive coach, *our* defensive coach, and *our* special teams. Aren't you here to fix all of our problems and save the team?"

"You have got to work on your self-esteem. Move over; you're really shit at this." Jax hip-checked Tom away from the cutting board, which didn't help with the achy hip situation or the self-esteem, and proceeded to chop the remaining six peppers into slices faster than Tom had managed one. Of course he could cook too.

"So, you hate me because you couldn't get a Cup without me?"

"I don't hate you."

"Strongly dislike me, then."

Tom sighed. "You make me feel deeply inadequate, all right?" He didn't have to admit his inadequacy stemmed not only from losing out on the Calder or the Art Ross or the Stanley Cup but, instead, also spanned the easy way Jax talked to people, the expertise with which he handled kitchen equipment, and the fact that he had no problem inviting men up to his hotel room.

Jax paused, glancing up from the zucchini he was decimating into precise circles. "Would it help if I let you cut the zucchini?"

"It would help if you would let it go. You're right about me being a shit captain. I'm talking to the rookies. I'm doing the barbecue. What more do you want from me?"

"I'll make you a deal. You give me an in with Easton and the other older guys, I'll help you with the rookies."

"And you'll stop saying I hate you."

"And I'll stop saying you hate me."

"Fine."

They shook on it, and then Jax explained how to chop vegetables like a one-man food processor, a skill Tom had never aspired to possess.

Tom hated to admit it, but the evening wound up being fun. The team trickled in one by one, and by five, Phil had a full house. Phil would never say it out loud, but he had the kind of dad energy that thrived on hosting low-key events; he was showing people around and getting more beers from the basement and shoving people away from the grill because they'd been doing it wrong all evening.

Breezy brought his girlfriend, a tall, slim blonde called Vanessa. She worked in interior design, and Tom asked her for tips to liven up his apartment. He didn't think he'd be investing in any of the designer furniture brands she mentioned, but an accent wall sounded tempting.

When she left to go to the bathroom, he told Breezy, "She's nice."

"You think so?" Breezy smiled brightly. He'd been on the team three years already, but he was still so eager to please. "Our parents know each other. My mom set us up."

Tom could not imagine a world in which his parents would set him up. He could not imagine a world where he would actually go on that date. "So, she's from Montreal as well?"

"Yeah, and her family's from Sicily. Which, I mean, it's not Calabria, but my mom still likes her." Breezy rolled the "r" in Calabria, a skill Tom found so momentarily distracting he didn't quite parse the idea of blonde-haired, blue-eyed Vanessa having Sicilian origins until he spotted her walking back, her sparkly beige sweater-dress catching in the light. Had he missed something about the dress code for a casual barbecue? There were at least three other women sporting similar tones of tan and light brown. The only woman wearing white was Hayesie's fiancée.

"So, Breezy, uh, Chris tells me you're Sicilian?" Tom asked.

Vanessa nodded eagerly. "Oh, yeah, my great-grandparents on my mom's side came to Canada in the thirties."

"Right." There went that particular avenue of conversation.

Except then, Vanessa opened her mouth and kept going. "Yeah, I mean, my dad has Dutch roots, I think, even further back, but the family decided to be lenient when my mom married him. It's a good thing I met Chris though. My sister's marrying a guy from Sweden!"

Tom had been aware that Breezy had an Italian last name despite being French Canadian. The knowledge had not prepared him for anything he'd heard in the last ten minutes.

At least he wasn't alone in being blindsided. Breezy had heard the word "marry" and gone as pale as a sheet.

"What about you, Cap?" Breezy asked in a tone so jovial it must have been forced. "When are you going to bring someone to one of these things? Isn't East's wife getting sick of having to make the WAG jackets?"

"Oh, Camille does those?" Tom frowned. He thought Camille had better taste. Last year, the WAGs had shown up to the playoffs in matching camo-print jackets with their partners' numbers in rhinestones.

Breezy's eyebrows shot up to his hairline, a feat only possible due to his curly hair covering half his face. "Bro."

"What?"

Jax chose the perfect moment to reappear with a hand on Tom's shoulder and a light beer shoved into one of Tom's.

Not for the first time, Tom wondered if anyone enjoyed light beer or if they accepted it as a necessary evil in order to somewhat stick to the meal plan while not sacrificing every small joy in life.

"Thanks," he said to Jax.

"No problem. And who is this lovely lady?" Jax smiled widely at Vanessa. The corners of his eyes crinkled, somehow making them appear more blue. He had dimples. It wasn't fair.

Vanessa clearly agreed because she giggled, a noise no adult woman had ever made in Tom's presence.

Unfortunately, nothing could distract Breezy from his new mission. Completely ignoring his girlfriend and how she appeared more than ready to jump ship straight to the next hockey player, he said, "Jax! You're just the guy. We gotta hook the Crow here up."

"Please don't," Tom said weakly.

"It's, like, the social contract," Breezy barreled on. "We follow your lead on the ice, so the WAGs need to follow your girl's lead off it."

Tom blinked. He had never thought his chronic lack of a date to team events was an issue, largely because he'd avoided planning and taking part in team events for a very long time. "I don't think that's what a social contract is."

"Also seems kind of sexist," Jax mused. "What if Cap had a girl but she had a real job or something? Not everyone has time to watch eighty-two hockey games a year."

Weak with relief, Tom nodded. "Right. I could meet a nurse or something. She could be working shifts. I don't think she'd want to design WAG jackets in her spare time."

Vanessa's eyes narrowed. "Are you saying I don't have a real job?"

"Uhhh…" Tom looked frantically to Breezy for help, but he appeared similarly panicked.

Jax, unperturbed, asked her, "What is it you do again?"

"I'm an interior designer. You can follow me on Insta and see all the spaces I've curated. Oh, and I do parties too. Like, it's so hard to coordinate florists and caterers and glassware, you would not *believe*."

Jax nodded. "Okay, so you have a real job. But I bet you get to set your own hours, and you're not hurting for money either."

"I guess."

He nodded, clearly satisfied he had won.

Vanessa tossed her hair over her shoulder. "I'm getting another drink." She stalked off and immediately starting whispering with another beige-clad WAG.

"Thanks for that," Breezy groaned.

"What?" Jax took a long draw of his beer. "You gotta admit she's not exactly working a nine-to-five."

"Do you know anything about the WAG ecosystem?"

Tom squinted. First "social contract," now "ecosystem." This was not what he had expected from Breezy.

Jax grinned, sleazy and wolfish. "Can't say I've ever had anyone stick around for long enough to become part of the pack."

"You gotta show some respect. Half of these women quit school to follow an NHL player across the continent, no clue when he's gonna get traded or where he's gonna end up. As soon as she commits to him, she commits to staying home and raising the kids because he's traveling half the year."

"She also commits to however many millions he's earning and the army of cleaning staff and nannies he can buy her."

Breezy smacked Jax upside of the head. "And to taking care of him if he gets his head bashed in one too many times or fucks up a joint so bad he has to stop earning millions. Anyway, when you might get uprooted any day *and* you have all the domestic responsibility, there's not much opportunity for finding your own career."

Jax looked set to argue. Tom couldn't see that going well, so he intervened.

"Vanessa is really lucky. You've put a lot of thought into understanding her."

Abruptly, Breezy blushed and stared down at his feet. "It's a big ask, y'know? My mom's a homemaker, and it didn't always make her happy. You gotta be super sure of someone if you wanna try and go the distance."

"Divorce is a thing."

Tom jabbed Jax in the side with his elbow.

"A thing I plan to avoid," Breezy says. "I need to fix this."

He wandered over to where Vanessa stood, surrounded by other women, explaining something to Vanderbilt's wife, Cheryl, with big, expressive hand gestures. On Cheryl's other side, Dmitriyev, their goalie, and Howie listened raptly. They were both ensconced on Phil's couch, sandwiched by beautiful blondes.

That boded ill.

Tom hoped none of the blondes were someone else's wife or girlfriend.

He made a mental note to talk to Howie again before he got any ideas.

Talking to Dmitriyev would be a much more daunting prospect. He'd put the conversation off until he absolutely had to address it. The language barrier alone… Tom shuddered and turned back to Jax, raising his eyebrows.

"I think you made an enemy for life, there."

Jax shrugged. "Guess you found out what I'm bad at, then."

"Women?"

"Rich women."

"You're rich."

"Yeah, well. I just don't get the whole WAG thing. It seems…I dunno, fake. How are you supposed to tell if they're doing it for the clout and the money?"

Tom frowned. He lacked the dating experience to know for sure, but he'd seen so many teammates get married and have kids, and he had to believe they were happier than he was. "I'm sure they all love their partners."

Jax squinted at him. "Spoken like a man who has never had someone suck his dick and then threaten to post pics on the internet."

The words "suck his dick" seemed to come out of Jax's mouth in slow motion, his full, full lips pursing and releasing and his pink tongue peeking out from between his teeth on the "*s*" sound.

Tom shook his head, trying to clear the image from his mind. "That happened to you?"

"Why do you think I got traded?"

"Oh." Oh, *no*. "I thought you, uh. I thought you wanted to come here."

Jax gave him a look so venomous it made Tom want to shrivel up and die. "I got drafted third overall in Philly. I had a house by the Schuylkill."

"The what?"

"The *river*, dumbass. I had at least three guys in town willing to drop everything when I texted them. I had a good thing going until…whatever. It doesn't matter. I'm here now, and I guess we have a better shot at a Cup than I ever did there."

Three guys in town. "What did you need three for?" The words left Tom's mouth before he could reconsider, and then he wanted to kick himself.

Jax raised his eyebrows and made an obscene gesture.

Tom flushed hot and turned away.

"Jeez, you don't get out much, do you? Why don't you have a girl anyway? Seems like you'd have some blonde chick you've been dating since preschool."

"Never really worked out for me."

"What?" Jax dragged out the "*a*" so long Tom found himself staring at his mouth again. "Handsome guy like you?"

Abruptly, Tom took a step back. "You wanted an in with the older guys. Come on."

He led Jax out to the patio, where they found Phil flipping steaks and muttering to no one in particular.

"Oh, there he is!" Phil cried when they arrived. "The man who forced me into hosting this shindig with no warning and can't even be asked to do the cooking."

Tom scoffed. "If I had tried, you'd have sent me inside. You never let anyone else touch the grill."

"You do it wrong."

"It's a fire pit. You put meat on it. What could I possibly do wrong?"

"Man, it's all about *timing* and *placement*. There's an art to it."

"You're avoiding going inside."

Phil pointed the tongs in his hand at Tom. "Don't say it so loud."

"What's inside?" Jax asked. "Besides what I *think* is Chamillionaire's second album, which, yikes."

"My house, my music. And inside are fifteen hockey players messing with my shit and getting crumbs in Camille's rug. She's gonna skin me alive when she sees."

Huh. It was a very ugly rug. So, Camille's taste? Actually awful, except when it came to husbands. Good to know.

Jax groaned.

"Don't mind him," Tom said. "He's learning to fear the WAGs. Speaking of, does Camille really do the WAG jackets?"

Phil nodded. "She's trying to get Allie to take over for her now Hayesie finally popped the question. Allie won't do it while she's wedding planning though."

"Isn't the wedding next year?"

"Yeah, the planning takes a good eight or nine months of work."

Jax looked over to Tom as if to say, *see? Rich women.*

"I went to your wedding," Tom said. "It took nine months to plan?"

"Yup." Phil poked a steak, deemed it finished and set it on a plate next to the grill. "Gotta book the venue and send out the save the date cards far enough in advance. Then, there's the music, the photographer, the dress shopping… It's a whole thing. This is Allie's year, man."

"Don't remind me."

The patio door slid open, and Jimmy Hayes stepped outside. He'd been Phil's defense partner for three years now, and for a six-foot-four fridge of a man, he appeared remarkably like an animal being hunted for sport.

"Cold feet?" Jax snagged the steak off the plate with a fork and bit straight into it. "Good stuff, East," he said with his mouth full.

"Nah. Just…you know. It's a lot."

As a matter of fact, Tom did not know, but he'd begun to realize he probably shouldn't advertise that. Instead, he steered the conversation away from weddings and toward the defensive coach, Trout. The mere mention of the man sufficed to get both Hayesie and Phil complaining immediately.

"Mm," Jax said, swallowing a bite of steak.

Tom watched the bob of his Adam's apple, the movement of his throat.

"Yeah, whenever we work with him," Jax continued, "I feel like I've maxed out my quad workouts for the week."

"You're telling me," Hayesie groaned. "I know we gotta practice this shit, but I swear, we were doing forechecking drills for a solid hour on Thursday, and by the time the game rolled around, I was totally out of gas."

Tom winced in sympathy. "Morris had you two on the ice for, what, twenty minutes during the game?"

"Twenty-two."

"Does he even talk to Trout? What the hell?" Jax's tone rose, sounding incensed.

Phil chuckled. "Calm down, man. You get used to it."

Jax shot Tom a pointed look.

Tom had noticed their coaching team pushing them hard but in very different directions previously. Edwards was all about finesse. If he got his way, the full team would perfect a passing drill before he moved on to the next one. Trout prioritized endurance; he was the kind of old-school guy who wanted to see his players skate until they barfed. Prior head coaches aligned more with one or the other philosophy. Morris, on the other hand, focused on the big picture, trying out different lines and special-teams constellations, sometimes seemingly at random. He usually managed to split the difference, but he'd been out sick on Thursday, and Trout had taken the run of things because Edwards never stood up to him. Now he thought of it, Tom remembered they'd worked on the forechecking drill for a long time. The forwards had rotated out regularly, but Trout had kept the same D-men in for much too long.

Food for thought.

Tom had always operated under the assumption that he'd been awarded the captaincy as a largely symbolic role. He had to be a good example for the younger guys, show up early, give it his all. Part of how he gave it his all was by respecting the coaches and the referees. Maybe he'd missed some room for him to improve things. Maybe Morris did want to hear his thoughts on the penalty kill. Tom had no idea what sorts of things he might have learned about coaching hockey in Utah, where a majority of the experience he'd told the team about when he introduced himself had taken place. Not exactly a hotbed of hockey. Perhaps he'd learned coaching other sports as well and really could bring in fresh new ideas. If Tom never asked, he'd never know. If he never offered his own expertise after years of playing on the same team throughout different coaches and front offices, how could he expect Morris to base his decisions on it?

Out of the corner of his eye, Tom studied Jax, watched as he tilted his head back and laughed at something Phil said. Before Jax had bullied his way into Tom's consciousness, he'd never considered how his own input might have an effect. Tom had been too busy shrinking down so small no one could see his failures. Maybe he could stop thinking about himself and start thinking more about the team's success.

Jax glanced over and caught Tom staring. His lips tilted up in a smile. His big, warm hand settled on Tom's shoulder. He had good hands. Deft and capable. Tom could feel his strength. It was a good quality for a hockey player to have.

"Come on, old man. You've still gotta talk to Mooney."

Tom let himself be led off again, but he shook off Jax's hand as soon as he could.

Some things weren't to be savored.

# Four

Kayleigh [off-screen]: Favorite hockey fights you've been in—go.

Hayes: Ooh, tough one. There was this time Turgenev crashed Dmitriyev in Buffalo. That was pretty good.

Kayleigh: What happened?

Hayes: Well, I dropped the gloves, obviously. Can't go after our goalie. He dropped his gloves, too, and I got him against the boards. But Jenkins—he's in Calgary, now, I think—came up too. And then East, here, joined in, and the next thing I know, the refs send both entire teams to the penalty box for five minutes while they figure out what even happened.

Kayleigh: Were you thinking of that fight, too, Phil?

Phil: I wouldn't say favorite. I don't have favorite fights. It's not really something you set out to do. I'll get in there if I have to, but I don't want to cost the team those penalty minutes, and I don't want anyone to get hurt.

## Top comments:

sealionsfan82: Glad Easton is so measured. Hockey fights are dangerous, and the incident Hayes talked about got a man in the hospital.

sealions4lyfe: @sealionsfan82—It's a contact sport. Let men be men. Easton's a pussy.

sealionsfan82: @sealions4lyfe—Have you heard of CTE? It's not the '80s anymore. Players whaling on each other isn't how you win the game

(Video posted in The Rookery, the direct-to-consumer streaming service of the San Francisco Sea Lions and all associated teams, on 11/10/2024)

Jax didn't sit next to Tom on the team bus to the airport. He also didn't try to join in the card game the old guys played on most flights. These things had to be taken slowly.

Anyway, he wasn't a huge fan of the way Tom kept jerking away from him whenever they touched or Jax mentioned anything to do with his love life. Tom might not be a homophobe in the classic, bible-thumping sense, but he wasn't exactly cool about it either.

Instead, Jax sat with Breezy and let Breezy talk his ear off about how Vanessa had forgiven him for Jax insinuating her job decorating rich people's houses made her less tough than a nurse. He did an excellent job pretending not to snort at how ridiculous he found her outrage. Sure, he might need to work on his own preconceived notions about WAGs, but he'd always been painfully aware it wasn't a life model he aspired to. Any partner of his wouldn't be welcome in the group, and that changed the way he saw them. To Breezy, a woman giving up her life to follow his career was a sacrifice, and maybe he had a point. But the same woman would never invite Jax's boyfriend, if he ever had one, along to the bridal shower or baby brunch or any one of the events they posted on Instagram.

Then again, maybe Jax, as a perpetual egoist, couldn't understand a way of life that entailed devoting your whole self to someone else's job. He just didn't think he could love a man who would be satisfied with an influencer career and coordinating outfits with twenty other people in his spare time.

Although...Jax played hockey professionally. He spent pretty much the entirety of his working hours coordinating his outfits with other guys.

The thought made him laugh, and then he had to share it with Breezy, who also chuckled.

"I never thought about it that way." Breezy turned to him, eyes wide. "I guess the WAGs really are, like, their own team, you know? Wedding season is their playoffs."

"You are going to make some woman very happy," Jax told him.

A huge smile lit up Breezy's face. "Thanks, man. Hey, you will too. You should try it sometime. I know you're all about the one-night-stand thing, but having a girlfriend is lit."

Jax smiled awkwardly, trying to formulate a response that wouldn't crush Breezy's hopes and dreams.

Thankfully, Mooney leaned over the aisle. "So, you think Vanessa's gonna be Mrs. Breezy? You know she's going dress shopping with Allie."

All the blood drained instantly from Breezy's face.

Good. He was way too young to get married.

The roadie went from south to north, so they started in Florida. On the bright side, awesome beaches; on the downside, even in November, the humidity climbed above 70 percent. Finally, a reason to be glad he didn't live on the East Coast anymore. At least the ice was decent in Sunrise. They must have paid a fortune to get an NHL-level rink installed there, and they didn't have Vegas money. The investment had paid off.

The other bright side was that they'd played a matinee game against the Wildcats—a loss. But they were 4–3–3 in the season so far, so Jax didn't worry too much; they had plenty of time to turn things around and eleven points in the standings. And it left the team with a free evening in Florida.

For the first time since Jax had joined the team, Tom agreed to go out for drinks. For the first time since Jax had joined the team, he begged off with a headache. The opportunity was too good.

No one knew shit about hockey in Florida.

Hooking up in Edmonton had been dumb as fuck. When the guy he'd matched with on an app he'd thought kept his identity reasonably anonymous showed up wearing his fucking jersey, he'd nearly called the whole thing off. He hadn't because he was drunk, horny, and still pissed about being traded for being queer. It would serve management in Philly right if he got outed after all, and everyone found out why they'd traded him.

Then Tom caught him, and Jax had a queasy moment of fear that his stupid, drunk revenge fantasy would become a reality. He still hadn't decided whether to be relieved or disappointed it hadn't.

Florida though. Florida was safe turf. Not to actually be gay, obviously. You couldn't pay Jax to live in this state, and if his agent had suggested he move here back when he was in contract talks and not just being traded with no warning, he'd have demanded some ludicrously high sum. Fifteen mil or bust. Something no team in the league could afford. Anything not to have to live in Florida while being queer. Visiting Florida as a gay man though? That shit ruled.

Jax considered going old-school, forgoing the apps, and heading out to the clubs instead. He'd packed a single pair of jeans for this road trip, anticipating very little cause to wear anything but game day suits and athleisure. Along with a tight, threadbare shirt, he could easily pass as one of many guys in a crowd out to hook up.

Of course, as soon as he'd gotten his wallet squeezed into the scant space in the back pocket of his pants and fixed his hair to appear artfully tousled in the little makeup mirror in the bathroom (Jax really had to get one of those installed whenever he finally found a place), there came a knock on the door.

He checked his watch. He'd switched out his usual Rolex for a leather band, which appeared less expensive, though it wasn't. Seemed safer for going out. Eleven thirty, too late for a casual visitor.

"Jax?" Tom asked through the door.

He was so soft-spoken for a hockey player, especially for such a tall one. He had a good three or four inches on Jax, but with the way he talked, the way he behaved, it surprised Jax every time to realize he took up so much physical space.

Jax pulled open the door. "What is it?"

"I, uh…" Tom looked him up and down slowly. "I wanted to talk to you about drills. Were you going somewhere?"

"And if I was?"

"Curfew starts in fifteen minutes."

Jax blinked. That explained why he wasn't still out getting drinks. "Tom, you are a thirty-two-year-old man."

"So?"

"So, have you never broken curfew to get laid?"

"Of course not!"

Right, of course not. Tom would never. He was so squeaky clean. Even when he got mad, his anger took the form of self-deprecation. Jax still wasn't over the revelation that Tom acted so weird around him due to his own feelings of inadequacy. This guy—with his knife-sharp jawline, his piercing eyes, his towering presence on the ice, and his aw-shucks Canadian manners off of it—felt inadequate because Jax could cut a fucking bell pepper faster than him.

It made Jax want to wrap him up in a blanket and then shake that blanket burrito until it made sense.

"You were, uh, going to get...going out to...um..."

"Go to a club and find someone to fuck, yep."

"Someone," Tom repeated.

The emphasis was weird, as if he wanted to insinuate something but didn't dare say what.

Jax rolled his eyes and pulled Tom inside his hotel room by the elbow. The door clicked shut. "A man, yes."

"Right."

Jax considered whether or not he had the patience to explain to Tom why his baffled confusion in the face of anything not entirely heterosexual was getting very old and somewhat insulting. Homophobia didn't only show itself in slurs and violence, but also in being treated like a space alien for being gay. He decided against getting into it for the sake of his sanity. A man only had so much time to spend staring at Tom Crowley's confused face before starting to think he was a little adorable. Jax didn't need the crisis *that* would cause for both of them in his life.

"Yes, I'm gay, and I like hooking up. We've been over this."

Tom appeared to digest this for a moment. Then his mouth set in a thin, stubborn line. "Well, I can't let you."

"Why? Because I might get my gay cooties all over you?"

Jax really had to stop saying purposefully outrageous things in Tom's vicinity. He just enjoyed the confused flutter of Tom's sooty eyelashes so much.

"Because it's past curfew."

"Have you ever broken a rule in your life?"

"Yes." The answer came instantaneously, Tom's voice so firmly haunted. Jax resolved never to ask.

"Okay, well, I don't want to stick around here talking about drills. I want to get laid in a place where no one will be wearing my fucking jersey."

Tom positioned himself so he blocked the door.

"You're being ridiculous."

"You're being reckless." Tom crossed his admittedly impressive arms across his admittedly very firm chest.

Jax considered the effort of getting past him. In a physical altercation, they would be pretty even. Tom was taller, sure, but Jax was broader and stronger. Tom was faster, but Jax was more wily. He could get through, but then his hair would be all fucked up again. He'd still have to get a cab to a club and get tipsy enough to have no trouble chatting someone up but not so tipsy he'd have trouble following through. Then he'd have to find a place to do it—after

Edmonton, he would never bring another man to a team hotel, and Jax was too old to be fucking in bathrooms.

It all sounded like a lot of work.

"All right, fine." He sprawled back on the bed. "Tell me about these drills."

He could hear the soft tread of Tom's feet on the carpet. "Well, I thought we could ask Morris for some more forward-heavy drills where the D-men need to stay on the ice but aren't getting totally gassed."

Jax peered up at him as he stood awkwardly at the end of the bed, hands folded together, looming like…well, like a crow.

"Sit down. You're making me nervous."

Tom eyed the chair by the table on the other side of the room.

Jax patted the bed. "Come on. I don't bite. Unless you're into that."

Tom took the chair.

Wuss.

Jax heaved himself up to a seated position, leaning against the headboard. "So, your plan is to get Morris involved but not tell him why?"

"I know it's dishonest and probably a bad idea, but I'd feel more comfortable if we could show him things are going well with what we suggested before we start criticizing the coaches, and—"

"No, no, it's good. It's sneaky. Didn't expect it from you."

Tom shrugged. The sharp points of his clavicles stood out in perfect relief against his smooth skin. "I guess I'm trying new things."

"Good look on you." Jax squirmed on the bedspread and pulled his wallet out from under his butt. It made sitting uncomfortable. While he was at it, he dug out the condoms and lube from the other pocket and tossed those on the nightstand as well.

A choking noise from the other side of the room let him know he'd gone too far.

Tom stood up again. "I should…go."

"Really? That's all you wanted to talk about?"

"I, um… Yes? No, wait. Will you help me ask Morris? Pretend it's because we want to practice working on a line?"

"Sure."

Actually, it wasn't a half-bad idea, and not only because Jax wanted to be on the first line. He *deserved* to be on the first line. Frankly, he should have been put there on day one. None of the team's other centers could hold a candle to him, and he didn't understand why the coaches hadn't done it yet.

Tom hesitated, halfway across the room. "You're not going out now, though, right?"

"What, are you gonna guard the door to make sure?" Jax rolled to his side so he could see Tom better, propped up on an elbow. "People might talk, Thomas."

Tom looked away immediately. "It's just Tom."

"You know," Jax drawled, fluttering his eyelashes lasciviously. If he wasn't getting laid, he might as well have fun in other ways. "I won't be closeted forever. Someday, I'll be out, and then everyone will wonder what you were doing in my hotel room, all alone so late at night."

Tom opened his mouth, then closed it again, and then he was gone.

Jax had to stop flirting with known homophobes. It was funny, but it was also very stupid. Long after Tom left, past the point when he should have brushed his teeth and changed out of his tight clubbing clothes, Jax remained in bed, staring at the ceiling and remembering Tom's built arms, long eyelashes, and flustered words.

He regretted the late night the following morning when he had to drag himself down to the team bus, bleary-eyed and groggy. They had an early practice in Florida before flying up to St. Louis for an evening game, and the back of Jax's neck prickled the entire time as Tom attempted unsubtly to catch his eye and remind him of the plan. When they did approach Coach Morris, Tom couldn't lift his gaze from the floor.

"You have no future in international espionage," Jax muttered to him. "Chill, would you?"

"I'm not good at this."

Tom's talents only seemed to include being handsome, being awkward, and stating the obvious. And hockey. Always hockey. *What am I going to do with him?* Jax thought fondly, then reminded himself he didn't want to do anything at all with Tom.

"Coach!" Jax pasted a brilliant smile across his face. "We wanted to ask you something."

Coach Morris peered down at his tablet, brow furrowed at a video of the penalty kill at last night's game. Fair enough. East seemed to be a solid dude with good skills on the barbecue front, but a brick wall he was not, and their goalie had been left out to dry when the Wildcats obliterated the defense.

Morris grunted in answer.

"We were thinking…" Tom started and then seemed to lose his words.

"We were thinking we want try some 3-on-3 at practice today."

Morris studied them. "Why?"

Tom opened his mouth, but nothing came out.

"Well, we lost yesterday, and we'd like not to lose today," Jax said drolly. "If we tighten up offensively…"

"The offense is not what I'm worried about right now." Morris glanced at his tablet.

Miraculously, out of nowhere, Tom came out with, "The best defense is a good offense, though, my dad always used to say."

Sensing an opening, Jax slung an arm around Tom's shoulder. "And look, between us, you've got Tom here, and you've got me. If you put us together, you won't find much better offense in the league."

Morris's mouth twisted. "I'm aware. I thought I'd keep you two separate to even out some of the deficit in the D-zone."

"True," Jax said slowly. "But you're not going to fix the D-zone by tonight, and if we know a lot of goals will go in, the best we can do is to score more ourselves."

Eyeing them speculatively, Morris said, "I guess I'll give you a shot."

Out of the corner of his eye, Jax watched Morris have a word with Trout. Trout was older, a man from whatever generation wore baseball caps with gas station brands on them and had a thick mustache but no other facial hair. He looked less than thrilled with the plans for the day's practice, but that could have just been his face.

Either way, practice went well. Jax had spent an embarrassing amount of time admiring Tom's game, so he had no trouble finding him on the ice. They got an easy four goals past Vladimir Dmitriyev, the starting goalie, and when Morris pulled him to let the backup get a chance, they scored more. The D-men took their turn in the 3-on-3, of course, but unlike the last few practices, they weren't taxed more than anyone else.

They still couldn't put up enough of a fight against Tom and Jax to stop them.

This left East in a good enough mood to start up the locker room tunes on the plane already, which was his God-given right as the only Black man on the team. Jax wished he would play something other than early-2000s club shit, but it got the people going. When the third song in a row that predated Jax's birth came on, he peered over at East, trying to figure out if he was catering to the masses or if his taste really had stalled out in 2010.

East wore a plaid button-up under his plain black suit.

Stalled out, then. Good to know.

Jax balled up his sweater, sending a silent apology to Louis Vuitton as he did it, and closed his eyes, trying to catch up on rest. But the plane was too loud, and every now and again the sound of Tom's low, reluctant laugh broke through the noise. Instead of falling asleep, Jax spent the flight imagining how his face must look.

He managed to nap at the hotel for a scant hour before the game, unbothered by thoughts of Tom, so it didn't mean anything that the idea of Tom's smile had haunted him for a half day there.

Of course, then Jax ended up walking into the arena just behind Tom and caught a glimpse of his frightened woodland creature expression when the media team tried to film him. Jax knew instantly that would be making his internal repeating loop of "Tom looking cute" moments. When had that started?

He shuddered, shaking the thought loose from his brain, and set about getting changed and warming up.

By the time the first period started, the team was pumped up and ready to go. Jax thrived on the pregame energy. Team sports, from peewee hockey to the highest available professional level, had one thing in common: when things went badly for someone, especially one of the team's big stars, it could drag everyone down. But when one or two of the guys were in a better mood than usual, they could buoy everyone up with them. Jax loved being part of what made the whole group tick.

The longer he played with the Sea Lions, the more he realized they all craved that same hype. Despite having some of the best stats in the league, Tom seemed to be under the impression that things were going badly, which made him quiet and withdrawn, making the team's communal spaces quiet as well. Between a captain with self-esteem issues and a coaching team in an identity crisis, the team's up-and-down stats ceased to be a surprise.

Good thing he was there to save the day.

And save it he did, if he did say so himself. Morris must have approved of what he'd seen at practice earlier because at the top of the second, with the score still nil-nil, he sent Jax out with Tom's line. After a period working with Mooney on his wing, it took Jax a moment to get used to top-line speeds again. But within five minutes, he and Tom were racing down the ice toward the opposing goal, the puck going tape to tape as they ducked around the opposition. The Arches backcheck sucked this season, relying too heavily on D-men who weren't as quick as the Crow. Jax shot him a neat between-the-legs pass, and all Tom had to do was tap it in from right beside the goal.

The horn blared; three sweaty guys in Sea Lion jerseys slammed into Jax and Tom.

On the bench, Morris nodded in stern approval as if this had been his idea.

They kept it up, and before the end of the period, Tom returned the favor, and Jax netted a sweet little goal over the opposing goalie's shoulder.

Jubilation filled the locker room during intermission. They were up two-nothing, which didn't mean much in hockey, but good energy in the room meant everything.

"Fuck, yeah!" East stood on the bench with the speakers in his hands, playing Nelly, which was lame as fuck, but also kind of great. "You going for the Gordie Howe, Jax?"

"I'm a lover, not a fighter," Jax said with a wink.

Next to him on the bench, Tom choked on his red Gatorade.

Jax clapped him on the shoulder. "Cap can do it."

Everyone laughed.

Tom excelled at getting out of tight corners, and if they gave out awards for legal shoulder checks, he'd win every year, but a bruiser he was not.

Of course, Breezy yelled out, "Oooh, sick burn!"

The other young guys took their cue from him and added their own chirps. Jax held his breath, waiting for their reticent, easily flustered captain to retreat into his shell. But when he looked over at Tom, he was smiling with his whole face, his eyes shining, and his nose crinkled a little with laughter.

"All right, all right, settle down. We haven't won this yet," he said. Still, the corners of his mouth remained curled up.

East ignored him and kept the party going. He turned up the music—from Nelly to 50 Cent—and shouted, "You listening, fellas? We keep it up, and we're gonna party like it's your birthday!" He hopped down off the bench. Maybe if he hadn't just been yelling at the top of his lungs, or if Trout hadn't been watching him closely, he'd have been able to hide the way he winced as he landed.

"Easton!" Coach Trout called. "That the knee?"

"I'm fine, Coach."

"You sure?"

"Yep."

Jax studied him. He seemed fine, but hockey players had been known to lie about these things. He glanced over to Tom, who watched East with concern written all over his face. God, he showed every feeling so clearly in his expression. It was truly miraculous he'd gotten this far in life.

His tells gave East away as well: he favored one leg. Jax only noticed because he watched closely as East circled the room, exchanging pats on the back and getting the guys excited.

Despite all the hype, they didn't get off to a great start in the third period. Jax took a face-off against the Arches first-line centerman and lost. It happened. Even he wasn't perfect. The guy had been talking his head off, all the usual shit guys said on the ice to get Jax off his game. But he'd ended on, "Bet you begged them on your knees to trade you to Cali, huh? Only thing your big mouth is good for."

To Jax's own annoyance, he flinched and lost the face-off.

Jax had hardly processed the puck being gone when Tom barreled into the man, gloves off.

"Tom!" he yelled, but Tom was locked in. He tried to drag Tom back by the jersey, but another one of the Arches got in on it, trying to start shit. And then the D-men made it across the ice, and East bullied his way between Tom and the opposing center, taking Tom's place in the fight. The center shoved, East hit the ice with his bad knee on an awkward angle, and that was all she wrote.

The refs finally whistled.

Jax almost laughed. Of course, the refs did nothing to penalize the initial chip. No one was miked up, so the audience couldn't hear anything, and when a tree fell in the forest, no one cared if it was a homophobic shithead. They didn't whistle when Tom did the stupid thing and dropped his gloves either. No, they waited until someone actually got injured, for maximum watchability.

East made it off the ice without a stretcher at least, supported by Tom on one side and Jax on the other. Coach Morris observed the whole thing with a thunderous expression.

"Congrats, Calabrese. You're in the first PK unit." Morris didn't bother looking at Breezy as he promoted him, watching instead as East walked down the tunnel supported by Coach Trout and a physical therapist.

"Shit," Breezy muttered. "Shit, shit."

The good vibes were going down the drain, and they were going fast. Jax tried to nudge Tom into action, but he stared down at his feet while a referee debated whether he ought to get two minutes for charging or five minutes for fighting.

Jax got up and clapped his hands together. "Come on, guys. We're up by two. All we gotta do is hold the lead for our man East! We can do it for him. Breezy, you can do it for him."

Breezy still looked a little nauseous, but he nodded. "For East."

Jax nudged their shoulders together. "Now, come on. You're on the penalty kill. Get out there."

Breezy hopped over the boards, a little shaky but gaining confidence as he went. Jax watched him for a moment before turning his attention to Tom, sitting in the penalty box. He was staring at Jax, but the second Jax caught his eye, he turned away.

Why had he dropped his gloves? He had to have known it wouldn't end well. Did he actually want the Gordie Howe hat trick? Jax studied Tom briefly, a picture of misery, not a man proud of or pleased with his accomplishment. So why had he done it? For a guy who never fought—a smart player with a two-goal lead—what could possibly make him do something so stupid? Jax thought back, tried to remember if there'd been anything special, anything noteworthy. The Arches center, now sporting a bloody nose but otherwise undeterred, grinned snidely at him across the ice and mimed a blow job.

Right. He'd been chirping Jax about his mouth. Distasteful, homophobic, and, unfortunately, not at all unusual. Jax shouldn't have let it distract him, but it was a little too close to the truth.

It still didn't explain what Tom had been thinking.

Unless… Jax checked Tom again, watching the same center with his lip curled in a sneer. Jax pursed his own lips. He didn't like that expression on Tom's face. It was made for laughter. What a shame he rarely showed it.

But why would he decide to break a career streak of no fighting because some idiot in Missouri thought Jax had blow-job lips? Jax *had* blow-job lips. In a nonwork context, he'd been known to remark on it himself.

The penalty ended. Jax vaulted over the boards with Tom and Vanderbilt. They won the face-off this time, but Jax couldn't seem to get Tom to meet his gaze, to read him the way he had before.

In the end, they won the game 2–1. A decent showing, for all they could have done more in the third to make it a real blowout. East waited for them in the locker room with his leg propped up on the bench. He gave them a lazy salute and made sure to pat Breezy on the arm for a job well done. Breezy sported a massive bruise on his thigh from a blocked puck but was so high on adrenaline he hardly seemed to notice. He wanted to celebrate the win (or more likely, his appearance on the first PK unit without choking and fucking up). Mooney and Howie were instantly down. The energy it took to play a full NHL season and party all the time… Jax was only a few years older than those three, but he could already feel it waning.

Ordinarily, he would have manned up and joined them, but processing Tom's odd behavior left him off-kilter.

"But you got a Gordie Howe!" Breezy wheedled, trying to get Tom enthused.

Tom smiled ruefully. "And I am not proud of it."

"You were awesome, Crow!" Howie said.

This was categorically not true. Jax had watched the replays on the big screens in the arena. Hockey fights were not dignified in the first place—two big, beefy guys standing on tiny little blades grabbing at all the excess cloth their gear provided. One of many reasons Jax didn't find other hockey players attractive: The shorts over pants and the dumb fighting were real boner killers.

"You guys should head out," Tom told the younger crew, kindly ignoring Howie's bald-faced lie. "You did great. Us old guys will man the hotel bar and ice Phil's knee."

It was about as close to official permission the guys would receive to get absolutely wasted on the road, especially since the schedule listed the next day as a rest day before they hit Carolina, Nashville, and then Philly. When Morris popped in to announce the coaching staff had decided to waive curfew for the night, the deal was sealed. Within minutes, Vanderbilt had picked out a bar that was "also part techno club" and sauntered out with an arm over Dmitriyev's shoulders, proclaiming he deserved free shots for his near shutout. Dmitriyev hadn't been starting goalie for long, and he'd done exceptionally well tonight, so it relieved Jax that someone was in the mood to celebrate him.

Based on the excited chitchat as Breezy, Howie, and Mooney—along with a good portion of the Scandinavian and Russian contingents on the team—followed them out, Jax had no doubt they would have an excellent night.

An hour and a half later, showered, changed, and fed, Jax dropped into place next to Hayesie at the hotel bar, giving East's leg and the spare chair it was propped up on a wide berth.

"Sneaky move from Coach, giving a curfew exemption in St. Louis," Jax said.

Hayesie snorted into his beer. Jax scanned the menu. Nothing but Budweiser products to be found, naturally. NHL players traveled a lot, but Jax had yet to find a city that screamed, "We're proud of mediocrity" as loudly as St. Louis. Still, Jax raised a hand to signal the bartender and ordered a Bud Select—about as close to water as an alcoholic drink could get. What more could a man want?

Tom was staring at him again.

"What?" Jax asked.

"You're not going out?"

"Again, St. Louis."

"What's wrong with St. Louis?"

The bartender brought over Jax's beer. He thanked her with a smile and a tip equivalent to the cost of the drink. Then he took a long sip and made a face.

"For a start, it's the home of the Anheuser-Busch brewery."

Hayesie clinked their glasses together.

"Okay, but wouldn't you rather be out with the other guys?" Tom stressed the word "out," making his meaning unmistakable.

"I don't have to go out in every city we're in."

East snorted. "Can you imagine? I think I would die before the All-Star Break if I tried."

A flush settled across Tom's cheeks, emphasizing his truly delightful cheek-bones. "I just mean...no curfew and all."

"Again, it's St. Louis."

Jax wasn't about to explain the risks he didn't feel comfortable taking. Hooking up in St. Louis, with its many country-and-western-themed bars and its dedication to the products of Anheuser-Busch, was one of them. True, the city might possess a thriving queer scene—St. Louis was a big place, after all—but he didn't feel as safe there as he did in the anonymity of a Florida club. Even if he'd been in the mood to explain the way local color affected his experience of app-based hookups and gay bars to Tom and deal with his wide-eyed confusion, Jax had no intention of outing himself in front of more teammates. Why Tom decided to mention it in this setting in the first place remained a mystery. Jax did the only thing he could to save the conversation and changed the subject.

"Anyway, how's the knee doing?"

East grimaced.

"I'm so—"

"If you apologize one more time..." East threatened Tom. "It's fine. You know I've been playing on a strain all season, and I never fully recovered the first time it tore. You can't stick a Toradol shot in a nonexistent ligament. It was bound to happen. And this way, I got to see you lose your cool for once."

Hayesie snickered. "Yeah, what was that about? No offense, Cap, but you should leave the fighting in our gloves."

Tom sank lower in his chair. "I don't know... He was saying...stupid things, and I wanted him to shut up."

East's eyebrows rose. "Jax, he said something to you, right?"

Jax wanted to make a quip about his cocksucking mouth, hiding the truth behind a joke as he had a hundred times before, but he caught sight of Tom's panicked face, eyes wide and frantic. His eyes were an odd color, a grayish blue which should have seemed cold but instead appeared deep. A man could get lost at sea in there.

His concerned expression triggered Jax's understanding. Tom worried other people would find out about Jax, and it would spread around the league that impeccable, impenetrable Tom Crowler had a queer on his team. Of course. "Not a homophobe," Jax's perfectly round left ass cheek. He might not be calling Jax names to his face, but he didn't want to be associated with his queerness either.

"Oh, you know," Jax said vaguely. "The usual bullshit about why I got traded."

Neither Hayes nor East had ever asked about his sudden appearance in San Francisco. Jax cursed himself for mentioning it and scrambled for a last-minute cover story involving a torrid affair with a fictional girl from the front office. But they continued their streak of disinterest despite having a perfect opportunity. Had hockey players always been so incurious, or was this a trait specific to the Sea Lions due to years of exposure to Tom's particular brand of never talking about anything if he could help it?

East even seemed satisfied with the nonexplanation of why Tom had chosen to fight for the first time in his career. Jax would have thought he'd know his own best friend better, but he seemed to take Tom jumping into a fight over a perceived slight to Jax, of all people, at face value. Maybe the knee was too distracting for common sense.

"Philly's coming up," Hayesie pointed out instead of asking anything pertinent about the trade. "How're you feeling about going back?"

Jax took a long draw of his shitty beer. "Pretty good," he lied.

# Five

Olivia Starling [off-screen]: Are you looking forward to seeing your old team?

Jax: Oh, yeah, it'll be great to see the guys. I'm meeting Fulls—that's Tyson Fuller, Philly's captain. We're going out for lunch before the game. Wish I could get a cheesesteak, too, but my nutrition plan says I can't.

Olivia Starling: Do you think it will be an advantage or a disadvantage, facing your old team?

Jax: Wow, you really want me to stay something stupid now, don't you?

## Top comments:

grant16rules: We miss you in Philly, Jax!

seelionssaylions: @grant16rules—Please take him back lol we will take a competent D-man and a tub of hair dye in his place

(From post-practice media availability, Sea Lions @ Magpies, posted to YouTube on 11/20/2024)

While the team flew to Carolina and the Twisters, Phil caught a commercial flight back to SFO and a waiting regiment of physical therapy. He told Tom to stop worrying; he told Tom it wasn't his fault; he told Tom he'd be rehabbing his knee and sleeping in his own comfortable bed.

Tom did not stop worrying.

It was as if Phil didn't know him at all.

He texted Phil from the team's charter plane to see if he'd made it okay. The team had sprung for business class for Phil, but the seats still wouldn't fully recline, and a six-hour flight was rough on a knee with a possible ACL tear. God, if he'd torn the ACL again, Phil would be out for at least the rest of the regular season, if not more. It could mean surgery. It could mean retirement.

Phil was only two years older than Tom. He'd hoped they would play together for a while yet.

To distract himself, Tom toggled to the text from his mom.

Mom: *What on earth did you get into a fight for? It's a good thing you still won!*

He imagined telling her about the idiot on the Arches who had made a crack about Jax getting on his knees and then shuddered. If he thought about those awful words for too long, he'd get angry all over again. Lacking an explanation for his behavior beyond white-hot rage, he responded as he always did.

*Thanks, Mom.*

In the time it took him to write to his mom, Phil gave Tom's message a thumbs-up but didn't reply otherwise.

Tom texted Camille next. She didn't even bother reading the messages.

He was debating whether he ought to text the team's physical therapist, asking to be kept in the loop, or whether that would be too much, when Jax slid into the seat beside him.

"So, Breezy's pumped, terrified, and sad he's been promoted to first D-pair."

"Sad?"

"Well, yeah, it means East is out."

Tom swallowed heavily. If he hadn't been so stupid, Phil wouldn't be out. He shouldn't have reacted to hearing someone talk to Jax that way. But the words were so casually hateful, and he could tell they bothered Jax even if he tried to play it off as nothing. Tom hadn't heard homophobic chirps on the ice in a long time. Hockey players talked plenty of shit, but no one had said anything so vulgar to him since Juniors. Naively, he'd thought the NHL better. Maybe he let himself be swayed into a false sense of security because people pretended not to be dicks when someone in their vicinity wore a microphone. But he hadn't heard such offensive language from his team, either, not even in their locker room. Maybe he hadn't heard it because he didn't talk to them enough. Maybe they said hateful things all the time, and he'd never stepped up enough to stop it.

"Do other players say things like that to you a lot?"

"What, homophobic shit?"

"Yeah."

Jax shrugged fluidly. His team-branded zip-up hoodie, one of the thin ones made from jersey cloth, no fleece, made his shoulders look obscenely broad. "Sure. You know how it is."

Tom swallowed. "What about from our guys?"

"I mean, they're not trying to make me lose face-offs most of the time."

"But do they say—"

"Yeah, Tom. Of course they say homophobic shit. Howie thinks the f-slur is funny."

"But you still hang out with him."

Jax sighed. "What am I gonna do, ignore every player who says ignorant shit? That's most of the league."

"Most of the league," Tom repeated dully. "Really?"

"Haven't you been listening?"

Tom had stopped listening, actually. At some point in his twenties, when other players started chirping his lack of success, he'd stopped hearing their words, focused inward on his own struggles and failings. It was easier to put his head in the sand than to hear everyone else calling him a failure when he could cut out the middleman and tell himself.

Jax shook his head at whatever expression Tom was making. "Half of them probably don't mean it. It's what they're used to hearing, so they say it too."

"Doesn't make it okay."

"I know. But you don't need to worry. They don't know about me. I don't fuck hockey players."

On the list of things bothering him about this conversation, that hadn't even crossed Tom's mind. He opened his mouth to say so, but before he could, Jax barreled on.

"And I don't need you out there protecting me or some shit. If you do, people will realize there's something to hide. Just keep your head down and play hockey."

"Stick to what I'm good at." The words left a bitter taste in Tom's mouth. He wasn't good at being team captain; he wasn't good at stopping all the hurtful, prejudiced words from being hurled at Jax; he wasn't good at keeping his best friend from getting injured. He was only good at hockey, and not even enough to win anything significant.

Jax nodded, pleased. "Right."

Despite the heaviness the exchange left in the pit of Tom's stomach, he played some of the best hockey of his life, decimating the Twisters 5–2 in Carolina and earning a shutout for Dmitriyev in Nashville. Morris seemed cautiously pleased, inasmuch as he ever showed human emotion on the ice. He kept them running more balanced drills during practice, more hands-on than he'd been before.

Trout chafed against it. He stalked around the rink as the team completed a drill he hadn't chosen, eyeing Breezy and Hayesie and the other D-men as if they were his property. There was no arguing the results though. With defense tightening up, the penalty kill did better than it had in years. Young as he was, Breezy stepped up for the team, showing he could handle the responsibility.

In Philly, a call-up from the AHL team in San Diego finally joined them for practice to cover the gap left by Phil. With a defensive core used to being worked to putty every practice, they'd managed admirably to keep up the energy for two games by subbing in one of the forwards who sat in the press box most games as a sixth D-man, but it was time and past they were given a little relief.

Luca Mazetti, a slim, fine-featured twenty-one-year-old, had nothing in common with Tom's mental image of a D-man. He was almost comically handsome, with wide dark brown eyes and long eyelashes, full lips and thick dark hair. With a few more years playing hockey, when his straight nose had been broken a time or two and he'd lost a few teeth, maybe he'd be less incongruous in the locker room. Until then, Tom had an educated guess as to why he'd been languishing in the Italian league for two years after being drafted.

He stole a glance at Jax, who gave their newcomer an approving once-over.

Of course, Jax would approve. He didn't fuck hockey players, and Luca looked nothing like a hockey player.

Breezy bounced up to Luca, interrupting Tom's thoughts. "Hi! Mazetti, right?"

The differences between the two young men were shocking. Breezy's appearance matched Tom's image of a picture-book defenseman to a tee, his stature tall and thick. His floppy brown curls and big brown eyes made him seem so harmless, but on the ice, he could take a man down. Next to him, Luca appeared elfin. Waifish. Other adjectives Tom rarely had cause to use about a hockey player.

"Yes, that's me."

God, even his voice was handsome, low and musical. He had an accent.

"Awesome! I'm Chris Calabrese, but everyone calls me Breezy. Anyway, it's so cool you're Italian! So am I!"

Luca studied him. "You…are?"

"Oh, yeah, my great-grandparents on my dad's side are from this town near Cosenza, and my mom's mom is from Vibo Valentia. Have you ever been there?"

"No."

"Cool, cool, yeah, me neither. But now I'm earning NHL money, I can totally go."

"Right." Luca gazed around the room as if trying to establish if they were all insane.

Tom walked over to interrupt before things could get worse. "Hi, Luca. I'm Tom."

"I know," Luca said. "You are a little famous."

Breezy cracked up. He clapped Luca on the shoulder. "Man, it's great to have you on the team."

So much for Tom's authority.

With the ice broken, the rest of the team introduced themselves in fits and starts. Hayes had been in the weight room with Trout, poor man, so he only met Luca when they got out on the ice, though he and Luca would definitely be working together on the D-core.

Jax was particularly welcoming. Tom couldn't help watching him shake Luca's hand enthusiastically and clap him on the back. Did they need to be touching so much? Or was Jax just being himself? He had certainly treated everyone else on the team with open friendliness. Tom had gotten off on the wrong foot with Jax for reasons of his own making. He shouldn't assume a romantic interest on Jax's part just because Luca was objectively gorgeous in a way hockey players usually weren't. Neither of them could help it.

He did wonder why Jax didn't sleep with hockey players though. Was there something wrong with them? Or did he prefer men who were as skinny and blonde as the women hockey players tended to date?

Jax was blond.

"Crowler! Joining us today?"

Coach Morris's voice snapped Tom out of his unfortunate thoughts. This was what happened when he stepped out of his comfort zone and started talking to the rookies and changing the team drills. Nothing fit his routine, and he got lost in his head.

Maybe that was the problem. Maybe he had to stop getting lost in his head. He'd never had a great time there, only made himself miserable.

He squared his shoulders. "Sorry, Coach," he said and glided out onto the ice.

Though the surface was smooth and clean, Tom couldn't shake a sense of unease as he cast his gaze around the stands at the Liberty Center. Some rinks felt wrong. Calgary had shitty ice and worse locker rooms, Toronto claimed the prize for worst media and closest proximity to Tom's parents, and Philadelphia just made Tom's skin crawl for no discernible reason. All the same, practice went well. Despite his size, Luca excelled. He was fast; he didn't mind using his stature to slip around and under where no one expected him. His stickhandling was ridiculous, delicate and skilled in a way Tom rarely saw from defenseman. More commonly, forwards used finesse to get the right angle at the goal. Having a D-man with skills in stripping the puck off the opposition and then using it himself was an advantage, no two ways about it.

Tom made sure to tell him as much when they finished practice.

He was unprepared for the full force of Luca's determined expression when he met Tom's eyes.

"Thank you," Luca said in his lyrical voice. "I have been waiting a long time to prove I can be here."

Tom thought of Jax, who showed his true self so unashamedly, so proudly—who toughed out hateful language from opponents and his own team with a belligerence that showed his desperate desire to prove them wrong.

"You came to the right team," Tom said firmly. He would make sure they had a place for Luca; he would make sure they had a place for Jax. He would make sure they still had a place for Phil when he was ready to return.

Tom had stepped out of his comfort zone, and he refused to go back.

During the bus ride to the hotel, he held on to the thought.

When they arrived, he followed Jax to his room, intent on discussing Luca and how he would fit, as well as what Tom could do to make him feel welcome on the team. He knew it wasn't his forte; maybe Jax would have pointers.

But Jax seemed surprised to see him. "Sorry, did we have plans?"

"No," Tom said. "I wanted to talk about—"

"Can we do this later? I'm meeting the Philly guys for lunch, and I don't want to be late."

"Oh." Tom stepped away. "Of course. I'll see you later."

It was good, Tom told himself as he walked back to his room. If they didn't talk now, Jax couldn't say anything to weaken Tom's newfound confidence. He ignored the jealousy. Jax could have other friends. He was social and personable, and the guys in Philly probably didn't know why he'd been traded. He probably wouldn't tell them.

The thought of Jax confiding in someone else made Tom's stomach tighten uncomfortably.

But Jax could do whatever he wanted. Tom could lead without him. He'd been named team captain for a reason, and it was time he started living up to the title.

Unfortunately, the game that night did not herald the triumphant beginning of a new era. It was more like when a washed-up popstar rebranded themselves and announced a new, different, improved sound only to end up performing their album at outlet malls to dwindling sales.

Jax's passes weren't connecting, unthinkable for him. His main skill lay in his strength, in his powerful, heavy thighs and glutes, propelling him into being one of the fastest men on the ice. His built shoulders helped as well; Tom remembered a particularly vicious check from Jax banging him into the boards last year. But what elevated Jax beyond any other strong, fast player was his hockey IQ. He had an innate sense for passing lanes and a sharp eye for positions and chances.

Tonight, the part of his brain in charge of finding the perfect angle had gone offline. Jax was still fast and forceful, but too often, he ended up in the wrong place on the ice to catch Tom's passes. Once, he nearly collided with Vanderbilt. Midway through the second period, Morris pulled him off the first line and reinstated Abrahamov instead, forcing Tom and Vanderbilt to adapt their whole play midway through the game.

It was no wonder they lost.

In fact, with Dmitriyev taking a maintenance day and their backup in goal, it was a miracle they only lost by two goals. A miracle provided by Breezy's blocking and Luca's deft hands, but a miracle all the same.

Back in the hotel after a subdued bus ride with a morose team, the text from Tom's mom read, *What was that? You should be better!*

He swallowed down the anger and responded, *Thanks, Mom.*

Because he enjoyed torturing himself, he looked up the postgame interviews on his phone. Kayleigh from PR had pulled Jax for media, and the interview he gave was a mess. Usually, Jax charmed every camera in a ten-foot radius with his smiles and jokes.

On the video, he had bags under his eyes. He appeared drawn and serious.

"What do you think went wrong tonight?" Olivia Starling asked. As the hockey beat reporter for the *San Francisco Herald*, Tom imagined she would be his sleep paralysis demon if he had one of those.

"What didn't go wrong?" Jax asked back. "I didn't show up for the team, didn't play a full sixty minutes. There were missed chances, giveaways, and those are on me. Gotta do better."

Tom couldn't watch the rest of the interview. Jax wasn't meant to look like that. He was supposed to be confident, cocky, even. Not whatever shadow of himself he appeared as on this video. Instead, Tom scrolled down his recommendations and found the interview Tyson Fuller, Jax's previous captain, had given after the game.

With some satisfaction, Tom noted Fuller didn't hop on camera right after a game runway-ready. He had what might have been the worst case of helmet hair Tom had ever seen, and he clearly hadn't been to the showers yet. He also wore the champion's belt, having received first star of the game after scoring two goals.

Tom should get one of those for the Sea Lions. They had a funny hat somewhere in one of the storage closets from five or six seasons ago, but most teams had a new novelty item every season to pass around to each winning game's MVP. Another captain's duty he'd been shirking.

A reporter asked, "Tyson, how did it feel to beat Jaxon Grant so decisively after he left the team suddenly in September?"

Fuller smirked. "Well, uh, it was good, not gonna lie. It blindsided the team, losing him right at the start of the season, and it's great to be out there proving it won't keep us down."

The interview went on to discuss playoff chances. The Sea Lions were tied for second place with Seattle in the Pacific division, while Philadelphia floundered in sixth place in the Metropolitan, which meant nothing anyone said in this interview had any weight. The standings didn't mean much at this point in the season. Tom only really started worrying in February. He closed YouTube and shut off his phone.

Why was Jax friends with Fuller? He seemed like a dick. Had he said something at their lunch to make Jax so off tonight?

Before this season, before Jax, Tom would have kept his head down and gone over his own game, found its flaws and worked to fix them. Now, Tom went over the game and considered, then decided, tonight, it wasn't his fault.

The anger living under his skin ever since St. Louis bubbled up. Righteous indignation at other players having the temerity to speak to *his* teammate in such a way, coupled with his own ever-present self-loathing for not doing something about it, had been his constant companion since the ill-conceived Gordie Howe hat trick. Now, outrage joined the swell of emotion in his gut that Jax had chosen to throw away the good thing they had going on the first line over Tyson fucking Fuller.

After changing out of his suit, Tom went to Jax's hotel room and banged on the door. Maybe ratty sweats and a Sea Lions shirt from eight seasons ago weren't the most authoritative clothing choices for this intervention. Back then, their logo had been a cartoon sea lion, not the current more intimidating line drawing with some vague similarities to aquatic mammals. Tom had also been a clothing size smaller at the time, and the shirt clung to him in a way his clothes normally didn't.

He didn't wear authority in his clothing though. It was in his voice and his face, and in the slow-burning anger he finally had the words to convey at least a part of.

Jax opened the door, caught sight of him, and turned away with a groan. Based on the track of shoeprints across the fluffy carpet, he'd been pacing the floor for a while. He still wore his suit, a light gray number with slightly darker pinstripes, and a crisp white shirt. The material strained across his thighs and shoulders. Whoever did Jax's tailoring had to be utterly obscene.

"What happened out there?" Tom asked. He was pleased, almost proud at how stern his voice sounded. "You can—"

"I know," Jax said. "I fucked up, Tom. I fucked up, and I let you down, and I'm so sorry."

Tom blinked. He expected belligerence or anger, not misery. He tried again, gently this time, banking the flames of his own outrage. Jax didn't need to be yelled at; he needed a friend. A confidante. Tom could be that for him. "You can do better."

"I know I can. I…" Abruptly, Jax collapsed at the end of the bed, hunched over, feet dangling off the side. "I met up with them after practice. My old team."

Carefully, gingerly, Tom sat beside him. "It didn't go well?"

A snort of derisive laughter emerged from Jax's throat. "Fuller fucking hates me."

Tom had no idea how he should respond.

"I don't care about people hating me," Jax said, which—well, it simply wasn't true. Tom had never met anyone who went out of his way to be liked quite as much as Jax. Jax had spent days trying to find out why Tom *didn't* like him and had done everything he could to fix it, albeit in the most roundabout way possible.

"I know it's going to happen, I get it, okay?" Jax continued. "You don't get to the top with everyone loving you. But it's…it's just not *fair*." He pushed one of his big, square-fingered hands through his hair, leaving it disheveled and falling over his eyes. Tom wanted to push it out of the way for him. Tom wanted to wrap an arm around him. Tom wanted to hold him.

"What…" Tom started to ask, but Jax beat him to it again.

"He thinks I asked for the trade. He thinks I wanted it. To play for a contender rather than the team that drafted me."

"Oh."

Jax got to his feet again, resumed pacing. "And what do I even say? If I tell him I didn't want it, he asks me why. And then I have to tell him I fucked up and some guy threatened to put pictures of my dick on Twitter, and I freaked out and told PR, and it got me fucking traded when I should have waited it out. And then what?"

He glared at Tom, his eyes bright with anger.

"I don't know, Jax."

"Then he gets to hate me for something true, and I'd rather he hate me for a lie, so I have to play along and pretend I chose any of this. But I can't live this way, Tom! I want to be out, I want not to care about all this shit, but every time I think about actually doing it, I find some reason it's not the right time or the right way."

"Jax." Tom stood, reached out awkwardly. He put his hand on Jax's shoulder, and Jax melted under his touch. He swayed forward, leaning into Tom's space. He smelled of some stupidly expensive brand of aftershave, and Tom wanted—wanted—

He wrenched away, took a step back.

Jax laughed, a bitter, hollow sound. "And the only person who *does* know is my fucking team captain who claims he's not a homophobe but can't stand to touch a queer man."

Something broke in Tom then. Something he'd hidden under his skin when he was eighteen, pimply, and with the worst haircut anyone had ever had, standing on the draft stage and going first overall to the Sea Lions. Something he'd kept safe within himself while he shut out more and more of the world around him. Something that had risen up through his gut, starting the moment he'd leaped in to defend Jax in St. Louis, and grew and grew, taking on the shape of anger to disguise its true form: fear and hurt and shame. He opened his mouth, and before he could think it through, that broken piece leapt right off his lips.

"I'm not a homophobe, Jax. I'm fucking gay, all right?"

# Six

Kayleigh [off-screen]: Okay, Hayesie, would you rather play with too-small skates or too-big gloves?

Hayes: Gloves all the way. If my skates don't fit right, I can't concentrate on shit. I'm falling on my face. It's not a good look.

Kayleigh: Jax, if you couldn't play center, would you rather be a winger or a D-man?

Jax: Winger. At least I kinda know what to do there.

Kayleigh: Hayesie, red or purple Gatorade?

Hayes: Purple.

Kayleigh: Jax, play in Philly or play in San Francisco?

Jax: Hah, good one. San Francisco, obviously.

## Top comments:

1682rox: Kinda rude to put Jax on the spot

sealions4lyfe: Grant needs to work on his media face. Hockey needs more guys like Crowler. All about the game, none of this wishy-washy shit

(From "San Francisco Sea Lions Play Would You Rather," posted to YouTube 11/08/2024)

There was no way Jax had heard right.

"What?"

"I'm gay."

Jax wanted to say something, anything, but the only thing he could think of was *what?* And he'd already said that. The answer still didn't make sense.

"I…you…" he tried, but nope, still no other words coming. "No way."

Tom didn't say anything.

"No," Jax said. "No, see, if you were, why would you let me squirm when you found out about me? Why would you let me think you had a problem with me? Are you fucking with me here?"

"Oh God," Tom said, pale now, his stormy eyes wide. "Oh my God."

Jax eyed his skin-tight, light blue team shirt, thankful they'd gotten rid of the cartoon mascot with its huge eyes before he joined. He could see Tom's chest rising and falling much too fast under it.

"Breathe, man."

"I'm trying," Tom said between heaving breaths. "I'm… Oh my God. I have to go."

As suddenly as he'd come, he vanished, leaving Jax standing alone in his hotel room, nonplussed.

No, not nonplussed.

Baffled.

Bamboozled.

Extremely, extremely plussed. He walked to the door to follow, then reconsidered and stepped over to the window again. It was raining outside. The drizzle turned the lights of the Philadelphia skyline into smears of yellow and orange against the windowpane. The team had booked a hotel near the airport, clear across town from where Jax's house stood empty. He couldn't stomach the thought of spending the night there instead, with nothing but dust bunnies for company. Not after today. Especially not after the last five minutes.

He could only think of one thing to do.

Jax pulled out his phone and called his mom.

"Jaxon!" She was always so thrilled to hear his voice. He really should call more often.

"Hi, Mom. How's it going?"

"Oh, you know. It's going. Your dad's still at work or I'd put you on speaker."

Jax rolled his eyes. "Is he still taking late shifts?"

"Only for your games, honey. You know he can't take the tension."

"I play eighty-two games a year, at least."

"Well, you know your dad."

Jax did know his dad. "What about the girls?"

"It's 10:00 p.m. in Minnesota, baby. They're asleep."

"Oh. Right. Did they like the piano?"

Her tone took on a soft, pleased note. "Yeah, sweetie, they loved the piano. No idea what we're gonna do if you keep sending such big gifts though. You know the living room's tiny."

Jax bit his tongue to keep from mentioning (again) that he'd be happy to buy them a bigger house. "So, join up with the neighbors. Make a music studio for the whole park. I'll pay for it."

She didn't say anything, but he could hear the lecture he'd gotten more than once about not throwing money at them. It wasn't the same as being there.

"How are they?"

"They're great! Lila wrote a poem about leprechauns, and it got printed in the school paper, and Rosa's thinking about the basketball team."

Jax smiled. They were such good kids. At fourteen, Jax had definitely not been writing poetry. He'd been all hockey, all the time, barely paying attention to his baby sisters and eating his parents out of house and home when he wasn't fighting with them about the electricity bill they could never seem to pay on time. He wished they would let him pay it all back.

"So why are you calling tonight?"

"Can't I check in on my family?"

"You always call on Sundays."

"Okay, Ma, you got me. I had a weird day."

"That why you played like shit?"

"Mom!"

"Just saying. Your pretty captain could barely keep you all in the game."

Jax drummed his fingers on the backrest of the chair, staring out the window. "Remember what I told you before I got drafted?"

He had been eighteen, and he had been terrified. He'd known the NHL was his best chance at a future where he didn't spend his whole life working nights at a diner the way his dad did, and after two years of billet families and bus rides in the USHL, he had to make it. Otherwise, the whole miserable experience wouldn't have been worth it. It had been two long years of missing his family and wearing smelly hand-me-down gear, always hungry because he was growing way too fast and burning too many calories to keep up, pinching pennies so he could afford fries when his team hit up fast-food joints. Two years of pretending to laugh along when his teammates joked about queers and fags, always with the secret, burning knowledge it was him they were joking about.

If he made it, he'd promised himself, it would all be better. He would have enough money to buy as many burgers as he wanted. He would visit home whenever he could. And he would be so good he could date whoever he damn well wanted to.

The night before the draft, he couldn't sleep. He'd been sharing a hotel room with his parents, and he tossed and turned until his mom made him go out onto the balcony, where he'd cried in her arms for all the homesickness he never told her about. It was the only time he mentioned that when he brought someone home, it would be a man.

She'd said, "Good for you," and then, a little later, "Be careful."

Now, six and a half years on, though he hadn't visited half as often as he thought he would, she said, "I remember every word."

Jax swallowed. "They found out. In Philly. They... I wasn't careful."

"And then they traded you."

"Yeah." His throat had gone dry. He cleared it, then cleared it again. "I...I didn't want to get traded. But..."

"Those assholes."

"Mom!"

"Well, they are."

Jax leaned his forehead against the window glass and smiled. "Yeah. Playing them tonight..."

"No wonder you sucked."

"Thanks, Mom. The team didn't even know. They thought I wanted to be traded. It was a management decision. But I wish I could tell them the truth about what happened."

She paused for a suspiciously long time. "Now, when you say you weren't careful…"

"You don't want to know."

She snickered. "Okay, then. I hope you're using condoms."

"*Mom.*"

"What? Your dad and I didn't, and look where it got us."

"Yeah, well, I'm not sixteen, and I'm also not getting anyone pregnant."

"You never know!"

Jax sighed. "Anyway. I might've told someone on the Sea Lions. And, uh…I think he just came out to me?"

"Wow."

"Yeah. And it doesn't make any sense because he's known about me for weeks now. Why didn't he tell me right away?"

For a long moment, his mom said nothing. Then, she asked, "When did you realize you liked men?"

Jax considered. He hadn't fully accepted it until he'd kissed his first boy at sixteen. But suspecting? "I was probably about thirteen, fourteen?"

"Did you think I'd have a problem with it?"

"No, of course not."

"So why'd you only tell me when you were eighteen?"

"I guess I wasn't ready."

"Mm-hmm."

Jax gently banged his forehead against the glass. "Right. Okay. Thanks, Mom."

"Anytime. Hey, do you have time to chat about the cute little defenseman you guys played tonight? Is he new?"

"Actually, I think I'd better go talk to someone." Talking to Tom would be awkward as hell, but not as awkward as that.

"Fine, spoil my fun. Love you, kid."

"Love you too, mom."

Jax slid his phone into the too-tight pocket of his suit pants. He grabbed his key and headed down the corridor. He didn't know which door was Tom's. Only the captain and the coach got a full list of everyone's room numbers, but he had a gut feeling a claustrophobic hotel space was exactly what Tom didn't need right now. Instead, Jax took the emergency stairs to the roof two at a time.

And there he stood, all alone on the rooftop terrace, rain sluicing off the tip of his nose.

"I'm sorry," Jax said. He'd always been direct, and apologizing was the most important part.

Tom started, and for a second, Jax could see the headline: NHL Captain Falls to Death From Philadelphia's Most Middling Hotel After Sudden Shock From Idiot Teammate. A bit unwieldy, but it would certainly catch the reader's eye.

"Jax."

"Jesus fuck, man, you're gonna catch a cold, and then we'll be out our best winger. Come inside."

"Jax, I…" Tom glanced away, shivering, still dressed in only his stupid sea lion T-shirt and the thinnest, clingiest joggers Jax had ever seen.

"It's okay," Jax promised. "I'm sorry I acted like a dick. I shouldn't have— I of all people should have known it's not always easy to tell people this stuff."

"I've never."

"Never?"

"Never told anyone. That's the first time I ever said it."

"*Never?*"

Tom shook his head, water droplets flying.

"Jeez," Jax said weakly. "Not even your parents? Or, I mean you must have an ex or two hidden in the closet. They'll know."

Tom shook his head again.

"Tom."

Finally, Tom looked at him. It was too dark for Jax to see his eyes properly, but the vulnerability writ large across every line of Tom's face bowled him over.

"Christ, Tom, you must have been so lonely."

Tom collapsed in on himself, taking deep, heaving, sobbing breaths. Jax stepped forward before he could think better of it, and then Tom leaned on him, shuddering against him. His skin was cool to the touch, and Jax wrapped his arms around him to keep him warm. He didn't know how long they stood there, but enough for the rain to trickle down the back of Jax's neck and all along his spine.

A siren blared in the street below, pulling them apart.

"Let's go inside," Jax suggested as gently as he could.

Tom still shook too hard to be much help, so Jax steered him to the emergency exit with an arm still wrapped around his shoulders. The bright fluorescents in the stairwell seemed sickening after being outside in the dark. Now, Jax could see Tom's red eyes; his skin, paler than usual, his wet-through clothes.

Jax's dress shoes squeaked wetly on the linoleum, the only contrast to the heavy sound of Tom's breathing. Jax wanted to speak, to say something to comfort Tom or lighten the mood, but he had nothing. They reached their floor in silence.

Behind the heavy emergency door, they entered the muted world of red-carpeted hallways and endless identical doors, another shock after the cold roof and the harshly lit stairway. Their footsteps squelched quietly against the floor.

Tom needed four tries to get his room key to work.

"Do you—are you—" Jax tried.

"I'm fine."

It was transparently the least true thing Tom had ever said to him, and he hadn't been truthful about a lot of things.

Tom seemed to know this because he corrected himself. "I'll be fine. I just need a hot shower and some sleep."

"You're sure?"

"Yeah." He paused. "You'll, um… You won't…"

A large part of Jax wanted to be insulted at the mere thought, but he held back. "Of course I won't tell anyone."

Tom nodded once, and then he disappeared into his room. The door clicked closed behind him, and Jax was left standing alone in the hallway in a wet suit at midnight. It wasn't the weirdest thing he had ever experienced—nothing could top the night of the NHL awards his rookie year—but it made an easy second place on his mental list.

He didn't sleep all night.

He tried, tossing and turning on the hotel bed. Hotel beds were always too soft or too hard, with no middle ground and always the wrong number of pillows. A two-pillow man, Jax preferred one big, firm one for his head and one long, squishy one to hug close to his body and throw a knee over. He had a great system at home, or rather, in the hotel room in San Francisco he currently called home. But in hotels they stopped at on the road for a night or two, the pillows were always too small, and he had to stack them under his head, leaving nothing to hold on to.

Still, he traveled professionally. He could fall asleep any place, any time. Except here and now.

He lay awake, going over every conversation he'd ever had with Tom. The way Tom shied away from him whenever Jax was too blatant, which he'd taken for a polite man's form of homophobia, had become a scared man's way of escaping being known.

He'd never told anyone.

How could he live that way?

Jax didn't shout it from the rooftops or anything, but he had his family. He had Grindr installed on his phone. He had a half dozen bars and clubs across the US he felt safe frequenting when there for work. He longed for a real community, for a bond with people who knew, actually knew, what it was to be rejected over and over again for who you were. Jax had only glimpsed those kinds of friendships and families in stolen moments in gay bars and stranger's apartments. But it had been enough to stave off the loneliness. Jax knew how to live off scraps. It was the same as the single order of fries in Juniors. He wasn't full, but at least he wasn't starving.

Now, he knew what starving looked like. Starving looked like Tom, standing alone in the rain and hyperventilating because he had never spoken the words aloud before.

Jax wondered what he told his hookups. Did he pretend to be straight and force his way through sex with women? Did he fuck men doggy-style so he could pretend they were women? Did he hook up in dark, shady clubs where no one could see his face?

None of the above matched Tom's MO. He was a shitty liar and a good person, especially now Jax knew his odd reactions to Jax's sexuality had nothing to do with homophobia, except for the internal kind. The idea of him compromising his goodness in order to compromise something much bigger made Jax's stomach hurt. He wanted to spare Tom that kind of hurt, which was ridiculous and stupid. What business did he have trying to comfort Tom? He'd only known Tom for two months and still wasn't convinced Tom even liked him. Which made sense. Jax threatened the way Tom lived his life, grandstanding about how he wanted to come out someday.

Jax could back off. He could give Tom the space he'd denied him since Tom had first caught him in Edmonton, let things return to their status quo, be an alternate in name only...but Jax didn't want to. He was a selfish creature, and Tom was the first person he'd met who would really get it. The first person who could be the community he craved.

The thought seduced him into daydreams of the friendship they could have, so intense that Jax hadn't thought once about Tyson Fuller, the Philadelphia Magpies, and the friends he no longer had here by the time he gave up on sleep at 5:00 a.m.

So, the next morning, when he got down to breakfast and saw Tom sitting alone at a corner table, he dropped into place across from him and dug into a plate of scrambled eggs and whole wheat toast.

"Why do hotel breakfasts always taste of sadness?" he asked with his mouth full.

Tom snorted around his coffee and held a napkin to his face to contain the spill. "I think it's the reconstituted egg product."

"Right?" Jax poked at the offending scramble. "I hated the hard-boiled eggs at the hotel in Nashville, but at least they were real food."

Tom grimaced in agreement. "Do you ever want to say fuck the meal plan and get the pancakes and the pork bacon?"

For a moment, Jax studied him, trying to work out if this was some metaphor shit and Tom meant the bacon as a stand-in for man-meat or something. But Tom looked at him earnestly, no hint of innuendo.

As if he could feel more sorry for this man.

"Yeah, Tom. You wanna know something?"

"Hmm?"

"Sometimes I do say fuck it and get the bacon."

A wistful expression stole across Tom's face, and Jax was surer than ever Tom had spent his entire time in the league denying himself every possible pleasure in an effort to be the best hockey robot he could. It made Jax a little insane. He wanted to put Tom in a bathtub full of maple syrup, cover him in bacon strips, and suck his cock.

Jax blinked.

One of those things was not like the others.

It wasn't as if he'd never noticed Tom before. He'd have to have been blind not to. Tom had a...presence in a room. Tyson, Philly's captain, acted more authoritative. Coach Trout took pride in being stern and immovable. In contrast, Tom was attentive. He watched and noted everything happening around him, and it made Jax want to show off for him in the worst way, which maybe explained some of his recent behavior. Tom was also tall, stupidly handsome, and very good at hockey, all of which Jax found attractive in a man. He didn't fuck hockey players as a rule because it was a surefire way to get in trouble, and most of them had other, less desirable traits, such as missing teeth and terrible personalities. But he'd also never known another queer hockey player.

Moreover, Tom desperately needed to be shown a good time and given some joy in life, and Jax specialized in those two things. So, the thoughts playing out across his mind's eye didn't mean Jax had a crush or anything. His brain needed to process the new information and did so by examining Tom under the new light his revelation shed. Jax would never act on it. That would be a catastrophe for the team, and they would probably kill each other within a week. Tom was so serious and humorless—no way would he put up with Jax.

The sex would be magnificent, of course. Jax gave himself a half second to mourn it, watching Tom's mouth as he ate his raspberry yogurt, his lips stained berry-red. Jax could make him feel so good that it might override his innate need for martyrdom.

But it couldn't happen.

"So, I was thinking," Jax said casually. "You and me, right?"

Tom froze, spoon halfway to his lips, a deer in the headlights.

Jax had to word this right to avoid being oncoming traffic. No mention of what unified them, nothing that would turn Tom into the scared, shaking shell Jax found on the roof last night. Just the reminder that while they'd been alone before, they weren't now.

"If the two of us can win it all, we'll show them."

A slow smile spread across Tom's face, beautiful as a sunrise. "Yeah," he said. "Yeah, we will."

# Seven

Kayleigh [off-screen]: We've got our captain, Tom Crowler, trying out the team beanie, goalie Dmitriyev in custom sweatpants with his number, and here's alternate Phil Easton in the brand-new Sea Lions lace-up hoodie. What do you guys think?

Dmitriyev: Yes. Is good.

Phil: Yeah, very comfortable. One hundred percent cotton, so that's nice.

Kayleigh: Tom?

Tom: Yeah, it's great.

Kayleigh: So are we gonna catch you wearing team swag around town?

Phil: [choked laughter]

Tom: Oh, uh, I don't really go into the city much. I, uh—

Kayleigh: Tom, you gotta give me *something* here.

Phil: How about some action shots of us wearing the merch on the ice?

[Clip show of Phil and Tom skating in Sea Lions merch while Dmitriyev lounges on his side in the goal, wearing the sweatpants]

# Top comments:

clions2010: Crowler and Easton continue to be a black hole of charisma off
ice and a sinkhole of playoff performance on it

seelionssaylions: Jeez, at least Dmitriyev has the excuse of not being a native
speaker. What reason does Crowler have to be so bad at words?

SFCLions: Tom...hey. Hey, Tom. I'm free on Thursday. I could introduce
you to some new hobbies on Thursday, when I am free

(Video posted in the outtakes section of The Rookery, the direct-to-consumer streaming service of the San Francisco Sea Lions and all associated teams, on 09/26/2024)

Tom was having a hard time remembering why he didn't want to spend
time with Jax.

At the beginning of the season, he'd been so sure he had to avoid
Jax at all costs. Jax acted outgoing and loud. He had a reputation as a
thoughtless party boy who spent big on dumb things such as luxury gadgets
and designer sweatpants. And he gave funny media soundbites. All of those
things sounded like the exact opposite of what Tom wanted in his life. Then,
when he saw under the surface and understood why Jax acted the way he
did, he'd been desperate to prove he was neither a homophobe nor did he
hate Jax, and he'd been resentful and scared Jax might see him for who he
was in turn. The combination made him clingy and skittish by turn.

Now that Jax knew, Tom couldn't get enough of him.

Jax was still loud and outgoing. He still had in-jokes with Breezy that made
Tom want to groan and order a strong drink. But now, Tom didn't worry Jax
would get too close and accidentally see too much. He liked Jax clowning around,

making everyone else laugh. He was never afraid to make a fool of himself if it made other people smile.

Two nights after their loss in Philly, the team congregated at a sports bar in Denver, the kind of place with five TVs broadcasting different games at once. Miraculously, none of them showed hockey thanks to ESPN's stupid regional blackouts. They'd lost the game against Colorado, but only in overtime, so they still got a point. Tom's mom had texted, *You win some, you lose some.* When he'd written *Thanks, Mom*, he'd almost meant it. Tomorrow, they would play in Boston, and then the road trip would finally end, so everyone was relieved and exhausted. No one wanted to go clubbing tonight. Tom hoped curfew wouldn't be too hard to uphold.

He was squished into the corner of the booth with Jax pressed up against his side, a solid wall of heat.

Across from them, Breezy held out his phone to show Jax a picture. "This is Chloe. She looks nice, right?"

The picture showed a blonde woman hugging a dog.

Jax frowned. "What about Vanessa?"

Breezy groaned. "So my dad found out her uncle runs one of the restaurants in Montreal we can't go to because my grandpa says it's, you know—" He lowered his voice. "—run by the mob."

"Did you ask her about it?"

"Yeah, man, of course. She got super shifty and didn't answer, and I think her family must be from, like, *that* part of Sicily."

"Right." Jax drew out the *i* for a long time. He caught Tom's eye and made a baffled face for a split second, and Tom had to take a long sip of his beer to avoid laughing. "So, Chloe?"

Breezy beamed. "Yeah, her great-great-grandmother's from Messina, which is almost in Calabria. She lives in Quebec most of the time, but we could do long distance or something."

Jax turned his attention to Luca, who was on his second beer already. "You have these kinds of problems too?"

Luca looked him dead in the eye. "I'm from Rome. We have joined the twenty-first century, unlike Montreal."

Jax collapsed into helpless laughter.

Tom glanced over at Breezy's offended face and laughed as well.

Luca clapped Breezy on the shoulder. "Come on, Casanova. I will buy you a drink and teach you how to talk to women not picked out by your parents."

They moseyed off to the bar just as Howie and Mooney returned with a platter of shot glasses and a handful of darts, respectively. Tom could think of a million ways in which that could go wrong, starting with any of the servers realizing they were underage and ending with a trip to the emergency room. He was about to say as much when Jax laid a hand on his knee under the table.

"I got this," he muttered.

A week ago, Tom might have pulled his leg away. Now, he kept it in place. It was easier on his hip anyway.

"All right, boys," Jax said cheerily. "Loser takes a shot?"

"Are you challenging me?" Howie puffed his chest out.

"Sure am."

Jax lost spectacularly to Howie. One of his darts bounced off the framed picture of Babe Ruth two feet above the dartboard. He picked up the shot glass with good grace, toasted Howie, and squinted at the bar. "Wow, check out the girl Luca's talking to!"

While their backs were turned, Jax dumped the shot in a potted plant.

The girl with Luca was gorgeous. She wore leggings and had her hair pulled away from her face in a half bun. Though she had a stack of textbooks with her at the bar, she seemed utterly engrossed in the conversation instead of her studies. Breezy stood beside them, looking as if he'd unlock the secrets of the universe if he listened close enough.

Jax threw the game against Mooney as well and, afterward, pretended to be so tipsy he absolutely had to go and dance on the little, makeshift floor in the middle of the bar. Mooney and Howie were young enough to be excited at the prospect, and while they flailed about somewhat more rhythmically than he expected, Tom took the opportunity to introduce a few more shots to the local plant life.

He wasn't quite quick enough. Breezy slid into place across from him and downed two of the remaining shots in quick succession.

"I will never be able to do what he does," he said mournfully.

"What, chat up a girl?"

"Chat up that kind of girl."

Tom made a questioning noise.

"She's writing a term paper about Fellini's use of shadow and light. Luca's seen, like, all of Fellini's movies apparently." Breezy stared down at the table. Tom twisted the platter until only empties sat in front of him. "I thought Fellini was a brand of freezer pizza."

"I wouldn't have done any better."

Breezy glanced up from under his thick curls. "Really?"

"Yeah." Tom hazarded a smile. "All I know is hockey. If I meet someone—a girl—who wants to talk about anything else, I'm screwed."

"Is that why you never pick up?"

Tom went hot and then cold all over.

"Because I thought you had some tragic backstory, and a girl back home broke your heart so bad you could never love again until you won the Stanley Cup."

"Um."

"'Cause you seem pretty sad a lot?" Breezy's fingers snaked out, and he grabbed a third shot while Tom tried to parse the words coming out of his mouth. "And I think the guys would love to help you be less sad, but we don't know how."

"Let's focus on winning the Cup, then."

With a loud groan, Jax fell into his seat, pressed up right against Tom. He was warm from the dance floor, and he smelled a little of sweat underneath his expensive cologne. "Yes. Cup. Breezy, our mission in life is to get this man a Cup."

"We can do it," Breezy said with the solemn conviction of the very drunk. "But also, though, I think I need to start watching smart people movies."

"You do you."

In the end, Tom and Jax had to walk to the hotel with Breezy propped up between them, no mean feat given he was taller than Tom and broader than Jax. Luca had gone home with his student friend, and Tom had extracted promises from Mooney and Howie, still dancing—although by then, attached to two scantily clad girls in matching cowboy hats studded with what Howie called "the good kind of rhinestones"—to be back by curfew. He had little hope they would remember if things kept heating up on the dance floor. Who knew Howie could move his hips like that?

"It's just," Breezy said, leaning heavily on Tom as he tripped over his own feet, "sometimes I think the girls I meet 'cause my parents talk up their hockey player son are kind of in it for the money? And that feels mean and wrong to say, right? And all relationships are about money at some point anyway, but…"

"Are they?" Jax asked.

Breezy was too drunk and too, well, *Breezy* to catch his tone of incredulity, but it made Tom smile.

"I mean, once you get married, all your money is shared. And one person always earns more, right? How can you not fight about it then?"

"Sometimes, couples earn the same," Tom pointed out. "Think of, uh, Brad Pitt and Angelina Jolie?"

"I guess," Breezy said doubtfully. "But, like, they didn't last. And even if I find a girl who earns the same, I'm away all the time, and then she'd have to take care of the kids and the house, and it's not any fun to be the responsible person all the time, so we would definitely fight about it."

Tom must have been drunker than he thought because Breezy made a solid argument. Responsibility was no fun.

"Breezy, my man." Jax wheezed slightly under the added weight as Breezy listed toward him. "You are twenty-two. You don't have a house. You don't have kids. You don't need to have either right now. Or ever."

Breezy came to a full halt for the seventh time since they'd left the bar. "I never thought of that," he said and then proceeded to vomit all over their shoes.

It took another twenty minutes to get him tucked into bed with a bottle of water, an aspirin on the nightstand, as well as strict instructions to call one or both of them if he needed anything. Thankfully, he appeared to have relieved himself of the worst of the intoxication, but he still seemed miserable.

Tom and Jax sprayed down their shoes in Tom's bathroom before collapsing onto the chair and the bed, respectively.

"He's a sweet kid," Tom said.

"He's gonna get hoodwinked by some gold digger."

Tom frowned.

"What?" Jax asked.

"You shouldn't talk about women that way. You shouldn't talk about *anyone* that way."

Jax groaned and squirmed into a different position on the bed. He was utterly incapable of sitting still, something Tom would be bothered by if he didn't enjoy watching all the different ways Jax found to arrange himself so much. "You're right. I don't mean... Ugh, I shouldn't have said it. You know, I got along great with some of the WAGs in Philly. They were nice women. You'll never meet better fans, probably, and they're the only ones who never get mad when we lose."

"So why say it?"

"Breezy's...he's a little naive."

"You don't say."

Jax threw a pillow at Tom, who caught it and threw it back.

"When I made the starting roster in Philly, I had this friend from Juniors. Well. Sort of a friend and sort of an ex. And it was no big deal at first—little stuff like covering his rent for a week when he lost his job. He always used to spot me cash in Juniors, you know? Seemed fair."

Tom nodded. He'd had similar friendships in the OHL, people he had lent to and borrowed from so many tiny sums no one could remember who owed whom what. He hadn't seen Sean in years, not since he quit the NCAA team in Michigan with a busted shoulder. He ought to call sometime.

"But then I got my big contract, and he needed help paying off his car, and then he really needed a designer couch for his place, and at some point, I had to say no, you know? And he got pissed, threatened to out me and everything. He never did it, but… Well. It sucked."

"I can't imagine." Tom had never been put under pressure by a friend in that way, maybe because he'd never let anyone close enough to try. He'd given one single blow job, once, when he was seventeen and drunk for the first time. He'd spent the next four years terrified it would come to light. It had been a secret relief when he stopped hearing from Sean.

"Yeah." Jax flopped down onto on the bed and stared up at the ceiling. "I still feel guilty about it. I mean, I have the money, right? He'll probably never earn a fraction of what I make in a year. But I don't want to be…beholden to someone because they know I'm gay. I'm not ashamed."

"I think most of the guys love their wives." Tom carefully didn't think of Vanderbilt, whose wife posted a cute pregnancy announcement online the other day. Everyone talked about it on the trip from Philly to Denver. Tom did try not to notice, but he found it hard to ignore when Vanderbilt turned down going out with the team tonight to meet with some girl he'd found on a hookup app he described as "discreet."

"And some wives accept their husbands don't give a shit in exchange for a comfortable life."

Tom swallowed.

"Sorry. I'm being depressing."

Tom hadn't been lying earlier. He really didn't know how to talk about anything except hockey. Emotional honesty was not his forte. If it were, maybe he wouldn't have had a very embarrassing panic attack directly after coming out for the first time. Jax deserved him giving it a shot though.

"What you told me about why you got traded…someone threatening to post pictures of you to out you. And your friend from Juniors threatening the same thing. I think it makes sense you would have a hard time trusting, um, romantic partners."

"Huh." Jax eyed him thoughtfully. "For a guy who doesn't date, you're shockingly insightful."

Tom laughed nervously. He wasn't insightful; he just spent way too much time thinking about Jax. "I have my moments." He grabbed his tablet from the desk, maxed out on emotional conversation for the night. "Hey, so… Want to rewatch the power play from tonight? I think we can make it better."

Jax scrambled to a sitting position. "You're on."

It ended up being a productive evening for all they were both a bit tipsy and warm, sitting too close to each other on the hotel bed. It was one of the softer ones, which they both complained about. That night, Tom secretly enjoyed how the mattress dipped toward the middle, pushing their shoulders together. When Tom pointed to the screen to show how the forwards had been neglecting to utilize Hayesie on the power play, too used to a weaker D-core, and Jax leaned in closer to watch, he could smell the mix of aftershave and sweat again. Tom should have gotten over thinking sweat smelled good about a minute and a half into puberty, when the locker room started to reek. And yet, here he was, inhaling it greedily.

They tried it out in practice the next day, making the power play unit more flexible and playing to all positions instead of trying to storm the opposing net on full power. And they beat the Redcoats 2–1 with a nifty goal during a 5-on-4, netting Hayesie his first goal of the season.

The next day, it seemed only natural for Tom to sit next to Jax on the flight back to California to rewatch the tape from the night before, searching for more opportunities.

"The strategy matches Luca's style of play better," Jax noted idly.

"Mm. He's too green for the power play though."

"Yeah. Hey, open up his minutes, though, just to check."

Luca had played fifteen minutes the night before. By the time they'd gotten through analyzing them and figuring out that what Luca needed to really shine was a more defensively minded partner, the plane had soared over northern California and begun its descent from the far side of the Bay. By then, Tom had an idea of what they could do to tighten up their defense and make it one of the best in the league.

"We could actually do this," he realized.

"Hmm?" Jax looked up from studying the tablet.

"What…you said." Tom lowered his voice, feeling foolish. Jax had probably already forgotten it—that little moment at breakfast after Tom had told him the truth and then panicked on a hotel roof like an idiot. He probably wanted Tom to be less terrified and had said whatever he could think of. To Tom, though, it was at once a comfort and the way to turn everything he thought was wrong with him into strength instead of weakness.

Jax smiled. His dimples dug deep into his cheeks, and his eyes were so, so kind. "About proving them wrong? Yeah. We will."

They had a rest day after the road trip ended. Tom took the half hour drive up to Phil's house to check up on him. He texted in advance, but Phil had been ignoring all of his texts since Raleigh. To be fair, he'd threatened to ignore Tom if he apologized again, and then he did it anyway.

He hadn't heard from Camille either, and the trainers hadn't given out any details on Phil's condition. Tom was worried. Besides, being injured and sidelined while the team went on without you couldn't feel good.

Phil answered the door in rumpled sweats, leaning heavily on a crutch. He hadn't shaved in at least a week, a forgivable look on him during playoffs and pretty much no other time.

When he saw Tom standing there with a case of Gatorade and a bag of groceries, he sighed, turned around, and hobbled over to the couch. He left the door open, though, which counted as an invitation.

Tom dropped everything off in the kitchen, then followed Phil to the living room.

A comforter lay balled up on one end of the couch, and at least a day or so of dirty dishes sat stacked on the coffee table.

"Are you sleeping here?"

Phil surveyed the area, clearly realizing there was no point in denying it.

"Stairs fuck with the knee," he muttered. "Damn open-plan houses. There's no guest bedroom down here or anything."

"Christ, Phil."

"Yeah."

Tom sat next to him. He ran his thumb across the weave of his track pants, slowly back and forth. "Is it bad?"

"It's not good."

"ACL?"

"Yeah. Apparently, everyone is still undecided about whether I need surgery or not."

Tom tried and failed to hide a wince. Surgery meant more time away for rehab, but either way, Phil was probably out for the whole season.

"This is a contract year for me," Phil said.

Tom had known that, of course, but he'd been trying very hard not to think about it.

"You don't think they'll re-sign you?"

Phil snorted. "Come on. We both know I'm past my prime."

"You're thirty-four."

"Which is three to five years from death, in hockey terms."

Tom had a mixed relationship with being honest about his feelings, but it had gone all right the last few days. He took a breath and gave it a shot. "I don't want you to leave."

Phil rested a hand on his shoulder. "I don't want to leave either. I'm…thinking about other options."

"Like what?"

Phil glared at him.

"No." Tom shook his head emphatically. "Retirement is not an option. No way."

"It might be my only option." Phil stretched out his bad leg and winced. "I want to keep playing hockey, but I also want to have two functional legs when I'm done."

"You will."

"Tom. I want kids someday. I want to take them to the park and push them on the swings, not be so broken I have to pay someone else to do it."

It sounded like a nice future. It also sounded lightyears away from sleeping on the couch because the stairs were too tricky.

Tom rubbed a hand over his face. "Where's Camille anyway?"

"Monaco."

"What?"

Phil laughed ruefully. "We got divorced. Six months ago."

Tom rifled through his brain for the right thing to say and came up empty. Instead, he blurted, "Why didn't you tell me?"

"You're my best friend, Tom. But we never talk about anything but hockey. Didn't know how to go there."

Right. The consequences of Tom's actions. Funny how those kept getting in the way of things. He'd done his level best to keep anything personal hermetically sealed off from his hockey life in case anyone found out about him. Found out he was gay. He ought to at least be able to think it, even if he'd only said it once. But him not getting personal with his friends meant they treated him the same. "I'm sorry."

"It's not your fault." Phil was so kind, so understanding, so…

A shiver of fear ran down Tom's spine. What if he knew? What if he'd always known? What if he'd been waiting for Tom to tell him, and Tom never had? What if… But this was Phil. They'd known each other for a decade. If Tom's reticence really bothered Phil, he would have said something. Instead, he absolved Tom of the blame for never sharing about his personal life.

"Well, that's bullshit."

It startled a laugh out of Phil, which was something.

"I know it's too late now, but I'm trying to be…better."

"Jax, huh? He brings it out in you."

"I…" Tom flushed hot, and then cold again. Could Phil tell, just from watching them, how attractive Tom found Jax? It was one thing for Phil to guess Tom's sexuality without Tom ever saying it. They'd been friends since Tom had been drafted. And Tom hadn't gone on one date with a woman in all those years; it would be a reasonable conclusion. But Phil's insight into the indignity of Tom's wild attraction to a teammate—a coworker years younger than him—with full knowledge that nothing would ever come of it, was far more embarrassing. "I guess."

"I knew I liked that kid."

"He's not a kid."

"I guess not. Hey, the call-up you guys got for me is looking sharp. Mazetti? Great on his edges."

Tom forced himself to look at Phil directly. "Luca's doing well. But don't change the subject. What happened, Phil?"

Phil sighed. "I want kids, Tom. She doesn't. Never has. I don't know. I guess we both thought the other person would change their mind down the road. And I used to think I would. I used to think it would be enough to love only her for the rest of my life, but…"

"I'm so sorry. Sounds rough." Tom couldn't imagine how painful it must be to promise to spend your life with someone only for it not to pan out. In part, he lacked the imagination to do so because, at over thirty, he'd never been in a relationship. Another part of him, buried so deep it couldn't be broken, still believed when you loved someone, really loved them, no challenge could be insurmountable.

Phil smiled weakly at him. "It is. It was. But we still talk, you know? And it's easier now there isn't always this…thing hanging between us."

"And she still couldn't come here and take care of you?"

"No way. She spent five years waiting around for me to come home from hockey. She's done her time. I'm not asking her to nurse her ex-husband back to health."

"Well, what about your family?"

Phil grimaced. "My mom would drive me insane in about five minutes."

Tom could relate. Still. "You can't be here all alone sleeping on the couch. What if something happens to you?"

"I'm an adult. I'll be fine."

"But—"

"So what about you, huh? If we're talking about real stuff now?"

Real stuff? Tom tried not to seem too scared. "What about me?"

"Why no wife? Why no girlfriend? You're rich enough, and you don't look like a potato, which is more than I can say for some hockey guys. You even have all your teeth."

Tom snorted. Not a potato. A damning, if accurate assessment of his appearance. He was no Jax Grant. At least Phil let him ease into this comfortably, asking about women first so Tom could have the dignity of saying it himself.

"Seriously, man. I've been wondering for years. Is it a married chick?"

Wait, what?

Phil read the confusion on his expression but not the cause. "It seemed like a reasonable explanation, you know? I thought maybe you fell for the GM's wife or something, and it could never happen. Why else would a single guy as handsome and rich as you literally never get laid?"

So, Phil didn't know. Phil had no idea Tom was gay. It should have been a relief. Thirteen years in the league, and no one had read the truth from his behavior, not even the person closest to him. Instead, it dismayed Tom. All at once, he realized how comforting the thought of being known so thoroughly without having to reveal himself had been, all of the reward with none of the risk.

He could tell Phil now. Own up to it, come out. It couldn't be as hard the second time around.

In the end, all he said was "You want some lunch?"

"All right, all right, keep your secrets," Phil said, but he seemed disappointed. Nowhere near as disappointed as Tom was, but still.

So, Tom cooked them lunch while Phil sat at the kitchen table with his leg up. Tom was the furthest thing from a proficient cook, but he had one or two recipes he'd made often enough he could fake confidence, and his salmon spinach pasta dish was one of them. They talked about the power play and Coach

Trout—"I should sue that guy; he broke my knee for good," Phil said, only half-kidding—and then Tom left.

He sat in the front seat of his car for fifteen minutes, debating whether or not to go back in and tell Phil the truth.

He didn't.

Instead, at practice the next morning, he pulled Coach Morris aside and told him Phil was living alone and sleeping on the couch because he couldn't do the stairs.

"I think the team needs to send someone by to help him," Tom said.

Coach Morris frowned. Since Tom had never seen him make any other expression, he couldn't gauge Morris's reaction. "I don't know. If Easton doesn't want—"

"He's thinking about suing," Tom blurted out.

Morris stopped dead.

"We all know his contract's not getting renewed. And if Trout hadn't been running the defensemen ragged, he might have—"

"Ah, fuck." Morris dragged a hand through his red-blond hair. "Thanks for telling me, Crowler."

Worry overcame Tom instantly about whether he'd made the wrong choice. He didn't know Morris well, and so far, his coaching had been inconsistent at best. Had telling him really been the right choice? "Will you—he won't—I mean, if he wants to sue, it would be his right."

"Oh, believe me, I know." Morris sounded grim, even more so than usual. "I'll take care of him. Of it."

He stalked off to his office, leaving the team in the less-than-capable hands of the assistant coaches. Trout, scenting opportunity for the first time in two weeks, brought out one of his most heinous drills, a full ice reverse drill for engaging with breakouts that left the defensemen gasping for air as they raced across the rink. Luca, the quickest of the six, was out of breath by the time they were halfway through. Their thighs had to be burning from the way Trout kept them crouching low half the time.

"Stop watching the others. Concentrate!" Coach Edwards encouraged. He used the scant free section of ice Trout had left him on either side of the playing field to practice passing across the entire rink. Tom thought Edwards would be too distracted trying to improve Howie's stance and Mooney's aim to pay attention to him, but apparently not.

"Coach?" Tom ventured to Edwards when Trout started yelling at Hayesie, calling him a waste of space who should be ashamed of the cap hit his contract caused the team. "Don't you think Coach Trout is...taking it a little far?"

Edwards peered over at the other group. Hayesie, a man with both the tact and the physical proportions of a tank, looked about twenty seconds away from decking Trout right in the face. Breezy intervened, asking Trout a banal question about the drill, which meant Trout screamed at him for being an idiot instead.

Tom breathed a sigh of relief. While he could be sensitive when the team chirped his taste in clothes, hairstyles, and women, Breezy remained impervious to yelling. It only made him double down and try harder. Tom made a mental note to thank him for taking the heat. The last thing they needed was for Trout to bench Hayes.

"I think they're doing fine," Edwards said.

"Um," Howie said, the closest he'd ever come to commenting on anything during practice.

Edward's statement was so ridiculous that "um" counted as a reasonable response. Trout treated NHL players like a bunch of hungover college students, and he had done so for months, totally unchecked. He hadn't been this brazen last year. Why had no one intervened? Why was Morris ignoring it? Had he been the same with his own college players before he joined an NHL staff?

Tom couldn't picture it. Everything about his manner spoke of a mild, polite, if grumpy man who wore authority poorly. Still, he was the head coach. So why hadn't he talked to the GM about how one of his team had been treating the players? If the players themselves had to intervene and suggest plays and lines, surely Morris saw that something was amiss. He might be new to the big leagues, but he'd been playing or coaching hockey for most of his life, so he had to know this wasn't normal.

Unless Morris didn't want the GM to know. Unless— No, Tom was being ridiculous. There might be a lot of money at play in the NHL, but not enough to make some sort of conspiracy lucrative. Coaches were just dicks sometimes.

Afterward, in the locker room, Jax fell into his spot beside Tom heavily. "You tried," he said.

"It's my fault. I should have waited to talk to Morris until practice ended."

"It's fucked up if Morris isn't paying attention to what his own staff is doing."

"True."

"What were you talking to him about anyway?"

"I…" Tom trailed off, wondering if he could tell Jax about Phil and his empty house and the comforter on his couch and the contract extension he'd already given up hope on. Tom wanted to. He wanted to tell Jax about all of it, especially the brief flicker of hope that Phil had known about him all along, how it had sparked to life a desire to be seen that had guttered and died so fast Tom couldn't enjoy it.

Jax would probably say something flippant and funny, and then he would feel bad about it and say something else earnest and heartfelt, and Tom would feel so much better afterward.

But Tom couldn't put all his feelings on Jax. Even if Jax didn't mind carrying the load, it was definitely too much to unravel in the locker room. So, Tom said, "I'm worried about Phil."

Jax nudged their shoulders together. "Hey, want to get lunch and talk about the PK?"

It was almost as good.

# Eight

Kayleigh [off-screen]: Best things about the NHL so far—go.

Howie: Wow, I mean, everything! Playing hockey on the big stage, my family seeing me out there—especially my dad. He's a hockey coach; it means a lot, you know?

Mooney: [snorts] See, Howie made the team straight off his first training camp. He doesn't know suffering.

Howie: Hey, I was in Juniors too!

Mooney: Okay, so I got drafted two years ago, but I went back to my Juniors team for a year, and then I was on the Pups—the Sea Lion's AHL team—last year. And we went everywhere by bus. Everywhere. That's twenty-plus sweaty dudes trapped in a bus for up to ten hours. Last year, one guy got food poisoning on our trip home from an away game. Worst five hours of my life. Then this year, I get here, I'm psyched already, right? And then we go on our first away game, and I get on the team bus, and it's, like, comfortable? How? What magic do they put into the NHL buses? I love it.

Kayleigh: So what would you tell all the guys out there trying to make it?

Howie: Um, keep doing your best?

Mooney: What he said. And shout-out to the San Diego Pups. I miss you guys!

## Top comments:

s_d_pups_official: Aww, we miss you too, Diego! Cuckoo says he's sorry for throwing up in the bus

seelionssaylions: Great to see these new guys rounding out the offense! Keep your heads up, boys!

[comment deleted]

Sea_Lions_Official: This comment has been deleted. We take personal attacks on our players for their race, religion, or personal lives very seriously. Keep your heads in the game.

(From "Meet this Year's Sea Lion Rookies," posted to YouTube on 11/10/2024)

When the trade to San Francisco went through, Jax spent the following weeks mourning the loss of the good thing he'd had going in Philadelphia. He missed his house, his friends, his booty calls, all of it. But by the next road trip in mid-November, two weeks after the East Coast swing, Jax realized what he'd missed most of all was the comforting reliability of a set routine and the steady hum of other people, present and familiar in his life.

Becoming friends with Tom gave him exactly what he needed. They went to practice, they had lunch together, and they played the game. Jax took the spinning bike next to Tom's in the cooldown room more often than not. Mooney even asked Tom for advice sometimes, especially with Jax there to make him less austere and threatening.

It was only natural to continue spending time together on the road.

After the game in Ottawa, they sat pressed up against each other all evening, shoulder to shoulder on Jax's hotel bed, watching video and pointing things out on the small screen. In Calgary, it was Tom's bed.

When Coach Trout got another half hour to unleash his not particularly well-hidden sadism on the D-core, they took Luca and Breezy out for lunch while Hayesie and the other vets chilled, literally, in ice baths so they could be something approaching fighting fit for the game in the evening.

"What is wrong with that man?" Luca groused over his kale and salmon salad.

"He's probably very sad." Breezy licked dressing off his knife. "You know, like, on the inside." A drop of dressing ran down the side of his chin.

Luca studied him. "It is a miracle you survived to adulthood. In Italy, we would have put you out in the hills for the wolves to find."

Breezy shoved a massive forkful of Cobb salad into his mouth before retorting, "In Montreal, you might have been hugged as a child, then you wouldn't be this way."

With every word, Jax watched, mesmerized, as bits of egg and bacon and chicken breast were compacted with lettuce.

"What way?"

"*Mean.*"

"Boys," Tom said with the air of an exhausted father.

Both of them looked over to him, appearing for all the world like kids with their hands in the proverbial cookie jar.

"Are you all right?" Jax asked them.

Breezy shrugged. "I'll be fine."

Luca nodded. "What he said."

"Okay, well, you two are the only ones."

Tom glared at Jax.

"What?" Jax said. "It's true. And so long as this coaching situation is going on, we're gonna need you two to step up."

"What do you mean?"

Tom and Jax exchanged a glance. They'd talked about it a few times now, and it became more and more clear with each passing game.

"We want Luca to have more ice time," Tom said. "Breezy, you're on the first D-pair now. What do you think about having Luca there with you?"

Luca took a slow, measured sip of his water and turned to Breezy. Breezy met his gaze, steadier than Jax expected.

"I think that's a good idea," he said. "Me and Hayesie do okay, but our styles are pretty similar. Luca's different enough we could really make something special happen."

"We thought so too." Jax leaned forward. "We were also thinking about the power play. Right now, we've got Hayesie on the first unit, but we think you would be a better fit, Luca, with Breezy and Hayesie on the second."

"Hayes will not be happy," Luca observed.

"That's your only objection?"

A smile stole across Luca's face. He was so extremely good-looking—with eyelashes some women would kill for and the face of an angel—it made Jax uncomfortable. It made Jax want to pat him on the head and make sure no one ever hurt him. Given everything he'd witnessed so far about Luca's personality, he would probably claw off Jax's face if he tried, but the urge remained.

Proving Jax's point, Luca said, "I obviously agree I am the best at everything."

Breezy groaned. "He's gonna be insufferable."

"We'll talk to Hayesie," Tom said, although it appeared as though he found the thought alone about as pleasant as chewing glass.

"I would like to be there." Luca returned to his salad once he'd said it, nodding in satisfaction.

"Why?"

When Jax laughed at the question, Tom cringed. He was such an awkward man. An awkward, gorgeous man who had put off his usual visit to the most aggressively heterosexual hairdresser in the Bay Area long enough his hair had begun to emulate something akin to style. It fell across his forehead, giving him a subtle delicacy, highlighting the sharp cut of his nose and jaw.

Also, he'd put on a tank top after practice, and Jax wanted to lick his biceps. Apparently, finding out he had a queer teammate was a gateway drug into fantasizing about that teammate. Jax couldn't wait for his subconscious to finish working through this so he could be the best platonic friend Tom ever had. Right now, he kept having to hold back his most id-driven thoughts.

"It seems…the right thing to do."

Breezy nodded at Luca in approval.

Luca's assessment turned out to be correct. They broached the topic with Hayes and Morris on the flight from Calgary to Montreal. Morris nodded thoughtfully, voiced a few concerns about Luca being a little too new to be a good addition to the special teams, but said he'd give it a shot. Luca, standing awkwardly next to the four-way seat, gripping the backrests when they hit turbulence, said very little except how glad he was for the opportunity. His expressive eyes remained steady when he added that he hoped Hayes would be open to giving him advice.

Hayes's expression darkened and darkened as the conversation went on. At the end of it, he shot Tom a nasty look. "Everyone warned me you were an asshole," he said. "I kept saying no, no, he's just shy. Guess I was fuckin' wrong."

"James," Tom tried, the first time anyone had used Hayes's full given name in Jax's hearing. Heedless, Hayes stalked to the rear of the plane and found a seat by himself, where he stayed for the rest of the flight.

Jax tried to distract Tom, first with more hockey talk, then with an increasingly desperate game of Would You Rather. But Tom was impervious to whimsy, and Jax ended up finding out Breezy would rather always have slightly wet socks than always be slightly too cold. As a consequence, Luca, who had been silent and dejected since Hayes's outburst, started ribbing him for being the worst Canadian in the world, for which Breezy blamed his Italian blood, which forced Jax to sit between them for the remainder of the flight to avoid bloodshed.

Things didn't improve in the locker room in Montreal. Hayes remained bitter and angry. As one of the team leaders—and especially with Phil out—some of the guys naturally took their cues from him. It made the power play awkward and uncomfortable, with Vanderbilt passing to Jax and Tom and summarily ignoring Luca's existence.

In the second break, with Montreal leading 3–1, Hayes graduated from icy glares to hostile barbs about how ineffective the new special teams were. Jax listened, feeling helpless and discouraged. Maybe it had been overly ambitious of them to change the lineup so fast. Luca *was* very new in the big leagues, though he had so much poise. Maybe Morris had a secret long-term plan he hadn't told them about, which explained why he didn't intervene with Trout. Maybe they'd ruined their chances at a playoff berth. They'd been doing so well this season, too, and now the locker room was poisoned.

By the intermission, Hayes had talked himself up enough to get to his feet and stalk over to where Luca sat, sandwiched between Breezy and Howie. He examined the rookie head to toe. "That's what you get for promoting his type."

A shudder ran down Jax's spine. "What exactly is his type?" He didn't want to hear the answer, but he would much rather take whatever came than make Luca face it alone. The kid was only twenty-one.

Simultaneously, Hayes spat, "Mexicans," while Howie said, "Queers."

Dead silence fell across the locker room.

This was Jax's moment. This was when he would intervene with a timely quip or a perfect takedown. This was what he had been preparing for his entire professional career.

No words came to mind.

Beside him, Tom got to his feet.

"Enough."

At some point in the last month and half, since joining the team and learning first to challenge Tom and then to support him, Jax had forgotten how imposing he could be. At full height, with his eyes glinting, steely and determined, he made Jax's breath catch in his throat.

"I will not have that kind of language on my team or in my locker room. If you're going to speak about your teammates like that, you can do it from the bench."

Then, he turned his back on the team and stalked out onto the ice.

Jax followed. He couldn't imagine doing anything else.

The third period was an unmitigated disaster. For the Montreal Wyverne, anyway. The Crow took to the ice, and he was not fucking around. He scored his first goal three minutes in off a pass from Jax. Jax hadn't even been going for the assist. He'd thought they'd have to deke it back and forth a few more times, but Tom saw some imaginary lane right between two opposing D-men, and a second later, the goal light went on.

One goal away from equalizing, they doubled down. Morris sent the first line out for longer, searching for chances, and Luca got them. With the puck on the wrong side of the ice, the Wyverne's first-line winger racing on a breakaway, Luca sped up to cut him off at every turn and stripped away the puck in a neat little game of keep-away.

He spun around and shot it over to Vanderbilt, the puck control breathtaking. The next minute, Vanderbilt had passed to Tom, who had hauled ass toward the blue line as soon as he'd seen Luca's play, and then the puck hit the back of the net.

The team barely paused to celebrate drawing even, not least because Vanderbilt had the assist, but he was clearly too much of a homophobe to get near Luca and too much of a coward to get near Tom.

Jax hugged them both as hard as he could.

"All right, boys," Morris said when they made it to the bench, blissfully unaware that the first line couldn't make eye contact. "We've got about seven minutes to wrap this thing up. I don't wanna go into overtime, you hear me?"

He wasn't great at reading the room, which made Jax wonder more than ever how he'd gotten the coaching gig, but he was absolutely correct. No one wanted to be here longer than necessary.

"Gotta get Cap the hatty," Breezy added, a much better motivation for Jax.

Jax did his level best, sending the puck Tom's way every time he had it on his stick. Tom, fucking on fire, tore across the ice at full speed. Jax remained firm in his belief of the unsexiness of hockey gear, but Tom made it work. He pulled his helmet off between shifts and pushed his sweaty hair out of his eyes, and Jax actually started chubbing up a little in his cup.

This was a disaster.

He had a lifetime track record of not making it weird with his teammates, a shining beacon with which to prove all the idiots wrong who said stuff like "I don't mind gay dudes, but I don't want them in the locker room, y'know?" And yet, he found himself here, at twenty-five, getting all boned up over his captain. It didn't matter that Tom was gay or that he was out there performing the sexiest feats Jax had ever seen on ice. It was the principle of the thing.

In the end, Jax didn't get him the hatty. He ended up with all of one assist on the board for the night, but he couldn't be mad about how it happened. Montreal got chippy as the clock ran down, equally unwilling as the Sea Lions to go to overtime. It made them sloppy. One of their forwards got called for slashing, and on the ensuing power play, all of Jax and Tom's strategizing paid off. Jax won the face-off. He took the puck forward, deked around a defenseman, and then doubled back, shooting to Luca. Luca picked up the pace, using his quick feet, right up the left side of the ice, and shot the puck neatly onto Tom's tape. Luca's aim had been so perfect Tom barely needed to tip it in, but it counted as his third goal of the night. With only two minutes left to go, the hats rained down on the ice for Tom.

A little smirk played around Tom's mouth when they hit the bench, only a tiny upward quirk of his lips revealing he knew exactly how good he was.

God, Jax wanted to suck his dick.

Right there on the bench, just shoulder his way between those thighs, pull down his layers of sweat-soaked, disgusting gear and swallow him straight down his throat. He bet Tom would stink of exertion and wet hockey gear, repulsive at best but also familiar and comforting. He bet Tom had a fantastic cock. Jax would make it so good for him, too, really pull out all the stops and make him moan. Make him beg. Tom was wound so tight, Jax bet anything he'd beg so prettily.

The game ended.

On the way to the locker room, Jax held his breath until his erection subsided. Mostly. Adrenaline erections happened all the time after close games and common courtesy was to pretend at selective blindness, but it seemed disrespectful to enter a team space while sporting a full chub because Tom fucking Crowler had been so hot decimating the opposition.

The locker room after the game was awful. On the one hand, they had won, which meant Breezy put on East's "winning" playlist (a lot of Nelly, some Jay-Z, some nineties rap, which, unfortunately, sounded very stupid to Jax's uncultured ears. He was used to much less upbeat hip-hop, a sign of the times he lived in). On the other hand, no one talked except Abrahamov and Dmitriyev, speaking in quiet Russian in the corner. Jax didn't want to know what they were saying. He doubted they felt differently than Hayes and Vanderbilt.

Jax escaped to a cold shower as quickly as he could. On his way out, he carefully didn't look too closely at Tom, stripped down to his base layers and talking to the media.

This was fine. Jax could deal with this. He'd go out tonight. It had been ages; he hadn't had sex since Edmonton, six weeks ago. No wonder he'd gotten pent up enough to fantasize about oral while at work. That was probably all this was, misplaced libido. He took a few deep, grounding breaths and washed his hair. If he went out tonight, he wanted to look good.

He returned to the locker room to hear Breezy loudly asking, "Hey, Ziti. You wanna come for dinner with my folks? They'd be so psyched to meet a *real Italian.*"

Luca, in the middle of tying his silver tie over an elegant dark blue suit, leveled Breezy with the most long-suffering expression known to man. "That is not my hockey nickname."

"Sure, it is! Mazetti, ziti, you're Italian. It's perfect!" Breezy threw an arm around Luca's shoulders. He wore a serviceable tan suit off the rack, given how it strained across his shoulders and thighs but wrinkled over his stomach, and one of the ties they sold in the merch store. The contrast could not have been more obvious if he'd tried. Breezy steered Luca out of the locker room still discussing the merits of baked ziti. Apparently, there were many.

In their wake, Hayes stared after the two of them, dumbfounded. "He's, uh. Italian?"

"Yup." Jax popped the *p* as obnoxiously as he could.

"What about the other thing?"

Mooney snorted derisively. "Ziti's wheeled a girl in every city this road trip. Howie's jealous; he could never."

Howie looked up, made a face as if he wanted to be insulted, but then seemed to decide it might not be worth drawing more attention to himself.

Rightly so. If Jax were in charge, Howie'd be doing nothing but bag skates and bench warming for the next three years.

"By the way," Mooney added, throwing his bag over his shoulder with enough force to smack Hayes in the side. "I *am* Mexican."

Hayes watched him leave. "Well fuck," he muttered.

Jax debated getting into it with him, telling him all the ways he'd been out of line. He debated walking up to Howie and asking him what the hell he'd been thinking. He took a deep breath and did precisely none of it.

He was too angry, too emotional, and weirdly, still a little horny. If he tried for confrontation now, he'd break things beyond repair. Better to try in the morning, when he could remember nineteen-year-old rookies like Howie spent their entire lives surrounded by bullshit and probably didn't know better.

Hayes, though, was old enough to know better. Jax might need two or three nights to stomach talking to him again.

The bus ride to the hotel remained quiet. If Breezy had been there, he might have livened things up, forced some sort of connection back into the team. But his family lived in Montreal, and he used his curfew exemption to stay with them (after dinner out with Luca, it seemed). Jax spent the time researching queer-friendly clubs on his phone. Normally, he'd have waited till they got there, and no one else could see his phone screen. Normally, he wouldn't have dared trying to hook up in Canada.

These were not normal times. Jax clung to sanity by a thread, and when it snapped, he'd either scream his sexuality in Hayes's face or kiss Tom on the mouth. Neither of which constituted a safe or sane option.

They got in around ten, but the clubs opened by eleven or so. Jax could post up at the bar and wait for things to get good. He changed quickly, keeping the tailored suit pants but switching the button-up shirt and jacket for a plain white T-shirt. If he had suspenders with him, he might have gone for a newsboy cap to round out the look. He styled his hair to be a little messy, just to make his highlights pop, then dabbed a little eau de toilette on his wrists and behind his ears because he was classy like that. He pulled on his shoes, checked he had his wallet, his phone, his room key, and a condom.

And then Tom knocked on the door.

Jax could tell it was Tom because even his knock was polite and a little reticent.

He yanked open the door. "No."

Tom held up his tablet. "I thought we could—the power play—"

"Tom," Jax said with all the patience he could muster. "It has been a very tense and emotional day, and I really need to suck someone's dick about it, all right?"

Tom's entire face went red. He stepped inside, and the door fell shut behind him. "In *Montreal*? Jax, you'll get recognized—"

Jax groaned. "I can't... How can you possibly want to talk about hockey right now?"

"I don't." Tom said it so quietly Jax barely heard it. "I, um, didn't want to be alone."

Well, shit. There went Jax's plans.

Unless...

"You got a fucking hat trick tonight. You deserve to get off. Come out with me."

Tom reared back, staring at him. "I...what? I couldn't. No, no I couldn't."

"Why not? You're gay. I'm gay. There's a club three blocks from here selling shots for two dollars."

"Jax." Tom said it as though he thought Jax might be kidding.

"That's two Canadian dollars. Come on."

"I don't go out."

Time to play purposefully dumb. "You do too, with the team sometimes."

"For team bonding, not for...you know."

Jax looked Tom up and down. He still wore most of his suit, but like Jax, he'd ditched the jacket. His shirt emphasized the length of his torso and lithe grace, despite his delectable ass and thighs. "You have needs, though, Mr. Hockey Robot, same as the rest of us. What do you do then?"

"I just...you know."

Heat rose in Jax's gut, clouding his judgment. He'd started a very stupid line of questioning for a man who was trying very hard not to sleep with his captain. "I don't know. What do you do? Get on the apps? Find a hooker?"

"No!" Tom appeared mortified at the very thought, focused directly on Jax for the first time since he'd admitted to wanting company. "I...take care of it myself."

Oh God.

"You mean you...never?"

Tom shook his head. "Well, once, when I was seventeen, I... But no. Not since then."

Jax did some quick mental math and wanted to jump into the nearest lake, no matter that it was November and they were in Canada. "Was it terrible?"

"No." A secret little smile stole across Tom's face. "It was…really nice. But afterward, I got so scared, and it never seemed worth the risk, you know?"

When Jax first thought Tom gave new meaning to the word "closeted," he decided Tom must be lonely. But "lonely" couldn't encompass how desolate Tom's life must actually have been. Jax had assumed he must be hooking up somehow. He couldn't picture a life without at least the animal comfort of skin and heat and pleasure when he lacked the human comfort of home and belonging and love.

Tom had granted himself none of it in fifteen years.

But maybe he didn't need that kind of connection as intensely as Jax. He could be ace, or more interested in romance than sex, or not interested in it at all. Before Jax went entirely off the deep end, he ought to at least ask.

"Is it something you want?"

"Of course I want it. It was always something I couldn't have until…" Tom waved his hand vaguely. "After hockey."

"After hockey could be *years*. Let me take you out. You could meet someone. You deserve…"

"Sex?" Tom laughed as if the idea itself was ridiculous.

Jax's very thin thread of patience snapped along with the entirety of his ability to be normal about Tom. "You deserve to be touched like you matter. You deserve to be held and—and fucking worshiped."

He'd stepped closer as he spoke. He didn't remember doing it, but he must have because they were so close Jax could see every fleck of gray in Tom's eyes.

"Jax," Tom said, husky and low as if he'd been drinking whiskey straight from the bottle. As if he was drunk on Jax's words.

Jax forced himself to step away. "So, yeah. You should come out with me."

Tom swayed closer as if trying to follow Jax. "I…I, um…I wouldn't know what to do."

"I'll show you."

"Show me?"

"Yeah." Jax cleared his throat. "I can teach you how to flirt, and dance, and get a guy to leave with you. It's easy."

Tom snapped to attention, back going straight and face going guarded. "It's still risky in Montreal."

"We'll be careful. There aren't many hockey fans in queer nightclubs, and the lighting is shit anyway."

For a long moment, Tom said nothing, and Jax was sure Tom would turn him down. And then he'd have to stay here, too, because Tom didn't want to be alone, and Jax would never, ever leave him, and then maybe they would open something from the minibar and sit down on the bed, and Jax could watch Tom's pink tongue lick the alcohol from his lips, and they would get closer, and—

"All right. Let's do it."

Jax didn't know whether to be relieved or disappointed.

The heating in the hotel must have been turned up much too high. The bracing air outside forced Jax out of the hazy headspace he'd been in. *You deserve to be worshiped?* What had he been thinking?

Clearly, he hadn't been thinking. Not with his upstairs brain anyway. He made sure to keep his distance from Tom as they walked. He didn't trust himself not to do something stupid if he got too close.

The club was mostly empty when they got there, a few groups standing awkwardly by the edge of the dancefloor, waiting not to be the first ones dancing.

Jax led Tom to the bar and ordered a beer for them both.

"Oh my God, relax. No one is watching us."

It wasn't strictly true. A group of college-aged guys had definitely taken note of their entrance. Jax doubted they were hockey fans. Based on the way they'd eyed Tom up, their interest had to do with his extremely nice ass. But with Tom's shoulders hunched practically up to his ears, he looked terrified. Jax would point them out later.

"I can't help it," Tom snapped.

Fifteen years. He hadn't been touched by another person (outside of hockey) in fifteen years.

Jax would allow a little snippiness. But only a little.

"And you're sure this is—"

"Tom, I have been doing this for six years, and the only person who ever caught me was you."

Incrementally, Tom's shoulders loosened. "Okay." He took a sip of beer. "Okay."

"Okay," Jax repeated. "So, Mr. Hat Trick. See anyone you want to have suck your dick?"

Tom choked on his beer.

Jax twisted in his seat to examine the room. It was filling up, albeit slowly. "So there's a group over on the left. See them? The guy in the purple crop top would absolutely blow you in the bathroom."

After wiping up his spilled beer, Tom turned to follow Jax's line of sight. "He looks a little young for me."

"Fair. You are a dinosaur. Okay, how about the guy heading toward the bar now, in the black T-shirt?"

"I don't know…"

"Tom. Do you or do you not want someone to blow your brains out tonight?"

Tom's eyes went a little wide. "I don't know?"

"You don't… *Tom*."

Tom mumbled something so low Jax couldn't hear it over the deafening sounds of a Dua Lipa club remix.

"What was that?"

"I don't know how to ask!"

Jax had always found honesty the best policy. If he wanted his dick sucked, he would go up to a guy and ask. To be fair, most of the time he asked to suck someone else's dick, which was an easier question both to ask and to answer.

He had a feeling his approach would not work for Tom.

"Okay. Pretend we've never met, and I don't know you."

Tom wore a deeply doubtful expression, but Jax hadn't gotten this far in life by letting other people's doubt deter him. He pasted on his sleaziest smile, the one most clearly indicating *here for a good time, not a long time*. Leaning in close, he said, "Hi. I'm Jax. You come here often?"

He only realized the tactical error when Tom blinked up at him. He'd never seen Tom at this angle before because Tom was taller than him, but with Jax leaning over him while he sat, Tom had to tilt his head back to make eye contact. The idea of Tom beneath him, Tom looking to him for guidance, for help, for pleasure, didn't so much occur to Jax as it left him bruised and battered by the wayside.

He could be so good for Tom. He could show Tom everything he'd been missing, pamper him with kisses and fuck him so good he'd never need to hit on strangers in bars. Jax could be everything he'd never known he needed.

Tom ducked his head, seeming for all the world as if Jax's lame come-on flattered him so much he couldn't help it.

Jax wanted him so much he ached.

"This is my first time," Tom said, low and smooth, not confident necessarily, but like a confidant, as though he was entrusting Jax with a secret.

"Can I buy you a drink?"

Tom gestured to his half-full beer. "I have one."

Jax rolled his eyes. "If you wanna get laid, you say yes to the drink."

"Oh."

"Yeah."

Tom ran a nervous hand through his hair, and Jax had to get out of there immediately before he suggested Tom cut out the middleman and fuck Jax instead, and then maybe marry him and have his babies while they were at it.

Jax drained the rest of his beer. "I'm gonna hit the head. Try it with the guy over there, huh?"

He escaped before Tom could answer. To avoid making a liar of himself, he went to the bathroom. He pissed, washed his hands, and spent a long moment staring into the mirror, mulling the inconvenience. He wasn't supposed to have actual feelings for Tom. Attraction to him was fine; Jax could ignore attraction. But all this wanting to care for him bullshit? Not happening. It wasn't something Jax could have. He'd spent enough of his life hungering for seemingly out-of-reach things to know the difference. An NHL career? Possible if he worked hard enough and ignored all the assholes who claimed he couldn't do it. Giving his parents everything they could possibly want or need now he could afford it? Possible if he did it without their knowledge so they couldn't turn him down. Having an active sex life while closeted in the NHL? Possible if he was careful enough. The second he hadn't been, he'd gotten traded.

Falling for someone, having a relationship? Not possible. He had enough self-awareness to know that when he loved someone, he couldn't hide it for shit.

Falling for Tom? A perfect, impossible dream. Not only would the secrecy of it kill Jax, Tom was too good for him. Tom deserved someone who didn't have such a hard time not fucking up by wanting too much, by hiding too poorly. Tom deserved someone who could support him through the difficulties of being a closeted athlete, not someone who faced the exact same issues, and definitely not someone who toyed ever more seriously with the idea of coming out.

Jax ran his wrists under cold water—he wasn't about to fuck up his hair by splashing some on his face—took a few deep breaths, and reentered the club.

The music, muffled in the bathroom, came at him too loudly, and the strobe lights were, by turns, blinding and too low. It took Jax a moment to make out Tom, even though he sat exactly where Jax had left him.

He was talking to the guy in the black T-shirt.

That...wasn't supposed to hurt.

Jax turned away purposefully. He took a deep breath. Good. Tom would meet someone, hook up, and learn he didn't have to deny himself everything. And Jax would learn to live with having had some small part in his opening up to pleasure.

A guy in cut-off jeans over fishnets and a tank top so tight Jax could count his ribs beckoned at Jax from the dance floor. Jax grabbed onto the distraction, and the guy, with both hands.

"Aren't you cold?" Jax shouted over the bass.

The guy laughed, tilting his head and exposing the line of his throat. A rhinestone-studded cross on a long chain hung around his neck. "Keep me warm?" He placed his hands over Jax's and slid them down from his waist to his hips, then twisted around so his back pressed against Jax's front.

In an ordinary world, Jax would have been into everything about this. He liked bold guys who told him what they wanted from him. He liked people who played fast and loose with gender expression. He liked hot and sweaty and ephemeral.

Tom was precisely none of those things. Tom had no idea what he wanted and presented as heteronormatively masculine as he possibly could. If something did happen, ridiculous as the thought was, Jax would never be rid of Tom no matter how badly it went. They played on the same team.

Jax glanced over at the bar again and found Tom alone, no black T-shirt man in sight.

"Your friend struck out, huh?" the guy in Jax's arms yelled in his ear.

"Seems so."

"You wanna go comfort him, or do you wanna come home with me?"

Jax watched as Tom turned to the bartender and signaled for the bill. He was giving up. He'd tried all of once and immediately called it quits. He'd return to the hotel, put his head in the sand, and spend another fifteen years "taking care of it himself."

Jax pulled away from his dance partner. "I'm sorry."

The guy shrugged and gave him a rueful smile. "Worth a shot. You should tell him how you feel."

"What?" Jax said. "I don't... No, that's not... I've got to go. Your eyeliner is awesome, by the way."

"Thanks." The guy gave him a bemused smile and a little wave, and then Jax had to hightail it out of the club. Tom was already gone.

Jax found him a block and a half away, walking way too fast for a man who'd been to hockey practice, witnessed the implosion of his hockey team, and played a full game all in one day.

"Tom!"

"You shouldn't be out here," Tom said without turning around. "You were having a good time."

Panting, Jax drew even. "We were there to get *you* to have a good time."

"We were there because you, and I quote, 'needed to suck someone's dick.'"

Oh, right. Jax had said that. Unfortunately, in the meantime, he'd been forced to accept he only wanted to suck one dick, and it was Tom's. "Yeah, well, maybe it was more of a want than a need."

"The guy you were dancing with looked like he wanted you."

"Plenty of fish in the sea. Which is why we should both go back so you can try again."

Finally, Tom turned to face him with an utterly anguished expression. "I can't do it."

Jax swallowed heavily. Had his stupid plan to get Tom out there somehow made everything worse for Tom? Had the man in the black T-shirt put him off sex for life? "What did black T-shirt guy do to you?"

"He asked me to dance."

Blinking, Jax tried to find the problem.

Tom continued, heedless of Jax's confusion. "I don't know *how* to dance with a guy. And even if I managed, what if he wanted to kiss me? I haven't kissed anyone since I was a teenager. I'll be terrible at it. I've given one blow job in my entire life. I've missed the boat. I can't do this."

He tried to stop himself, really, he did, but Jax couldn't help it. He burst out laughing.

Tom turned away, ready to keep power walking toward the hotel.

"No, no, Tom! I'm sorry. But...do you only ever do things you're good at?"

"All I do is play hockey or talk about playing hockey."

Good God, this man. Didn't he cook meals or do his laundry? Or had he performed some crazy leap of logic to make believe he only cooked meals as fuel for hockey and did his laundry so he'd have clothes to wear to hockey?

"So firstly," Jax said, "you're lying. I've seen you play cards, listen to music, and watch the news. Secondly, were you born with a magnificent slapshot?"

"No."

"How did you get good at it?"

Tom crossed his arms like a petulant child in the body of a very large hockey player. "I practiced."

"And what does that tell you?"

"I can't just...practice kissing on some guy."

*Practice on me!* Jax wanted to shout. He didn't because he was an adult with self-preservation instincts.

"Actually," Tom said, peering at Jax under the light of a digital display panel at a bus stop, "could I practice with you?"

Jax opened his mouth to turn Tom down flat. It was a terrible idea. He'd only realized he'd romantically fixated on the man five minutes ago; practice kisses would be a handy exercise in self-flagellation. Which was much more Tom's deal than Jax's, whose MO trended toward avoiding pain at all cost.

"It's perfect," Tom said before Jax could so much as get to the *n* of no way. "You know what you're doing. You can teach me. Neither of us runs any risk of being outed, and you're not into hockey players, so it can't get messy."

Tom had said so many incorrect things in a row Jax didn't know where to start. To begin with, no one had ever accused him of knowing what he was doing except for maybe the NHL. As further evidence for this claim, when Tom stepped in close to him and ducked in for a kiss, Jax did absolutely nothing to stop him.

# Nine

Jax: Most likely to get called out on social media? Hmm, tough one. Besides me, I'm gonna have to go with Howie on this, 'cause he's a young guy, and he's on social media more than the older guys on the team. And, well. Sometimes he puts his foot in it.

[Smash cut to Howie]

Howie: Jax said me? Well, then, I'm going to say him. Most likely to get called out on social media. Jax Grant. Boom. Next card. Person on the team you would go to for advice? That one's easy. Tom's the captain for a reason, yo.

**Top comments:**

seelionssaylions: this just in, Sea Lions most wholesome team in the league

stickstickpuck: Crowler team dad confirmed. Who's Grant, team crazy wine uncle?

(From "San Francisco Sea Lions Call Each Other Out For Fun," posted to YouTube 10/15/2024)

The kiss was nothing to write home about. Tom only managed to brush his lips against Jax's, dry and close-mouthed, before Jax wrenched away.

"What are you *doing*?"

For a queasy moment, Tom thought Jax was so incredibly repulsed by him that the kiss angered him. Or Tom was so bad at kissing that he'd hurt Jax.

"We're in the middle of the street! In Montreal! People could see us."

Oh. "I forgot."

Jax stared at him, so handsome, especially with his eyes all wide and dark in the streetlight and his lips red from the cold. Tom wasn't in the habit of letting himself look for too long, but he'd already kissed Jax in public, so he might as well.

"I cannot believe *you're* making *me* be your impulse control." Jax turned on his heel and started walking.

Tom followed. "Are you—did I—" He couldn't think of a way to finish the sentence without apologizing or begging for feedback vis-à-vis his kissing skills.

"We are going to the hotel," Jax said, his voice calm and measured, which was how Tom knew he was extremely agitated. "And then we are going to your room, and then I am going to kiss you properly."

"Oh. Okay."

The three blocks they walked side by side might as well have been ten miles. An unbearably tense elevator ride up to their floor followed. Chief among Tom's worries, besides whether there had been any CCTV cameras by the bus stop, was how to exit the silent detente they found themselves in and resume kissing. It seemed impossible, as if they'd left the potential for kissing outdoors in the cold, and now, they were two people who had kissed and discussed further kissing but were unable to do so until they found the magic words to reengage.

Tom didn't know the magic words. He wasn't sure he knew any words.

Fortunately, Jax knew the words. The door to Tom's hotel room had hardly closed behind them, and then he was in Tom's space, walking him backward toward the nearest wall. "You're sure about this?"

If Tom took a moment to think, properly think, about it, he would retreat into the safety he'd been living in for so long. But ever since he'd stood up in the locker room, for Luca and Jax and Diego, and finally, finally for himself, there had been a reckless thrumming in his pulse. The part of him that had sat up and took notice back in St. Louis, that burst out of him screaming in Philadelphia, that guided his words and actions tonight, had enough of being buried. It wanted out, and Tom lacked the strength to keep denying it. Even knowing he might regret it later wasn't enough to stop him following through, taking the feeling to its natural conclusion.

"Yes."

Before, Jax had said he would kiss Tom properly. Tom had taken him to mean "longer" or maybe "with tongue." When Jax leaned in and kissed him, he realized his mistake.

They hadn't kissed at the bus stop. Tom had barely done more than graze his lips across Jax's face. The way Jax cupped his cheek in one hand and looked straight at him right up until they were too close to see anything but the blurry outlines of each other's faces. The way his mouth moved, soft and gentle against Tom's, a whisper of sensation which left Tom parting his own lips, asking for more—*that* was a real kiss.

He really was bad at this.

Jax was not. The hand not holding Tom's face in place settled on his hip, and Tom found himself anchored. He didn't have to consider how to move, where to put his own hands, what to do. Jax took care of it. Jax angled his head a little so he could kiss Tom more deeply. Jax grabbed Tom by the hand and guided him to hold on to Jax's waist. Jax carded through the short hair at the nape of Tom's neck, sending shivers down his spine.

Hazily, Tom became aware kissing probably had to end at some point. He didn't know when the end point was, though, and he felt so good he left difficult things like decisions up to Jax. At some point, Jax's tongue licked lightly against his lips, and it was only natural to open his mouth. Their tongues slid together, Jax pressed closer, and Tom let himself melt back into the wall.

Was kissing supposed to feel this good? Or did Tom just think it did because he had no idea what he was doing? Could Jax tell he was totally out of his depth? Should he be more active? Or could he just let go and allow Jax to be in charge of things? Tom tore his mouth away.

"Am I—is this okay?"

Jax ran his thumb up Tom's jawline. "You're perfect."

Tom grabbed hold of the front of Jax's shirt and pulled him in.

Now Tom knew what to expect, and desire for more took the place of his nerves. Jax pressed forward in deep, slow surges, licking into Tom's mouth and then drawing back for short, soft, close-mouthed kisses. His hands ran all along Tom's sides, making Tom sigh and arch into the touch. He had nothing to worry about; Jax would take care of everything, and Jax said he was perfect.

Tom couldn't say how long they stood there, kissing up against the wall. At some point, he needed to take a full, deep breath instead of the little puffs of air he could get with their lips connected. He pulled away. Jax, apparently above such minor concerns as oxygen, switched to pressing soft, light kisses down Tom's jawline and his neck.

No one had touched Tom there before. He didn't know it would feel like *that*. He groaned, a soft little "ah" sound.

Jax stepped back. Cold air rushed into the space between them, and Tom reached out for Jax, missing his heat and his touch. His chest rose and fell, so visible in his tight T-shirt. Maybe Jax would take it off if Tom asked. Maybe he could run his hands underneath and feel warm skin.

"So that's, uh… That's kissing. You've practiced. You're good."

Did Jax want to stop?

Tom couldn't fathom why anyone ever stopped doing this.

"I want—" he started.

"I should go," Jax said hurriedly before he could finish. "Let's, uh… We can…touch base? Tomorrow?"

He was out of the door before Tom could sum up an answer.

On autopilot, he brushed his teeth and changed into a loose top and sweats. He lay down in the bed and turned out the lights. Then, he double-checked whether he'd set his phone alarm with enough time to get breakfast before the flight.

He thought about checking his messages, but he knew what awaited him there.

Mom: *Great game, sweetie! So proud of you!*

He didn't want to thank her. Not when she didn't know why he'd played so well in the third period, what had fueled him.

The lights from passing cars illuminated the whole room through the open curtains. Tom got up and pulled them shut properly.

A little cold under the sheet, his skin prickling all over, he got up again and turned off the air conditioning. Who needed AC in mid-November anyway?

The pillowcase was rumpled under his cheek. He propped himself up to fix it.

Then he rolled over to his other side.

Finally, onto his back.

He'd *kissed* Jax.

No, that wasn't right. Jax had kissed *him*. Jax had kissed him thoroughly and deeply, right here in this room. Jax put his hands all over Tom, over his shirt, sure, but still. He'd run his fingers through Tom's hair. Experimentally, Tom ran fingers through his hair. It felt good, but it didn't make him shiver. He trailed his fingers down his sides. Nice, a little ticklish. It didn't make him melt. He traced a fingertip across his neck. It sent a little spark down his spine, but it didn't make him groan.

He'd rather have a pale imitation of Jax's touch than lie in the dark, trying and failing to sleep. He let his fingers continue their journey across his skin, skating lightly over places on his body he'd never touched with intent. His hand, warm on his bad hip, soothed the ache. The touch of his fingertips on his ribs sent goosebumps in their wake.

Eventually, Tom realized he was hard. He hadn't noticed getting there, but he was unmistakably extremely erect, straining against the fabric of his boxers, tenting his sweats. When he dragged his hand across his chest, his fingernail caught on a nipple, and his cock twitched.

Carefully, delicately, he trailed his fingertips across the outline of his dick. The touch, so light he could barely feel it, made him strain upward for more. He kept his right hand there, barely touching the swell of his cock with his index and middle finger. With the left, he retraced all the places Jax had been: up his sides, through his hair, down his neck, across his swollen, sensitive lips.

It should have been nothing, those light, delicate touches. Tom was used to being checked into the boards or slammed from all sides with teammates to celebrate a goal. Surely, his body shouldn't even react to such gentle handling.

But something about being kissed the way Jax had kissed him, as though he was precious, as though he was worth taking time over, had awoken a tender craving for softness within him. If he had managed to say something, if Jax had stayed, could they have tried it in this position, lying on the bed? Tom underneath Jax, Jax with his big, strong hands barely skimming over Tom's body?

His cock gave a painful throb, and Tom gave in to temptation, pushing his clothes down far enough to pull it out. He stroked along the underside with the pads of two fingers, and that barest of touches drove him insane.

It wasn't as if he'd never been desperate for someone else to touch him. It had been such a long time, and toys ordered off Amazon could only do so much for him. His one experience had been fumbling and over so fast. Before tonight, Tom had never realized what a difference it would make for someone else to evoke these feelings in him. He'd never known how different it could be to long for someone specific to touch him, or how startling it was when they did. He hadn't known to want any of Jax's touches. His body's reaction had been so natural, so unhindered by expectation.

He wrapped his fist around his cock and stroked, properly, the way he did at home in the shower when he wanted to get it over with so he could go to sleep and stop feeling restless.

After all the buildup, he reached the edge in seconds.

And then he stopped. Trailed his fingers across the head again and gasped, loud in the quiet room. Pressed his other hand to his lips, remembered how Jax had tasted, how he'd felt, crowding in close to Tom.

Tom pictured him in bed, above him. He imagined Jax grinning at him, teasing and happy, the dimple in his cheek popping. He imagined Jax pushing him down into the sheets and kissing him again just like before, and then he came all over the bottom of his T-shirt in long, shuddering pulses that left him wrung out and hollow, satisfied but aching for more.

He rolled onto his side, clutched the second pillow tightly to his chest and went to sleep.

The next day, they played Toronto, Tom's least favorite game every year. He was thankful he played in a different conference, so he only had one day of dread leading up to it.

This year, he'd been distracted, preoccupied by other things. Coming out to Jax. Fixing the power play and fucking up the team. Kissing Jax.

He managed to forget all the way onto the team plane, still thinking about that last thing and wondering if he needed to talk to Jax about it and, if so, what he ought to say. *Thank you? Please do it again?*

And then his mom texted.

Mom: *Hi honey, we'll be waiting for you by the dressing rooms. Got a table at the Italian place we always go to. Good luck tonight!*

Nothing unusual or particularly noteworthy, but it made his stomach sink. Not least because hardly anything at most Italian restaurants was compatible with his diet.

With a sigh, Tom dropped his phone into his lap and surveyed the plane.

Hayes and Vanderbilt sat together in stony silence. Breezy had nabbed one of the four-way seats usually occupied by the vets, and he, Luca, Mooney, and Jax were laughing loudly at something on one of their phones. The coaches occupied the other four-way seats, all of them on their tablets, firmly ignoring one another.

Howie sat alone at the rear of the plane.

Tom wanted to stay in his seat, maybe put in his headphones so everyone would think he was listening to music, and then spend the flight staring out the window and thinking about last night. It wouldn't destroy his resolution to be different, to be more present as a captain and as a human being. Previously, he'd never conceived of having anything like last night to think about. But peeking over at Jax, he could see the tension in his body and the strained way he smiled. Jax would be disappointed if he didn't at least try.

So, Tom heaved himself up and joined Howie.

"I'm sorry," Howie said before Tom finished sitting down.

Tom studied him. Kilian Howard wasn't overly laden with dignity. For some awful reason, he'd chosen to shave the sides of his head, leaving his curly hair an unkempt mess on the top. He had helmet acne. He struggled to keep on the weight he needed for hockey. By March, he'd be mainlining protein shakes to stay upright on his skates. He compensated for it by being a pest on the ice, goading other players into taking penalties.

Unwillingly, Tom felt a sort of kinship rise up in him. At nineteen, he hadn't been too different from Howie. He wasn't an agitator; he'd never had the personality for it, preferring to be as unseen as possible in the fishbowl of the NHL. But he, too, had been a mess of insecurities and bad skincare choices.

"What are you sorry for?"

"For saying…you know."

"Why did you?"

Howie swallowed, his Adam's apple bobbing visibly. "I, uh…I dunno. Luca's supposed to be the new guy, but he's all…suave and confident. Everyone treats him as if he's part of the team for good already. I guess it made me…jealous."

At least he knew.

Taking a page out of Jax's book of blunt honesty, Tom asked, "Do you hate gay people?"

"No!" Howie considered. "I mean, I don't know any, but I've been doing some research ever since, and I swear I get why it was so shitty and why some people think it's a slur. And I know there's more to it. I made a list of stuff to look into later."

"When you say words like that as insults, you make it sound as if you do hate gay people." Tom winced. Here he was, pretending what Howie had said hadn't hurt him on a deeply personal level he'd never shared with the team, acting as though he knew so much better. In a way, he did; he'd never resorted to slurs or hateful language. But in so many other ways, he wasn't much different than a scared teenager.

"I know," Howie said miserably. "And I'm sorry. I really am."

Again, Tom lied. "It's not me you should be apologizing to."

Howie nodded and looked away.

Tom could leave it there, but the truths he hadn't shared itched under his skin, forcing him to keep going. He might not be able to tell Howie the truth, but he could give him something honest.

"Look, Howie. Hockey players…we do a lot of chirping about a lot of things, and that isn't okay."

"You never do."

Tom smiled. "I try. I'm a lot older than you, and I'm the captain. I have responsibilities. But I'm sure you've heard slurs thrown around in locker rooms your whole life."

"Yeah."

"And your style, the way you play, getting under people's skin…it's easy to do it with that kind of word."

"Yeah." Howie still wouldn't look at him.

"If I wanted to get under your skin, you know what I'd say?"

Finally, Howie peered up from under the curls falling across his forehead, confusion written across every inch of his face.

"I'd tell you to invest in some skincare products for those pimples." Tom flicked at Howie's cheek.

Howie ducked away, utterly outraged. "Cap!"

"Sensitive subject for you, huh?"

"Yeah."

"Mm-hmm. And how much more would it throw you off your game if I said *that* to you on the ice than if I threw slurs at you?"

An expression of pure glee stole across Howie's face. "I think I should start looking up every embarrassing thing the Toronto Huskies have ever said online."

"Attaboy."

Finally, Howie smiled properly at Tom. "Thanks, Cap. And I really am sorry."

"I know you are. Next time, think about who you're trying to insult and why. When you use homophobic language, the person you're hurting most is the innocent bystander who actually is gay and too scared to say anything."

Howie went quiet and pensive. For a moment, Tom thought he'd overplayed his hand, revealed too much. Sweat broke out on the back of his neck and cooled immediately in the recycled plane air.

Howie said, "I don't want to be a bad person."

Tom breathed an internal sigh of relief. "Leave the agitating on the ice. And remember, hockey players are stupid enough all on their own. You don't need to use slurs."

"Right. Um, I think I have to go talk to Luca."

Tom let him out of the seat, wondering if he should have also discussed that the problem wasn't the word "queer" as much as the way Howie had said it. Jax called himself queer sometimes, after all. But no, a political correctness lesson wasn't in the cards, not today and not from Tom. Howie ought to get his LGBTQIA+ education from someone who knew what they were talking about, not a man so afraid of his own sexuality he could barely even think the words.

"Don't I get a nice captainly pep talk?" Hayes asked snidely from across the aisle.

Tom contemplated it. "I don't know what to say to you."

"Written me off already, huh?"

Tom rubbed at his temples. "No, but you're not a rookie I can teach something to. I thought we were friends. I thought you and Phil were friends."

"Don't bring Phil into this."

"You did that yourself by saying racist shit."

Hayes's chin jutted out stubbornly.

Tom was so tired, though he'd slept well. Jax kissing him until his brain shut up seemed like a dream he'd had months ago rather than yesterday's reality.

"If you're mad at me, be mad at *me*, not Luca. And if you're going to be a bigot, do it where I can't hear it."

He slumped into his own seat and stared out the window. Instead of pleasant kissing thoughts, worries flitted across his mind about what to do with Hayes and the text from his mom.

Halfway through the flight, Jax sat next to him. "Whatever you said to Howie worked like a charm."

Howie had taken Jax's place in the four-way, the young guys all back together where they belonged.

"I'm glad."

Jax had brown eyes. Previously, Tom hadn't many thoughts either way on eye color, but Jax had a way of looking at him, his eyes so warm and understanding it made Tom feel safe.

"Are you okay?" Jax asked him.

Tom wanted very much to tell Jax he'd never been as okay as he was after kissing him. But they were on a team plane, and the team was in shambles, and he had to see his parents tonight.

"I'll be fine," he said instead and let his arm rest against Jax's between their seats.

# Ten

["Anyone can play hockey" logo]

Tyson Fuller: Anyone can play hockey.

[Image: Instagram picture of Jaxon Grant in a Magpies jersey hugging another player after a goal. Top comment reads: "tfulls87: kinda gay bro lol"]

Jimmy Hayes: Everyone is welcome in my locker room.

[Image: Jimmy Hayes's Twitter likes. Camera zooms in on Allie Jenkins's post: "tfw you're the only white people in the bar. Guess we're not coming here again!"]

## Top comments:

sealions4lyfe: hockey is for men, bro. real men. not for fags and affirmative action whiners.

seelionssaylions: best sport worst league

(From "Anyone can play hockey (except you)," Supercut posted to YouTube by hockeyfanofcolor88 on 11/30/2024)

They lost to Toronto 5–1. Jax scored the lone goal off an assist from Tom, but that was cold comfort. The team couldn't function this way. At least whatever magic Tom had worked on Howie had been effective. He apologized sincerely to Luca and everyone else, even if he still sounded like a dumbass doing it. But not every problem could be fixed so cleanly.

Before the game, Hayes asked Luca in full hearing of the entire locker room, "Why didn't you say you weren't Mexican?"

Luca stared at Hayes for so long Jax felt uncomfortable standing in the vicinity. "If I had the right kind of tanned skin and dark hair, you would be all right with me on the power play, then?"

"I…" Hayes blinked rapidly, frowning.

"If I am only ever an accident of birth away from losing your respect, it isn't worth very much."

Breezy, stripped down to his novelty boxer briefs featuring tiny pizzas on skateboards, leapt to his feet. "Boom!" he shouted. "What a comeback. Shit, Ziti, do you write this stuff down?"

Luca gave him the most long-suffering look Jax had ever seen. "It is not hard to appear clever in this locker room."

It didn't exactly set a solid tone for the team.

Morris had watched the entire game in near-silence, his mustache twitching. By comparison, Trout yelled himself hoarse at everyone he could reach. Edwards tried to get a few breathing exercises going on the bench. No one had been in the mood.

To make matters worse, Jax had to do media because he'd gotten the goal. Media in Toronto was brutal. Questions about every aspect of their failure abounded. Olivia Starling, the beat reporter for the *San Francisco Herald*, got in on the fun by asking him whether the team had made a mistake using Luca in the first unit of the special teams so soon after calling him up.

Jax said, "Well, you know, we're still getting used to working together. But I think we can do great things together."

Someone from Toronto asked him whether Tom had the leadership skills it took to get them to the playoffs.

Jax said, "Tom's been to the playoffs seven times, six of those as captain."

Then, Starling asked him if he thought Tom had gotten too old for the job.

Jax lost his shit a little. Maybe back in October, when he thought Tom hated him, he'd have been able to play it off with a little joke. But now, remembering Tom's serious face on the plane as he talked quietly with Howie, though Jax knew how vulnerable the topic made Tom? No way. And compounding his excellent captaining with the other memories of Tom he now had and was trying actively not to think of in the middle of a media session? Double extra no way.

"I'm sorry," he said. "Did you watch the game last night? Did you see someone else get a hat trick in a single period? If Tom's too old, then you might as well take me out back and shoot me. I've never gotten a hat trick in a single period. Anyway, being captain is about more than staying fit. It's about being there for the team and sacrificing your time and your energy into making sure everyone is at their best. I've never known anyone who does that the way Tom does."

Then, some chucklefuck in a Huskies Nation T-shirt stood up and asked, "So you don't regret leaving Philly, then? They're currently in a wildcard spot."

Jax leaned into the microphone. "Given that leaving Philly wasn't exactly my choice, you gotta wonder if they're the ones who regret trading me. Our playoff chances aren't looking half bad either."

Almost instantly, Kayleigh from the media team pulled him away from the throng of reporters.

"Sorry," he muttered to her. Poor girl, stuck wrangling guys who either hated media (Tom and Phil) or who always said the first dumbshit thing on their minds (Jax and Howie). They'd even dragged her on a winter Canadian road trip to manage their shit, and he couldn't make it through one interview without causing more work for her. "Should've had Tom do it."

"It'll be fine," Kayleigh said with far more cheer than she probably felt. "Tom had a family thing tonight."

A family thing? He hadn't said anything to Jax. But when he got to the locker room, it was entirely devoid of captains.

Fine. Tom didn't owe him an accounting of his movements just because they made out one time. Tom had no responsibility to comfort Jax when he put his foot in his mouth in front of the press. If Tom had family stuff in Toronto, Jax would occupy himself with something else. He didn't *need* to spend all evening pressed against Tom's side in a shitty hotel bed analyzing game tape they would talk about in video review anyway.

He turned down Breezy's offer to join him and the other boys for Mario Kart, aware he'd bring the mood down, and completely discarded the possibility of talking to Hayes. In this funk, he would only make things worse.

Instead, Jax took an angry shower. He'd already gotten cleaned up in the locker room, but angry showers were different. They weren't for hygiene. They were for blasting loud music and drinking a beer under the spray. They were also a hotel-only indulgence. He liked to take his time under there, driving up the water bill. Though Jax knew he didn't have to worry about whether he could afford it anymore, when he was out of sorts, he couldn't turn off the niggling feeling in the back of his mind.

Afterward, his irritation persisted. He put on his favorite flannel pajama pants and flopped into bed only to find it was one of the too-hard hotel beds, making flopping summarily unsatisfactory. There was nothing on TV. It was a Thursday, so of course there wasn't. He debated going out, but the Toronto-ness of the city put him off. If he were to be recognized anywhere, it would definitely be in Toronto.

Besides, what would he do? Pick someone else up? When he knew what it felt like to kiss Tom? When he'd heard the little noise Tom made when Jax kissed his neck? Definitely not. Nothing could compare.

He texted his sisters in the sibling group chat for a while. They were doing homework, and he hypocritically berated them for working on assignments due the next day at 11:00 p.m. as if he had been any different in school. Apparently, Mom had picked up macramé again, and they'd spent all afternoon making bracelets and lost track of time.

He lost another half hour checking up on his mom's Etsy shop, making sure people were actually paying for her arts and crafts and that she was on top of the shipping orders. She'd never been good at money management and often got so invested in a project she forgot all about the practicalities of life.

At midnight, his phone chimed. Hoping to hear from Tom, he immediately toggled to his messages.

*U didn't want to get traded???*

Tyson Fuller. Who hadn't written to him once since he left Philly.

Jax groaned and tossed the phone somewhere into the bedsheets. People would ask about the trade now, and he'd have to play it cool and pretend nothing had happened or lie about it. He would have to do his level best not to burst out with the truth because as much as he might hate lying, he had no idea what the league would do with him if he told the truth.

He had no idea what San Francisco might do with him.

Jax didn't dare hope they would go to bat for him. Especially not when Tom—well, Tom would have to do everything he could to distance himself from Jax publicly if Jax were to come out. No more kissing practice.

Not that they'd be practicing again. Tom didn't need it. He'd been so pliant and…lovely in Jax's arms yesterday it made Jax's heart hurt. Any man would be lucky to have him.

Jax buried his face into a pillow and screamed.

At twelve thirty, as Jax debated going for a run to get out of his own head despite the sleet rain pounding against the window, Tom knocked on the door.

Jax bounded over and opened it. "I thought you were with your family."

"I was," Tom said, grim and gaunt, as though he had aged ten years in one evening. "Can I come in?"

He'd never asked before, had only pushed his way in and tried to stop Jax from doing anything he deemed too dangerous.

"You can always come in," Jax said before his mouth got any input from his brain. Oh well. It wasn't wrong.

Tom smiled. "Careful, or I'll get a second key and barge in all the time to talk about the power play."

"I wouldn't mind." Jax needed to reel this in, change the subject, and move on, or else Tom would realize he'd been thinking about having Tom in his room, in his bed, in his heart. "Are you okay?"

Sitting on the edge of the bed, Tom looked up at Jax. "It's been a lot, the last few days." He smoothed down the edge of the sheet. "And, um…yesterday? When you were…when we were…"

*Kissing!* Jax wanted to shout. *We kissed, and you ruined me for life! There's now a section of my brain devoted entirely to replaying those kisses over and over again!*

Tom squared his shoulders the same way he did when meeting an opponent in the face-off circle. "I haven't felt so good in years. It was like I…like I wasn't in charge, like I could just feel. I want to feel that way again. I know you said I don't need practice, but I think I do. I don't know if I could trust anyone else, you know? I feel safe with you."

Jax sat next to him on the bed, primarily because his knees had lost the ability to keep him upright. He took Tom's hand in his own. "You can practice with me as much as you need to."

Tom's fingers tightened around Jax's. "Good. Can we, um…can we be lying down this time?"

Jax wouldn't survive this. There'd be a scorch mark left on the bed where he'd burned to a crisp from wanting a man utterly unaware of the devastating effects he had on his surroundings.

They scooted up the bed until their heads rested on the pillows.

Jax made a face. "Why are there no good pillows in hotels?"

"I have a memory foam one at home." Tom turned to his side to face Jax. "You should try it sometime."

Was Tom inviting Jax into his bed? Was he aware of how those words sounded? No, this was Tom Crowler. He would probably have Jax come over and lie in his bed and test the pillow, which would definitely smell of the shower gel brand he'd done a sponsorship deal with a couple years ago. He had a dozen bottles of the stuff in his stall at the practice rink, but grimaced every time he used them. Then, he'd wander off to the kitchen to offer Jax a Gatorade or something instead of kneeling over Jax's face and letting Jax eat him out. Tom was too oblivious to his appeal for his own good.

Jax turned so they were nose to nose. "Sounds good."

With an impatient sound, Tom pulled him closer. "Aren't you going to…"

"What?" Jax rubbed their noses together.

"Aren't you going to kiss me?"

Feeling a little puckish, Jax asked, "Why don't you kiss me?"

Tom rolled onto his back and dragged Jax on top of him. "I want you to do it."

If Tom'd had any sort of contact with any aspect of queer culture, Jax would have teased him for being a pillow princess. As it was, the combination of his pouty, pleading look and the full spread of his body under Jax's sufficed to make Jax give in.

He leaned down and kissed Tom, long and thorough and so good.

It had been good yesterday, up against the wall with the hot line of Tom's body against his. Something could be said for the intimacy of a bed, though, with both of them in soft clothes at the end of a long day. More adventurous this time, Tom let his hands trail up Jax's bare skin. Jax rewarded him with more neck kisses, which in turn made Tom tilt his head and arch up to grant Jax better access.

Six weeks ago, Jax had a hookup come to his hotel room and beg Jax to fuck him while wearing a jersey with his number on it. It hadn't been the first time he'd been with someone who was absolutely desperate for him.

And yet, somehow, Jax had never felt more wanted, with Tom shifting his head back a little more and sighing in pleasure.

He kissed Tom's neck again, with his mouth open this time.

Tom's hands went tight on his ribs, and he pulled Jax up to his mouth. So pliant, so eager. If Jax had thought about it, he'd have expected Tom to keep tight hold of his self-control. The way he presented himself to the world—serious, masculine, kind of humorless—was so at odds with the way he gave in to Jax's slightest touch.

Jax's wrists started to ache, propped up over Tom, so he rolled to his side again and pulled Tom to him. Tom nestled closer, hands wandering up and down Jax's sides, making Jax squirm.

"What?" Tom said against his lips.

"Ticklish."

"Hmm." His touch went even softer, even gentler, as if savoring the chance to touch Jax. The idea was so ludicrous Jax couldn't take it without biting something. In this case, Tom's neck.

Tom moaned, as sweet a sound as it had been yesterday. This time, he dared returning the favor, letting his teeth scrape along Jax's shoulder while Jax attacked his neck. At the same time, he pressed in again, his leg brushing against Jax's. Jax threw his own leg over Tom's, giving in to the full heat of Tom's body.

He returned to Tom's mouth, ravenous, and kissed him deep and hot, moving his lips and tongue faster and more demanding. Tom met him step for step, seemingly satisfied for Jax to set the pace. The end-of-day stubble on Tom's cheeks scratched against Jax's lips and jaw and would probably leave some intense beard burn, but Jax didn't care. All he cared about was getting more. More of Tom's kisses, more of the little sounds in the back of Tom's throat, more of Tom's body clinched tight against his own.

He slid his hands under the hem of Tom's T-shirt and touched warm skin, drinking in Tom's shuddery intake of breath under his fingertips and in his mouth, and Jax—Jax was extremely close to being extremely hard with one leg thrown over Tom's and nothing between his cock and Tom but a thin layer of flannel.

For a moment, Jax pushed his advantage, let his hips nudge toward Tom's, and then pulled away reluctantly.

Tom hadn't agreed to anything more than kissing.

Tom wanted someone to practice with, not someone to maul him in a nondescript shitty hotel room after he'd had several emotionally taxing days, including two back-to-back hockey games.

Jax could give him that.

Jax would give him that.

Just because Jax wanted him so badly he could feel it in his teeth didn't mean he'd burden Tom with his desires.

He pulled his leg off Tom's, leaving some distance between their hips. He slowed the tempo of their kisses, allowing them to become ever softer until their mouths barely slid against each other, lips closed.

Tom's body grew heavier and heavier against Jax as his breath evened out.

"'S'okay 'f I stay for a bit?" Tom mumbled against Jax's lips.

"Yeah."

With permission granted, the last of the tension left Tom's body, and he sank into the subpar hotel pillow completely, mouth still a hair's breadth away from Jax's.

Literally kissed a man to sleep. That was a new one, even for Jax. He tried not to take it as an insult to his prowess. He rolled onto his back to stare at the ceiling, then turned the lamp by the bed off as quietly as he could. Beside him, Tom breathed in and burrowed deeper into the sheets.

Jax closed his eyes and tried to will his arousal into submission.

Lying in bed and thinking about Tom instead of sleeping had become a habit over the last weeks. Jax expected he'd be awake for hours, so close to the real thing, but it turned out, with Tom lying beside him, the sound of his breathing and the heat of his body close enough to touch, he drifted off in mere minutes.

In the morning, Jax woke first slowly and then all at once, wrapped around Tom with his heart pounding and his cock hard enough to shoot pucks. So entirely subsumed in each other, with his arm slung over Tom's chest and their legs tangled together, Tom woke up with him.

His eyes immediately went wide. "Shit!"

"It's okay," said Jax, a bold statement for a man who had no idea what "it" might be let alone how it was doing.

"I should never have fallen asleep. I'm so sorry. I—"

"Tom, it's okay. Breathe. Breathe." Jax searched for his phone and found it underneath his left knee. He checked the time. "It's fine. We're flying out late today, remember? No one's awake yet."

"Right," Tom said, still breathing much too fast. "Right. I can just…sneak over to my room. No one will know."

That hurt a little. Jax was aware of what he could expect from Tom and how deeply closeted Tom was. He hadn't pictured Tom dancing for joy at the thought of a hotel full of their teammates realizing they'd spent the night together. Jax had reached a point in his life where he chafed against secrecy and pretending, but he couldn't expect Tom to share his sentiments, especially when

Tom didn't feel the same way about him. Still, a petty part of Jax wished Tom could be proud of being seen with him.

"Your first walk of shame," he joked.

Tom rubbed a hand across his face. "Oh my God. I can't believe I fell asleep here."

"It's okay. Hey, don't tell anyone I'm such a boring kisser I sent you to sleep."

"I wasn't bored."

"I'm kidding. It's fine."

Tom shook his head. "No, Jax, I don't...I don't even sleep on the team plane. I fell asleep here because it was the first time all day I wasn't worried about anything."

He sat up and rolled out of bed. Stretching his arms above his head, a little sliver of his treasure trail became visible where his T-shirt rode up, and Jax had to swallow hard against the swell of saliva. He was literally panting over this man like a fucking dog.

He had a problem.

He had a lot of problems.

In particular, he had six-foot-three of this particular problem, and it kept getting worse.

"Glad to be of service," he said weakly, while his brain assaulted him with several other ways he could be of service.

Tom rewarded him with a heart-stopping smile.

On reflection, it looked no different than Tom's usual smiles, but Jax had trouble imagining a time when he didn't find everything Tom did heart-stopping. Thank God he hadn't tried having feelings for someone earlier on in life. It was fucking debilitating.

"I'm gonna..." Tom said with a nod toward the door.

"Oh. Right. Of course. Um, bye."

Ignoring Jax's sudden inability to form full sentences, Tom leaned down and kissed him, just a little brush of their lips against each other. "I'll see you later?"

"Uh-huh."

It occurred to Jax later how stupid a question that was given they were staying at the same hotel, riding the same team bus, and getting on the same flight. At the time, his heart had skipped a beat in joy that Tom wanted to see him later. After a reasonably healthy breakfast of fruit, yogurt, and shredded oats—Jax could not face the thought of more reconstituted scrambled eggs—and enough coffee to replace at least part of his bloodstream, he regained the ability to think rationally.

So he'd had another make-out session with the Crow, and they'd slept in the same bed. Weirder things had happened. Probably. Somewhere. So he wanted to go home with Tom, continue where they'd left off, and take him out to dinner during a nice weekend on the coast. It was probably nothing more than a crush. Jax had a thing about taking care of people, and Tom needed taking care of. Jax had let his instincts run away with him a little, but he could keep it together and be professional about this. Tom did not need or want some guy panting after him at work.

Breakfast eaten, Jax sipped his second coffee and distracted himself by scrolling through Instagram on his phone, which was at 12 percent battery after lying in the sheets all night instead of charging like good little phones were supposed to. Vanessa's interior design channel still showed at the top of his feed. Since Breezy had dumped her for being in the mob or something, Jax could probably unfollow. He did find something about the room transformations she posted hypnotizing. Every time, she'd start with a perfectly livable room and end with a place where Jax would be scared to sit down on anything in case his butt left a print.

The official NHL channel had posted an interview with the captain of the Magpies and tagged him in it.

He dug an earbud out of his pocket, prayed it was still charged, and pressed Play on the interview.

"Yeah," Tyson said on the tiny little video. (They used to keep a tally in the Magpies locker room of how often he said "yeah" in interviews. When he did it more than ten times, he bought the team a round at the sports bar they frequented.) He was sweaty, his hair the rat king of cowlicks, so this must have been postgame, probably before his shower. "I mean, as far as I knew, Jax asked for the trade? He didn't really talk to me about it."

Jax closed his eyes. Definitely postgame if they asked him about what Jax had said in his own interview last night.

"He's not the best at impulse control. Maybe he regrets it now or something."

The feed cut out then, replaced by the NHL's blue-and-white logo. Jax googled the full clip before the audio ended. There wasn't much more to it, though, just some talking points about the Magpie's new second-line center, who couldn't hold a candle to Jax. Tyson must have realized immediately after that he shouldn't gossip about former teammates to the media.

So much for impulse control.

Appetite gone, Jax went back to his hotel room to gather his things before the bus left. He kicked the door shut a bit too loudly, which took some doing as it was one of those doors that fell shut automatically and resisted when he tried to slam it. Poor impulse control. Ugh.

One glance around the hotel room showed the rumpled sheets where Tom had slept, the charger by the bed where Jax hadn't plugged his phone in last night (because Tom had been here). The beer he'd taken with him to the shower, now empty. The room was a monument to his shitty impulse control.

Couldn't a man have faults? Sure, he was a bit impetuous, but it had never gotten him in real trouble. Sometimes, he put his foot in it with the media or spent too much money on something stupid, but he played hockey for a living. They might as well put those in the job description. None of that was why he'd left Philly. He'd left Philly because some asshole wanted to blackmail him with pictures of his dick, and once they'd dealt with it, PR decided they wanted no part of a queer hockey player, although Jax *knew* they'd dealt with worse shit from straight dudes.

Kayleigh, the Sea Lions media rep, might be aggressively perky and into annoying fluff content, but at least she hadn't called him a liability for something he couldn't change.

The reasonable, rational voice in the back of his head, which sounded suspiciously similar to Tom asking for tips on how to be a better captain, reminded him that people with decent impulse control didn't usually have other people blackmailing them with explicit photos.

Jax didn't particularly want to listen to reason. Reason had never done shit for him.

To prove he had impulse control, instead of bagging the seat next to Tom and maybe holding his hand during takeoff back to California, Jax took the one next to Breezy.

"Oh, good," Breezy said. "I wanted to run something by you."

Jax raised an eyebrow, a trick he'd practiced for over an hour in the tiny bathroom at home when he was thirteen. It had served him well ever since.

"So everyone is super fucked up over the whole—" Breezy waved a hand. "—thing."

"Uh-huh."

"Like, Howie feels like shit, and Mooney's super pissed, and I think Luca feels guilty, but he'd never say."

"Yeah." Jax leaned against the headrest, closing his eyes.

"And we need to fix it."

"Don't see how I can help."

Breezy punched him in the arm, hard.

"Hey!"

"This is *serious*, dude."

Jax opened an eye. "I *know*. That's why I'm useless."

"I don't know what your deal is today, but you're the guy who got us from being a bunch of dudes sharing a locker room to a real team. You got Cap talking to us. You got him to talk to the coaches—"

"That was all Tom."

"Okay, well, it was your influence."

"And it all turned to shit two months into the season."

Breezy narrowed his eyes. "This is about the thing the guy from the Magpies said last night, isn't it?"

Great. So, people had already seen the interview.

"Who cares what he thinks?"

"I do," Jax snapped. "I should have kept my mouth shut. He's right about me."

"Hmm."

"What?"

"Well, I always kinda thought your interviews were awesome. You just say whatever. Made it feel like you didn't care what people thought about you."

Jax swallowed. If he really didn't care, he'd have come out years ago. He wouldn't be so miserable every time someone mentioned Philadelphia. The sting of rejection was so sharp, and he hadn't even enjoyed living there half the year, with the unbearable muggy summers making training camp awful.

But he had to concede Tyson's point. If he'd had any impulse control, he wouldn't have spent two evenings in a row kissing Tom until he got so hard he could barely see straight, and he wouldn't still be desperate for more despite knowing Tom didn't want that with him. Tom needed someone who would keep his secrets, not someone liable to lose his shit and spout off at the mouth.

Tyson was right about him.

Philadelphia was right about him. He was a liability.

"So what if you're impulsive or whatever?" Breezy said, barreling on. "You're, like, real."

Jax snorted. If only Breezy knew how real he wasn't. Better to get off this topic before Jax lost his mind and started telling him truths he couldn't take back. "What did you want to talk about?"

"I think we need to do something as a team."

Jax opened his messages and showed Breezy the team chat. "Thanksgiving at Phil's house for everyone who's not going home." He'd seen the message last night, before Tom came over, and figured he'd stay home and sulk. But if it was important for team unity or whatever, he supposed he could make an appearance. They did have three full days off with only weights and light practices scheduled, a concession after the Montreal-Toronto back-to-back.

"Yeah, I mean, that's good and all, but I thought…" Breezy sighed and shifted in his seat. "I think we should *do* something."

"What, one of those team-building courses? I am not doing trust falls with you fuckers. Especially not on skates."

"No! I mean, like…charity."

Surprised, Jax looked directly at Breezy, which was his first mistake. For all he was an absolute tank of a defenseman, Breezy had the biggest, brownest puppy dog eyes Jax had ever seen. Coupled with the thought he'd put into this, Jax crumbled like cheap drywall. "Okay, hit me."

"Okay." Breezy cleared his throat and sat up straight. "So, what happened in the locker room in Montreal was shitty. And dumb, and wrong. And Howie's apologized to us all, but I mean, Howie's a kid."

Howie was all of three years younger than Breezy.

"But Hayes hasn't said anything," Breezy continued. "And we all started hearing this shit in the room when we're about twelve, right?"

Jax nodded wordlessly.

"So, now that we're in the NHL, and we've actually made it, I think we should do better. And also help other people do better."

A burning sensation stung in Jax's nose and behind his eyes. "Yeah," he said roughly. "That would be…that would be good."

"Right, so, um…I know it's kind of vague so far, but—"

"You're right. You're so right. And we *can* do better. We're the fucking San Francisco Sea Lions. There's so many charities for gay rights literally on our doorstep."

"Oh, yeah." Breezy scratched his head. "I almost forgot. You know, my mom was super worried when I got drafted to the Sea Lions. I think she thinks the Castro is a den of iniquity or something. She kept going on about what if some beautiful Asian-American 'transsexual' seduced me or something." He used air quotes around his mother's words, but frankly, there weren't enough air quotes in the world.

A snort of extremely undignified laughter escaped Jax. "Yikes."

"I know, right!" Breezy grinned. "I told her it's transgender now. And also, that I would only fall for Italian dudes."

"Only you, Breezy." Jax patted him on the shoulder. "I should take you to a drag show. They would eat you alive."

"What?" Breezy's eyes went wide and scared.

"Uh, nothing," Jax said, attempting to emulate a person who had never been to a drag show. "You were right. This is a really good idea."

A broad smile spread across Breezy's face. "Wow. I don't think anyone has ever said that to me before."

Jax spent the rest of the flight buried in his phone, looking up charities and sending emails. It was far more rewarding than his original plan of deep-diving the comments on Tyson's interview. Halfway through the trip, he switched to sit next to Kayleigh to talk over what he'd found so far. She supported the idea enthusiastically.

"Honestly it's a relief," she told him as they narrowed down the possible charities. "I'm running out of ideas for new content I can do with you guys, and it's only November. Every time I get Tom in front of a camera, I feel like he's about to run away. And then I watch the footage, and I wish he had."

Jax wasn't interested in "content"; he was interested in doing something good. But if content got this project off the ground, he would do it.

He followed Tom off the plane as a matter of course. On the bus ride to Cyberian Arena, he showed Tom the research he'd collected in his notes app and the ideas he and Kayleigh were percolating on.

Tom answered in a series of hums and head movements, which had Jax increasingly concerned.

"Don't you think this would be good?" he finally asked when they'd disembarked, and Tom had yet to say anything more substantive than "hmm."

"No, I, uh…" Tom rubbed the back of his neck. "Why don't you come over so we can keep talking?"

# Eleven

[…] Over in the NHL, it's not much better. While hockey has been known to have theme nights, including Pride Night, in a show of cowardice the world hasn't seen since the last time France capitulated to an invading army, the NHL forbade its players using Pride tape. (For those playing the home game, as it were, hockey players tape their sticks, usually in plain black or white). The league gave a spurious reason for doing so, allegedly trying to keep the game apolitical by banning themed practice jerseys and gear. With players all but lining up to declare their disinterest in supporting LGBTQIA+ causes (follow the links to statements by the Hodgson brothers in Tampa Bay and New York Pioneers Captain Jack Côté at your own risk), it's clear hockey is anything but apolitical. The ban might have been reversed, but it being instated in the first place speaks volumes. Say it louder for the people in the back: Not caring about human rights is a political stance! The only other initiative hockey as an institution has managed to muster is the lukewarm "Anyone can play hockey" initiative, where NHL players who most recently got caught saying something awful on social media step in front of a camera and pretend not to be bigots for about five seconds. Even here in San Francisco, the nation's capital for queer culture, there has been nothing but silence from team leaders on the subject of Pride tape, Pride Nights, and bringing the sport into the 21st century. […]

(From "Why Gen Z Won't Watch Sports," op. ed. in *The San Francisco Herald*, published 10/13/2024)

Jax remained quiet on the way to Tom's apartment. Tom tried not to worry about it too much. It wasn't that he didn't like Jax's idea; it just seemed so risky.

When he said as much, standing at the kitchen counter and offering Jax a glass of water, Jax's expression darkened.

"Risky," he repeated.

"Well, yeah. I mean, we've never done anything of this scope before, and now all of a sudden, it's important for us to engage in the local community? Won't people suspect…"

"What? That someone on the team must be queer? Newsflash, two of us are."

"Exactly!"

Jax rolled his eyes. "You don't have to be involved, okay? Breezy got the ball rolling; it should be him and me."

Tom blinked. Had he heard correctly? "Breezy?"

"Yeah."

"Why?"

With a loud sigh, Jax plopped onto one of the bar stools at the counter. "Because he's a decent human being?"

"Oh." Guilt swamped Tom. He wasn't a decent human being. Nothing new there; he would add it to his list of personal and professional failures. His efforts to be a better captain maxed out what little emotional energy he had. He wasn't ready for this. "I guess that works. No one will think Breezy's gay."

"No," Jax said, shaking his head emphatically. "Let me try to get something sorted with PR and one of these charities, okay?"

"Okay."

"Seriously, you don't have to be involved. But I think it would be good for Howie and Luca and stuff. And for the kids."

"The kids?"

"Yeah, the kids. Weren't you listening? We want to work with a shelter for kids who got kicked out for being queer. Donate some stuff. Play hockey with them."

"Would they want that?" Tom had no idea how it felt to be homeless as a teenager, but he didn't think playing hockey would be high on their list of priorities.

Jax shrugged. "If my parents had kicked me out when I told them, I'd have needed help."

"You *told* your parents?"

"Yeah, of course."

Of course. Tom's head hurt thinking about it. Or maybe the headache was a byproduct of too little sleep after a long dinner in which his mom had gone over every minute of the disaster of a game against Toronto, picking out his mistakes. And then…well, what had happened in Jax's hotel room last night. "And you think this would be good for the team?"

"Not everything is about hockey."

"No, I know, but I thought you were doing this for the team."

"I *am*, but it's also really important to me."

Tom swallowed heavily. "Okay. It's a good idea. It is, Jax. I'm only…" He turned and opened the fridge to avoid saying "scared" out loud. He should probably offer Jax something for dinner. All he had were precooked meal plan deliveries.

"I know. I'll keep your name out of it."

"No, it's a team thing. If it's all of us, I have to support it."

"Tom."

"What?"

The stool creaked, and Jax's footsteps came nearer, but it didn't prepare Tom for having Jax's arms suddenly wrapped around his middle and his chin hooked over Tom's shoulder.

"This isn't something you have to sacrifice yourself for," Jax said. "If you don't want to be involved, we'll do it as a volunteer thing. You don't owe anyone the truth about yourself, and if you don't feel safe doing this, I won't ask it of you."

Tom let himself lean back into Jax's embrace. "If it's a team thing, it'll be fine." Maybe if he said it enough, he'd believe it. "But I can't take the lead."

"It'll be me and Breezy all the way."

"And if people think…"

Jax pressed a kiss to Tom's shoulder. "Fine by me. I hate living this way. You know I do."

Tom did know, but selfishly, he wanted Jax to keep on hiding. If Jax came out, there would be no more shoulder kisses or hugs in Tom's kitchen. They'd only kissed twice—or, well, had two discrete incidents of kissing—but Tom already needed more. Was this what addiction felt like? He'd been clean and sober of this thing he wanted more than breathing for half his life, but now he'd had it, he was jonesing for his next fix.

"I understand," he said.

"And I get that you don't want people to know. It's fine. If anything gets out, we'll just...stop meeting up, the two of us. No one will have any reason to think anything of you."

*We'll just stop.*

Tom closed the fridge and twisted around, capturing Jax's mouth with his.

If they had to stop at some point, he would get everything he could from this beforehand.

They kissed right there in the kitchen until Tom's hip complained about standing still for so long, and then they moved to the gray sectional in Tom's living room. Jax separated their lips for long enough to critique Tom's sparsely furnished apartment, the main room devoid of anything besides the couch and a TV. When Tom pushed him into the cushions, he shut up about it. They only stopped after Tom's stomach growled so loudly Jax could hear it.

After dinner, which Jax also complained about because it was bland and reheated, Tom took Jax to the bedroom to test out the memory foam pillow. Since Tom cared about only two things in this apartment, the bed and the couch, it pleased him when Jax groaned in pleasure as he lay down. He was even more pleased when Jax refused to get up.

They didn't kiss again—Jax had emails to answer about the project Tom didn't want to think about, and Tom wanted to watch the East Coast games. They'd be playing New York and New Jersey soon, and it paid to know your enemy. But when Tom cautiously curled closer during the intermission between the first and second periods, Jax made space for him to rest his head on Jax's chest. He fell asleep before the third period started.

The next day, they woke late, so he offered Jax access to his home gym and spare clothes to do a light workout routine. He staunchly ignored the hum of pleasure at Jax's continued presence in his home and in his clothes.

"Oh, thank God," Jax said when he saw the spinning bike. "I'd have to go to the practice rink or for a run otherwise."

"Rookie mistake. Literally. I went running twice my first year, and it messed me up for the next game both times." The Bay Area hills weren't easy on the joints, even for fit hockey players.

"I can imagine. Whoever thought building a city here was a good idea?"

Tom, who at this point had a dedicated drawer for masks for when the air quality got too terrible during fire season and paid an extra insurance premium for earthquakes on his apartment, said, "Christian missionaries, I think."

Jax shook his head in consternation. "Man, why did people keep listening to those guys? They never got anything right."

After their workout, they had a light breakfast (also from Tom's meal service, also something Jax complained about), and because they weren't expected at Phil's until noon, they spent another two hours making out on Tom's couch.

By the end, Tom's skin buzzed with arousal. They lay on their sides, Tom caged between the cushions and Jax's body. Jax had been toying with the hem of Tom's shirt for a while, running his hands underneath and skimming across the skin in a very distracting way. Tom wanted him to repeat what he'd done the other night in Toronto, when he'd touched Tom more firmly, when he'd used his teeth, when he thought he'd felt Jax, just as affected as him, through the layers of their pants. Jax seemed determined not to go there again, though, as he kept backing off, leaving his touch light and his kisses sweet.

Maybe if he did to Jax what Jax had done to him? Tom set his mouth against Jax's throat and sucked at the column of it, light at first and then harder when Jax made a low, pleased sound.

"Oh, fuck, Tom," Jax said, breathless and deep. His hands slid down, suddenly cupping Tom's ass and hauling him closer, and Tom wanted—wanted—

Taking a great, heaving breath, Jax wrenched away. "We should probably go. Phil's…thing. Thanksgiving."

Still breathing unsteadily and with an erection throbbing in his pants, Tom said, "Thanksgiving was last month."

"I'm not having this debate with a Canadian." Jax slid to his feet.

Tom could see the outline of his dick, straining against the zipper of his pants. He licked his lips.

"Shit," Jax said. "Stop looking at me like that."

"Like what?"

"Like you want me to… Never mind."

"Like I want you to what?" Tom hadn't really thought any further than kissing. He'd been turned on every time they'd done it, sure, but he'd enjoyed the arousal in an idle, passive sort of way. Usually, being turned on was a nuisance, an urge he couldn't fulfill the way he most wanted: with another person. He'd take care of it quickly, treating it as yet another bodily maintenance function. Even when he ventured into trying out the toys he'd dared order to a PO box, the experience had left him largely unsatisfied.

With Jax, being aroused became not a problem in need of solving but a natural consequence of skin and mouths and sparking heat. Tom found himself savoring the feeling without wanting or needing it to end.

"Like you want me to tie you to the goddamn bed and make you come so much you pass out," Jax snapped all in one breath, aroused and angry at the same time.

"Oh," Tom said, then checked his phone. It was already eleven thirty. "I told Phil I'd bring stuffing, so we need to go to a store. I don't think we have time."

Jax made a wordless noise of frustration. "Stuffing takes hours to make. What—"

"I was going to buy the ready-made kind."

"Absolutely not."

So, Tom followed Jax through the grocery store two blocks from his building. He'd never made stuffing—why, when it was literally the furthest he could get from adhering to his meal plan—so he had no idea what Jax needed.

Instead, he turned over what Jax had said in his mind.

Just because Tom hadn't done most of the things his teammates talked about when they were two or three beers in didn't mean he remained ignorant of them. He'd always found it somewhat distasteful when they talked about bondage. It was always "she let me tie her to the bed with my game day tie," or "I gagged her with my socks." It sounded disgusting for the girl involved. Hockey player socks smelled awful, and a washing machine could only accomplish so much. It also sounded as if it would be a lot of work, tying someone up and then having to think of things to do to them.

Rarely had teammates mentioned doing it the other way around, but even then, the phrasing left something to be desired. One time, Vanderbilt bragged about an extramarital hookup by saying, "I let her put me in handcuffs."

The way Jax had said it didn't sound as if Tom would be *letting* him do anything. It didn't sound as if Tom would be in control. It sounded as though Jax would take the reins and do whatever he wanted to Tom, and Tom could lie there and take it.

"What are you smiling about?" Jax asked, dumping a truly ridiculous amount of celery in the shopping cart. No one even liked celery, which was nothing but crunchy water, only more unpleasantly so than cucumbers and lettuce.

"Thinking about what you said before."

"What did I—*oh*."

For a minute, they stared at each other, Tom's cheeks going hot. He wondered idly if Jax would forget about everything and take him back home.

But he turned around and started piling herbs on top of his celery.

The nice thing about being distracted by thoughts about sex was that Tom didn't worry about much of anything else. They took Tom's car from the garage under his Palo Alto apartment, where it had been since the last time he'd driven to Phil's. He didn't need it to get to the practice rink since he lived next door to it, and he usually took rideshares to Cyberian Arena for games, unwilling to deal with the traffic when he had to get his head in the game. Going to Phil's house, a newish construction in Cole Valley he and Camille had completely redone when they moved in, meant a good half-hour drive through the city.

It was a lot more fun with Jax in the passenger seat, fiddling with the air conditioning and complaining about every radio DJ in the Bay Area.

He only remembered he had things to worry about when Phil asked, "You came here together?"

Things like being seen with Jax. Being close to Jax. People knowing he spent time alone with Jax.

Because Jax wanted to work with queer charities. Because Jax would come out at some point, and Tom wouldn't.

Panic quickened his breath, and before he could come up with an excuse, Jax spoke up.

"Yeah, we both live near the rink, and I don't have a car yet. Made sense. You should thank me for it. This guy wanted to buy a hockey team's worth of supermarket stuffing."

Phil wrinkled his nose. "Ew, Tom."

"What? I don't know how to make stuffing."

"It's *Thanksgiving*."

"Not in—"

"We're not *in* Canada," Jax interrupted. "How are you at onions?"

Tom blinked. "Fine?"

Jax eyed him. "So, the same as you are with bell peppers?"

"Yup."

In the end, Phil and Tom sat at the kitchen table, drinking beer and watching Jax chop vegetables. Phil had ordered out for the turkey and assigned sides to everyone who RSVP'd, meaning he only needed to put out plates and silverware.

"Why didn't I get a side?" Jax asked, midway through cracking an obscene number of eggs into a mixing bowl.

"I didn't think you could cook," Phil admitted. "You didn't seem the type."

"Oh, so you just assigned the most important side dish to Tom, who you *know* can't cook."

"Tom can cook," Phil argued loyally. "I've seen him make at least one thing."

Jax pulled open three different drawers until he found a wire whisk and then shot them both a look of extreme skepticism.

"Where did you learn to cook anyway?" Tom appreciated watching Jax move around the kitchen, very in charge. Feeling rebellious for even entertaining the thought, Tom acknowledged it was pretty hot.

"My dad's a line cook at a diner. Or he used to be. I guess he's the owner now."

"Huh." Tom's dad was an investment banker. He couldn't imagine either of his parents doing anything involving getting their hands dirty.

"I used to work shifts with him when I needed money for new hockey gear. And in the summers."

Phil's eyebrows shot up. Much like Tom, his family was upper-middle-class enough that hockey gear had never been an issue. Also, much like Tom, he didn't talk to them when he could avoid it.

For lack of anything better to say, Tom threw in, "Cool."

Phil asked, "So how'd the road trip go? Why'd you all fuck up Toronto so badly?"

Tom dropped his forehead to the table.

It took the better part of an hour to tell Phil about everything, from the line changes leading to Hayes's outburst to Howie's apology tour to the communication shutdown leading to their massive loss in Toronto, ending with Breezy and Jax's master plan.

"Wow." Phil said. "This will be a fun evening. Why did no one warn me? Heck, why didn't— Where was Morris in all this?"

Jax shrugged. He finally finished assembling the stuffing, using every oven-proof dish Phil owned. After topping it all in a truly concerning amount of butter, he pushed it into the oven. Thankfully, Phil had one of those designer kitchens with the oven at waist height.

"Around," Tom said. "I don't think he heard any of the…racist, homophobic parts?"

Phil grunted in displeasure and levered himself out of his chair in his crutches. At least he had crutches now, a definite improvement from ten days ago when Tom had last seen him.

Jax took his vacated seat and cracked open a beer, then made a face. "Light beers. Blech."

"You're a massive hedonist, aren't you?" Tom realized.

Jax glanced away shiftily.

"I mean, the hotel pillows, the reconstituted egg thing, the beer…"

"Okay, I know you think life will reward you for denying yourself or something, but some of us can enjoy nice things *and* win awards."

Tom opened his mouth, but he couldn't get any words out.

Pointing at him and narrowing his eyes, Jax went on. "And I know you feel the same way about the eggs and the hotel beds. I've seen your couch. Talk about hedonism."

"I…" Tom looked down.

"I'll make you enjoy life if it kills me."

He was about to ask Jax what enjoying life would entail and if it could involve tying him to the bed when they were mercifully interrupted.

"…this is exactly the sort of shit a coach is there for, Ben. What were you *doing?*" Phil's voice and the uneven thump of his crutches preceded him by mere seconds before he returned to the kitchen, Coach Morris in tow.

"I can't do my job if I have to spend all day babysitting temperamental hockey players!"

"Babysitting temperamental hockey players *is* your job."

"Phil—"

"Nope. You're doing Thanksgiving with us, and you're going to solve this clusterfuck."

"*Phil.*"

"We all want a functional hockey team, don't we?"

Phil stared Tom and Jax down until they agreed.

With a sigh, Coach Morris fell into place next to Jax. He wore glasses and a T-shirt with a graphic of a seal making a thumbs-up gesture with its fin. The caption read, "Seal of Approval." Tom wondered if they sold that in the merch store now or if Morris just happened to have it.

"Stuffing smells good," Morris said.

"Uh…" Tom wasn't sure if he was allowed to ask, but he didn't see how he couldn't.

"My apartment is being renovated," Morris said. "I moved in here to help Easton until his knee is better. Win-win."

Given what Tom knew about how long it took to rehab an ACL tear, the renovations must be set to last a long time, but at least Phil wouldn't be alone.

Phil maneuvered his way onto a stool next to Jax, and Morris wordlessly pushed the spare chair into place for him to put his leg up. Their silent interaction, more than anything Morris had said, convinced Tom he'd done the right thing in letting Coach know Phil needed help. Morris remained a mystery in terms of coaching style, neither authoritarian like Trout nor interested in the team's psychological wellbeing like Edwards. Tom wished he could get a sense of Morris as a player to help him understand, but the highest level he'd reached before switching to coaching was college hockey in Utah, which no one filmed in the early 2000s.

"So the new lines were a bad idea," Morris summarized.

"No!" shouted all three hockey players in the room.

"Luca really is good," Phil said. "Did you see his assist in the third period in Montreal?" He whistled. "He plays smart. That's a defenseman who can stop goals going in and rack up his own points while he's at it."

"But Hayes—"

"Jimmy's thirty-one," Phil said bluntly. "He's not bad, but he's slowing down, and if he can't accept playing less minutes for the good of the team, it might be time to pursue other options."

Tom winced. Both he and Phil had a few years on Hayes, and Phil, in particular, faced the same issue about his longevity in the league. His estimation of Hayes's skill profile came out more than a little bitter because of it. While Tom remained angry and disappointed at Hayes, as team captain, he couldn't let the one-sided analysis stand.

"Hayes isn't bad by any means," he said. "I could see him doing well on the second D-pair and PP2. And from his perspective, we did petition to trade him out for the new guy three votes to one. He might be worried about losing his place on the team entirely."

"And getting traded from a team you've been on for years is rough." Jax didn't look at anyone as he said it, but Tom thought immediately of the interview he'd seen with Philly's captain. He'd always had questions about Tyson Fuller, who got a little too intense when he went after referees who made calls he didn't agree with.

Morris raised an eyebrow. "But he reacted by using a slur against a fellow player."

"Technically, 'Mexican' isn't a slur," Jax pointed out. "The way he said it made it sound like one, which is shitty and racist, but it is not, in fact, a slur."

Phil shook his head. "I can see Howie saying something thoughtless and cruel. Kid's been in the show for five minutes, and we all know what that's like. He just wants to fit in. But Jimmy? I've known him for years. Camille and I used to go on double dates with him and Allie."

"How has Lunes reacted?"

Morris asked a good question. Unfortunately, neither Jax nor Tom knew the answer. They exchanged a helpless glance, both aware they'd been too wrapped up in other things the last few days to check in with Diego.

"Is he coming tonight?" Tom asked.

Phil shook his head.

"Fuck. He said he was flying down to see his family." Jax pushed a hand through his hair. "He's been missing them all season."

Morris, Phil, and Tom made varying degrees of the same uncomfortable face.

"Oh my God," Jax muttered. "Okay, leaving aside that you all need therapy, I'm gonna try calling him." He pulled his phone out of his pocket and left the room.

Phil watched him leave, then turned to Tom. "I am so glad he joined the team."

Tom smiled tightly. "Me too."

"No, really. He's been good for everyone. He gives the younger guys someone cool to look up to, and he helps you figure out how to channel all your drive into something helpful for the whole team. If we can get the defense situation sorted out, this could be our year."

Partially because he wanted not to talk about how good having Jax on the team was for him personally and partially because he didn't want Phil to get his hopes up, Tom eyed Phil's crutches conspicuously.

"If we make the playoffs, I'm playing," Phil said darkly. "Count on it."

"Why don't we let a medical professional decide." Morris wandered to the fridge. "Tell me there's a real beer in here."

"Buy your own damn groceries," Phil told him.

"Do you think it's a good idea?" Tom asked Morris. "Jax and Breezy's charity scheme, I mean."

"Yes," he said without hesitation. "I mean, no clue if it'll fix what's wrong with the team, but it will definitely be a net positive for the world."

The healthy outlook surprised Tom. He'd never had a coach who saw a bigger picture outside the team's successes and failures. While Tom appreciated the perspective, he couldn't understand why a man so measured seemed unwilling or unable to see the bigger picture when it came to the coaching situation with Trout. Tom made a mental note to research Ben's past teams, to see what other players said about him. Good people could be bad hockey coaches.

The evening proved to be awkward. Breezy and Howie were too jovial, palling it up and trying too hard to be friendly to everyone. Hayes and Allie kept to their corner of the room, though Allie still wore all white, and the other WAGs conspicuously didn't. Chloe, the new girl Breezy had been dating for less than a month, wore the same dark green color scheme as the rest. How had Tom never noticed they'd done this before?

Chloe was lovely and spoke English with a French accent. Apparently, she came from a more rural part of Quebec, where French was more frequently spoken than English. But her family, she assured Tom, hailed from Messina.

"And that is what matters," Luca muttered into his wine glass. "Inbreeding."

Breezy shoved him none too gently into the wall and changed the subject to Chloe's studies toward a degree in social work. She wanted to be a high school counselor, something Tom would never do even if it paid more than his NHL contract. When he told her as much, she laughed as though he was kidding.

Tom enjoyed the food. The turkey was great because someone else made it. Breezy and Luca, who had moved in together, brought cranberry sauce, the one dish they were both sure they couldn't fuck up despite Luca having never eaten a cranberry. Howie had played to his strengths and brought store-bought rolls, and Hayes and Vanderbilt had let their partners make the vegetable sides so they would be edible.

Jax's stuffing tasted magnificent.

Tom had three helpings of it.

No one asked why Coach Morris got an invite to a usually team-only event.

Over dessert, Breezy and Jax brought up their plan. Jax had found a shelter for LGBTQIA+ teens that was thrilled with the offer of pro athletes donating time and money. Meanwhile, the team's PR office, excited about engaging with the local community, planned a rollout of the project across all their platforms, headed by Kayleigh Williams. San Francisco remained a long way off from being a hockey town, but this might help.

"We're going live on Wednesday in two weeks," Jax explained, which was news to Tom. Two weeks. So soon.

Reactions were mixed. Gustafsson and Nieminen, Swedish and Finnish defensemen respectively, nodded in agreement but appeared more interested in the pie. It was pecan, the best kind of pie, so Tom understood. Dmitriyev and Abrahamov, on the other hand, exchanged laden looks and said nothing.

Howie expressed his support loudly and enthusiastically, right up until Vanderbilt said, "Can it, kid. You said what you said. You can't undo it."

Howie squared his jaw. "I can learn to do better though." But he stared down at his dessert and didn't meet anyone's eye for the rest of the meal.

A protracted, awkward, awful silence followed before Hayes finally spoke up.

"Fine, I said a shitty thing, and I can't take it back. And I'm still not thrilled about the line changes. But I hate losing. So if you guys need this to feel like a team again, okay."

Though more akin to begrudging acceptance of mandated community service than enthusiasm for charity work, Tom would take it. In his role as captain, anyway. As a gay man, he didn't know how he could stay friends with the guy.

With a start, he realized that at some point in the last few weeks, he'd become comfortable using those words to describe himself, albeit only in the confines of his own head. Before Jax, he'd thought about it obliquely, in ellipses, or not at all. It turned out the words themselves didn't threaten his safety, only the reactions others might have to them. This was who he was, a gay man, and being around people he couldn't trust to respect him as such didn't feel good.

He left the get-together alone, still chewing on the revelation on the drive home. Tom didn't want anyone to get the wrong idea, and Jax had cottoned on fast enough. His Uber followed, probably only a few cars behind Tom. It was silly, with Tom's apartment and Jax's hotel only a few blocks apart.

Jax must hate living in a hotel.

He could invite Jax over again, let him sleep in Tom's comfortable bed on his superior pillows. He wanted to. He wanted Jax to make good on his promise from before, to know how it would feel when Jax went further. He wanted more kisses; he wanted less clothes; he wanted all of it with Jax, and thinking about it had him squirming uncomfortably in the driver's seat.

It would be good. Tom had no doubt. But being around Jax and hearing him talk passionately about wanting to be out was changing Tom. It was changing him fast, which scared and thrilled him in equal measure. Going there with Jax, granting himself permission to feel all the things he so desperately wanted— Tom couldn't help thinking there would be no turning back.

He went to bed alone.

It was safer, even if he could still smell Jax in his sheets.

# Twelve

Kayleigh [off-screen]: We've seen a lot of amazing goals coming off your line this season, even though you've never played together before. Why do you think that is?

Tom: Well, we have very complementary playing styles. And Jax is such a great player. It would be hard to play badly with him.

Jax: He's being modest, like always. He's so fast it's insane. I can barely keep up. We work hard in practice to get used to each other, and the rest is just…

Tom: Chemistry.

### Top comments:

grant16rules: So great to see Jax on the first line and really shining!

1682rox: When your hockey crush on a guy is so intense it turns into a real crush

(Video posted in The Rookery, the direct-to-consumer streaming service of the San Francisco Sea Lions and all associated teams, on 12/02/2024)

Jax had never been this horny in his entire life.

It was getting a little worrying.

Thanksgiving had been such a downer it hadn't surprised him Tom didn't want to hang out afterward, although Jax had been replaying that pleased little smile on Tom's face at the thought of Jax tying him up and driving him crazy ever since.

He had plenty to occupy his time with getting the partnership with Pot of Gold, the shelter housing homeless LGBTQIA+ teens, up and running. Their three days of downtime were eaten up quickly with meetings. Jax had to wear a suit on an off day. He hoped it would be worth it.

And when they found a bit of time to spare between practice skates and planning sessions, Tom would ask Jax to lunch, ostensibly to talk about the power play.

There wasn't much left to say about the power play.

Instead, they spent hours making out on every available surface in Tom's apartment until someone's phone chimed with an alarm for the next meeting or workout or media opportunity. Jax felt weird when he *wasn't* uncomfortably erect in his pants.

Despite the frequent kisses, Jax got the impression Tom had slowed things down intentionally. He never asked Jax to stay the night (a travesty, his bed was much more comfortable than Jax's hotel bed) and never moved his hands below the waist.

Jax did the same on the ice and off: he followed Tom's lead and hoped he'd be allowed to stay a little longer.

On Sunday, Washington came to town.

Their first game since the shitshow in Toronto had everyone tense.

Mooney retaped his stick three times, taping and untaping it over and over. He'd been pretty chill about everything, all things considered, and fully supportive of Jax and Breezy's charity plan. He'd said he neither expected nor needed an apology from Hayes. Watching him unravel the tape for the third time, Jax couldn't help but wonder if this was more of a "prove Hayes wrong" situation than Mooney wanted to admit.

He had that in common with Luca, who had been practicing like a lunatic. He clearly wanted everyone to know his promotion to first string wasn't a fluke, and their faith in him hadn't been misplaced.

As for Hayes, he and Vanderbilt kept to their corner of the locker room, laughing and shooting the shit as though nothing had changed.

Morris gave a rousing speech before the game about team unity. It was a surprisingly good speech, but somewhat out of place for a random game in the middle of the season and uncharacteristic for someone who tended more toward calm and quiet.

Weird quality in a coach, now Jax thought of it. At least Phil's Thanksgiving intervention seemed to have awoken some sense of responsibility on Morris's part to actually coach the team. While convinced most hockey coaches had at least a screw loose, if not a whole bit set, Jax had never before experienced such a strange coaching setup. He ought to ask Tom about Morris—maybe he knew more about the man—if only he could stop getting distracted every time he and Tom found themselves alone.

Awareness of the stakes thrummed throughout the locker room. So many players felt wronged—Luca and Mooney, for obvious reasons, Jax and Tom for reasons only known to themselves, and Hayes because straight white men hated getting called out for their behavior. If the team succeeded tonight with the new D-pairs, it would prove the tension had a worthwhile outcome. If they didn't…Jax refused to think about it.

They got through the first period scoreless, which was something. In the second, a wily right winger got past Hayes and tapped one into the net on a breakaway.

Hayes broke his stick.

Easton waited for them in the locker room. He'd been watching from the visitor's lounge in one of his game day suits, leg propped up on an extra chair. The cameras had been sure to catch him for the jumbotron, and he'd gotten a round of applause. Home game crowds could be so gracious.

"You've gotta get your shit together," he told them bluntly. "Tom, what the fuck are you doing out there?"

Tom blinked, clearly shocked.

"You keep playing to Mazetti like you're trying to prove your line switches were a good idea if you try hard enough. Stop it. Mazetti's doing his job fine, but he's still a D-man. Use Grant."

A never-asleep part of Jax's id sat up and took notice. *Yes, please, use me.*

"I…okay." Tom had probably been avoiding playing to Jax too much because they were…because he didn't want people to think…

Jax pushed the thought from his mind and forced down a protein bar and half a Gatorade.

They came out swinging in the third period. Jax won the face-off, passed to Breezy on the back-check when an opposing D-man got too close, and then hauled ass up the ice. The puck went to Luca, to Vanderbilt, to Tom—and then Jax had it. He was at a bad angle, almost too flat, but went for it all the same. He aimed and shot and the goal light went off, and then Tom crushed him into the boards in a hug so hard it hurt, followed by Breezy and Luca and finally Vanderbilt.

The equalizer lit a fire under them. Over the next ten minutes, Jax had another five shots on goal. The goalie was good, but no one could hold out under that kind of barrage forever.

With five minutes left on the clock, their line kept right on killing it. Vanderbilt seemed to have forgotten his hesitance from the previous periods and fed Jax the sweetest passes. Tom, on their other side, made good on his nickname, looming over the opposition and stealing the puck away. It was only a matter of time.

When it happened, what Jax would remember afterward was how he didn't even have to look. Tom might as well have been on his wing forever instead of only a few weeks. Jax deked left around one of the Washington Wolves, right around another, the puck at the tip of his stick, and he knew instinctively he couldn't make it all the way, not with all of them on him. But he also knew where Tom would be as if they'd been practicing their whole lives for this one moment. He shot the puck blind, aiming halfway between the blue line and the goal, and it hit Tom's stick right on the tape. An instant later, the goal light went on.

It took a moment for him to process, and then he threw his arms in the air and crushed Tom to the boards.

"Fucking beauty!" Jax roared, meaning the goal, meaning Tom, all at the same time.

"That *pass*." Tom had torn off his helmet, his hair dripping sweat, his eyes dark. Jax might die if he didn't get Tom exactly like this, in bed, as soon as possible.

It wasn't a close game in the end. Washington pulled their goalie with two minutes to go, hoping to equalize and go to overtime. But their defense was gassed, and no one knew what to expect of Luca yet, so when Breezy got him the puck and he sniped it straight across the ice and into the empty goal, the home crowd roared, and the game ended 3–1 in their favor.

The locker room tension gave way to jubilant relief in the aftermath. Jax didn't mind when he got pulled for media; he'd gotten first star of the game, though he thought it should have gone to Tom, who got second. The two of them crowded next to each other on a locker room bench while the reporters arranged themselves in front of them in a semicircle.

"Jax, what were you thinking when you sent Tom the assist for what ended up being the game-winning goal?"

"I wasn't really thinking." Jax would probably regret the word choice later. He could already see himself becoming a meme. "I just…knew Tom would be there."

The reporters turned to Tom.

"We've heard some criticism of Jax this last week for being impulsive," Olivia Starling said. "How do you think his impulsivity plays out on the ice?"

Tom considered. "I'm the kind of player who thinks everything through. And Jax has been very patient with me. He lets me bug him on the plane to go over video and stuff. But he doesn't really need to; he's got such great hockey IQ all on his own, you know? And would you call it impulsivity if your instincts are fed by years of experience, of knowing yourself, your team, and the game?"

The interview went on with questions they'd both been asked hundreds of times. Yes, the team showed up and played a full sixty minutes. Yes, the back-check could use a little work. No, they weren't guaranteeing Luca would stay on the first D-pair forever, but so far they were thrilled with the results. No, they didn't know when Phil Easton would be back.

Jax couldn't concentrate on any of it. Tom had played a game like *that*, and then he'd gone in front of a microphone and said *that* about Jax? Casually taking everything Jax hated about himself and turning it into a compliment?

With only a hair's breadth of space between their bare legs, Jax could feel the heat emanating from Tom's skin. He could smell the stupid body wash he used even though he didn't like it. Jax wanted to inch closer, to let their thighs press together on the bench. He wanted to put his hands there on the soft, hidden skin.

He kept his hands on his own lap and his eyes on the camera.

The team had to celebrate Luca's first NHL goal. In the name of bonding, Jax agreed to join them. He made sure to sit on the opposite end of the table from Tom. He didn't think he'd be able to take it otherwise. Not for a full evening. He drank his beer—regular, not light; he couldn't deny himself everything all at once; he wasn't Tom—and teased Luca for only making it on an empty net.

"I suppose I will have to keep trying," Luca said. Flushed with alcohol and pleased with how the game had gone, he didn't even mock Breezy too much over his sudden crisis of faith about Chloe. It turned out the great-grandmother she thought was from Messina actually came from La Massana, which wasn't even in Italy.

Mooney and Howie stood at the bar, trying to chat up two women who were clearly out of their league but might be interested in telling their friends they'd hooked up with professional athletes. Jax was glad to see their friendship had survived intact. Dmitriyev hovered beside them, silent. Jax couldn't help but wonder if it was a bit. He knew a Russian guy on the team in Philly who swore up and down the best way to get girls was by using the line, "Sorry, no English," despite being fluent. Dmitriyev didn't seem the type for subterfuge, but you never knew. He and Vanderbilt were friendly, which could only mean questionable things about Dmitriyev's sexual history.

Jax looked away. If he didn't see what they got up to, he wouldn't have to think about it later. He had no intention of ruining his perfectly happy position, surrounded by team members. Phil Easton ruled over their table, a benevolent king with everyone except Tom, whom he reminded every ten minutes or so that he'd been right and didn't even need to be in skates to win the damn game for them.

It was a good evening.

Good enough to make Jax complacent. When Phil caught a ride home with Vanderbilt and Hayes stepped out to meet Allie, he found himself suddenly alone in the booth with Tom. Howie, Dmitriyev, and Mooney had left for a club with the girls they'd been talking to. Only Breezy and Luca remained, sitting at the far end of the table and debating intensely whether the best pizza in the world could come from Montreal. This topic had them so intent on each other they didn't notice when Tom turned to Jax.

"The shelter…you start in ten days, right?" This was the first time Tom had asked about anything to do with the shelter.

"Yeah?"

"Hmm. Are you coming over tonight?"

Jax swallowed tightly. He wanted to—God, did he want to—but… "I don't know if I can."

"Why not?"

"You were so fucking good tonight, Tom. And I don't wanna take things too far, or—or fuck things up, and I don't trust myself."

Tom blinked. He had these long, sooty eyelashes. Jax wondered what they'd look like with mascara. He bet Tom would be fucking gorgeous. Not that he wasn't already. "Don't trust yourself how?"

"If I go home with you, I'm gonna want more than kissing," Jax said, low and fervent.

When Tom didn't answer, the words kept coming though Jax tried to fight it, aware he could scare Tom off for good.

"I...fuck, Tom, I wanna get on my knees for you. I wanna swallow you down and make you feel like you won the Stanley fucking Cup of blow jobs. I want you to pull my hair and make noise for me and tell me how good I am for you—"

The table shifted when Tom banged his knee into it.

Luca and Breezy glanced up, momentarily distracted from their debate about whether there was such a thing as authentic cheese-stuffed crust.

"Sorry," Tom said. "Guess I'm a little tired. I'll see you guys tomorrow."

He slid out of the booth without a backward glance.

Jax watched him go. His ass in those suit pants was a crime. Maybe he should have gone whole hog, straight-up admitted he had no preference which part of Tom's physique he got his mouth on. He'd be perfectly fine burying his face in those cheeks and never coming up for air again.

Probably not. If the mere mention of a blow job scared Tom off, Jax would have to learn to keep his stupid mouth shut. Good thing Tom had self-control because Jax was clearly all out.

His phone chimed in his pocket. Jax pulled it out.

*I'm waiting around the corner. Give it two minutes and follow me out.*

Very carefully, Jax resisted the urge to fist pump. No impulse control, huh? If only Tyson Fuller could see him now. He drank the rest of his beer, told Breezy he was a caricature of a human being, and let Luca explain what he meant. Then, he moseyed off toward the bar to settle the tab for the team. He was feeling generous.

It took way too long to get to Tom's place in Palo Alto from the city. Convenient it might be for practice, but not when Jax desperately needed to see Tom naked. They spent a full half hour in the back seat of an Uber, not touching each other. Finally, they reached Tom's cold, impersonal apartment, and once again the urge struck Jax to fill Tom's life with things he'd enjoy instead of sticking to the purely practical. Tom deserved a place that suited him rather than one that just made sense for hockey. He deserved furnishings he liked, food he enjoyed, and a little mess crowding the corners of his hermetically sealed-off existence.

Jax could be the mess.

Jax was already a mess, kissing Tom wet and sloppy as soon as the door shut behind them. "Tom," he said between kisses. "Tom, Tom, I want you so much, you can't imagine."

Tom groaned with his head thrown back against the wall while Jax ran his teeth down his clavicle. "I think I have an idea."

Fifteen years, Jax reminded himself. It had been fifteen years since Tom had done anything, and even then, he'd admitted he hadn't done a lot. "Are you sure about this? We've been drinking, and—"

"I had one light beer," Tom said. And then he said, "Please."

Jax's tenuous hold on his impulse control snapped.

He fell to his knees, hard. He didn't care about the pain when they hit linoleum. He didn't care they were both still fully dressed. He needed, and he needed now. His hands shook as he undid the fly of Tom's pants and pushed them down to fall around his ankles. It had been months since he'd touched anyone else, weeks since he'd started wanting this, and his entire life since he'd touched someone and meant it the way he meant this.

Tom's cock was long and uncut and already mostly hard. Jax pressed a kiss to the head before running his tongue all around it.

"Oh," Tom said somewhere above him, vaguely surprised.

With his mouth open, Jax drew a sloppy line down the entire length of Tom's cock, getting it wet. The taste, the smell—body wash, sweat, Tom—being on his knees for this man, all of it conspired to send any blood still in Jax's brain south. He was hard and straining, and it comforted him in a weird way because, really, nothing had changed from all their make-out sessions. He could give something to Tom, something Tom wanted to experience, and his own intense arousal was a happy by-product.

He took the head of Tom's cock into his mouth and sucked.

"Jesus."

Jax groaned around his mouthful in agreement. He loved how Tom sounded, how overwhelmed. He wrapped his fist around the base and set a slow rhythm, up and down with his mouth.

"Uh," Tom grunted, and, "fuck."

With his free hand, Jax grabbed one of Tom's and deposited it on his head. Tom kept his grip gentle at first, petting at the strands, but when Jax started really using his tongue, drawing snaking patterns along the underside of Tom's cock, his hand clenched down. Jax's eyes rolled up, and he moaned. The vibrations made Tom pull harder, and Jax sucked more in response, and from there, it was all heat and spit dripping out the corner of his mouth and the inexorable weight of Tom's cock on his tongue.

Jax lost a little time, bobbing his head up and down, sucking and tonguing and changing his rhythm up when it got to be too much for his jaw. He liked how little he needed to think. He palmed himself through his pants every now and again when he got too desperate, only barely enough stimulation so his body knew he hadn't forgotten it.

"Please," Tom said eventually, and *oh*. His voice had gone so breathy and deep. He said it again, and the desperation in it made Jax *throb*.

He pulled off long enough to say, "I'll take care of you, baby."

Then he opened his mouth wide, let the head of Tom's cock rest there, and started stroking him frantically while he drew wild patterns with his tongue.

The hand in Jax's hair clenched tight. Tom's hips shook with the effort of staying still. He said, "Jax!" And then he came all over Jax's tongue in long pulses that left him shaking and bent over.

Tom slid to the floor, naked from the waist down, and pulled Jax onto his lap. Everywhere he touched Jax, shoulders, waist, legs, lit up as though an electrical charge passed between them.

"I can't," Jax gasped out. "I have to—"

Fumbling between them, Tom got his pants undone. Jax had leaked so much his underwear was wet clean through, and he nearly came the second Tom touched him. All he needed was a little extra push.

"Tell me," he half begged, half demanded. Their movements became rhythmless and clumsy, Jax thrusting his hips up into Tom's hand, Tom trying to meet his frenetic pace. "Tell me I was good for you."

"So good," Tom told him, his eyes still hazy, his lips kissed red. "I've never felt like that. You were *so* good for me, Jax."

Jax came hard all over Tom's dress shirt. He shuddered his way through it, gasping, hips pushing up—up—up until he got too sensitive to keep going.

He collapsed onto the floor next to Tom. "Jesus Christ."

"Uh-huh."

Jax let his head thunk against the wall. "As good as you remember?"

"I wouldn't know."

Jax raised his head again to shoot Tom a quizzical look.

Tom shrugged, a little embarrassed. "I *gave* one blow job once. He never returned the favor, and we never talked about it again."

Something a little possessive trickled down Jax's spine. He tried his best not to notice it. "I should have made it more special, then."

"It was plenty special."

"Could have at least made it to a bed," Jax said around a yawn, the word alone reminding him how sleepy he was.

Tom scrambled to his feet. "Come on." He offered Jax a hand. "We can make it there now."

Jax let himself be dragged to bed. They shed their clothes somewhere along the way, and then his head hit Tom's fancy pillow and his arms wrapped around Tom's body. He thought, I could get used to this.

He fell asleep before he could remember he shouldn't.

# Thirteen

Breezy: Hi, everyone! So, we have an exciting announcement to make. Um, in about a week, the Sea Lions will be starting with Pot of Gold—

[beep]

Breezy: Sorry. In about a week, the Sea Lions will be starting a sponsorship program with Pot of Gold, which is a shelter for homeless teens in the BLT community—

[beep]

Breezy: Sorry, the LGBTQIA-plus community, not the sandwich. It's almost lunchtime. Kayleigh, are you sure you want me doing this?

## Top comments:

sealions4lyfe: If there were a BLT community, I would donate to them, not to this shit

HockeyIsForEveryone_Official: [clapping emoji] The San Francisco Sea Lions are making history

(Reel posted to the Sea Lion's Instagram with the caption "He tried!" on 12/04/2024)

Part of being a leader meant being willing to admit your own mistakes.

Tom had thought having sex with Jax would change him for the worse. In fact, having sex with Jax was possibly the best thing that had ever happened to him. Despite the late night and the intense game, he woke up refreshed and happy. Then, Jax followed him into the en-suite shower and jerked him off from behind, his arms wrapped around Tom's middle, anchoring him and keeping his knees from giving out when Jax twisted his wrist just so.

He tried to return the favor with the water still streaming all around them, fogging the glass walls and Tom's mind. But when he started to sink to the floor to get his mouth around Jax's erection, Jax stopped him.

"I've seen how you baby your hip. If you fuck up your knees, too, we'll be out a playoff spot."

So, Tom steered him to the couch, both of them with their hair still damp, and sucked him off without any of the finesse Jax had shown the night before. Jax still narrated the entire thing as if Tom was the best he'd ever had. By the end of it, Tom's erection had renewed, and Jax flipped them over and blew him all over again.

When practice rolled around, Tom felt loose and easy in his own body, relaxed and buzzing. All went well, with the team gelling, buoyed off last night's win.

Afterward, Breezy passed around a sign-up sheet with dates for visiting the kid's shelter. He'd marked the dates PR would be with them, filming content for the team's Instagram, with a sparkly purple gel pen because: "I don't know, it seems kinda fitting."

"Why do you even own this?" Luca asked.

Breezy muttered something indistinguishable. Next to him, Mooney choked on a laugh.

Luca's eyebrows shot up. "I'm sorry. Could you repeat that?"

Letting out an aggrieved sigh, Breezy said, "It makes writing grocery lists more fun, okay?"

Tom used the ensuing mass hysteria to sign up for dates when no one would be filming him. For most of them, he'd be working with Dmitriyev and

Abrahamov. Tom was pleasantly surprised they'd signed up. They'd spend the whole time talking to each other in Russian and only speak English when spoken to, which Tom could live with. It might even be nice, he thought guiltily, to get through his time at the shelter without much conversation. Only two of the dates he picked were at the same time as Jax, but maybe it would be good for him not to spend too much time in public with Jax. Sitting next to Jax in the locker room, pretending he hadn't seen him naked, pretending he didn't know what Jax looked like when he came, made Tom break out in a sweat he had to blame on practice.

Good, was the answer. Jax always looked good, but when he came, his eyes went wide and shocked, and his lips parted, and Tom wanted to see it again. Maybe after practice.

After practice, it turned out Jax had to talk to PR about a video series of him and Breezy at the shelter.

Tom tried to ignore the surge of guilt for not doing his part. It wasn't only that Jax was doing something good for people like him—like them—he'd also been right about it being good for the team. Even the guys who blustered about not being able to remember all the letters in "LGBTQIA+" were checking timeslots with their friends and asking Jax what PR would expect during filming. No one questioned it, and no one opted out despite it not being mandatory.

To have somewhere to put the feelings caused by this realization—feelings Tom neither understood nor had words for—he hit the spinning bikes in the team exercise room after practice. When Jax asked where he was headed, he called it a "cooldown." But he ended up going for so long that his posture, hunched over the bike, worsened his hip from a mild twinge to an ache. He forced himself to slow down and stop. He really needed to find a way to get out of his head without doing more damage to his body. Long walks, maybe. But walking around town alone just to get out of his apartment seemed like the kind of thing a seventy-year-old would do. He could go with someone, but Phil wasn't up for it, and asking Jax would be futile. The shelter project started in nine days. Only nine days until Tom couldn't go on walks with Jax, or invite him over, or…

"Hey, uh, Cap? Tom?"

"Hmm?"

Howie edged around the corner of the bike. "Hi. Do you have a minute?"

"Sure. What's up?"

Howie cast an anxious glance toward the free weights, where Hayes and Vanderbilt spotted each other for deadlifts. "Maybe somewhere, uh, private?"

They ended up in an upscale sushi bar on the main drag in Palo Alto. During his time with the Sea Lions, Tom had tried nearly every sushi place in the area as the food met their need for large amounts of healthy protein and little to no dairy. Howie eyed the prices suspiciously, which reminded Tom he was still on an entry-level contract. He resolved to pay for them both. Good seafood didn't come cheap, but the sooner Howie learned how worthwhile those macros could be for his conditioning, the better.

"So what's going on?"

Howie sighed and pushed his sashimi around with the fork he'd asked for specially. Someone had to teach him how to use chopsticks, and Tom was afraid he might be the someone. "Um, so Vanderbilt was talking to me before."

"Oh?"

"Yeah, uh, he said all this stuff about how the project Breezy and Jax are doing is only for show, and if I want to make it in the NHL, I need to, um, pretend to be into that sort of thing?"

Tom dipped his sushi into the low-sodium soy sauce. "Uh-huh."

"I mean, what he said was more 'you need to talk the talk; you don't need to walk the walk.' But I think he meant the shelter thing is all for show. And then he said I should go clubbing with him and Hayes sometime, just the three of us."

"Do you want to?"

"I—" Howie peered around the restaurant as if anyone here cared about ice hockey, let alone about intra-team gossip. "I don't know? Like, I don't think the shelter stuff is about image. I've been researching this all week, and if we wanted to look good, we probably should have gone with a children's ward in a hospital or an animal rescue center or something. Did you know the shelter takes in trans kids too? A lot of hockey fans could get pissed about this."

Tom hadn't because Tom had been trying very, very hard not to know anything about the shelter.

Howie picked at his sushi. "But Vanderbilt has been one of my favorite players since I was twelve. I watched all his interviews, and I even bought this water bottle he did a sponsorship deal for. It cost me three months' allowance."

Christ, Tom felt old. Vanderbilt was a rookie during Tom's third year in the league. It did make sense. Vanderbilt played a fast, physical game similar to Howie's. It was why Vanderbilt rounded out their first line so well while Howie played on the second with Mooney. Vanderbilt couldn't reach the same speeds as Tom nor make the intuitive leaps Jax did, but he was fierce and relentless, and sometimes those were necessary skills.

Unfortunately, he was also a dick.

"But, um…all the stuff we talked about on the plane is also really important to me."

Tom breathed out a sigh of relief and stuffed some sushi into his mouth to avoid saying as much. As captain, he had to at least playact at being vaguely neutral. At least, he thought he did. The NHL rulebook and the CBA had no helpful insight on how a captain ought to react to homophobia when he himself was gay. He chewed and swallowed and took his time collecting reasonable words.

He finally came up with, "You can look up to someone's playing style and professional accomplishments and not want to follow their example in other ways."

Howie parsed that slowly over the course of several different slabs of uncooked fish. "Okay, but I don't want to make him angry if I don't hang out with them. And I don't want to disappoint Jax. Or Breezy." He made a face. "Breezy's disappointed face is awful."

"You won't," Tom promised instantly. "You're putting thought into it; you want to do the right thing. That's all anyone can ask. You're doing more than you have to with all the research. It shows how much you care."

Tom had never watched a flower turn toward the sun, but he imagined it was similar to the way a smile spread across Howie's face and his back straightened. Sitting up properly and actually meeting Tom's eyes even made his haircut appear less stupid. Positive reinforcement. Who knew it was so effective?

"The research stuff is pretty cool," Howie said. "I always liked doing independent study at school. Did you know there's a whole code based on handkerchiefs?"

Tom had never carried a handkerchief in his life. A sense of guilt overcame him at being so bad at being gay that he'd never heard of the things Howie had discovered in under a week. At least it made for a good cover. "What kind of code?"

"You know what? It doesn't matter. Um, Vanderbilt and Hayes—what do I do with them?"

"Just don't follow up with them." Tom had perfected the art of escaping social interaction. Teammates sometimes said things like, "We should hang out sometime" or "We should go golfing this summer." Tom's proven tactic to avoid making definite plans was to say, "Yeah, for sure," and then never mention it again. Only Phil had ever nailed down a time and a place with him.

"And if they ask?"

"Then you tell them you're not comfortable with the way they've been acting."

Howie's face went white.

"I can help you," Tom promised, with no idea how he would. It seemed to comfort Howie at least. They spent the remainder of the meal talking about different back-checking drills and wondering why things had gone so quiet with Coach Trout recently, which relieved Tom immensely. He'd maxed out his capacity for emotional conversation.

Howie suggested Morris might be taking the Trout issue more seriously since he'd been a little more involved in practices lately. It didn't seem probable to Tom; taking the issue seriously ought to mean actual changes to the way things were run rather than a constant push and pull between the two coaches.

"Maybe we could talk to Pulvermacher, then, if Trout starts up again," Howie suggested, his mouth full of rice.

The thought made Tom's heart race with anxiety. "Maybe."

He'd met Martin Pulvermacher, the GM, a few times and had never gotten the impression he cared about what happened in practice so long as they made the playoffs. But Howie wasn't off base. Tom and Jax suggesting plays and line changes wasn't a long-term solution, and the rest of the coaching staff and management should have gotten involved a long time ago. Tom hadn't considered talking to them about it because he never talked to them, but fixing team issues should have been their job. Where was Pulvermacher? Didn't his staff report back to him? Didn't any of them notice or care what happened on the team?

The waiter offered them sake with the check, and Tom gulped his down too fast. How had he gotten so bad at this? His first year or two as captain, when he still believed he could take the team all the way on his back, he'd done this kind of thing more often: meals out with the rookies, checking in with their coach. But the older he got, the more he failed, and the more he wanted to hide away from everyone.

He might never have seen his own failings if not for Jax.

"Thanks for this," Howie said, gesturing both to the check and vaguely between them. "It was really...yeah. You're a really good captain."

Emotion swelled in Tom's chest, which he was neither prepared for nor particularly enjoyed. "Uh. Thanks."

"No, seriously, when I made it through training camp, everyone warned me that you weren't easy to talk to or something, but they were wrong."

Tom snorted. "They weren't wrong. I've been...practicing."

Howie shot him a confused look, but only one confused look for the entire conversation counted as a success in Tom's book.

Tom walked home, trying to empty his mind of all the things pressing down on it: Being captain and what it meant to lead a team, when he could change things, and when he ought to get other, higher-ups involved. His own successes and failures. The awkward, awful dinner with his parents in Toronto, when Tom had once again started a sentence with "Mom, Dad, I wanted—" only to be interrupted before he could get anywhere. Jax's charity efforts. Jax's inevitable coming out. The end of their…whatever in nine days.

Tom had heard words like "fuck buddy" and "situationship" thrown around the locker room. He'd always assumed no one would ever apply them to him because he couldn't date, much less have casual relationships, until he retired. If then. He hadn't been able to imagine anyone wanting a washed-up hockey player deep in the closet with no experience even after retirement. Then, Jax had kindly ignored his inexperience, which meant there might be hope for Tom in the distant future. When he'd suggested they practice together, Tom had half hoped Jax would turn him down flat so he could go on believing this was all an impossibility. But Jax hadn't, and kissing once became kissing daily and then more than kissing. Tom had gotten too caught up in the newness of it all to think about it in depth.

Now that he had a moment to process, Tom didn't know what to call the two of them. They weren't dating, but they were more than friends. They weren't *together*, but when it ended, Tom wouldn't be able to ever see Jax as nothing more than a teammate again. He'd always remember the thrill of Jax's touch and the care he'd taken with Tom. There was no way Tom could keep from missing what they'd had however briefly, longing for it, even before he lost it. Tom would have to accept the loss, and the earlier, the better.

Jax wanted to live authentically, and Tom wanted that for him too. It would hurt when Jax called it quits in nine days. But Tom had never met anyone quite so unapologetically himself, and he couldn't stomach being the reason for Jax compromising who he was.

It would be better to keep his expectations realistic. They could enjoy this for as long as it lasted, and when Jax came out, he'd find a partner he could bring to team events and post couples pictures on Instagram with. And Tom would go back to the way things had been before, only a little better for knowing Jax and having been with him, however briefly.

Until then, he'd have to make the most of it.

The team homestand was coming to an end. Tomorrow, they had a matinee game against Chicago. The day after, they'd fly to SoCal for a quick roadie against the LA teams and then on to Arizona. With the end of his time with Jax looming so close, Tom texted him to come over. It would be their last chance for real privacy for at least a week or so.

He stopped off at a CVS on the way home.

He had lube, the same bottle he'd bought three years ago and hadn't often used for a variety of reasons, all of which were too embarrassing to think about for too long. He didn't have condoms; he'd never had any need to buy them. It appeared the market had exploded since he'd been a teenager getting awkward talks from his billet mom.

What size was Jax's cock? He'd had it in his hand and his mouth, but Tom didn't know how to translate the haptic knowledge to inches. It was cock-sized. Not huge, but definitely not small. Should he get magnums? What was the point of flavored condoms? Could he text Jax and ask if condom size was important?

Tom shuddered at the mere thought.

He delayed the decision by perusing the more limited lube selection in case his had gone bad. If lube could go bad. The brand he chose promised it didn't dissolve condoms—a fear Tom had never even known. Then, he grabbed a variety pack of normal-sized condoms from the bottom shelf and called it a day.

Never before had he been so glad for the invention of self-checkout.

Jax waited for him outside his apartment building, leaning casually against the wall near the entrance and typing on his phone. He smiled when he saw Tom, and a part of Tom he hadn't known was tense, unclenched.

"Hi," Tom said as if they hadn't woken up side by side and then had practice together.

"Hi," Jax said back, grinning now.

Tom loved his smile.

"So, you want to…" Tom gestured toward the building with the hand holding the CVS bag.

Jax eyed the bag. The black packet labeled "Condoms" in big white letters showed through the cheap plastic. Tom really ought to start using the canvas bags he had stashed somewhere in the apartment, but he so rarely went shopping. Why bother when he had a service deliver tasteless, dietician-approved meals weekly?

"I want to," Jax said hoarsely.

They took the elevator up without speaking. What was there to say? They were about to have sex, and now they both knew it. Tom *wanted* to have sex, had purposely gone out and bought the materials to have sex, and Jax had seen and agreed.

Strangely, Tom wasn't nervous.

Half the reason he'd put it off for so long, besides the blinding, ever-present fear of discovery, was that at some point, he'd gotten so nervous about not having done it he couldn't fathom ever overcoming the anxiety enough to actually do it. He hadn't counted on Jax though. Jax's enthusiasm, the way he seemed to want everything with Tom so much, made Tom feel…warm. Appreciated. Something hot and excited deep in his core. Watching Jax fall onto his knees yesterday—how eager he'd been, how good he'd been—soothed his fears of inadequacy. Tom knew Jax had exaggerated the experience for his benefit, at least in part, because Jax had as good as said hockey players didn't do it for him. But it still felt good to be appreciated.

Inside the apartment, Jax took the bag out of Tom's hands gently and set it on the table. Then, he reached for Tom's hands and pulled him close. He pressed a soft kiss to Tom's lips.

"What do you want?"

Tom stiffened. Jax had seen the bag, so Jax should know. If this was some power move, some way to make Tom beg—

"Hey, shh." Jax kissed his cheek. "I just mean…I need you to say it. There's a lot of things I'd do with you, and I don't wanna overwhelm you."

"You don't have to baby me," Tom snapped. "I'm a virgin, not an idiot."

He'd never used that word in reference to himself. Virginity was something for hyper-religious people or teenagers. Tom was a grown man who happened not to have had sex. He didn't appreciate Jax turning it into something that made him lesser.

"I'm not babying you. I'm trying to respect your boundaries." Jax stepped away and took a deep breath. "Look, I get this is new for you, and I love how into it you are. But I don't want to be something you'll regret."

"Oh."

"Yeah, oh."

"Sorry."

"It's okay." Jax gave him a smile, a little more tired than before.

As if Tom needed a reminder about why he had no future with Jax. He couldn't even talk about sex without freaking out.

"Talk to me," Jax coaxed, reaching out once more to trace his fingertips across Tom's arm.

Heat flushed up Tom's neck. "I want, um…I want you to…"

"Yeah?" Jax sounded encouraging, eager even.

Tom closed his eyes. "I want you to fuck me," he said into the darkness, directed at no one. "I want you inside me."

Jax kissed his cheeks again, first one, then the other, and then his lips, soft and slow and comforting in a way Tom never knew kissing could be. "Thank you."

Leading Tom by the hand, Jax brought him to the bedroom. "Have you ever, uh…had something inside you?"

Tom nodded. "I have, um…a toy."

"Jesus fucking Christ." Jax closed his eyes briefly as if overwhelmed by the thought. "Okay, so…do you want to shower first?"

"Yeah."

"Alone?"

"Uh, yeah." The process of getting ready for this wasn't really something Tom wanted Jax to witness. He was running low on dignity anyway.

He escaped to the bathroom and turned the shower to hot. Ordinarily, he kept his showers lukewarm and brief because the trainers had mentioned the benefits for his circulation and because California's water supply problems kept him up at night. The massive shower stall, with the rainforest fixture and adjustable side nozzles, had been an indulgence when he bought the place.

Preparing for anal sex though? Turned out having a fancy shower paid off. Tom leaned against one of the marble walls, aiming the nozzle at his ass while spreading his cheeks—a very strange feeling. While he'd experimented by himself previously, this part kept him from doing it more often.

He stayed in the shower a while past what he deemed necessary; he just…needed a minute.

Jax lay on the bed waiting for him, naked except for black Armani boxer briefs—Jax loved an expensive brand—and scrolling on his phone. When Tom entered, Jax looked up and smiled, his hair falling over his eyes, one of the particularly blond strands right over his eyebrows. He was so handsome.

"How're you feeling?"

"Not very sexy," Tom admitted.

"Still wanna?"

Tom nodded.

"Okay, I can fix the feeling sexy thing, then." He beckoned Tom over, then pulled away the towel wrapped around his waist. Tom made to throw it toward the laundry bin, but Jax stopped him and kicked it to the end of the bed. "We might want that in a bit."

Then, he pulled Tom on top of him, and they didn't talk for a while.

Kissing Jax had become familiar by now. Tom wondered if anyone else used his technique of gripping his partner's face so firmly but tenderly, directing them. Was it only Jax who used his whole body, his hands and arms and legs, to hold someone in place on top of him? If Tom had any future partners, would they make him feel this held and protected even when he was on top?

The slide of their bare skin against each other was still new for Tom. He liked the way the hair on their legs rasped together and the swell of Jax's pecs, firm yet comfortable. He liked the heat of it, the warmth, some animal instinct in him for pack and comfort he'd been denying his entire adult life.

"You feel so good," he told Jax, rubbing up against him with his whole body.

"Thanks." Jax grinned. "I work out, you know."

It startled a laugh out of Tom, and the movement shook them apart until they lay intertwined on their sides, so close Tom could almost believe he'd never be alone again.

"Feeling better?" Jax asked, low and intimate.

"Yeah." Tom nosed in closer to the long, tempting curve of Jax's neck. "I got...lost in my head, I guess."

"'S' okay. Sex can be weird sometimes. Sorry if I ruined the mood before."

"No, I'm glad you asked." It was, Tom found to his own surprise, the truth. He hadn't expected it to be, too caught up in the embarrassment of voicing his desires, but he felt better for having been able to tell Jax what he wanted. He'd made a choice rather than letting fate run its course.

"Good. In that case, I'm gonna do my best to make it worth your while."

"Huh?"

Before Tom could fully articulate a question, Jax pushed him over and straddled him. Briefly, Tom was thankful for the ridiculous size of his bed, allowing them to roll all over it. Soon after, most of his thought processes vanished into nothingness.

He'd enjoyed it before, when Jax boxed him in while they kissed, when he took what he wanted and let Tom accept what he gave. The night before, he'd gotten a taste of what it meant not to be in control during sex, but Jax had been so desperate that the loss of control felt mutual.

This, though… Tom lay flat on his back, staring up at the ceiling while Jax did his level best to touch every inch of Tom's skin. His thick thighs caged Tom's hips, already an incendiary image. When Jax used one hand to trail his way up and down Tom's arms, Tom shivered. He wasn't even particularly sensitive there; it was the mere idea of lying still under Jax, letting him do as he pleased that got to him.

What Jax pleased next was to attach his mouth to Tom's collarbone, a place he'd previously established made Tom whimper, and thumb his way around one of Tom's nipples. Tom had never touched himself there purposefully, at least not to get off. The skin was surprisingly tender, getting more so the longer Jax stroked against it. When he replaced his fingers with his mouth, Tom's hips arched up, only to be stymied by the weight of Jax spread across them.

"Oh," he sighed, tilting his head back in pleasure.

"Mm," Jax agreed against his skin. He continued his perusal of Tom's upper body with his tongue. Tom didn't pack on muscle as easily as some players; he tended more toward skinny. In order to keep his weight up, he had to eat massive amounts of fish and chicken with pasta the longer the season went on. He might be a professional athlete, but he'd never had a sixpack.

Jax didn't seem to mind. Instead, he sank his teeth into the pronounced divots of muscle above Tom's hipbones, which had resulted from his work to keep his bad hip from getting worse.

"So hot," Jax said. "Fuck, you are so hot."

An undignified snort escaped from Tom.

Jax raised his head enough to see Tom's face. "What?"

"*You're* one to talk. You're the hottest man I've ever seen in real life."

Jax smiled frequently, and Tom always thought he was handsome when he did, but he'd never seen this smile, crooked and bashful. "Aw, thanks. I mean, I'm all right for a hockey player, but you could be in *GQ* or something."

All right for a hockey player? "Jax, if you were in a magazine, I'd be jerking off to your pictures for weeks, no, months, whether you were a hockey player or not."

Jax shook his head. "I do okay, I guess, but you…"

Tom was tall and awkward, and he'd grown out of the terrible haircut he'd had his first few years in the league, but otherwise, he was nothing special. He cupped Jax's cheek in his hand. "I think you're gorgeous."

Jax's cheeks flushed so red he hid his face, and then he slid down Tom's thighs, peppering them with kisses. Keeping his legs open for Jax made heat prickle along the back of Tom's neck, too intimate and not enough all at once.

He tried to stop thinking, which became easier when Jax nipped at the thin, sensitive skin while firmly gripping the outside of Tom's thighs before sliding around to squeeze his ass.

The myriad of feelings distracted Tom so much he didn't notice Jax going for the lube. When Jax's slick fingers slid down his taint and farther, he jerked, biting the inside of his cheek to keep from shouting.

"Shh, it's okay. I've got you," Jax said as if soothing a frightened animal.

Distantly, Tom thought he should be insulted. Maybe he should do something—anything—to regain control of the situation. But Jax's fingers circled his hole gently, his tongue on the head of Tom's cock, so it didn't seem worth it to risk ending any of the sensations.

"Oh, that's good," he sighed as Jax's first finger slid inside.

"Yeah?" Jax gazed up at him with heat in his eyes. His finger slid in farther.

"Yeah," Tom said. "You make it feel so good, Jax; you're so good to me."

Without breaking eye contact, Jax swallowed down half of Tom's cock in one go and slipped a second finger inside him. He crooked his fingers, and Tom had to yell out. He couldn't keep the noise in *and* keep his hips still.

"I love the way you sound," Jax told him, his voice hoarse from how much cock he'd sucked over the course of the last day.

"Keep going," Tom begged.

Jax fucked him on two fingers and then, eventually, on three, for an interminable length of time. Tom had done this alone, but it hadn't been the same. He'd been responsible for every moment, had to choose when to add another finger, how to position himself, what to do when. With Jax, Tom could let go and feel.

"Please," he said when it got to be too much. "Please."

"Hmm?" Jax asked around his cock.

"I need you to stop, or I'll come."

"Fine by me." Jax's eyes were dark, pupils blown wide. He leaned down to take Tom back into his mouth. Tom jerked away.

"Please, Jax."

Jax took a breath and rested his forehead against Tom's hip. "God, you're hot."

He crooked his fingers again, right where Tom needed, and for a moment, Tom thought it was too late. His cock jerked and drooled against his lower belly, Jax following the entire motion with the expression of a man who'd been starving for years.

"*Now.*"

"Right. Yeah." Jax scrambled away, stripped off the boxer briefs he some-how still wore, and fumbled for the box of condoms. He didn't seem to care about the size or the color, though looking at him now, Tom thought maybe he did need those extra-large ones after all. That was a lot of cock to be going inside him. Jax's fingers were big, but were they enough to prepare him?

"You're sure," Jax said, rolling the condom down his dick. He stroked lube over the condom—one of the normal ones, not flavored or ribbed or any of the other dozens of options—and jerked himself a few times. The tendons in his forearm corded. The blood roared in Tom's ears.

"Tom?"

"Huh?"

"You sure?"

Tom flipped over onto all fours. Over his shoulder, he said, "Please, Jax. Fuck me. Please."

Jax was on him in an instant, a line of heat down his back, his fingers hurried and clumsy as he lined up and then pushed inside.

The heat of Jax's body warmed Tom's. They stuck together with sweat in some places and slid against each other elsewhere. Jax's loud, panting breaths in Tom's ear came second only to the pounding of his own heart. Jax pushed into him, Tom's body gave way, and suddenly, wonderfully, everything was out of Tom's control.

He could have asked Jax to stop at any moment, of course, but the angle, the pace, the inexorability of the slow slide of Jax's cock into his body—Tom didn't decide any of it. His arms collapsed under him, leaving him propped on his elbows, face buried in the sheets, while Jax slid inside him.

Jax kissed his shoulder blade. "Let me hear you, baby."

Tom let out one single sob before Jax started to move, and then he couldn't stop.

"Oh," he moaned on the outstroke, and when Jax changed his angle and pushed in again, he started talking. "Just like that. There, please, Jax—"

"I got you," Jax said calmly, as controlled as the way he fucked Tom. He kept it slow and steady, hitting the perfect angle over and over.

"Jax!" Tom could barely breathe.

"How's it feel?"

"Perfect, it's so good, it's—*fuck*!"

Jax fucked in harder, a staccato metronome. His hot breath puffed out against Tom's spine.

Tom shivered all over. "I need, I need, please!"

He had no idea how Jax did it, where he got the coordination, but a warm hand closed around Tom's cock in an instant. Combined with the way Jax pounded against his prostate, there was no way Tom could hold out.

His orgasm blindsided him, hitting him right in the gut and exploding outward. His thighs and stomach clenched, his balls tightened, and then his spine melted as he shot over and over again, making a mess of the sheets. "Yes," he panted, and "Jax," and "so good."

Finally, Jax's composure cracked. "Oh thank God," he breathed, all one word, and then his hands went tight on Tom's hips and he fucked Tom with all the strength in those massive thighs and glutes for a few short uneven thrusts before letting out a broken groan and filling the condom. His hips kept moving, grinding little circles like he wanted to get it in deep. The movement sent sparks up and down Tom's oversensitive nerves, and he fell forward, his knees and elbows giving up.

He became aware of the world outside his own body again when Jax gently, gingerly patted him down with the still-damp towel they'd left at the end of the bed.

"Should've put this under you. Sorry. Here, roll over. You're in the wet spot."

Tom let Jax turn him, still wanting to move the way Jax moved him.

"You doing okay?"

"Mm." Tom nestled closer to Jax. He was warm, and Tom slept so well when he stayed over.

"You're like a cat, you know that?"

"Thought I was a bird," Tom managed around a yawn.

Jax laughed so softly it was more of an exhale. "Somehow, you manage both."

He sounded so happy, so fond, so in the moment here with Tom. When Tom remembered it couldn't last, it felt as if a barbell had settled over the back of his neck, pushing him down and keeping him there.

"I'll miss this," Tom said drowsily. He turned toward the wall and squirmed until he could feel Jax behind him, then placed Jax's hand on his hip to hold him while they slept.

"What?"

"When the charity stuff is up and running, and you can come out. I'll miss this."

Jax's hand went tight on his hip, and the sensation of being firmly in his hold sent Tom to sleep.

S.B. BARNES

# Fourteen

Kayleigh [off-screen]: Okay, so tell us a little about what you have planned.

Jax: So, today we're shopping for gear for the teens in our new sponsorship program at the Pot of Gold shelter. We've got skates in all sizes and, of course, helmets and pads so no one gets hurt, and—

Kayleigh: And what message are the San Francisco Sea Lions aiming to send with this program?

Jax: Um, right. We really just want to help kids who need it. Living in San Francisco, the local queer—

Kayleigh: LGBTQIA+.

Jax: Right. Sorry. Although, you know, it's not a slur. Some people in the community—

Kayleigh: Jax, we talked about this. And now we have to start over. Again.

(Unpublished outtake from the making of the Instagram reel subtitled, "SF Sea Lions are proud to announce their sponsorship of the Pot of Gold shelter for LGBTQIA+ youth! Follow the link in our description to donate!" posted on 11/30/2024)

It was a hell of a thing to be given a date and time for when someone would break his heart.

After Tom fell asleep in his arms, trusting Jax to hold him in his sleep after the most intimate and intense sex of Jax's life, Jax stared at the wall for an hour. It was only around four in the afternoon. He'd been thinking about ordering in for dinner, then watching something on Tom's ridiculous couch. He'd planned on staying the night.

When had that happened?

Sometime between Tom kissing him at a bus stop in Montreal and Tom buying a ridiculously large multipack of condoms, Jax had let himself believe this had a future. It had only been a *day*, and he'd thought...what, that he could casually insert himself into Tom's domestic arrangements? Jax kept mentally repeating that this was only for now, and Tom didn't want anything more than a practice partner who would keep his secrets. He'd skipped the part where he actually believed it.

This whole thing had an end date, and Jax needed to remember that, or he'd screw things up more than he already had. Tom had set the date, like pulling the goaltender off the ice after he lost three easy shots in a row, a mercy and an arrow to the chest all at once.

Had he given Jax a choice with his mumbled words? Keep Tom or work with the shelter? Keep Tom or come out? How was Jax supposed to make the right call? No matter what he chose, he'd be missing out.

No, he had to remember how they'd gone into this. The last thing Tom needed in his life was Jax's impulsivity, his burning need to remain true to himself at all times. Jax was convenient, and when he stopped being convenient, Tom would stop being his.

Unfortunately, Jax would remain Tom's.

His silent, senseless devotion would have to stay a secret between Jax and the plain white walls of Tom's bedroom.

When Tom woke up, sleepy-eyed and warm, Jax pulled away. He had to call home, he claimed, because they'd be on the road on Sunday when he usually talked to his family. It wasn't really true; he could call his parents whenever and wherever. But the concept of people who actually liked to talk to their parents seemed to baffle Tom so intensely that he didn't question it.

Back in his impersonal hotel room, Jax immediately missed the impersonality of Tom's apartment. Tom kept everything in neutral tones, all grays and browns, but once Jax knew how to look, he'd found Tom's fingerprints on everything. The massive, plushy sectional that swallowed them whole when they lost an hour kissing on it. The absurdly high thread count on the sheets. The twenty different presets in the shower. Tom just wanted to be treated nicely, gently, softly. He might make fun of Jax's expensive tastes, but he was the real hedonist.

Jax had to stop thinking about Tom.

He called home.

Because the Sea Lions didn't have a game tonight, his dad wasn't working the late shift. He answered the phone after two rings.

"Kiddo!" he cried. "How's California?"

Jax peered out of his hotel window. "Foggy."

"Aw, I thought it was all sun all the time."

"Nah, that's a couple hundred miles south."

"Hmm. Shame. See if I'll come visit."

Jax rolled his eyes. His parents had left Minnesota precisely once in their lives when he got drafted in Boston. It had been an enormous production, and they hadn't visited him in Philadelphia. "Who knows how long they'll keep me here anyway. Maybe I'll get traded to the Minnesota Fury next." The team hadn't made the playoffs in seven years, but the location might be nice. Close to home.

"Hold on. Jax is being emo," his dad called, and then a door clicked shut on his end of the line. "What's going on, kid?"

Jax could picture it precisely: Dad on the tiny little deck at the back of the house, standing by the railing, squinting out at the patch of grass they called a garden. To his left, the rickety, fifteen-year-old IKEA table held the tin cup he'd bought Mom at the state fair when he was fifteen. The whole family pretended it wasn't actually a secret ashtray for Dad's secret smoking habit. He had a fantastic view of next-door's fence, which they probably still hadn't repainted.

"Did you ever fix the gutters? Must be coming down hard in St. Paul already."

"Don't change the subject."

That was a no. Jax would have to call the gutter guy.

"Jax."

"Sorry. Got a lot on my mind."

Dad grunted. "You finally get an apartment?"

Jax looked around his hotel room at the clothes strewn over every surface, his bag from the last roadie only half unpacked. "Not so much."

"But you love buying real estate."

"Let it go, Dad."

"Nope, I'ma be salty forever."

"I could still sell the trailer and buy you a mansion," Jax threatened. They both knew he wouldn't follow through. He'd tried, as soon as he had his ELC, to buy his family a better life, but they resisted. All he'd managed was paying off the trailer they'd lived in since Jax turned four and helping his dad start his own diner instead of working shifts at someone else's restaurant for the rest of his life. Dad, at forty-two, should not have as much gray hair as he did.

Someday, his dad might notice how every check he'd sent to repay Jax for the start-up costs of the restaurant bounced, or how the charges for internet and electricity in the family trailer never showed up on the family account. Jax wasn't holding his breath. If his parents tracked their accounts properly, their power wouldn't have been cut half as often when he was a kid.

"You wouldn't dare," Dad said easily. "So. No fancy digs in SF?"

"Not yet."

"Why?"

Jax sighed. "I'm scared they won't keep me. I only have two years left on my contract. If they're smart, they'll trade me early to turn a better profit. What's the point in settling down if I have to leave again in a few months?"

"I remember some upstart eighteen-year-old with dumbass blond highlights telling me real estate is always a good investment when he bought my house."

"Sounds like a smart kid."

"Jax." There it came—Dad's cut-the-shit voice. He might have been a solid five to ten years younger than all the other dads in the PTA, but he had a voice meant for shouting orders in a busy kitchen, and he wasn't afraid to turn it on his kids.

"I'm doing a thing," Jax said. "With a shelter for homeless queer kids. A team charity thing. There'll be media and everything. People might find out about me."

"That sounds good."

"Which part?"

"All of it."

"Dad."

"You haven't been happy, kiddo."

Jax sat on the bed heavily.

"You think I don't watch your games because, what, it's too violent? I showed up when you were in peewee, and those kids were ruthless *and* clumsy."

"Mom said—"

"Your mom didn't want to hurt your feelings. I don't give a shit about hurting your feelings when your feelings are already shitty."

He gave Jax a moment to process.

"I don't think I was *un*happy."

Dad sighed, gusty and loud down the line. "You weren't you. I don't know. Maybe it's something I never got to go through, this part of your life where you try on being different people to see who fits, but the kid I know was the sweetest little boy."

Jax flushed and laughed. "Dad."

"No, seriously. You never got mad at us, you know?"

"Why would I?"

"Well, we kept forgetting the power bill. And the phone bill. And the gutters. All your hockey friends had their own gear, you had to borrow used stuff, and I know how gross those gloves get. But you were always smiling, always making your mom smile, always trying to find a way to help us out of whatever money trouble we got in. Half the reason we had the girls was because you were the best thing in our lives."

*Don't cry*, Jax told himself and then immediately failed.

"Of course, that came after the screaming, crying, pooping phase. Kinda thought I'd go insane before you turned one, but once you could walk, you were great."

Jax laughed wetly. "So what are you saying?"

"I'm saying you found a way to take care of me and your mom and your sisters, and you found a career you love enough to pour your energy and your passion into. And you're fucking fantastic at it. But the person you have to pretend to be while you do it, Jax Grant, hockey superstar—"

"—I can *hear* the jazz hands, Dad. Quit it—"

"He's not you. He's got parts of you, the sense of humor, the playboy act."

Jax didn't confirm or deny the playboy accusation, and his dad was kind enough not to elaborate.

"But he's not as kind as you or as generous with his time and his money. And if this shelter thing and coming out lets you be you again, I'm all for it."

"What if everyone hates me?" The words slipped out, tiny and scared.

"No one important will."

"Thanks, Dad."

With nothing else pressing left to talk about, Jax let his dad go on about the Reindeer's chances at the Super Bowl this year, a covert excuse to bitch about how having a professional athlete in the family still hadn't netted him free football tickets. Jax made a mental note to get him some for Christmas. He had Dad pass the phone on afterward so he could talk to Lila about basketball and Rosa about poetry. By the time his mom took her turn, Jax was all talked out, so she let him listen quietly while she told him all the neighborhood gossip.

He fell asleep with his phone on his chest, feeling not entirely at peace but closer to it than he'd been before.

In the morning, refreshed or maybe resigned, Jax skipped the optional skate. He and Breezy had decided to head out to the shelter to meet everyone before the roadie and get the lay of the land before there were cameras everywhere.

To Jax's surprise, Mooney joined them.

"This is a public service," Mooney told him. "Have either of you ever been to the Tenderloin?"

"No." Jax hadn't even known there was a part of the city called that until he'd pulled the shelter up on Google Maps.

"Yeah, if you leave without getting pickpocketed, I will be fucking amazed." Mooney shook his head at the both of them. "This is a cool idea and all, but I'm not sure if you guys know what you're getting into."

"We'll make it work," said Breezy from the driver's seat. He had a light blue pickup utterly unfit for parking in San Francisco. He also had boundless optimism and apparently no need for caffeine in the morning.

Mooney shook his head again.

"And you're sure you're okay with doing this?" Jax checked in again. "We kind of jumped on this idea after what Howie said that day. But what Hayes said—"

Mooney pushed his sunglasses down his nose expressly to roll his eyes at Jax again. "They're not, like, separate issues. And if you think a homeless shelter for gay or trans or whatever kids in California will not be full of Latinxs, I don't know what world you're living in."

He turned out to be right.

They'd scheduled a meeting with Mara, the coordinator for the shelter who'd been emailing Jax. From her emails (professional, cordial, and frequently organized using bullet points), he'd imagined her to be about forty. It turned out she was twenty-four and had blue, pink, and purple stripes dyed into her hair. She was also the only white person on the premises, besides Jax and Breezy.

She caught Jax eyeing her hair. "We had a hair night last night," she said in lieu of an actual explanation.

"Looks dope," Mooney said.

"Thanks. So, come on through, and we'll go over the basics."

The basics turned out to be a comprehensive list of rules outlining what they could and couldn't do, mostly centering on the kids' safety.

"Um," Jax said. "You know hockey is a contact sport, right? We won't try to get anyone hurt, but—"

Mara shot him an unimpressed glare. "Yes, I am aware. This is to cover my own ass and to make sure the big-shot hockey players understand what it means to be responsible for teenagers. They will try to use the hockey sticks as weapons to hit each other with. Ice skates are basically knife shoes. Someone might try to use them as such, and many of them will use them as such unintentionally. If this whole partnership deal lasts for more than one session, you will end up calling 911 at least once."

Jax's pulse quickened. He'd imagined fun, happy times explaining to kids how to get a sweet pass and what the five-hole was. Why, he had no idea. His dad had made a good point: Peewee hockey was a fucking bloodbath.

"Knife shoes," Mooney whispered. "That's metal as fuck."

Mara glared at him.

He shrank back in his seat.

Mara steepled her fingers, elbows leaned on her desk. "Okay. Last question. Are you sure no one on your team will say something shitty and homophobic to my kids?"

"That's kind of why we're here."

Jax closed his eyes. Why couldn't Breezy think before he spoke?

Mara's eyebrows rose, the piercing in the left one shifting with the movement. "Explain."

"We had an incident in the locker room," Jax said. "Some…things were said. Not just homophobic things, racist, too, and, uh… We don't want to be a team where it's okay to say hurtful or prejudiced things. The captain shut it down when it happened, but we, um, Breezy and me, felt like we should be doing more. We earn a stupid amount of money, so we can do something good with it instead of being bigoted shitheads."

For the first time, Mara smiled at them.

"Really?" Mooney asked. "Telling you we've already fucked up makes you trust us?"

"Oh, no. I'm pretty sure you're all idiots, but your hearts are in the right place, and I can work with that. This captain of yours, he coming too?"

Jax had managed to go a full ten minutes without thinking of Tom. Now, he couldn't help but remember. When the charity stuff was up and running,

Tom would miss him. Because they couldn't see each other anymore. Because Tom was so deep in the closet, he couldn't be associated with this. Or Jax.

"Yeah," Breezy said enthusiastically. "He signed up for a few dates. None of the ones with cameras and PR, though, which is Tom all over. He's a humble guy, you know?"

Humble. Sure. Humble, self-loathing, and terrified.

Jax shoved the feelings down and smiled brightly. "So can we meet the kids?"

Despite it being a school day, a few of the kids hung around Mara's office, very conspicuously trying to catch a glimpse of what was going on in there.

"Late night last night. I let them have a sick day," Mara said with a shrug. Jax wondered if there was more to the story, but her closed-off expression forbade him from asking.

Some of them couldn't have been older than twelve or thirteen, and Jax abruptly remembered none of these kids had a home.

His parents might have been kids themselves when they had him, they might have been disorganized and chaotic and shit at remembering to pay the bills on time, but he'd never for an instant doubted whether they loved him. He'd never been scared to come out because of them. He'd only been scared because of hockey.

Mara drummed everyone together while Breezy and Mooney grabbed the sticks and pucks they'd brought with them from the car. The shelter had a courtyard out back, a shitty asphalt patch with two rickety basketball hoops. It would do, but Jax made a mental note to ask about getting a landscaper in here. Kids needed trees, for oxygen or something.

"All right, any questions?" he asked once they had gotten through explaining the rules of street hockey.

"Yeah," said a short, skinny boy with an Afro probably meant to make him appear taller. "What's the point?"

Jax blinked.

"I mean," the kid continued, "you guys are gonna get filmed playing hockey with us, great for you, but what good does it do us?"

"It doesn't have to do you *good*." Breezy's expression was utterly crestfallen at the thought. "It's just *fun*."

Mooney's eyes might as well have permanently rolled to the top of his head at this point. "We're not only playing hockey; we're sponsoring you guys. We're giving you clothes, sports gear, notebooks, school supplies, whatever, from the team store. Also, you get seen playing with us on the team Instagram or whatever and next thing you know, you've got hockey fans all over the country donating you shit."

"Stuff," Mara corrected out of the corner of her mouth.

"Right. Stuff."

The kid still looked skeptical. "All of it have that dumb-ass sea lion on it? You know sea lions are the laziest animal. It's no wonder you guys never win anything."

Breezy's face crumpled in devastation. "Sea lions are awesome. They can stay underwater for twenty minutes."

Jax stared at him.

"What? There's a fact sheet in the locker room. We have a donation box for a research center underneath it and everything."

"Okay." Jax grabbed a stick and a puck. "Everything they said is true. We're gonna get you guys noticed, and we're gonna try to help. But also—" He took aim and shot. The puck slammed into one of the basketball hoop stands with a loud clang. "—hockey's really great if you ever feel angry."

The kids—teenagers, most of them about the same age as Jax's sisters—were ruthless once they got the hang of things, enthusiastic and energetic. On the court, Breezy shone. His easygoing nature and cheer worked there in a way it hadn't beforehand. In another life, Jax could see him as the rare PE teacher all the kids at school loved.

They wound down after half an hour, most of the teens already heading inside or helping Mooney liberate the snacks and drinks they'd brought from the car while a few stragglers asked Breezy for tips on checking. He did great, making sure to teach them how not to hurt anyone, first and foremost.

"So how did you know?"

"Huh?" Jax turned to Mara.

She studied him, assessing. "How did you know how angry they all are? Most people who donate expect everyone here to fall all over themselves being grateful for every little bit of help we get."

Jax swallowed.

He thought again of Tom, half asleep under the sheets, tugging Jax closer and at the same time announcing his intention to push him away if he ever dared be himself out loud.

"I know how I'd feel if the people who should love me no matter what turned me away for…this," he finished lamely.

Mara gave him a sad little half-smile, and he thought she knew. But if he was doing this, it wouldn't be with rumors and half-baked non-statements.

"I got lucky."

"I'm glad you did. Worked out pretty well for my kids."

Jax grinned, relief loosening the ever-present fear gripping his chest. It made way for the sadness, the impact he'd been bracing for since last night. Maybe if he mourned losing Tom now, before it happened, it wouldn't hurt so much when it did.

"So, Mara," he said, trying to sound upbeat, a little smug, and, in general, like Jaxon Grant. "Can I pay to get a landscaper out here?"

"You know what?" Mara linked her hand through his elbow and led him toward her office. "I would be thrilled to take more of your money."

# Fifteen

[…] Forty years ago, when you thought hockey, you thought big, beefy guys knocking one another's teeth out and maybe occasionally scoring goals in there somewhere. To say things have changed would be like pointing out that Istanbul is, in fact, no longer Constantinople.

These days, hockey players pride themselves on speed, agility, and the combination of intuition and practice referred to as "hockey IQ." Summer isn't downtime, it's training season; penalty minutes aren't something to be proud of, they're something to avoid. Looking at the San Francisco Sea Lions, star left wing, Tom Crowler, plays a game based on speed and agility while his center, Jax Grant, brings the muscle and the intuition to back it up. In the defensive zone, they've got new, rising star Luca Mazetti, who is slight enough to be a figure skater but has a deft hand with the puck, relying on his quick feet and soft hands instead of stature. And while none of these guys are overladen with dignity (Grant in particular is known for wearing hideously colorful suits and whatever designer object is the newest trend), they're a far cry from the toothless buffoons of yore. So where does that leave old-school players in a new league? The guys who're still out there to rile everyone up and smack their stick in someone's face? Well, the Mike Vanderbilts of the hockey world are still trucking, but a new kind of player is on the rise to bridge the gap. Smart and quick, yes, but also annoying as all get out, Kilian Howard is the Sea Lions' answer to the changes in the hockey landscape. He's our youngest player, a kid no one expected to make the team his first year after being drafted, but already he's got the speed and the know-how. In addition, he's such a pest the other teams can't help but take penalties trying to shut him up. […]

(From "So You Want to Watch Hockey: the Bay Area Native's Guide For Sports Fans Tired of Football," posted on http://sfhockeyftw.blogspot.com on 12/02/2024. Found in the search history of Ben Morris's private laptop.)

Morris called in sick for the Chicago game. After his absence from morning skate with no notice, Tom's black mood only worsened. He'd felt off since Jax left the night before, lonely in a way he hadn't been in all the years he'd spent alone.

Jax probably knew he was getting too attached after spending the night together, sleeping with Jax curled around him. That couldn't become a habit. Jax didn't even like hockey players. So, while it was very kind of him to claim he found Tom attractive, to compliment him, and teach him all the things Tom had been missing out on, Tom benefited from their arrangement far more than Jax.

Jax had made the right call leaving yesterday, and it was good he hadn't been at the optional skate this morning. This meant Tom had almost a full day to get his head on straight, and Jax wouldn't go apoplectic after suffering through one of Trout's practices.

Tom had nearly forgotten what a mess they were.

The good news was that Trout had decided to stop systematically over-working the D-core. The bad news was that he'd moved on to including everyone else. Tom tried to ask about it, midway through a prolonged, full-ice special teams drill, which had both power play units racing across the ice at full speed over and over till none of them could get enough air.

"Coach?" he tried, still panting. "I thought this was a light practice?"

The SoCal games were back-to-back. The team would need some breathing room.

Trout snorted derisively. "You're not paid to think. Get going, Crowler, or do you want to be a healthy scratch tonight?"

By the time the team dressed for the game, Tom's skin prickled, stretched tight across his body, wired from wondering if he'd messed things up with Jax by being too needy. At the same time, exhaustion from the practice drills weighed him down so heavily it would be a struggle to get through the whole game.

Jax, Breezy, and Mooney returning together, full of excitement and stories about the shelter, did not help his mood one bit.

For the first time, he was thankful for Trout's perpetual bad mood.

"No one wants to hear about you holding hands with orphans," he bellowed. "Get fucking dressed."

"They're not orphans," Breezy said. "They're teenagers who've been—"

"Do I look like I care?"

Trout ducked into the office to get something—possibly a whip, given the way things were going—and Phil chose that moment to arrive, which seemed a little too convenient for Tom's taste.

"What's wrong with Morris?" Tom asked.

"He'll be better in time for the roadie. How're you feeling, boys?"

The boys groaned.

Phil took a seat on the bench. "Okay, well, the good news is Chicago's starting goalie's on IR. Keep the D-line tight, let Jax do the heavy lifting offensively, you'll be fine."

"Easton!" Trout barked. "What the fuck is this?"

Phil smiled at him innocently. "Just giving the boys a little moral support, Coach."

"Sounds like backseat coaching to me."

It not only sounded like backseat coaching, it also looked like it. Whatever issues plagued the coaching staff, Phil knew about them and hadn't told Tom.

"Nah, I wouldn't know the first thing about coaching. Oh, hey, Howie?"

"Huh?" Howie glanced up from taping his stick.

"Denisov—on Chicago's second line? He put something really stupid online the other day. Lemme show you."

Howie went over to check it out and immediately broke into a braying laugh. "Oh, damn. I bet I can lose him at least a face-off if I time it right."

"But don't let him crush you to the boards too much, kid. The man's six-foot-seven."

Jax elbowed Tom lightly. "You think we can hire him as a coach?"

Trout's eagle eyes narrowed in their direction.

"I wish," Tom muttered. It would certainly solve a lot of problems. Maybe Tom could talk to the GM when he wasn't seeing Jax anymore. He'd have too much time on his hands then anyway.

The game ended up being an overtime loss, with an incensed Denisov scoring on them two minutes after the end of regulation. Still, a point was a point, and he had lost several face-offs against Howie.

"It's as if Trout doesn't want us to win," Tom complained to Jax as they headed for the showers. They were the last two in because they'd been tapped for media, the endless curse of the captain and alternates.

Jax winced. "I heard he went hard on you guys this morning. Hope Morris gets back in time for the roadie."

"Yeah." Although, the longer he led the bench, the more Tom noticed Morris wasn't particularly helpful on his own either. It had taken their intervention to get the team up to a solid winning record. Tom had a tab open on his phone to research drills, and he worried he ought to be watching the video review for the goalies on top of everyone else, but he didn't have the time or the eye for it. None of these things were in his job description. "I never want to be a coach."

"No? I thought for sure when you retired..."

Tom realized, suddenly and sharply, that he had no clue what he would do when he retired. He didn't want to coach, didn't want to spend time on any of the annoying parts of hockey and none of the actual playing. He definitely didn't want to be in the public eye anymore. But as for something he *did* want to do? Tom had nothing.

It was as if Jax could see the sudden existential crisis on his face. "Guess you'll be one of those millionaires who spends all year on the beach, huh? Get a little house in Cabo, drink cocktails all day..."

"Burn to a crisp and die of skin cancer."

Jax stared at him. "Wow. What crawled up your ass and died?"

Tom wanted to tell him nothing had ever crawled up his ass besides Jax's dick, but that was neither appropriate for the workplace nor sexy. "Nothing. Weird day. Come over?"

He hadn't meant to invite Jax. He'd meant to play it cool, act as unaffected about it all as Jax. But Jax was right there, naked under the showers, and Tom was only human. He had eight days left. He wanted all of them.

Jax hesitated, chewing on his lip. "Yeah," he said eventually.

"You don't have to—"

"No, no, I want to."

"Okay, um, see you later?"

"Yeah."

At home, Tom showered thoroughly despite having just cleaned up at the arena. He didn't want to repeat yesterday's awkward interlude; he wanted to be ready for everything. Thinking about what "everything" entailed left him a little glassy-eyed and wobbly-kneed under the stream, making the whole process take longer than it should have. After, his skin was so sensitive from the lingering heat of the water and the memories of last night he couldn't handle the thought of the tough, scratchy fabric of any of his pants, so he pulled on threadbare sweats and his most washed-out T-shirt. He realized too late he hadn't given Jax a time, which left him wandering aimlessly around the apartment, dusting off surfaces he hadn't bothered cleaning in years and wondering what Jax would do to him this time.

By the time Jax got there, Tom had run through most everything his imagination had to offer, leaving him flushed and horny already.

"Okay, whoa, whoa!" Jax laughed when Tom dragged him through the door by his shirt collar and kissed him thoroughly. He snaked his arms around Tom's waist and slowed the kiss into something more tender. "What's gotten into you?"

"I was hoping you would," Tom said, and then he had to stop and laugh at himself. He rarely watched porn because it used exactly that kind of cheesy line he'd thought no one ever said in real life.

Jax smiled, too, indulgently, as if he didn't get the joke but enjoyed the sound of Tom's laughter all the same. Tom's stomach swooped. He kissed Jax again to keep from saying anything stupid. It escalated quickly as he slid his hands under the hem of Jax's henley, the fabric soft—something designer and likely costing more than all of Tom's shirts combined—though not as soft as Jax's skin, warm under his touch.

He was vaguely aware of Jax moving them, walking him backward through the apartment, but Tom couldn't focus on anything except how to get more. More touch, more heat, more of Jax's tongue, teasingly dipping in and out of his mouth. When the backs of his legs hit the couch, he nearly fell.

Jax caught him around the waist and held him steady. "I want to make you feel good," he said.

"You always do."

Jax groaned as if he was the one who had revealed something embarrassing. He pulled away to look at Tom. "I love you this way."

"What way?"

"All…soft." He tugged at Tom's T-shirt. "I know you're probably not…into that, but I want to wrap you up in cashmere and silk and make you feel so…fucking…good." He punctuated each word with a kiss.

Tom had never owned anything made of either material, but the thought of it, of Jax picking out nice fabrics for him to wear, pretty things, made Tom flush with agitated desire. He *wanted* intensely at the mere thought, but he knew he couldn't have. He wasn't the kind of guy who got to have pretty or gentle or soft. Jax had seen the embarrassing core of him that wanted to be held and touched as though he were precious. When whatever they were doing ended, Tom would need to live with having been known for every pathetic part of himself and then losing that unbearable intimacy. If Jax left a physical reminder—some pretty clothing he'd chosen with Tom in mind—Tom wouldn't be able to handle it.

"Just...fuck me," he said, lightyears from what he wanted and yet as close as he would get.

"In a minute. First, I wanna try something."

Jax pushed Tom's sweatpants off his hips and spun him around until he leaned over the couch in only his T-shirt. "Tell me if you hate this."

Tom had enough time to wonder about the location of Jax's voice, coming not from right behind Tom's head where he'd expected to hear it but farther away. And then Jax licked into him.

"Oh!" Tom cried out, hips bucking away on instinct. They had nowhere to go, though, except deeper into the plush cushions of the couch. Jax followed him down, his hands firm on either side of Tom's ass. He held Tom open so he could reach with his tongue, the sensation odd, warm, and wet where Tom expected neither of those things. Beyond the shock of it, at first it didn't feel of much. But the longer Jax kept at it, licking over and over that patch of skin, the more sensitive it became. Jax had a little stubble, and Tom could already tell he'd be sensitized, itchy, raw, and squirming in his seat tomorrow—a heady, sensual thought.

Jax pulled away. "Your ass is the most perfect thing in the world, I swear to God." He dove back in immediately.

Tom reached behind to grab onto Jax's hair, and Jax groaned into his skin, the sound making goosebumps break out all over Tom's body.

Eventually, Jax moved on to stabbing right into Tom's hole with his tongue. It felt good, though still nowhere near as good as Jax's fingers or his cock. But when Jax pulled away and rose to his feet, he said, "Tom, I need to be inside you now, or I'm gonna die." He accompanied this by pressing the entire length of his body against Tom's, and oh, he was so hard, a hot line against the curve of Tom's ass, practically shaking with how badly he needed to get inside. If rimming did this to Jax, Tom would take it.

Neither of them had thought to leave lube or condoms by the couch before Jax crash-landed them there, making an interruption necessary.

"Stay here," Jax said, with a firm pat to Tom's tailbone. He returned so quickly Tom didn't so much as get cold. Somewhere en route, Jax had lost his shirt and his pants, and he plastered himself to Tom's back, all hot, naked skin and slippery fingers.

Prep went faster this time. The rim job had relaxed Tom, and it had only been a day since they'd last had sex. Eagerness made Jax sloppy. He kept a running commentary on how hot he found Tom, how turned on he was, and how badly he needed it as he raced through slicking up Tom's hole. That more than anything else made Tom squirm against the cushions. The soft fabric dragged against his cock, and with Jax behind him, surrounding him on all sides, heat and desire cocooned him.

"Please," he said, wondering if there'd ever be a time when Jax touching him didn't make him beg for more.

This time, Jax was right there with him, needy and wanting. He lined up and drove home, chin hooking over Tom's shoulder. "God, Tom, you don't even know. The things I'd do to you. You're—"

"Do them," Tom gasped, and then Jax gripped his hips so tight Tom knew it would leave bruises. Jax fucked him then, nothing like last night, not as slow and gentle and exploratory. He didn't slow down to make it good for Tom; Jax took what he needed, and Tom discovered he loved being what Jax needed.

"Come on," he said. "Come on, more."

Jax made a nearly inhuman sound. He fucked into Tom harder at just the right angle, and Tom cried out into the cushions. The pace drove him against the couch harder and harder, the friction of the velour softer than he needed, a teasing pressure which gave under his hips when he wanted to rub up against it.

"I need you to come," Jax said.

Tom felt every word on his skin. "For you," he said nonsensically. "I wanna come for you."

"You're so perfect." Jax bit into the side of Tom's neck, ground into his prostate exactly right, and Tom came all over the couch cushions, too much and not enough and hot and wet and good.

After, every inch of his skin went oversensitive. It made him sob when Jax kept moving. He would have taken it anyway, wanted it, even, but Jax pulled out before he could say anything.

"I'm gonna," Jax said, followed by the slap of skin on skin, and then only a few seconds later, Jax's come hit the back of his thighs and his ass.

It was warm, and when it dripped down between his thighs, it tickled. Tom squirmed on the couch.

"Shit," Jax panted. He sounded more winded than a practice with Trout had ever gotten him. "Shit, sorry. I'll get you cleaned up."

He stumbled off toward the bathroom. Tom let his head rest on the cushions as he drifted.

Jax returned with a warm, wet towel and carefully dabbed across Tom's ass and thighs, spreading his legs to get the drops that had slid down between them. "You okay to move, baby?"

Didn't sound appealing, but Tom figured he had to at some point. He got to his feet slowly and examined himself. His come stained the bottom of his shirt as well as the couch cushions where he'd been lying.

"You should always dress this way," Jax said, sounding oddly sincere.

"I look like Winnie the Pooh."

"You look like you got fucked within an inch of your life."

Tom considered. "Two things can be true." He hitched his discarded sweatpants up and sat on the clean side of the couch while Jax dabbed ineffectually at the cushions with his towel. "It's fine," Tom said. "I'll turn them over or something."

"It will just happen again on the other side."

Would it? Good to know.

Jax came around the couch and collapsed next to Tom. "Was that, um…was that okay for you?"

"What do you mean?"

"I kind of went for it. I was…so into it. So into you."

Tom gave it a moment's consideration. "I really liked how much you liked it. The rimming, I mean. Sensation-wise, it felt fine, I guess, but I mostly enjoyed the part where you were desperate to have me."

Jax let his head fall back with a groan. "You can't say sexy things for at least an hour. Forty minutes, maybe."

"You staying for dinner, then?"

A troubled expression stole across Jax's face, but it cleared away so fast Tom didn't have a chance to react. "If there's a round two after, sure."

Good. A clear objective would keep Tom's mind from romantic daydreams.

They ate Vietnamese takeout on the couch with some dumb home improvement show on in the background. Tom's mom texted about the game, and he tapped out a thank-you without reading what she'd written. He didn't want to waste his time with Jax thinking about her.

Jax told Tom about the shelter, the kids he'd met, the coordinator who had scared the crap out of him. Tom forced his shoulders to relax and his expression to reveal nothing as Jax spoke. He pushed through the discomfort the way he'd work out a sore muscle. The more Tom focused on the end date, the more he'd be ready for the hurt. He couldn't make Jax smile the way talking about the shelter did, excited and wistful all at once. He couldn't fill Jax's life with purpose. All Tom had to offer were thoughts on the penalty kill, and as much as Jax appreciated those, Tom knew he needed more.

After dinner, they were both tired and lethargic. They'd agreed to something, to give Jax a reason to stay, but the best Tom could offer was lazy hand jobs on the couch. They left the TV on, and it took a while for Jax to get off because he kept getting distracted by the baffling choices on *House Hunters*. He had thoughts about sconces, apparently. By the time they finally finished, it had gotten so late it only made sense for Jax to stay over.

In the morning, Tom woke to Jax easing away carefully and picking his clothes up off the floor. Tom kept his breathing even and his eyes closed, but he couldn't help the sharp intake of breath when Jax kissed his cheek.

"I have to go home and pack," Jax whispered. "Get some more rest, baby."

After he left, Tom stared at the ceiling for twenty minutes before giving up on sleep and getting up.

He was in such deep shit.

# Sixteen

[Images of Jimmy Hayes proposing to Allie Jenkins on a beach in the Caribbean]

The Sea Lions family congratulates the soon-to-be Hayes family! Looking forward to the pics [eyes-emoji]

## Top comments:

sealions4lyfe: Finally some good off-season content!

Camille Easton: Congratulations! You will be the most beautiful bride!

SFCLions: I don't care who gets engaged this off-season. So long as Crowler's still on the market, a girl can dream.

(Posted to the San Francisco Sea Lions official Instagram on 7/14/2024)

Jax spent the entire road trip sharing Tom's hotel room.

He knew it would blow up in his face. He could count the ways it was a bad idea on both hands, and somehow, "it'll fuck up the team dynamics beyond repair" didn't even make the top five. He just couldn't help himself.

On the plane ride down to Los Angeles, PR sent out an email announcing the launch of the shelter project on social media for Wednesday,
reaffirming the deadline for whatever Jax had with Tom.

Tom caught his eye on the way out of the plane, and Jax knew he had
to make the most of the seven days he had left.

It had only been a few weeks since they'd first kissed. A month was not
enough, not when Jax wanted years. He wanted so many things with Tom.
He wanted to cook dinners for him, real dinners with unhealthy carbs and
butter and all the things they couldn't eat during the season. He wanted
to sit on Tom's ridiculous couch with Tom's feet in his lap, rubbing them
while they watched something mindless. With no outlet for his want, he
spent the bus ride to the hotel looking up increasingly pricey sweaters soft
enough that Tom would feel like he was wearing a cloud.

He wanted other things too. He wanted to know who Tom had given
his one and only blow job to in Juniors. He wanted to know what Tom
thought about Coach Morris living in Phil Easton's spare room and hear his
theories about why the coaching staff did the things they did. He wanted
to gossip about Breezy's newest girl—Brittany. Breezy had talked to her
grandmother on the phone to make sure she actually was Italian. He wanted
to discuss his concerns about Hayes and Vanderbilt and whether Howie had
gotten even more obnoxious since learning to be less of a dick. But since
they'd started sleeping together, they'd lost the ability to talk about hockey
when they were alone, as if bringing the team into what they shared would
blur the boundaries, and they wouldn't be able to leave this thing behind
them.

Jax didn't *want* to leave it behind them.

So, he followed Tom to his hotel room in the evening and left at the
crack of dawn so no one would catch them. He played like shit, and they
lost against Los Angeles; the next night, he did it again, and they lost against
Anaheim as well.

They beat Arizona, but winning against the Prairie Dogs was akin to
playing chess with a five-year-old. Sometimes, Jax thought it would be good
to let them win, to help them build confidence.

The words "impulse control" rattled around Jax's brain, but what little
he had, he'd used up not falling on his knees and begging Tom to keep him
a little longer.

On Monday, they returned to San Francisco, and Tom invited him
over one last time.

Jax made good on his earliest promise. He tied Tom to the bed with his ugliest game-day ties (there were a lot to choose from) and took his time. Tom was perfect under him, pliant and relaxed and staring up at Jax as if he'd hung the moon.

Jax did his level best to live up to it. He started at Tom's ankles and kissed his way up his legs, then did the same thing from wrists to shoulders. He pressed their bodies together from thigh to chest and kissed Tom as thoroughly as he knew how. With Tom distracted, Jax opened up quickly and perfunctorily. He rolled a condom down Tom's cock, hard between them, settled one knee on either side of Tom's hips, and sank down slowly.

Tom's eyes flew open, wide and shocked. His hips bucked up, hindered by the clamp of Jax's thighs around them.

A high, keening noise left his throat.

"You've never been inside someone, have you?" Jax realized.

Tom shook his head mutely.

Jax rolled his hips as slowly as he could. "Good," he said fiercely. "I want all your firsts. I want you to remember this for the rest of your life."

Wrapped in the hideous teal-and-orange tie, Tom's right hand flexed as if he wanted to reach out and touch. "I could never forget."

Jax leaned down to kiss him again and began moving properly.

He'd planned to take his time, and he tried, but he couldn't. He sped up by accident and then forced himself to slow when it got too good, over and over until they both panted for breath.

Under him, Tom bit his lips red, head turning from side to side. "Jax," he begged. "Jax, please."

"A little longer," Jax said, hanging on by the skin of his teeth and by virtue of the fact that he hadn't touched his own cock yet. He didn't want it to end.

Tom strained against the ties. The tendons in his neck stood out. His mouth dropped open, and a flush crawled up his cheeks.

Jax didn't decide to speed up again; his body was beyond his control, bucking up and grinding down. Tom groaned, his whole body tightening and then going loose again as he came. Only his hips moved, pushing up and up and up as deep as he could go into Jax.

Jax reared up, reaching for his own cock, but the realization came faster than he could.

It was over.

He paused a moment too long and bitterness overwhelmed him, killing his arousal.

Swallowing around the lump in his throat, he pulled off of Tom. He discarded the condom—that was a first Tom could have with someone else—and set about untying Tom. His hands shook a little, his eyes blurring.

"Jax?" Tom's voice was hoarse from begging. "Jax? Are you all right?"

"Mm-hmm."

"Did you—did you finish?"

"It's fine." Jax's voice cracked.

"Jax." As soon as Tom's hands were free, he grabbed for Jax, pulling him close. "What's wrong?"

"I…" Jax tried to turn away, to hide his face, but Tom wouldn't let him. "Please."

"I don't want this to be over," Jax burst out. "Why can't we keep—why can't we—"

Tom's face fell.

"Sorry. I know this was just…practice to you."

"Don't be ridiculous."

The dismissal irked Jax enough to forget his reticence. Tom might not share his feelings, but he didn't get to pretend they didn't exist. He opened his mouth to snap back, but Tom got there first.

"Of course I want to keep doing it!" Tom said it as if it were a given, and Jax should have somehow known.

"You do?"

"Of course I do! If it were just practice, I wouldn't keep asking you to stay the night. I wouldn't want to spend all my time with you. You were always running out the door."

"Because I knew I'd get my heart broken if I stayed!"

"Oh."

They stared at each other for a long moment.

Finally, Tom asked, "Could you untie my legs?"

Jax's hands still shook as he did, this time from the hope clawing its way up from the pit of his stomach, making him jittery.

With his legs free, Tom drew them up under himself. "I'm sorry."

"Why?"

"For hurting you."

"But if I—and you—can't we?"

Tom looked away, tugging at the bedsheets to pull them up. "Are you still doing the shelter thing tomorrow?"

As fast as it had come, Jax's hope cratered. "Yeah."

"Well. Then."

"But, Tom, no one would have to know about—"

"You want to come out."

He said it with such finality, as if it were a certain death knell for any possible relationship.

Anger overwhelmed Jax. How dare Tom make the shelter, the one worthwhile thing Jax had done with his career, his first possibility to take a stand, something he might regret for the rest of his life? "Yeah, I do. That's about me, not you."

"If we do…this, then it is about me."

"So you've decided we can never happen because you're too scared?"

"So you've decided we can never happen because you need to tell everyone everything?"

"It's not *about* me! The shelter…we're doing something great, and I want to be a part of it. I want my legacy to be more than hockey, and I wish you could see why."

Tom sighed. "I do see you're doing something great. But the shelter project is a great legacy without coming out on top of it."

Jax ran a hand across the back of his neck. "It's who I am, Tom. My name is Jaxon with an *X*. That's not how you spell it. I dye my hair blonder than it already is, and I wear thousand-dollar watches and branded fucking track pants. Everything about me screams 'my parents never finished high school, and I grew up in a trailer park.' The only reason *I* didn't end up in a shelter is because I lied to CPS when my parents forgot the power bill for the third time one winter. And I fucking own it. You think I don't know what people say about me? That I'm impulsive and loud-mouthed and classless and not very smart? I'm fine with being those things."

Looking as if he wanted desperately to interrupt, Tom opened his mouth, but Jax barreled on.

"It's all true. It's who I am. I got this far by being myself and borrowing used hockey gear and believing I could make this world accept me. I don't make myself smaller for others, and I don't apologize for being who I am. And who I am is queer. If I can't own being queer, too, I'm not being me. I know it's different for you, but can you try to understand?"

Tom studied him for a long, painful moment. Finally, he said, "Yes. But I can't be there with you."

The tension fell out of Jax's body, anger giving way to bargaining. "Why not? You've done so much this season, changed so much. For the team and for yourself."

"And for you. But I can't— I never even said it out loud until I met you, Jax. I can't undo my entire life to fit into the way you need to live yours."

Tears burned behind Jax's eyes. He knew an impossible dream when he saw it. One more tilt at the windmill, and then he'd give up. One more try to convince Tom how good they could be. "Have you ever tried? I mean, just because you haven't doesn't mean you couldn't. What about your family? They—"

Tom laughed hollowly. "They know, Jax."

"What?"

"They know. I've been trying to come out to them since I was fifteen."

That didn't make any sense.

"The first couple times, I thought it was a coincidence, how when I'd try to start a conversation about it, my mom would have something really important to tell me first, or she'd forgotten something at the store, and we'd need to go shopping. But it kept happening. Eventually, I realized she was stopping me from saying it out loud. And that's when I knew once I did tell her, things would change for the worse."

"Tom." Jax ached to reach out and touch him.

"So I know. Okay? I know how it feels when the people you care about most turn away from everything but the parts of you they want to see. And if I can't bear it from my family, how would I take it from the team or the whole world? I can't. I made the choice to keep quiet and keep my family and my captaincy. I made that choice fifteen years ago, and I still make it every day. If I let myself go there with you, I lose who *I* am, Jax."

Jax's heart hurt, and he couldn't stop the tears from leaking onto his cheeks.

"Okay," he said. "I understand." He rested his hand on top of Tom's on the sheet. They were both still naked, and a used condom lay somewhere on the bed. Jax was exhausted, and tomorrow, he'd have to play street hockey with twenty teenagers in front of running cameras.

He stayed there for as long as he could stomach, holding Tom's hand. When he pulled away, he felt the hot drip of Tom's tears on his skin.

"You know what I never got?"

"What?"

"Why use a body wash you don't even like? You don't have to use up the free shit they send you, and you don't have to keep doing endorsement deals you hate."

It startled a laugh out of Tom, which was what Jax wanted. If this had to happen, he didn't want to cause Tom more pain than necessary.

"The scent is called 'Sport.' That isn't a real smell, or if it is, it's sweaty gym socks. You could use anything. You have the money."

"Are you going somewhere with this?"

Jax took his tone down a notch. "Yeah. I'm gonna miss how it smells. I'm gonna miss your million and one Sea Lions T-shirts because you never let yourself buy nice things. I won't miss your stupid reheated meals, but I'll miss everything else. I could have been in love with you."

Tom inhaled, startled.

"And I'll only say this once. You deserve to be happy, Tom. You're settling for safe, but you can have both. You will have both, someday. Even if it's not with me."

Jax nodded once, more to himself than to Tom. "I'm leaving now. If I stay, it'll only hurt more. But if you care about me at all, if you care about *you* at all, think about it."

He left Tom's apartment feeling as though the inside of his chest had been scooped out with a grapefruit knife. It hurt, but the weight had lifted.

# Seventeen

## San Francisco Sea Lions Launch Sponsorship Program with local LGBTQIA+ Shelter

A week ago, San Francisco's NHL hockey team announced its partnership with local LGBTQIA+ shelter for homeless queer youth, Pot of Gold. Today, the first posts about it hit social media. In it, we see the young core of the team, center Jax Grant, defenseman Chris Calabrese, and left wing Diego Lunes, handing out pucks and sticks, playing street hockey, and getting mercilessly roasted by queer teenagers. The pushback on social media has been exactly as stupid as could be expected, but we at sfhockeyftw are happy to see our team engaging with the local community and taking a stance on important issues.

### Top comments:

CLions2010: Spare me the mushy social justice bullshit. These guys are hockey players. I want to see them playing hockey.

Susannah Lindenberg: Anyone can play hockey!

(Posted on http://sfhockeyftw.blogspot.com on 12/13/2024)

On Tuesday, Tom downloaded Instagram.

He tried to follow his normal off-day routine first. He hit the gym and did a light weight routine. He ate lunch, a prepackaged, precooked wild rice pilaf with tilapia and green beans.

Jax was right. The food contained hardly any salt and no fat, and it tasted of very little.

After, he had no idea what to do with himself. Restless energy filled him, leaving him jittery and by turns excited and miserable. His body hadn't caught up with his brain. His restless limbs still sang *he could love me, he could love me*, forcing him into action, while his mind chanted *I can't give him what he needs*, dragging him down.

He didn't want to be alone, but the only people he knew were other hockey players. He wanted to tell someone about this massive, life-changing thing that had happened to him (sex, love, heartbreak, *Jax*), but he couldn't without doing the exact thing he wanted to avoid so badly it made him let Jax go.

At two, he went for a run.

The spinning bike wasn't cutting it, he needed the cool breeze off the bay and the light drizzle in the air. He needed to be part of the world, not somewhere off to the side while life happened around him.

He regretted it soon enough. After twenty minutes, his calves were killing him from the uphill stretches, and the impact to his ankle on the downhill parts jarred his bad hip. After forty, he called it quits and went home. Showering reminded him of Jax, standing under the spray with his heart in his throat while Jax waited for him in bed, so he kept it quick.

When he got out, the digital clock at his bedside table read three thirty, and six and half hours stretched out ahead of him before he could reasonably go to bed. If he hadn't slept after Jax's departure last night, he might have been able to justify a nap. But the truth was, after the travel, the sex, and the emotional upheaval of it all, he'd slept like a rock if only to escape reality.

So, with half a day's worth of time to kill, he opened his phone, toggled to the app store, and downloaded Instagram.

Beyond basic messaging, he mostly used his phone to follow the news and track stats or watch YouTube compilations of other NHL players. It stubbornly insisted on sending him recommendations to watch his own highlights as well, but he ignored those. If being present for his own goals wracked his nerves, watching them back, with running commentary about how good he was, made Tom want to curl up in a ball and never leave the apartment. The commentators couldn't see his thought process, which was mostly *oh fuck, oh fuck, oh fuck, did I make it?*

Having to watch himself in the short videos Kayleigh shot of the team would be even worse. He relied on his teammates to show him when something noteworthy showed up on Instagram or TikTok, such as the video of Tyson Fuller badmouthing Jax. But maybe he'd been missing out. When the app finished installing, he chose the username "sealionsfan8216" as if he were a teenage girl scrawling his and Jax's jersey numbers in the margins of her notebook with a heart around them. He didn't add a profile picture or any photos of his own. Instead, he followed everyone on the team he could think of. Finally, when he couldn't put it off anymore, he followed the official team account.

The top post showed Jax in a Sea Lions hoodie and shorts, holding up a hockey stick wrapped almost entirely in Pride tape. More images popped up in the post: Breezy surrounded by teenagers, blowing a whistle, wearing the most ridiculous rainbow-colored knee socks Tom had ever seen; Mooney peeking out from behind a stack of boxes full of snacks he was carrying while a woman with multicolored hair directed him.

A long, explanatory post scrolled under the photos, but Tom didn't bother reading it. He knew what it would say; he'd gotten the emails. He clicked on the profile picture—the Sea Lions logo, of course—and watched the stories. In one, Breezy explained an around-the-world drill while a loud-mouthed kid with a sky-high Afro interrupted him every other word. In another, Mooney played goalie, which he was truly terrible at, while the kids rained pucks down on him.

Finally, he swiped to a video of Jax, giving everyone a handshake at the end of the game.

One of the kids grabbed his hand and pulled him into a hug instead.

It was only then that Tom realized Jax's smiles for the camera had been fake because it was only then that Jax smiled for real.

Good. They'd made the right choice if these kids made Jax smile properly. Some deep, achy part of Tom's psyche that wanted to legitimize his heartbreak turned his pain to satisfaction. Jax's happiness was the only way to make sense of what he'd done in turning Jax down when he'd offered everything Tom wanted.

He watched the video six times before he made himself close the app.

It was still only four o'clock.

On a game day, Tom could have followed his routine. A nap, followed by a carb-heavy meal, a ride to the stadium, getting dressed, warming up with the buzz of the locker room around him. And then the comforting cold of the ice, the clarity of winning or losing, the roar of the crowd, and the shrill whistles signaling stops and starts of the game.

On the other hand, if it were a game day, he'd have to see Jax, and he didn't know how he'd handle the first confrontation with his…ex? Tom's stomach rebelled against the idea of defining Jax as his first relationship now that it had ended. He'd been changed enough by Jax without conceding that as well, especially when he hadn't even been able to enjoy it before it was over. Every part of his life touched Jax's now, and all the good parts of hockey had been changed irrevocably by his presence. The buzz of the locker room, the warm, comfortable atmosphere? Before Jax joined the team, it hadn't been half as comfortable. And it had to be said, with Jax on the Sea Lions roster, they'd been winning a lot more, which made everything way more fun.

Tom's phone vibrated in his lap. He checked it immediately, like a dog hoping for a treat long past snack time.

Instagram had recommended accounts for him to follow. The notification showed the orange logo of the Philadelphia Magpies. Tom was sorely tempted to crush his phone under his heel. But then, hadn't he'd also taken what he had with Jax and thrown it away just as the Magpies had?

Another notification followed. For a minute, Tom thought it might be his mom. He'd never answered her text after the Arizona game, too caught up in Jax, and the thought of doing it now filled his brain with lead, making him unable to complete the task. Maybe she was worried and wanted to check in.

But when he opened his messages, he found something far better.

*Phil: Want to come over for dinner?*

Tom jumped up, grabbed his keys and wallet, and made it to his car in less than five minutes. He turned on the radio, focused on the street, and, for the first time all day, managed to turn his brain off.

Phil still opened the door with crutches jammed under his arms, but leaned on them less than he had after the ill-fated East Coast road trip.

"You're looking better," Tom said.

Phil studied Tom. "Wish I could say the same for you."

Tom glanced down at himself. He wore his favorite sweatpants, soft and comfortable, but admittedly worn at the knees. He had another old Sea Lions shirt on, and he hadn't shaved. There didn't seem to be much point. Who would he want to look good for? He didn't need to make an effort for Phil, having seen each other in worse states. Speaking of, though, he hadn't heard about Phil's progress with the knee in weeks, his own fault for getting lost in Jax. "So what's the prognosis? Surgery?"

Phil shook his head. "I got a second opinion. She thinks I can rehab it without operating. Better recovery time."

"That would be great."

"Yeah. Only chance I've got of making it onto the ice in time for playoffs."

Playoffs again. "Phil…"

"Chances are this is my last season either way. I want to actually play in it."

"There's more to life than hockey." Even as the words left his mouth, Tom winced at the lie. There wasn't more to his life.

Phil allowed him to keep some semblance of dignity by not answering. "You want chicken or steak for dinner?"

The right answer was chicken. He preferred the taste of red meat, but with the amount of protein a hockey player needed, chicken and fish were safer bets.

Tom was so fucking tired of safe bets.

"Steak."

"Good man."

Phil led him out back and fired up the grill.

"It's December," Tom pointed out.

"It's always barbecue weather in Cali."

Outside, the day was gray and drizzly. But Phil had few passions in life, all of which were extremely boring, so Tom let him have it. Plus, a roofed part of the patio protected the grill. Tom could take the chill, and he'd rather this than Phil's other favorite hobby. Fishing in the bay would be a million times more annoying in the rain.

"Is Morris joining us?"

Phil shook his head, scowling. "He's apartment hunting with his nephew."

The way Phil spoke gave the impression Morris was committing a heinous crime. Tom had no idea what to do with that. He hadn't known Morris had any family in the area, let alone any he was close with. Apartment hunting sounded innocuous to Tom. Coach Morris couldn't stay in Phil's guest room forever.

Eventually, he'd let the pause go on for too long and couldn't address it anyway. "The PK's doing better," Tom said instead.

Phil flipped their steaks and stirred a bunch of vegetables in an aluminum dish. Soaked in oil and herbs, they would be so much better than Tom's lunch.

"Yeah, it's looking decent. Mazetti's gotta stop trying so hard to make his passes pretty though. He's only gotta make 'em work."

"You should tell him."

Phil snorted

"Seriously," Tom said. "Your advice has been great so far. And no one is taking Trout or Morris seriously anymore. Anyway, it'll mean more coming from you."

"Morris too?"

Tom picked at a fingernail. Before stalking Jax on social media, he'd tried to be productive by looking up info on their coach. All he could find were two grainy photos of an intramural college hockey team with a very young Ben Morris on right wing. The accompanying article from the school paper didn't so much as mention him. Reports about his previous coaching career were also thin on the ground.

"I think he lets us make too many decisions," Tom said. "Promoting Luca to first string—Jax and I suggested it. And getting the team to gel again, Breezy and Jax's shelter plan. Keeping us fired up in the locker room when things were going to shit—you."

Phil took the steaks off the heat and covered them with a lid. "Taking rookies out for lunch and talking them through existential crises—you."

Tom flushed. "How'd you find out about that?"

"Howie told Breezy. Breezy told me."

Last year, Tom and Dmitriyev, their goalie, had gotten invited to the All-Star Game. Tom kind of hated it. Not only did it ruin the one week off he had during the season, it meant hours and hours of socializing even after the games were over. If he didn't show his face, he would be talked about; if he did, he'd be talked at. Dmitriyev, who drank enough to be mildly tipsy—an amount which made Tom feel sick just watching—had said a Russian grandmothers' knitting circle had nothing on the NHL in gossip.

Tom was starting to think he had a point.

"When I'm gone—"

"*Phil.*"

"You should give Breezy the *A*."

"You're not gone."

"I will be eventually. And he should have it."

Before this season, Tom would have laughed at the idea. In the three years since he'd made the team, Tom had known Breezy as a goofy jokester, always ready for a good time, never someone to think too hard. It might have been true once. But this season?

Tom paid attention this season. Breezy stood up for Luca; he got Jax started on the shelter idea. He kept up the energy and good spirits in the locker room when everyone else fell apart. As players, he and Luca were the only ones whose conditioning was on par to keep their stats steady despite Trout's insane workload.

He wasn't sure if Breezy had always had this potential or if he'd grown into it, but Tom knew for a fact he'd have never seen it if Jax hadn't made him open his eyes.

Still, he wouldn't let Phil go without a fight. "We'd have to start listening to music from this decade in the locker room, then. I'm not ready."

Phil snapped the tongs he'd used to flip the meat at Tom's nose. "Someone had to be in charge of it. If I let you do it, all we'd listen to would be your Canadian indie shit."

"Hey! The Barenaked Ladies are in the Canadian Music Hall of Fame."

Phil gave him a pointed look.

"At least I've updated my playlists since high school."

"Who has the time?" Phil asked. "We hear enough new shit when the rookies drag us to the clubs, and honestly, I'm not into it. Like, Migos? What is that? You can't even dance to it. How's it supposed to get you pumped up for a game?"

Tom had no idea whether "Migos" meant a band or a solo artist, let alone what kind of music they might make, so he just shrugged. "This is why we're the old guys on the team."

"I like being old. If I had to keep up with the charts to be an *A*, I'd pick the letter off my jersey myself."

"Do they even still do charts?" Tom asked. "Isn't everything streaming now?"

Phil considered. "You know what? I have no idea. Breezy would know though. Or if he didn't, he'd look it up. Maybe he'll even let the other guys pick a song for the playlist too. Give him a chance, and he'll make something of it."

Tom sighed deeply. "You're right. But I'm not ready to take the *A* away from you yet."

"Good."

"And I'm not ready for Russian techno in the locker room."

They ate in the living room, thankfully, because even Phil had to admit it was too cold to eat outdoors. Phil put the game on—the Winnipeg Pirates against the Minnesota Fury. The Fury's goalie was on fire, and the Pirates had been struggling as a whole this season. By the second intermission, the score stood four–nil with the Fury headed for a shutout.

"Brutal," Phil said, wiping up the last of his steak juice with garlic bread.

"Don't remind me. We haven't played the Fury since they got their new tendy."

"Eh." Phil wobbled his hand back and forth. "You'll be okay. Dmitriyev isn't quite as good yet, but with the defense tightened up, he should be okay. And you and Jax can decimate *their* defense easy."

Tom's face did something between a smile and a grimace. What cruel joy that he and Jax were so good together on ice. On the one hand, it filled Tom with pride. They were playing some of the best hockey of his career, both as a team and him individually. On the other, he wanted to hide their chemistry, protect it from the world, so no one could see how good he and Jax were together, not when they couldn't *be* together the way they were supposed to be.

The way Tom wanted to be.

As the TV went into an ad break, Phil pressed mute and turned to Tom, maneuvering to keep his leg stretched out straight. "So."

"Hmm?" The TV ran an ad for men's shampoo, the same brand Tom had done that stupid sponsorship deal for five years ago. With the color scheme all dark and red and the sound off, it really brought to the fore the ridiculousness of the industry gendering soap of all things. But Tom couldn't help thinking about Jax and the supply of body wash he didn't particularly like but felt duty-bound to keep working through. Maybe he should buy a different brand, just to switch it up. Just to make it easier on them both.

"What happened with you and Jax?"

Tom jerked away from the TV to stare at Phil.

"See, last I checked, you two were tearing it up on the ice and actually becoming friends off the ice for once in your life. But then today, I get a text from Jax telling me to invite you over because you need to, and I quote, 'Get out of your head,' but not to ask why."

Tom's throat closed up. Jax couldn't help but always take care of him.

"I made friends with you," Tom pointed out.

"Nice try, but no." Phil flicked his ear. "We were road roommates before the NHLPA bargained their way into single rooms, and I wore you down by proximity. That's not the same thing as going out of your way to spend time with someone."

Tom forced a laugh. "I wasn't *that* bad."

"Oh, buddy, you were worse. You'd have stayed in every night of every road trip if I had let you. The first month sharing a room, the only things you would talk to me about were how to fix your back-check and the *weather*."

It had been a long time since Tom had thought about his first season. He'd been eighteen and brand-new in the NHL. Everyone had expected great things from him, but the nerves caused by heightened expectations combined with the grueling travel schedule and the media attention made him so anxious it took a month or two for him to hit his stride. A slow start meant everyone called him a draft bust both in the press and sometimes to his face, which didn't help. To top it off, he still lived in fear that each new day would be the one Sean slipped up and told someone about the time first-overall-pick Tom Crowler got drunk and sucked him off. All he had going for him were the texts from his mom after every game, telling him honestly whether or not he'd done well.

"I was so scared," Tom said, caught up in the memory. He'd only felt safe on the ice or holed up in the huge apartment the team had organized for him.

"Of me?" Phil frowned.

Belatedly, Tom remembered the things hockey media said about Phil. People *still* called him an overpaid draft bust, even though he'd been a solid wall of a defenseman for a decade before his knees started giving out. Whenever he took a penalty, they called him a goon or, worse yet, a dangerous player. Tom could name twenty guys off the top of his head who played a much more dangerous game than Phil—Vanderbilt and Howie among them. Anyone could play hockey, but most who did were straight white men.

"No, not of *you*." Tom took a deep breath. "More of you...finding out about me."

Phil's brow furrowed. "What about you?"

Tom's pulse sped up. "I felt like such a liar that season. I thought I'd tricked everyone into thinking I was ready for the NHL, and I was terrified they'd realize their mistake and I would get sent down."

"I think we all feel like imposters our first season in the show."

"Yeah." Tom tried and failed to smile. He could leave it there. Phil believed him. Phil had no reason to question him. Tom could move on, and the whole conversation would end without him revealing any more about himself than he had to.

"Think about it," Jax had said. About being happy. Well, the joke was on him because Tom couldn't think about anything else.

"I was terrified you'd figure out I'm gay," he blurted out. "I thought that would be what got me sent down if anyone knew."

For a terrifying moment, Phil didn't say anything. Tom stared straight ahead, clutching his plate on his lap. The TV now played an ad for antidepressants. A man walked a dog while an endless text of possible side effects scrolled past him. If Tom lost Phil and Jax in one fell swoop, he would probably need to get a dog, or he really would be all alone.

"Oh my God," Phil said. "Oh my God, Tom."

"Yeah." Tom looked down at his cleared plate. He was glad he'd asked Phil to make steak instead of chicken if this would be their last meal together. He should have made fun of Phil's grill less; he should have let him know how much he appreciated the food if—

Phil took the plate out of his hands gently and set it on the coffee table. Then, he turned to face Tom as best as he could, sitting next to each other on the couch, and hugged him tightly.

One by one, Tom's muscles unclenched, until he slumped over in Phil's grip, his arms slack between them, his face buried in Phil's shoulder. "You don't hate me?" he asked into Phil's T-shirt. It smelled of barbecue.

"No," Phil said emphatically. "Jesus, Tom."

He held Tom for longer than Tom thought he could get away with for a hug between friends. He couldn't bring himself to pull away.

When they finally did separate, Tom muttered, "Thank you."

"Well, that explains why you never had a girl all these years."

"Yeah. I thought for sure someone would guess eventually."

"Wildly overestimating the average intelligence of hockey players there, bud."

Tom laughed, half relief and half genuine amusement.

"No, whatever you're doing, it works. You're not someone people look at and think 'could be gay.'"

"I mean...who is?"

Wincing a little, Phil admitted, "Luca Mazetti, I guess?"

"What? Because he's pretty, well-dressed, and smart?"

"Yeah, basically."

"Honestly, I think that's being European."

"All the Russians in the league would disagree."

"Denisov would *murder* me."

They both laughed again, mostly at the thought of Russian giant Damir Denisov having to parse out whether or not he was being complimented or insulted. English subtleties were not his strong suit.

"What did you have Howie chirp him with the other night anyway? He went nuts," Tom asked.

Phil opened his mouth to answer and then paused. "Wait. You changed the subject. What happened with Jax? Was he shitty about…"

Tom forced his attention to the TV. The third period had started. Winnipeg, getting desperate, had taken a stupid penalty and barreled toward a 5–0 score with the Fury on the power play. "No. No, I was the shitty one."

"Tom?"

An empty Gatorade bottle sat on the table—a yellow one, Tom's least favorite flavor. He picked it up and toyed with the label.

"I, uh…I don't think I can talk about this?"

Phil hummed contemplatively. "Spitballing here, but if Jax thought you needed a friend tonight, and he also thought he couldn't be that friend— Did something happen between you two? As in, romantically?"

Tom flinched, an automatic reaction, and in doing so, he confirmed it. "Shit. I didn't ask him if I could tell you. He's…not out. Yet."

"I think he hoped you would."

Probably. Why else would Jax message Phil?

"He wants to come out," Tom explained. "He will at some point. Maybe not right now, but I don't think he'll wait long."

"Okay," Phil said slowly. "Good?"

Tom stared at him.

"I mean, someone has to be the first, right?"

When Tom still had no answers for him, Phil shrugged.

"Or not? I don't know," he said. "I thought someone would do it way before now."

"Really?"

"It's 2024, buddy. They make Pride tape and everything."

"Yeah, and then the NHL banned it." When he woke up to that press release, Tom considered calling in sick to work for the first time in his life.

Phil waved a dismissive hand. "Then they un-banned it again. The league is run by older, even stupider hockey players. Someday, we'll take their place, and things will get marginally less dumb."

It should have been a comfort, Phil's hope for the future, but all it did was remind Tom of Jax. Jax and his desire to do better, to be better, to *be* the future. A future with no place for someone like Tom, clinging desperately to an image of a person he didn't want to be. Where would he be in a future more tolerant NHL? He had seven or eight years at most until he was done and only if he continued to be outrageously lucky and not get injured. If he hit the boards wrong just once, he could be down to two years. Or none. And then what would he be? A sad, lonely man, haunting an empty apartment, watching a sport he couldn't play, wanting a man he couldn't have. He didn't have any other plans or hobbies or goals. He wanted to play hockey, and he wanted to be loved. He could only have one of those things, and he'd chosen wrong. He'd chosen—

"Tom, breathe." Phil's hand steadied him, warm on his shoulder. "Come on. In, out, slowly now. What's gotten into you?"

"I've got nothing, Phil," he managed between desperate, panting breaths. "I thought I could put it all away. Thought I would be better. I would win us a Cup if I wasn't…gay. If I didn't want things I couldn't have. But it's been fifteen years, and I haven't won anything. And I lost—"

"Jesus Christ, Tom, we don't keep missing out on the Cup because you're gay!"

It startled Tom into stillness. When he finally breathed in, it tasted like the first breath out on the ice, crisp and sharp. "I don't think I ever realized how ridiculous that is."

"This is what happens when you keep everything to yourself. You don't have anyone to tell you when you're being an idiot."

"When I got drafted, it seemed impossible, you know, being gay and being in the league. I spent so much time trying to disappear so no one would notice me too much. Never let myself look at anyone too long, never hooked up, never dated."

Phil made a wordless, hurt noise.

Tom leaned back into the couch, playing with the Gatorade bottle again. "Then Jax showed up, and he didn't care, you know? He hooked up, and he flirted… Hell, he even flirted with me before he knew about me, and he still played hockey so well it made the rest of us look stupid."

"Good for him."

"Yeah." It *was* good for Jax. It was so good for Jax, and it could never be for Tom. "That's why—that's why I can't be like him, and I can't ask him to be less than he is."

Phil studied him. "When a buddy has a rough breakup, mostly I offer him junk food, beer, and a dumb-ass movie if he doesn't wanna talk about it. And I'll offer you the same thing in a minute."

"Okay," Tom said, nonplussed.

"I'm gonna ask you something first though. If you can't ask Jax to be less than he is, why are you so bent on asking it of yourself?"

# Eighteen

The SF Sea Lions begin their sponsorship of the Pot of Gold LGBTQIA+ shelter! Follow the link in our description to find out more & donate!

**Top comments:**

SFCLions: Disgusting how these kids are being indoctrinated to believe that men aren't men and women aren't women

sealions4lyfe: Remember when hockey teams still cared about hockey and not this social justice shit?

Camille Easton: [hands clapping emoji]

sealionsfan8216: So proud of Jax Grant and Chris Calabrese for spearheading this! We need more people like them in the league!

(Posted to the San Francisco Sea Lions Instagram on 12/10/2024)

Jax finally caved and leased a car the weekend after Tom dumped him. (Or he dumped Tom. Hard to tell which way around made more sense.) Public transit had no direct connection between Palo Alto and the Tenderloin, so using it to get out to the shelter every other day irked him after less than a full week.

On Friday, with a game-free Saturday ahead of them, Breezy suggested a Halo tournament at his and Luca's place. By then, Jax was crawling out of his skin alone in his hotel room.

He'd known in the abstract it would be a big change, no longer seeing Tom, but he'd been thinking in emotional terms. Purely practically, Jax didn't have anyone to have lunch with or watch tape with or talk to at the end of the day. Going to Breezy's felt necessary so he didn't start chewing the wallpaper of his hotel room. They'd just scraped an overtime win in the matinee game against Vegas, so the mood was tentatively jubilant, if exhausted. Hanging out with four other hockey players and trash-talking each other over video games didn't fill the same emotional void as having Tom's head in his lap on Tom's stupidly comfortable couch. But listening to Breezy and Luca bicker while Mooney and Howie ate all the snacks let him feel part of something bigger all the same.

Breezy and Luca lived way up in Haight-Ashbury, though, and getting an Uber to his hotel at two in the morning was such a pain Jax bitched about it for half the evening. By the time they stood outside, waiting on their rides, Mooney had heard enough and said, "Dude, get a car already."

Despite having the cash for it, Jax hadn't managed to work up an interest in cars. Growing up in the Twin Cities, buses had been available if not comfortable, and it wasn't as though his parents could afford a second car for him. The temptation was to get something really flashy, maybe a convertible in an outrageous color. Lime green and blush pink called to him. Thankfully, he took Mooney with him to the dealership on Saturday. Mooney rightly reminded him he'd be using this vehicle to get to and from the Tenderloin, so he'd want something that wouldn't stall getting up and down the hills and wouldn't be a flashing neon target for every car thief in the city.

"Why leasing and not buying anyway?" Mooney asked as they drove away in Jax's new, sensible, four-door Sedan. "You have the dough, Mr. Art Ross trophy winner of 2022."

Jax shrugged. "Waiting to see if they keep me around here."

Mooney scoffed as though the idea of another trade was ridiculous, but with every stoplight they passed on the way to the shelter, Jax could feel the urge growing stronger and stronger under his fingernails, in the balls of his feet, in the back of his mind. Today could be the day he said it to the cameras, to the kids at the shelter, to *someone*. Today could be the day he got traded again or became so undesirable that his NHL career would be over. The only fear holding him back was that he'd be doing it for the wrong reasons. He'd be doing it to justify losing Tom. He couldn't make this decision on a whim or a snap choice because he'd had a bad breakup. It meant too much.

So, he bit his tongue on Saturday when he and Mooney took the shelter kids to an ice rink for the first time. No hockey, just learning to skate. Lots of cute footage for the cameras. Mooney wasn't the biggest guy, but with two teenage girls who had yet to hit a growth spurt thanks to puberty blockers, one on either hand, he looked fucking massive. People loved to see a big guy with cute kids.

Jax kept biting his tongue on Sunday, which was easy because of another grueling practice under Trout. Not much talking to be had there. He even managed to keep his staring-at-Tom time to a minimum, only giving in every other minute or so.

By Monday morning, Jax thought he was finally approaching something like equilibrium. He thought maybe he could make a decision on the whole coming out question without flashing back to the sense memory of Tom's perfect ass spread open for him over the couch. The last few days, he'd been alternating between the hope-fueled delusion that if he didn't come out, he'd get to keep Tom and the frustration-fueled desire to do it right away. But time had a way of eroding urgency, and as he took the elevator downstairs, Jax thought today would be a good day to make a plan. He could talk to Mara about it; she would probably have good ideas about how to do it in a classy way.

Of course, he wouldn't see her for another few days since the next scheduled shelter event wasn't till Thursday. Waiting to see Mara before making any big decisions sounded like something a normal, not pathologically impulsive person would do. Wait a few days, sleep on it, ask for advice. Maybe even loop in his agent, though Jax didn't relish the thought of someone else getting a say in this, especially not someone who had a vested interest in how much money Jax made.

As he passed through the lobby, the receptionist called him over. She handed him the package with the Prada logo stamped on the outside. Jax loved the packaging for expensive things. No cheapo cardboard with a logo on the outside for Prada, oh no. They sent sleek black boxes with the letters embossed on the sides. That kind of quality meant Jax had paid north of four thousand dollars for the contents.

He had the money. He lacked the recipient.

He threw the box on the passenger seat and drove to the rink, all the calm and equilibrium from the morning in tatters.

Morris was in, so practice stayed light and mostly effective, largely due to East sitting in the stands with his leg propped up on the chair in front of him.

He called out drills every now and again, and when Morris didn't protest, the team did those drills. Occasionally, East yelled out an individual name, and the person in question skated over to get some feedback.

He never called Jax's name or Tom's. Not for the first time in the last week, Jax wondered what Phil thought had happened between them. He hadn't said anything more to Jax after their brief text exchange on Tuesday, and Jax had no idea what, if anything, Tom had told him.

Knowing Tom, he'd probably said they'd had a disagreement about the power play or something. God forbid he had an emotion not about hockey.

After practice, Jax had a meeting with Breezy and the PR department about how things were going with the shelter program. They went over statistics, and Jax understood a charitably estimated 14 percent of what Kayleigh said. What he did understand interested him about as much as watching the staff sharpen skate blades for six hours at a time. The takeaway was that PR had hit their goals. The videos had caused an uptick of engagement on the team's social media.

"Um," Breezy said when Jax thought they were finished. "I mean, there was a lot of engagement, but there were also kind of a lot of nasty comments."

Kayleigh smiled brightly. "That's to be expected with such a political topic. But it drives engagement, you know, people discussing stuff in the comment sections."

A nasty, unclean feeling stole down the back of Jax's neck. "By discussing, you mean…"

"Oh, you know, debating whether this stuff has a place in professional sports."

"And I assume you're deleting every single one of those bigoted comments before the kids we're working with have a chance to read them?"

"Ah." Kayleigh paused, fingers steepled. "We haven't really been moderating commentary so far."

Blinding rage filled Jax's lungs, stole his breath and his words. He was seconds from exploding, a hair's breadth from calling Kayleigh every name in the book, when Breezy interjected.

"Why?" He acted it as if it were a valid question asked purely out of interest, and Kayleigh took it as such.

"Well, the whole point of this from our perspective is to generate more buzz around the team. We don't have as much strong local support as, say, Chicago or Toronto."

No one had as much strong local support as Toronto.

"And not to put too fine a point on it, but our department has been struggling to generate content that will get the team noticed on social media. You know how Tom and Phil are." Kayleigh sighed as if it was a crucial failing in a hockey player not to be particularly good on camera. Did she know their actual job had nothing to do with Instagram?

"Okay, well, San Francisco's pretty LGBT-friendly, right?" Again, Breezy sounded as if he genuinely didn't know the answer.

"Yeah, definitely."

"I don't want people thinking we're using kids to get views, you know? Like, if people think this is just for clicks, they'll like us even less."

"Hmm." Kayleigh pursed her lips. "I guess you have a point there, Chris. So, some comment moderation is important to you guys?"

"I think we'll send a much stronger message against homophobia if we stop letting it run rampant in our spaces," Jax said. "And it should go without saying, but any personal commentary about any of the underage participants shouldn't see the light of day." He couldn't quite keep the rage out of his voice.

"Okay, noted. We'll look into some moderation in the comment section. You two will be on media tonight. Make sure to mention the project," Kayleigh told them cheerily, and then turned back to her computer, ending the meeting.

Jax literally shook with anger on the way to the parking lot. "Is it bad I kinda wish we'd had practice with Trout today?" At least then he would have somewhere to put the rage.

Breezy snorted. "That makes one of you. You doing okay, Jax?"

"Nope."

"It wasn't so bad. We got them to fix the comment sections."

Jax patted him on the shoulder. "I have no idea how you kept such a cool head."

Breezy shrugged self-deprecatingly. "You always tell people what you really think. I admire that about you. Whenever I do, people end up calling me an idiot. I guess my thoughts aren't as deep as yours or something. The good thing is, when people think you're dumb already, they don't usually second-guess what you say."

"Breezy," Jax said, "I mean this with my whole heart. You are the least dumb person I have ever played with."

At least one of them left the stadium in a good mood.

The package still sat on the passenger seat, mocking Jax. What was he even doing? Tom got it right when he asked why Jax couldn't stop at sponsoring the shelter. The project was about the kids who needed help, not him. Using them as a springboard to satisfy his own selfish need for public visibility left his skin crawling after the conversation he'd just had. In addition, Kayleigh's blind hunt for clicks at the cost of the teenagers who could be harmed convinced him. The Sea Lions would be equally shitty about him being gay as the Magpies had been. He might as well give up now and get Tom back. He would spend his life in hiding, always rattling at the bars of his enclosure, but at least he wouldn't be alone.

In a state of capitulation, he left the package in Tom's stall.

On the way home, he acknowledged he was going through more emotions than Destiny's Child had in 2002. Human beings weren't supposed to feel so many things in such quick succession. Worse, as a consequence, he felt himself slipping into spur-of-the-moment decisions he would probably regret.

More than anything, he wished he had an easy way to tell what the right choice was. Usually, when he faced a hard decision, he pretended he'd already made it, and whatever alternative he'd picked either delighted or disappointed him.

Granted, the hardest decisions of Jax's life so far had been whether he wanted Indian or Thai takeout or if going out or staying in would feel better that night. Everything important in his life had been a no-brainer (choosing hockey as a career) or he'd made the decision before he realized the consequences (hooking up with a guy who thought taking pictures during was sexy). Jax had never been in a situation where both decisions had made him feel miserable in wildly different ways. Ever since he'd left Tom's apartment last week, he'd been hollow, cut off from his own emotional core. He thought about Tom constantly, about how he hid his need for soft fabrics and comforting touch but leaned into it as soon as it was offered. He thought about how seriously Tom took his job, how hard he worked trying to be as good as he could be, and how happily surprised Tom was whenever something made him laugh.

Jax knew all these big things about Tom now, things no one else knew. He could never unknow Tom's sexuality, his loneliness, his need to be held. Worse, he had a collection of tiny details about Tom living rent free in his head. Tom had shared his abhorrence for hotel scrambled eggs and light beers. He liked to be anchored by a hand on his hip when he slept on his perfect memory foam pillow. The only things he'd ever splurged on were his couch, his bed, and his shower, and he still felt guilty about those. Jax didn't know where to put all that knowing, all that care now that Tom had closed the door on him. It formed a yawning pit inside him, pulling him down, down, down, away from everything he'd previously thought important.

At the same time, he'd told Tom he understood, and he did. He'd left. He closed the physical door. And the thought of staying—staying in Tom's apartment, keeping what they had right there, behind closed doors, possibly forever—made Jax want to chew his own leg off like an animal in a trap. Even the brutal reminder that the Sea Lions were a business and would see him as a faulty return on investment the second he started expressing nonconformist traits such as being queer as fuck couldn't stop him from wanting to do it. But now, the thought of using the shelter and the kids there to satisfy his own need for authenticity in his life felt wrong as well. What would he end up doing besides feeding the sports media machine with a new scandal? All he wanted was to play hockey and live his life without feeling as though he could lose it all in an instant if he stepped a toe out of line.

Could humans go feral?

Jax thought he just might.

He managed to eat before the game, but a nap was out of the question. Instead, he paced around his hotel room considering and reconsidering what he might say to the media that night, whether it would be stupid and impulsive, or worse, exploitative to rip the bandage off.

When he got to the arena for the game—early because he couldn't wait around any longer—the box still sat on the bench in front of Tom's stall, and four other guys eyed it contemplatively.

Jax was such an idiot.

All this, and he still hadn't learned to control his idiot impulses. Now, half the team knew the captain had a gift waiting for him in the locker room, meaning Jax couldn't take it back. At least Kayleigh pulled him for media before Tom got there, a small mercy.

The usual reporters crowded around the area set aside for pre- and postgame interviews, waiting for him. The Sea Lions played Seattle tonight, who were about as close as they had to a rival since the LA teams had their own thing going and Vegas couldn't care less about a divisional rival when half the Eastern Conference wanted their heads on platters. Most of the rivalry consisted of bored interns shooting one another vaguely catty mentions online in an attempt to gear up interest in hockey in football towns. Beat reporters who actually cared about the sport ignored it.

All of which made media before the game an excellent time to advertise the shelter.

Jax took the first opportunity when Olivia Starling, wearing an SF Bobcats hat—which seemed out of place given she was at an ice hockey rink and not a football stadium—asked how he felt after the team's up and down week.

"Yeah, um, we had a few bad days down in Los Angeles for sure, but we really turned up on Friday, and I think we will today too. And the week's been awesome. Thanks for asking."

"What have you been up to?" someone called from the back.

Jax grinned, making sure to show off as many teeth as possible. "I'm *so* glad you asked." He outlined the project, making sure to mention Mara and where people could donate to the shelter as many times as possible in about three sentences.

He spent a good ten minutes after answering questions about the shelter and what the team's sponsorship entailed. At that point, Breezy wandered past, shirtless and with his hair all over the place, his novelty boxer briefs (Christmas trees this time) peeking out over the waistband of his athletic leggings.

He slid onto the bench next to Jax, threw an arm over his shoulder, and said, "We're playing hockey with them. It's kind of all we're good at."

The ensuing laughter sounded a little too mean for Jax's taste.

He let the questions go on, time ticking by while he weighed his options. Coach Trout eyed him vengefully from the corner in a way that screamed, "Are you not done yapping yet?"

Finally, Olivia Starling in her stupid football hat asked, "Jax, is working with the gay community an important message to you, personally?"

This was what he'd been waiting for, the moment he could come out neatly and instantly and have it all out in the open. Ever since the first idea for the shelter project had come up on the flight home from Toronto, he'd known he wanted this, needed it even. But as soon as someone actually asked him, something in Jax stalled out.

He didn't owe her anything. She'd shown up to Cyberian wearing merch for the wrong fucking sport. Jax wanted to live authentically, but he didn't want to do this lady, in particular, any favors. He also found, now that he had the chance, he didn't want to make this about him. The shelter needed donors, and the kids needed to be seen and helped a lot more than Jax needed to have everyone all up in his business. He was a fucking millionaire; he'd be fine.

"Yes," he said. "It's very important to me."

He left it at that.

In the locker room, Tom had moved the box from the bench to the floor in front of his feet so he could sit and tie his laces.

"Jax!" Howie bounded over. "Crow won't open the gift from his secret admirer!"

Jax hoped the heat in his face would be attributed to the twenty cameras he'd just had in it. "Secret admirer, huh?"

"Who else would send him something from Prada?"

Even Hayes and Vanderbilt had left the comfort of their corner to peer at Tom curiously. Jax wanted to apologize, wanted to tell Tom he didn't have to open it in front of everyone, wanted to say *something* to defuse the situation. But everyone had stopped, listening and watching, and all he could do was shoot Tom the most apologetic look he could muster.

"Come *on*, Cap!" Howie wheedled.

Tom glanced around the room. "We have a game in ten minutes. Surely—"

"If we spend all game wondering what is in the box, we will play much worse." Betrayed by the Italian. Jax frowned at Luca.

"Wait, do you know who it's from?" Betrayed by the French-Canadian Italian too. Jax wanted to shut them all up, but Breezy seemed so honestly excited it would have been heartbreaking.

Tom didn't meet anyone's eye. "I have an idea, yeah."

Wolf-whistles and cheers sounded around the locker room. Jax had to turn away and start pulling on his pads or someone would catch on to whatever his face was doing.

"Damn, Crow, I thought you were a monk all this time. Turns out you've got some crazy rich mistress!" Hayes sounded far more enthused by this development than Jax would have thought. Maybe he wanted to see Tom being human and fallible. Maybe he hoped he wouldn't be the only guy in the locker room with something to be ashamed of. Maybe Jax was reading too much into it.

"Ooh," at least three guys went.

"Is she hot?" Howie asked.

Jax thought for sure Tom would clam up, would hide in his turtle shell. But then something magical happened. Tom laughed, loud and bright.

Jax had to turn to him. He had to see the lines around Tom's mouth, the crinkle in the corners of his eyes. He never wanted to look away.

"All right," Tom said. "I'll open it. But I'm not telling you anything."

He picked the package up and ran his fingers around the edges, searching for an opening. One of the equipment guys gave him a pair of scissors. Apparently, this was an event for the whole team *and* the crew. The locker room fell totally silent as he lifted the top off the box.

Tom pulled out the contents.

Howie groaned in exaggerated disappointment. "Bo-ring!"

Vanderbilt pushed to the front. "Are you kidding? Those are cashmere. That's fucking expensive as shit."

Hayes and Howie stared at him while Dmitriyev nodded as if this should have been obvious.

"What?" Vanderbilt shrugged. "I like high quality menswear."

Tom pulled the top sweater out of the box carefully, thumbing the fabric. There were three total, one in blue to match Tom's eyes, one in black to match Tom's hair, and one in cream because Jax thought he would be incredibly soft and comfortable in it. He'd gone a bit wild on the site, deciding between different styles and colors for almost the entire flight back from Arizona.

He'd only wanted Tom to have nice things.

"Just saying, if someone got me something from Prada, I'd want, like, bling, not some sweaters."

Breezy cuffed Howie around the head. "That's not important. What do *you* think, Crow?"

Tom looked up from the sweaters. He didn't seem aware he was still running his hands across the fabric. "I love them."

Jax's heart did something it had previously only done during a VO2 max test.

Breezy beamed. "Well, then."

"If y'all are done with…whatever this shit is," Trout barked. "Warm-ups. Now."

"Ignore him," Hayes muttered on the way out. "Bet no one's ever given him a present in his life."

Oddly, the team hit the ice thrilled by the whole thing. Jax had expected confusion, maybe even some resentment. Instead, everyone was excited, laughing and joking during warmups. Seattle's season had not gone well so far. Their star forward had an undisclosed upper body injury, which probably meant "concussion we're hoping isn't serious." Their defense tended toward the slow side of things, and their goaltender lacked experience. No way they'd match the Sea Lions in a really good mood for the first time in a month.

Still, Jax hadn't counted on a seven–one blowout.

He had a three-point night, assisting on two of Tom's goals. He got one of his own on a breakaway in the starting minutes of the third.

He should have been on top of the world. Instead, he felt exactly the same as he had in the morning—anxious, empty, and less surefooted than he'd been in years. Tom careening into him to celebrate after every goal, reminding Jax he'd never again hold him without six layers of hockey gear between them, did not help.

Postgame, the locker room filled with buoyancy the way only a win could ensure.

"Drinks! We are all going for drinks," Breezy shouted. "Keep your suits on. We'll hit the clubs after!"

Vanderbilt cheered. Who knew the only thing it would take for him to act like part of the team again was Jax humiliating himself and Tom in front of the whole locker room?

While Tom did postgame media—the curse of the captain, and the guy who'd just gotten his second hat trick of the season—Jax wanted desperately to congratulate him. He also wanted to apologize for the stupid sweaters, but he couldn't with everyone around.

Olivia Starling, still in her Bobcats hat, had a question. "Tom," she asked, overly familiar. "Before the game, Jax was telling us about the team's new sponsorship project. How do you feel about it?"

Tom smiled his media smile, not the real, shy little thing Jax liked so much he wanted to wallpaper pictures of it all over his bland, terrible hotel room. "Jax and Breezy—sorry, uh, Chris—have started something really great in their work with the shelter. I haven't been out there yet myself, but I'm scheduled to go next week. I'm excited to see what the kids have learned about hockey so far."

"Crow'll make them run sprints and learn to use a foam roller," Mooney yelled from across the locker room.

A real grin stole across Tom's face. "I will not. They're kids."

"Ooh, he likes them better than us already!"

Shaking his head ruefully, Tom turned back to the reporters. "It's a wonderful program, and I'm so proud of Jax for doing something so good with our platform. And, uh, Breezy, of course. Chris." Tom's eyes darted over to Jax, and Jax couldn't take it.

He ducked into the shower and spent about twenty minutes trying to boil his skin off. Tom was proud of him. Tom thought he was doing the right thing. Even now, with Jax fucking him over by leaving a very personal gift in the middle of the locker room, Tom was *proud* of him.

Maybe Jax did need to get traded again. Staying here might kill him.

By the time he got out from under the water, the locker room had emptied. No one remained except Tom, sitting in his stall right by Jax's, softly petting the fucking sweaters.

"Where is everyone?"

"Headed out. Breezy called some bar in the Marina. Everyone's on their way over there now."

"Ugh, that's so far away."

Tom laughed at him. "Careful, you're sounding like one of the old guys."

Jax finished toweling off his hair and pulled on a pair of athletic shorts before sitting down on the bench next to Tom. How much of a mindfuck would being naked around his ex multiple times per week be? He guessed monumental. He'd had reasons for not sleeping with hockey players. They'd been good reasons, too. Just not as good as Tom.

"I'm sorry about the sweaters. I wasn't thinking. I got them this morning, and I was going to return them or something, but…"

"I'm glad you didn't."

"I shouldn't have put them in the locker room. I was upset, and I wasn't thinking, and I guess I really am an impulsive idiot, and—"

"Jax, stop."

Jax swallowed hard and forced himself to stop.

Tom picked up the cream sweater and held it against his skin. "It's not stupid or impulsive to buy a thoughtful gift for someone you care about."

Unable to stand the sight of Tom holding his present so tenderly, Jax examined his hands, braced on the locker room bench. "I care about you so much," he admitted. "I don't know how to turn it off."

Carefully, gently, Tom placed his hand on top of Jax's, right there in the locker room.

"Don't."

# Nineteen

Spotted around town: Tom Crowler on a night out with his teammates, wearing a cream cashmere sweater from Prada's new winter collection. The SF Sea Lions' forward usually dons team merch or black game-day suits, and we think the change really works for him! Has a new leading lady upgraded your style, Tom?

## Top comments:

SFCLions: Mystery woman's taste is terrible! Tom, you can get the same sweater for 100$ at an outlet mall, and I can do things to you she never could!

sealionsfan82: If it gets him two hat tricks in a season, Crowler could wear a pink tutu for all I care

(From: "Talk around Town" on hockeygossip.net, posted on 12/15/2024)

Tom's heart thundered in his rib cage. His hand, resting on Jax's, was sweaty. Anyone could walk in, one of the equipment guys or a teammate who had forgotten something. For Jax, Tom could learn not to care.

"You haven't come out yet," Tom observed. He'd watched Jax's media appearance before the game closely. Eyes on the ostentatious box in his stall, he'd waited for Jax to say it. The gift, he'd thought, was a goodbye, an unnecessary apology for Jax choosing himself over Tom.

He'd stood by, expecting the moment to come, understanding all the while that it was so, so stupid of him to force Jax into making the choice.

And then Jax didn't.

"I've been thinking about it," Jax said. "What if I don't need to?"

"But you do. We talked about—"

"No, I mean…" Jax flipped his hand upside down so he could lace his fingers through Tom's. "I mean, what if I don't need to tell people outright? What if I could just…do my thing? Date a guy. Be in a relationship. And not worry about getting caught."

"You mean…"

"I mean, there's a middle ground between me telling the press I'm gay and staying in the closet forever."

Tom considered.

"It would be risky," Jax added. "There's every chance I could get caught taking…my guy out to lunch or whatever. But I don't actually owe the press or even the team advance warning if I want to go out for lunch, or stay the night, or take a guy home to meet my parents."

"You do? I mean…" Tom backtracked, flustered. "I mean, if you mean me."

Finally, finally, Jax turned to look at him properly. "Of *course* I mean you, Tom. I've never felt this way about anyone. Until I met you, I thought I'd be happy hooking up on the down-low for however long I was in the NHL, and then I fell for you and realized I've never been anywhere near as happy as you make me."

The words were a warm bath, subsuming Tom in peace. "I've been thinking too."

"Yeah?"

"Phil told me I would never treat anyone else the way I've been treating myself."

"You told him?"

"Yeah."

Jax lifted Tom's hand and kissed the back of it. Tom let his eyes slide closed. He had to get this out before he lost the ability to talk.

"I think he was right. I think you were right. I want more than what I've let myself have. I want you."

"Even if we get caught?"

Tom opened his eyes again. "It's not getting caught if we're not doing anything wrong. We wouldn't…we wouldn't be doing anything wrong."

A smile spread across Jax's face like the sun coming out after a long winter. "You believe that, huh?"

"Yeah." Tom rested his forehead against Jax's. "I think I finally do."

Jax dipped down to kiss him. They'd never shared a kiss so sweet, soft, intimate, and, for the first time, hopeful.

It was entirely Tom's fault when things escalated. He put a hand on Jax's shoulder and encountered only warm skin, and it made him lose his mind a little. The next thing he knew, he was tugging on Jax's hair, with Jax moaning into his mouth, and Tom wondered if they would still not be doing anything wrong if he got onto his knees right there in the locker room.

Tentatively, someone cleared their throat behind Tom.

They jumped apart.

"So, uh," Breezy said loudly from the showers. "If anyone was wondering, I'm still here. In the showers. Having a shower. I'm done now though, so I might be heading into the locker room any minute. In case that might affect what anyone's…doing there. Yeah."

Jax rested his face in his hands. "Oh my God," he said, muffled between his fingers.

"You can come in, Breezy." Tom tugged Jax's hand back into his own, where it belonged.

"And if I did hear anything, which I definitely didn't, I sure wouldn't tell anyone about it," Breezy added, beelining for his stall, making eye contact with no one. "Should I, uh, be telling the guys you two won't make it?"

Tom glanced at Jax. Jax wobbled his head from side to side, as if weighing the options. On the one hand, they weren't doing anything wrong. On the other, the team had finally come out strong after weeks of inconsistency. They could wait a while to be alone for the good of the team. The drive to the Marina took about half an hour, and they'd need to stay at least two hours before trekking back to Palo Alto, another forty-five minutes.

Three and a half hours.

Tom could wait three and a half hours to touch Jax again. He'd been waiting his whole life.

"We'll be there," Tom said.

Breezy's face split into a wide smile. "Cool! Wanna share a ride?"

When Tom pictured the most romantic night of his life in idle fantasies over the years, sitting in the back of the Uber with Breezy strapped in the middle, his long legs pushing Tom up against the door, never made the cut. But every time Tom looked over at Jax and found him already looking back, steady, wanting, *caring*, he was glad of the buffer. He wouldn't have been able to keep his hands to himself.

Tom seemed to have gained an extra sense, a constant awareness of where Jax was in relation to him: Sitting next to him at the team's table in the bayside gastropub Breezy had booked, their legs brushing up against each other under the table. Ordering drinks, leaning up against the bar, the top two buttons of Jax's shirt undone. Talking to Luca, his elbows on the table and head bent to hear him over the din, the material of his shirt stretched across his shoulders and biceps.

Before, Tom would have spent the entire evening worrying someone would catch the way he was attuned to every little thing Jax did. Now, he reveled in it.

"How's the sweater working out for you?" Hayes asked from the other end of the table, eyeing Tom's outfit of choice. He hadn't been able to resist pulling the cream sweater on over his dress shirt. Not ideal for the heat of the crowded bar, but every time he touched the soft fabric, it sent a tingle all down his spine.

"Good. It's good." He couldn't have hidden the smile if he'd tried.

Hayes whistled, long and low. "Wow. You must be really into her, huh?"

Tom was physically incapable of not stealing another glance at Jax. He'd pushed his shirtsleeves up to his elbows, and the corded strength of his forearms made Tom's mouth water. "Yeah," he said. "I am."

Hayes clapped him on the shoulder. "Good to know you're human after all."

Tom thought of Phil, who had known him for fifteen years and never once suspected. Hockey players really struggled with subtext. He thought about all the years he'd spent worried, lonely, and tired, trying his best and getting nothing in return. He'd wasted so much time hating himself.

But that was a sad thought, and tonight wasn't for sad thoughts. Tonight was for catching Jax's eye and sharing a secret smile. Tonight was for indulging in a decent beer, a sweet, chocolatey stout, because he'd gotten a hat trick, and he deserved it. Tonight was for letting his fingertips ghost across the fabric of his new sweater and thinking about what else he deserved for his hat trick.

His mom texted at eleven thirty, the telltale buzz of her after-game message in the pocket of his suit pants a giveaway. The feeling alone made his heart sink in his chest.

Mom: *Good job sweetie! We're so proud of you!*

Tom swallowed heavily. "No, you're not," he said and put the phone away, text unanswered.

Around one, when the Swedes had split off already and Dmitriyev had gotten a cab home after what appeared to be a half bottle of clear liquor, Mooney and Howie started making noise about heading over to some club they liked.

"There are four floors!" Howie said excitedly. "And a different DJ on each floor. Who's in?"

"Sure," Breezy said. "Let me text Brittany to see if she's up for it."

Behind his back, Luca and Mooney exchanged a deeply long-suffering glance.

"I'm in," Vanderbilt announced. "Cheryl's in bed already anyway."

Cheryl was nine months pregnant and due pretty much any day, last Tom had heard, but he didn't say anything.

Hayes yawned widely. "Nah," he said. "I'm too old for that shit."

"Same," Tom said with some measure of relief.

Jax heaved a sigh and got to his feet. "Come on then, old man. Let's find a ride home."

"Aww, Jax," Mooney pouted. "Come on, bro. You gotta start enjoying what the city has to offer."

Jax winked, deliberately sleazy. "Who says I'm not? Never said *I* was going home. I'm just not going clubbing with you losers."

His words were both absolute truth and also deeply misleading. Whole new vistas opened up for Tom as to what they could get away with on the tacit understanding it wouldn't be terrible if someone noticed. Sure, the respect Hayes and Vanderbilt granted them now would vanish, but at this point, Tom could safely say it wasn't mutual.

They left the bar together and took a car down to Palo Alto. They sat in the darkness of the back seat, and if the driver saw they were holding hands, he said nothing. It still made Tom's heart race, but for entirely different reasons than it might have before.

Finally, finally, they reached Tom's apartment building, then the elevator, and finally the door.

"Alone at last," Jax said with a crooked smile. "I didn't dream earlier, did I?"

Tom wrapped his arms around Jax's waist and rested his chin over Jax's shoulder. With no hesitation, Jax melted into his hold and wrapped his own arms around Tom in return.

"God, I missed you," Jax told him.

Tom kissed the patch of skin behind Jax's ear. "I missed you too."

Then, he pushed Jax against the wall and slid down his body.

"Hey, hey, what?" Jax protested weakly. "You got the hat trick. I should be—"

"My hat trick, my choice of blow job." Tom unbuttoned and unzipped Jax's pants and rested his forehead against Jax's bare hip. He smelled of his expensive shower products and a little of the sweaty, gross locker room. That was what dating a hockey player meant. Lots of locker room stench. The familiarity comforted Tom.

It didn't take long to get Jax hard. And he remained gratifyingly vocal about everything, gasping and sighing and moaning when Tom so much as breathed on his cock. He knew he couldn't be very good at this as, all told, it was only the third time he'd given a blow job. But from the way Jax reacted, he felt like the sexiest person alive.

"God, Tom," Jax groaned when Tom took him down as far as he could (about halfway). "Just like that. Oh God, please."

Tom sucked and used his tongue. When it got to be too much for his jaw, he pulled off and used his hand. He kept the head in his mouth, drawing circles around the bottom with his tongue. Under his hands, Jax's hips shook.

"You can move if you want," Tom said, pulling off for a second.

Jax's hand clenched tight on his shoulder. "I can't—we can't—"

"If I hold you this way…" Tom squeezed his fist around the base of Jax's cock. Above him, Jax made a noise as if all the air had been punched out of his lungs.

"Yeah, yeah, okay."

It wasn't clean or elegant. Within moments, Tom began drooling, spit slicking down around his hand. He couldn't do much more than remain still, mouth open and tongue ready for Jax to push forward. He wasn't *giving* a blow job; he was letting Jax use his mouth. It felt filthy. It felt fantastic.

Distantly, Tom became aware he was hard and throbbing in his pants. His jaw ached, his knees ached, and spit wet his face and hand. Jax's rhythm had gone haywire, all fast, jerky motions.

"Yes," he gasped out. "Yes, yes, keep—Tom!"

He came on the stroke inward, shooting almost to the back of Tom's throat. Tom struggled to swallow, drops leaking out of the corners of his mouth.

When Jax pulled out, he licked up the rest.

Jax whimpered.

"What? I didn't want to get any on the sweater."

Tom rocked onto his heels, intending to get up slowly. He didn't expect to be dragged up by the armpits and then unceremoniously shoved toward the bedroom.

"Off," Jax ordered, tugging at the sweater.

"Careful!" Tom said. Jax had spent so much money on it. On him.

Jax glared at him. "Take your clothes off, Tom. I am going to wreck you, and if you're not naked in two minutes, I'll do it with you fully clothed."

Cheeks a dull red, Tom fumbled the buttons on his dress shirt, shaking a little. Jax wrapped them in his own hands for a second and then took over.

"Someday, I'll buy you a silk shirt."

That sounded impractical.

"Yeah, silk. I'm thinking mother-of-pearl buttons. They'd look so perfect with your skin tone." With Tom now naked, Jax pushed him down onto the bed.

"Why?"

"So every time"—Jax pressed a kiss to Tom's sternum—"you feel the fabric whisper over your skin, you'll remember"—another kiss to Tom's stomach—"it was me who gave it to you"—a kiss to the swell of Tom's cock—"me who made you feel good."

Tom managed a shaky inhale. "Oh."

"Uh-huh." Jax propped his chin on one of Tom's thighs. "Pass me the lube?"

When he pulled it out and tossed it onto the bed, Tom found Jax staring at him hungrily. "Your body...Tom, it's... I *just* came, and I want you so much."

Shivering a little at the earnest desire in Jax's tone, Tom said, "You once told me you didn't fuck hockey players. So, I thought you wouldn't want me."

Jax laughed. He grabbed the lube and slicked up his fingers. "I said that because before you, I didn't *know* any queer hockey players."

"Oh."

"But also—" Jax kissed Tom's hipbone. "I have a thing about guys who dress pretty and let me take care of them."

Tom laughed a little breathlessly. Jax had gotten his finger into him up to the first knuckle. "One out of two...one out of two isn't bad."

"Baby." Jax kissed the other hipbone. "You like the sweater?" He nodded to the soft, luxurious cream fabric on the floor. "That's only the start." He pushed his finger in farther and crooked it up.

Tom gasped, knees splaying wider.

"Thought about silk sheets for your massive bed, too," Jax continued, voice heated. "So I can watch the fabric slide over your naked body. But they're too slippery, and I know you like it when I hold you down and fuck you."

Tom could only whine in agreement.

"So, I'm gonna go cotton, maybe bamboo, something with an even higher thread count than you have now. But ties, we can definitely do silk ties. You can slip them through your fingers when you're doing interviews, remember who gave them to you."

Two fingers slid inside Tom now, pushing and prodding against his prostate. Jax wasn't so much fucking Tom with them as he was massaging, slowly and gently.

"And toiletries. Tom, there's a whole world out there."

How could anyone sound so smooth and seductive talking about toiletries of all things?

"I'm gonna get you a decent shampoo," Jax continued, "and some bubble bath, and then I'll sit you down in your massive bathtub and wash your hair for you."

That sounded…unbearably intimate.

Tom shivered all over.

"Mm, and there's lotions to think of as well. I could lay you out one night and rub down every inch of your skin till it's all soft and smooth."

"I…" Tom tried to protest.

"Hmm, what is it, baby?" Jax paused his fingers' assault.

"What would I be doing for you?"

Jax grinned. "Remember when you let me rim you till I was so turned on I nearly cried?"

"Yeah."

"That."

"Oh—" Tom didn't ever get to the "kay" part of the word. With no warning, Jax fit his mouth around the head of Tom's cock and sucked hard as he continued to massage Tom's prostate, and Tom lost the ability to form words.

He dropped his head fall back into the pillows and let his body just feel.

Pleasure unlike anything he'd ever done to himself, unlike anything Jax had done to him before, overtook him, direct and intense but unhurried. Instead, the prolonged assault on the most sensitive parts of him made him clench and squirm away, not because it felt bad but because it was so, so much.

Tom didn't know how to recognize the feelings rising in him, different from the usual friction, motion, and increasing tempo to build a crescendo. With

Jax not backing away from any of his pleasure centers, a long, solid wave rose from the soles of his feet through his knees and up into his belly, taking him higher and higher until he gasped for breath.

"Oh," he managed, and "yes," and "Jax, Jax," over and over.

And then Jax came to a full halt, fingers still inside Tom, mouth still around his cock.

The wave receded, leaving Tom at the shoreline, floundering. "Why—"

Jax winked at him and resumed sucking.

He did it twice more, took Tom higher and higher until nearly at the precipice of something unknown and terrifying, then stopped without letting him go all the way. The last time, Tom broke.

"Please," he begged. "Please, Jax, please let me, please, I need you, please—"

"Maybe," Jax said, his breath a whisper against Tom's overheated, oversensitized skin, "you'll even let me buy you something pretty in lace. For me."

Tom sobbed.

"Shh." Jax kissed the head of Tom's cock. "I've got you. You can let go now."

He started again, and this time, he moved his fingers just a bit faster, sucked just a bit harder, and the wave dragged Tom under.

He heard nothing but his pulse thundering in his ears, saw nothing but the black flicker behind his closed eyelids, felt nothing but Jax, always Jax. Then, his hips jackknifed off the bed, and he came so hard he blacked out for a moment.

When he was able to form words again, Jax had tugged the blankets over them both and wrapped himself around Tom.

Tom nuzzled into Jax's chest. "Thank you."

"For the orgasm?" Jax snickered.

"For taking care of me. And for giving me another chance."

With a hand in his hair, Jax pulled him up gently to look him in the eyes. "Hey, Tom? Thank you for *taking* a chance on me. I hope I'll get to take care of you for a long time."

Tom didn't have the words to tell Jax how that made him feel, but as he let his head rest against Jax again, he figured he would have time to find them.

# Epilogue

After a mixed start to the season with a solidly middling record for the first ten games followed by a few truly embarrassing losses (see: <u>Sea Lions lose 5–1 to Toronto Huskies</u>, <u>Sea Lions drop both LA games back-to-back</u>), the San Francisco Sea Lions have clawed their way back to place three in the Pacific Division standings. With Tom Crowler putting up a career year alongside ex-Magpie Jax Grant and new first-string D-pair Chris Calabrese and Luca Mazetti, the Sea Lions have a solid chance at the playoffs despite inconsistent performances by the lower lines. A shout-out also to their starting goaltender, Vladimir Dmitriyev, with a save rate of 0.916, making this a career year for him, too, if he keeps it up.

## Top comments:

seelionssaylions: Go Sea Lions! Always knew they could turn it around!

sealions4lyfe: That's my team! Vanderbilt, Grant, and Crowler are the best top line in hockey

(From "Pucks to Watch Out For: Playoff Teams for 2025," published to nhl.com on 02/12/2025)

Jax woke up with his ass on the floor.

He groaned and pulled Tom tighter on top of him so Tom's hip wouldn't end up on the linoleum. The movement woke Tom as well, and he made a distressed sound.

"When I said I would take care of you," Jax said, "I hope you know this isn't what I meant."

Tom huffed against him. It might have been a laugh; it might also have been Tom's perpetual inability to deal with mornings. That had been a delightful discovery. Given a morning off and someone who actually cared enough to alternate ice and heat packs on his hip, Tom was not a morning person.

"C'mon, babe. We should get up. Morning skate, remember?"

"Ugh."

It took some doing, but eventually, Tom managed to struggle upright, bleary-eyed and messy-haired.

Jax was definitely, definitely in love with him. Now was not the moment to tell Tom though. He would make it special, maybe after a candlelit dinner at a restaurant on the bay, maybe after Tom's next hat trick. He'd know when he found the right moment.

Waking up on the floor of his parents' trailer because the air mattress in the living room had deflated overnight was not the right moment.

"Jax? You awake, honey?"

Jax rubbed his eyes. "Yeah, Mom. We're up."

"Oh, good!" She popped her head in through the door. "You can have breakfast with the girls before school, then. I'm making waffles."

"Not sure Tom can eat those," Jax said, leaving out that he also didn't eat store-bought waffles, at least not during the season.

Mom clucked her tongue. "I'll have Dad whip up something gross and healthy for you two."

She'd been married to a cook for twenty-five years yet couldn't make anything not from a package, though she was handy otherwise. He followed her to the kitchen, still in his Sea Lions sweatpants, while Tom headed for the bathroom. When Jax had floated this visit, he didn't expect Tom to agree for a myriad of reasons, such as the duration of their relationship or his own preference for a hotel bed as opposed to the literal floor. But Tom had only stipulated not sleeping naked in Jax's parents' house.

It was a reasonable request.

This way, Jax got the pleasure of sitting at the breakfast table in his pajamas, the way he never had as a teenager, too busy with hockey games and working shifts at the diner. Maybe this was better, watching his sisters get ready for school when he didn't have to go himself.

With the water running in the bathroom, Jax took his opportunity. "So, what do you think of him?"

Rosa peered up from slathering her waffles in butter and syrup. "Tom?"

Lila, who had a knife neck-deep in a jar of Nutella, didn't bother looking at him. "We like him, so he's probably too good for you."

Jax heaved a sigh. "Should've taught you to fear me."

"You wish, asshole."

"Language," Dad said idly. Given he said worse things during every football game, no one paid him any mind.

"He seems…" Mom trailed off with a sigh. "He seems like you make him happy, and you seem like you love to make him happy. That about right?"

"Yup." Heat spread across Jax's neck. Something about moms, the way they looked straight through you.

She tousled his hair. "Good. Maybe if you finally get a place in San Francisco, we can come visit you two."

"I'm working on it." Jax had hired a realtor to find a house somewhere in the city, maybe near the park so they could be close to Phil and Breezy, and Tom could still go on those long walks he'd started. A place big enough for both of them and the dog Tom so clearly wanted. Once he found the right place, he'd start talking Tom into moving his nice, soft couch and big bed out of his soulless apartment and in with Jax.

Dad made his patented egg white scrambles with spinach and mushroom. They were mostly edible because he used so much butter, but Tom didn't say anything about it. And then, they had to leave already, first for morning skate and then for the game against the Minnesota Fury.

Everyone hugged them both at the door, which left Tom a little shell-shocked and quiet while Jax said his goodbyes.

Very seriously, Dad told them, "I hope you lose tonight. Love you, kiddo."

"Love you too, Dad. I hope we crush your team's dreams and spirits."

Dad tried to give him a noogie, but Jax was bigger and stronger and escaped scot-free, laughing.

They waved goodbye and got into the rental car. Jax still knew his way around St. Paul well enough they didn't need GPS, so it was only them and the crisp, cold Midwestern air.

"So?" Jax asked eventually.

"Hmm?"

"You okay? I know they can be a lot."

"They're great. I can't believe your dad roots against you."

"Oh." Jax rolled his eyes. "I think he's kidding about that? Mostly? It's hard to tell. I don't think he actually cares how my team does."

Tom hummed.

"What?"

"No, it's just…I never realized how different it could be. He loves you no matter whether you succeed."

Jax bit the inside of his cheek. He ran a policy of not commenting on all the horrifying things Tom said about his parents, letting Tom uncover the layers of misery on his own, one by one. Like the long walks, it was good for him, therapeutic or something. Jax could listen and maybe go a few rounds with a punching bag later.

"You ready for skating or should we stop for coffee first?" Jax asked.

"Nah, I'm ready. Remind me to stop in with the physio after though."

"Hip?"

"Yeah, only a little, but I figure…"

"Good call." Perhaps this was Jax's proudest moment in his ongoing mission to let Tom have nice things: All of his own accord, midway through January, Tom had gone to the team physical therapist in San Francisco and let her examine his hip. He'd even missed a game for the first time in three years, and by his own account, it was now much better. "Any thoughts on the other project?"

"Nope," Tom said cheerfully. "Still no clue who I am without hockey. I'll get there."

"I know you will."

"You can stop sending me links to random stuff you want to do though."

"I don't—"

"You do."

"Fine, fine. There's always the shelter."

"Yeah, but that's your thing."

"You still like it there."

Tom had been right when he said he wasn't much of a coach, but he was still a good captain, and the kids reacted well to him during games. When some of them, especially the quieter ones, came up to talk to him afterward, he always made time for them. Whenever Jax scheduled himself for the same time slots as Tom, he lost long minutes watching his boyfriend interact with the teenagers, listening to them with the same seriousness he brought to game tape analysis.

After the third time Jax got distracted, Mara snapped her fingers in his face to make him pay attention.

"Anyway, you'll be playing for years once I'm retired," Tom said. "I need to find something you don't want to do."

Jax tried not to grin too hard at the thought they'd still be together years from now. He failed. Chancing a glance over at Tom, he saw Tom smiling, too, so it was a win-win. Still, it had been a big couple of days, and there was only so much emotional conversation either of them could take, especially on game days. Time to change the subject.

"So, what do you think we'll get today? Trout trouble or Morris mayhem?"

Tom shook his head. "I never should have let Luca teach you about alliteration."

"Seriously, though, what do you think's going on? I swear Morris has missed more games than he's coached this month."

"It's only the twelfth. And Morris flew out with us. He won't just vanish. Besides, Phil came along for this one. He can usually make the best of it."

That didn't calm Jax's nerves about the whole situation.

Tom placed a comforting hand on his thigh. "If it's still this bad when we get home, I'll try calling the GM."

Jax smiled at him, aware the promise was a lot for someone as unwilling to rock the boat as Tom. It needed doing though. The coaching situation had only gotten odder as the season progressed, with Phil all but taking over the reins from Morris and Trout trying his level best to enforce his draconian methods as soon as they turned their backs. Phil remained on LTIR, so he should have been in California rehabbing his knee instead of flying halfway across the country. At least he'd stopped needing his crutches. He'd been allowed some light skating in a no-contact jersey at the start of February ten days ago, and now he joined them on the ice for most practices, correcting form and giving tips because the actual coaches were too busy one-upping one another to work with the team.

The season had taken a positive turn for the Sea Lions, but with practices such a drag, morale had started to flounder again after the high of a solid win streak following Tom's hat trick against Seattle.

Today was no exception. They started off well enough, a little keep-away, a fun start, Phil shouting encouragement to Luca when he went up against Vanderbilt, who was roughly twice his size. Then Trout started in on one of his routines, a particularly grueling down-low exercise which left Breezy wheezing and the remaining D-core barely upright. They all needed to conserve energy this late in the season, and the arena ice was scratched to shit. Hayes fell on his ass more than once, getting more and more angry as Trout mocked him.

Finally, Jax turned to Morris. "Aren't you going to do *anything*?"

"Huh?" Morris looked up from his cell phone. "Oh. Shit. Um." He glanced to Phil.

Phil made a gesture with his hand, a sort of circular motion with his pointer finger.

"Right. Around-the-world drill." Morris patted down his jacket, searching for his whistle.

"Christ, Ben, seriously?" Phil muttered.

Morris snapped, "I've got a few other things on my mind."

"When you're on the ice, you've gotta eat, sleep, breathe—"

"Oh, for fuck's sake, Phil, I'm not even a real hockey coach."

He said it just as the D-men finished a repetition of their drill. They gasped for air on the sidelines while Edwards, off-ice to grab a few extra sticks, had the forwards working through a similar deep breathing exercise. As soon as the words echoed around the rink, everyone came to a halt, not a single inhale to be heard.

A single puck scraped across the ice and hit the boards with a dull thunk. No one moved to follow it, everyone too busy staring at Morris.

"Well, shit," Phil said.

# Hockey Jargon

A glossary for the non-sports-fan reader. Use in casual conversation with sports fans at your own risk.

- 3-v-3—"Three versus three" or "three on three," a primarily offensive drill in which three players and a goaltender face off against the same amount of opposition. Also used during regular season overtime.

- AHL—American Hockey League, the league below the NHL. NHL teams have so-called "farm teams" in the AHL, where they send players they drafted but don't want on the season's starting roster for development. An AHL salary is over 50,000 per year. The (fictional) San Francisco Sea Lions AHL affiliate is the (fictional) San Diego Pups.

- All-Star Game—Every year, one player from each team deemed best by the NHL, as well as other players voted in by fans, compete in a just-for-fun tournament and a skills competition. Unlike in this series, in 2025, the All-Star Game was cancelled in favor of the Four Nations Tournament.

- Alternate/A—Part of team leadership. Each team has two or three alternate captains. The alternates' jerseys have an *A* sewn in the same spot as the captain's *C*.

- Arbitration—When a player's contract expires, in some cases their team retains the right to be a part of the negotiation. Frankly, if you are interested in learning about the difference between restricted and unrestricted free agent contracts, I have to assume you are either a lawyer or you have crossed the event horizon into true sports fandom, in which case you do not need this glossary. For our purposes: When the original team is part of the negotiation and disagrees with the player about salary, they can call in a third party to deliver an assessment. By all accounts it's an unpleasant process for the player, whose performance is put under the microscope.

- Around-the-world drill—A warm-up drill in which each player has a puck and tries to carry it all the way around the opposing goal while defenders try to knock them off the puck.

- Art Ross—The award for the most goals (not points) scored in a season.

- Assist—Points are awarded to players not only for goals but for the passes leading to a goal, called an assist. Or sometimes an "apple," but I could not force myself to write a human being saying that, despite having heard multiple players use the term.

- Back-to-back—When a team plays two games on two consecutive days. Generally seen as a disadvantage.

- Blue line—The blue lines separate the ice into three zones: offensive (i.e. closest to the opponent's goal), neutral, and defensive (i.e. closest to your team's goal). They help determine offsides: if a player from your team crosses the blue line before the puck with both skates, any attempt at a goal is considered offsides.

- Boarding—A minor penalty assigned when one player checks or pushes another into the boards violently.

- Breakaway—When a player has the puck and no one between him and the goal but the goaltender.

- Calder—The award for the best rookie (note that a rookie can be any age as long as it's their first NHL season).

- Captain/C—Each NHL team has a captain. While in some cases the captain is a veteran player chosen for the role due to leadership skills, often it's the team's most talented player, regardless of their social role or age, which explains why Tom Crowler is a captain despite having the leadership qualities of a frightened Pomeranian.

- Center—The forward who plays in the middle, typically a fast skater who sets up plays and operates more defensively than the wingers.

- Charging—A minor penalty assigned when one player checks another player with excessive force by jumping, building too much momentum, or checking from their blind side.

- Checking—Techniques used to put an opponent off the puck. These include both methods using the body (such as shoulder and hip checks), methods using the stick (such as sweep checking), as well as game-play strategies to regain control of the puck (such as a forecheck in the offensive zone when the players are near the opposing goal or a back-check in the defensive zone when the players are near their own goal). Cross-checking, which means hitting another player with the stick held in both hands, is a penalty. A check gone wrong can turn into boarding or charging.

- Chirp—A cute, friendly way to refer to trash talk.

- CHL—The Canadian Hockey League, the umbrella organization in charge of all Canadian Junior teams. The highest level, Major Juniors, comprises the QMJHL (Quebec Maritime Junior Hockey League), the OHL (Ontario Hockey League), and the WHL (Western Hockey League). The OHL and the WHL have teams in the United States as well as Canada. Someone should have told the OHL that specific geographic names are a bad idea in hockey. Players are drafted into the teams, including a limited number of overseas players. Multiple members of the Sea Lions were in the CHL, including Phil, Tom, Jax, Howie, Breezy, and Luca.

- Coach's challenge—The coach can challenge whether a goal should be allowed to stand (see goaltender interference). If unsuccessful, it counts as a penalty for the team.

- Conn Smythe—The award for the playoff MVP.

- Contract negotiations—Broadly, contracts have a few big talking points: length, salary, and restriction. For a good player in their prime, between five and eight years are the usual length. Older players and players with less renown sign for shorter periods. Salaries depend on the teams' cap space, a set amount of money the teams can spend on player's salaries, which rises with inflation. At time of writing, the highest awarded annual salary is 14 million, but it is likely to be eclipsed before this book is released. In terms of restriction, a contract decides whether or not a team can trade a player at will. Players generally want no-movement clauses and negotiate for them, but even when they have an NMC, they are sometimes asked to waive it when the team's situation demands it. They also often have shortlists of teams they would accept a trade to.

- CTE—Chronic traumatic encephalopathy is a brain condition that worsens over time and leads to dementia. It's caused by repeated head injuries. Definitive diagnosis is only possible after death. Studies on donor brains have revealed that hockey players have a high likelihood of being affected by CTE, which rises with each year of hockey played (though the sample sizes for studies are quite small). There are a number of measures in place to protect hockey athletes at every level of play, but head injuries continue to be very common despite the danger.

- Deke—To feint or fake the direction in which a player plans to take the puck in order to confuse defenders and the goaltender.

- Division—The NHL is separated into four divisions, the Atlantic and the Metropolitan, which make up the Eastern Conference, as well as the Central and the Pacific, which make up the Western Conference. San Francisco, which is in the Pacific division, plays the other Pacific teams four times per season, twice at home and twice away. They play the teams in the Central Division three or sometimes four times, and teams in the Atlantic conference twice. The conferences make geographical sense, but especially in the eastern one, geographical knowledge of major cities in North America is only occasionally helpful in figuring out which teams are in which division.

- Down-low—The area behind the goal.

- Draft—The ceremony in which new players are selected. Teams pick in order of their success in the previous season, with the best team going last. However, there is also a lottery which affects this order, meaning the order changes prior to draft, though the first few picks always go to non-playoff teams. Why do a lottery? Possibly to avoid a team purposely dropping to the bottom of the list to get the number one pick when it's clear they won't make the playoffs. Possibly to level the playing field between the bottom-ranked teams. Possibly because it's another big event the NHL can televise and make money with (though the NHL continues to have the worst ratings of any of the big four sports in the USA). Players must be eighteen on or before September fifteenth of that year to be draft eligible and cannot be older than twenty. Europeans can be twenty-one.

- Draft bust—A player who is drafted among the top prospects and fails to live up to his promise (according to sports media).

- ECHL—The league below the AHL. The letters no longer stand for anything. The ECHL also has affiliate AHL/NHL teams, so some ECHL players are drafted by the NHL and then sent down. But unlike the AHL and NHL, undrafted players can try out without being drafted. Salaries average between 525 dollars and 575 dollars per week. But back to that letter thing. You read right. It used to stand for East Coast Hockey League, but then the league expanded beyond the East Coast, and the name stopped making sense, so they just kept the letters but not the words they stand for. Do they know they're allowed to change abbreviations? Also, if the ECHL can decide the letters mean nothing, why doesn't the NHL do this to address their "National (actually, two nations are involved) Hockey League" issue?

- ELC—Entry-Level Contract. The first contract an NHL player under twenty-five can sign. Depending on the age of the player, it lasts up to three years, and the annual salary is capped at 950,000. To assuage this pauperism, players on an ELC can earn up to 3.5 million in bonuses per year. The contract also allows them to be sent down to the team's AHL affiliate at a lower salary or, if they choose to attend college or remain in a junior league after signing, "defer" for a year or two.

- Equalizer—A goal that ties the game.

- Expansion—Sometimes the NHL expands by adding a new team. To do this, there is an expansion draft in which players from other teams can be drafted. In real life, the most recent team added to the NHL was the Seattle Kraken in 2021. The Minor Penalties series takes place in a groundbreaking, fantastical alternate universe where absolutely everything is the same except that instead of Minnesota's team moving to San Jose in 1991, they moved to Seattle, and San Francisco got an expansion team in 2011.

- Face-off—The start of play in which the referee whistles and drops the puck between two opposing players, who attempt to gain control of it.

- Five-hole—The space between the goaltender's legs.

- Five-on-four—Refers to the number of players (minus goaltenders) on the ice. If the game is currently five-on-four, it means the team with four players has one player in the penalty box (see Power play and Penalty kill)

- Five-on-five—The standard play formation when no penalty has been called, consisting of three forwards and two defensemen on either side.

- Forward—The group term for all offensive players playing in a line of three (center plus left and right wingers). A team typically has four lines of forwards which rotate out in short shifts of usually under a minute. The expectation is for these players to generate more scoring chances and garner more points than defensemen, though they are also criticized if they don't contribute to defensive efforts.

- Game misconduct—When a player is forbidden from reentering the game after an infraction

- Gassed—Out of breath, exhausted

- Goal—I'm going to be honest. If you don't know what a goal is, I don't think I can help you. There are a few terms that define the goal more closely, like "top shelf" (describing the area of the net the puck hits) or "bar down" (meaning the puck hit the top bar of the goal and then fell into the net).

- Goaltender—Exactly what you think. This is the player wearing the most padding (understandably), as well as a full cage helmet, which is personalized with images they choose. Goaltenders (also sometimes called "tendys") have a reputation for being "odd human beings," which seems mean until you watch about 0.2 seconds of one of them speaking to a reporter.

- Goaltender interference—Sometimes when an opposing player stops a goaltender from blocking a shot by getting right up in their personal space, it counts as interference and the goal is deemed invalid. Sometimes when this happens, the goal stands. There is a rule governing when it should be allowed, but the phrasing is open enough to interpretation that many people get angry about this up to one hundred and ten times per year.

- Gordie Howe Hat Trick—A player getting a goal, an assist, and participating in a fight in the same game.

- Half-ice drill—A drill using only half the available ice.

- Hart—The award for the league MVP (taking only regular season games into account, not playoff games).

- Hat trick—Three goals in a game scored by one player. Shootout goals don't count. A natural hat trick is when no one else scores in between that player's goals.

- Holding—A minor penalty assigned when one player restrains another.

- Home Ice Advantage—In sports in general, playing at home is seen as an advantage because the crowd is on your side, and the setting is more familiar.

- Juniors—The leagues in which players aged sixteen to twenty (fifteen, if deemed exceptional) play prior to the NHL draft. Different leagues exist in different countries. Like the NHL, AHL, and ECHL, there are different tiers depending on quality of play. Unlike the NHL, these teams count as amateurs, though in Canada, players receive a stipend, while in the States, only expenses are covered.

- Keep-away—A game in which one side tries to keep the puck and the other tries to steal it.

- Lady Byng—The award given to the player showing the most sportsmanship or "gentlemanly conduct." The definition of the latter remains unclear.

- Losing an Edge—When a skate isn't sharp enough, causing the player to stumble or fall.

- (LT) IR—(Long Term) Injured Reserve. A player who is out, either short or long term, for injury recovery. Putting a player whose return is uncertain on Long Term Injured Reserve can be beneficial because that player's salary no longer counts toward the salary cap, meaning the team can bring in other players.

- Major penalty—Five minutes in the penalty box for the offending player (usually).

- Minor penalty—Two minutes in the penalty box for the offending player (usually). Minor penalties can become major, or even game misconducts, if the opponent was injured.

- NHL—National Hockey League, the highest professional men's hockey league. Despite the name, teams are situated both in the USA and Canada. (There was once an International Hockey League, which included many of the same locations consisting of minor league teams. The NHL already existed at that point. There is also a tier 2 Junior league called the North American Hockey League. All of its teams are in the USA. Furthermore, there exists a semiprofessional Ligue Nord-Américaine de Hockey, but it operates only in Quebec. None of these leagues appear to have considered choosing a name that either makes sense or at least doesn't include an inaccurate geographical reference.)

- Overtime—When a game ends in a tie, the game goes to overtime. During the regular season, an overtime period is five additional minutes played three-on-three until one team scores. If no one scores, they might take it to a shootout. During the playoffs, they play for twenty minutes at full strength. An overtime loss during the season gives the losing team one point in the standings.

- Peewee—One of the age ranges in Junior hockey from eleven to twelve. Other ones that sound less funny as a throwaway line in a romance novel include Mini Mites, Mites, Squirt, Bantam, and one more that I'd rather not put in print because it really hasn't aged well.

- Penalty Kill—One of the special teams with two units who switch into play after a penalty is called, replacing the regular five-on-five lines. When your team gets a penalty, one player is benched for two or five minutes, meaning the other team has more players on the ice. The penalty kill is tasked with defending against the other team's advantage. If the penalty passes with no goals scored, they have "killed" it. It's rare for a player to be on the first units of both penalty kill and power play to avoid overtaxing them. Usually, a player with strong offensive and defensive capabilities will be on the first unit of one special team and the second unit of the other.

- Period—A hockey game is split into three periods of twenty minutes each.

- Playoffs—The sixteen teams of the NHL that finish highest in the standings of the regular season go to the playoffs to compete for the Stanley Cup. In the first two rounds, teams face off against their own division (mostly, see Wildcard Spot for exceptions). In the third round, they play for the conference championship, for which there is also a big shiny trophy. Some teams believe it's bad luck to touch that if they want to go on and win the finals against the champion from the other conference. Each round of playoffs is won by the first team to reach four wins, so there are a maximum of seven games per round.

- Plus-Minus—A statistic measuring how many goals are scored by or against the team while a player is on the ice. A player with a plus-minus of plus 1 for a game could have been on the ice when one goal for his team was scored and off the ice when all the other goals were scored, or he could have been on the ice when four goals were scored by his team but three goals were scored against. Power play goals do not count toward a plus-minus. The relevance of this statistic in determining a player's quality is subject to some debate. If you want to know more about that, wait for book three.

- Points (Player) —As covered elsewhere, players get points for assists and goals which are counted together toward their stats for the season.

The best players in the league average above a point per game during the season. Sometimes a player's point production can vary between the season and the postseason because playoff games are more physical, and also because, at that point, they have already played eighty-two games of hockey (barring injury). Just for comparison, (American) football teams play seventeen games per season, and they only play once a week rather than three or four times.

- Points (Team) —Not to be confused with player points, a team also collects points. Two for each win, one for each overtime loss, zero for each regulation loss. The teams with the most points reach the playoffs.

- Power play—One of the special teams with two units who switch into play after a penalty is called, replacing the regular five-on-five lines. When the opposing team gets a penalty, your team goes on the power play. This means the other team has one player less on the ice, so your team has a greater chance at getting past the defense and scoring. The two power play units will contain the team's best offensive players, often including one unit of four forwards and one defenseman tasked with strategizing plays. Also called the PP because there aren't enough acronyms.

- Reverse drill—A drill in which players pass the puck behind themselves to avoid the defense or create a better scoring chance.

- Right/Left Wing—Forwards playing on either side of the center closer to the boards. Typically, the players playing the least amount of defense.

- Roughing—A minor penalty assigned when one player uses "unnecessarily rough play" that doesn't cross the boundary to a more serious penalty such as head contact or fighting.

- Salary Cap—The total amount a team can spend on the roster's salaries. This limits the contracts they can give players, meaning they might need to trade expensive contracts for cheaper ones to provide the team with everything it needs. In theory, because all teams have the same funds available for players, the playing field is leveled. In practice, different places in North America have very different tax laws, and there are a number of loopholes in the salary cap, including LTIR and contracts with bonus structures.

- Shootout—When a game remains tied after overtime, the game goes to a shootout. Three players from each team take a shot on goal, and the team to get more goals in wins. If they stay tied, they just keep going until one team scores and the other doesn't.

- Shortie—A shorthanded goal, meaning the team currently on the penalty kill with one less player on the ice scores.

- Shutout—When a goalie doesn't let in any goals during a game, thereby "shutting out" the opposition.

- Smaller ice—European characters in this and the subsequent books occasionally mention "smaller ice." International competitions and European leagues use a different size rink than the NHL because they measure things in meters and don't base every rink on the one the first game was played in in 1875. (What gives, Canada? You use the metric system—why not for your hockey rinks?) Because the international size is both generally larger and also has a different length to width ratio, adapting play can be difficult both for European players joining the NHL and for NHL players playing in international competitions.

- Stanley Cup—The trophy awarded for winning all four rounds of the playoffs. Seen by some as the hardest trophy to win in professional sports, which is an honorific I will not be touching because I don't know anything about any other trophy in any other sport. Once a team has won, they get a parade and a big party. Over the course of the following summer, each player gets a Cup Day, where the trophy comes to their hometown with them and they party some more and also do a variety of charitable things. Many babies, foodstuffs, and types of alcohol have been inside that cup, usually not simultaneously. The Cup travels with an official keeper, whose job is to make sure it doesn't get damaged, though he has not stopped players from taking it into the Atlantic Ocean or tucking it under their covers and going to bed with it.

- The "D"/D-man—Look. You know the abbreviation "the D" doesn't stand for "defense" in real life anymore. Hockey players know this. Hockey media knows this. But they have all practiced not laughing even a little bit when they say things like "splitting the D" or "D-zone coverage," and they're going to keep doing it. Defensemen work in pairs. Typically, a team has three pairs who rotate in shifts somewhat longer than the offensive shifts because defensemen are expected to cover less ice by spending more time in their team's defensive zone. Defensemen can play an offensive game in which they take more risks and generate more chances, or they can be more focused on defending their own goal.

- Unsportsmanlike conduct—A minor penalty assigned when a player behaves disrespectfully. What is disrespectful? Well, there are many very funny things I could write here and probably also a few poignant ones about the concept of respect, but I will restrain myself and instead say: imagine an NHL referee as a harried substitute teacher, sending one student to the principal's office for using a bad word while he says, "But Brad did it, too, and you didn't send *him*," to which the substitute has to respond, "That might be true, but I didn't hear Brad. I heard you."

- USHL—The highest Junior hockey league in the United States, also hosting the development program for the national team. Generally seen as not as good as the Canadian equivalent but catching up in recent years. Many players also go on to the NCAA and attend college as student athletes before joining the NHL.

- Vezina—The award for the best goaltender.

- Waivers—When a team wants to send a player down to the AHL but they don't have a two-way contract, meaning the team has to first offer the player to all other NHL teams before they can send him down. The other teams can then claim the player or waive their claim. If all teams waive their claim, the player is sent down. Imagine your boss demoting you, but first showing you off to all the other departments and asking if anyone else wants to take you on, even though you suck, before he docks your pay and makes you move to a different city.

- Wildcard Spot—To get a place in the playoffs, the top three teams of each division are automatically selected. After that, the remaining teams from the conferences are ranked by points during the season, and the two highest point totals get the remaining playoff places. So five teams from the Atlantic Division and three from the Metropolitan could get in.

S.B. BARNES

# Acknowledgements

Writing a book is a strange process because it's both something you work on alone and something you cannot possibly complete by yourself. So many people helped this book come into being, and I hope those of you interested in reading it enjoy the finished product.

First, thanks to Elizabetta for her tireless efforts to help me make this book the best it can be.

Thank you to NineStar Press for their interest in and work on this entire series.

Tuisku, I cannot thank you enough for agreeing to read a half-finished draft of a book in a genre you had no experience in and then getting so invested you watched me live-write the rest and volunteered yourself as cover artist! Your input and enthusiasm kept me motivated more than you probably know, and your feedback is always thoughtful and helpful!

Jui, thank you for taking a look to help me decide on whether or not this counts as slow burn (I'm still not sure, but talking to you helped).

Michelle, thank you for staying friends with me even though I got unfortunately fixated on hockey, and thank you for asking, "But will this book have an Italian in it?" Thank you even more for saying, "No, I mean a *Canadian* Italian" after I told you about Luca.

Anina, Sabine, Nandita, and Toni, thank you for being supportive of my weird side gig and letting me talk about it so much, and also thank you for Wednesday dinners. They've been a high point in my week.

Fabi, on the off chance you see this, thank you for sticking with me through all the ups and downs of the last year and for helping me carve out the time and space to write.

Jamie, you will never see this, but thank you for developing a vested interest in examining carrot sticks for a whole half hour when I started this manuscript—I really needed that time!

Finally, if you picked this book up either as an ARC or just in general, thank you for taking a chance on it! Less than a year before I wrote it, I knew nothing about hockey or hockey romances. Then my life took a few weird turns, and I spent a month and a half in 2024 feverishly following the playoffs while staying up half the night with my infant son (hockey games happen between about midnight and six AM where I live). In many ways, I miss not caring. We live in a time when it's hard to be a fan of men's professional hockey for a lot of reasons, and more than one of those reasons spilled over into the writing of this series. But care I do, so much so that I wrote four books about it. I hope you enjoyed your time with the San Francisco Sea Lions, and I hope you're interested in hearing more from them!

(P.S.: Apologies to St. Louis, I'm sure it's wonderful there!)

# About the author

S. B. Barnes attended college in the Hudson Valley, studying English Language and Literature and Anthropology (although unlike her characters, her time there was not interrupted by crime-solving). She grew up split between the USA and Germany, attending university in both countries before eventually settling in Germany. Today, she works as a teacher and lives with her husband, son, and two cats. Fiction has always been one of her greatest loves, as a reader, as a teacher, and as a writer, and she hopes you enjoy reading her work as much as she enjoys creating it.

## Email

sbbarnesauthor@gmail.com

## Website

www.sbbarnes.com

## Instagram

www.instagram.com/s.b.barnes

## Tumblr

www.tumblr.com/sbbarnes

## Bluesky

@sbbarnes.bsky.social

# Threads

@s.b.barnes

# Also by S.B. Barnes

**A Hudson Valley Murder Mystery Series**
*Heart First*
*Second Chance*

# Coming Soon

## Two for Boarding

Minor Penalties, Book Two

If there was one thing about professional sports Ben would never get used to, it was the noise.

The editor Ben had worked with in Wisconsin, before he took the job as head coach, had called Ben a shut-in. He'd vehemently denied the accusation—he had no problem getting out of the house and talking to people when work demanded it. Ben even sometimes enjoyed it. But his previous jobs mostly involved doing interviews in coffee shops or, if they demanded subterfuge, posing as a patient in a hospital or a customer looking to buy large amounts of produce from agricultural businesses.

None of that had prepared him for how an NHL hockey rink sounded on game night.

There was the blaring noise over the loudspeakers, shitty music for warm-ups and intermission. There was the constant swish and scrape of skates. There was the never-ending dull roar of the crowd. There was the nonstop babble on the bench—players and staff discussing lines and plays and watching video footage of events that had occurred seconds previously—a din Ben was somehow supposed to speak loudly enough over to convey when line changes ought to occur, something he remained unclear on even after ten games. And then there was Ben's personal nemesis, the thirty-two slightly different goal horns, one for each team in the league, which combined poorly with obnoxious excerpts from obnoxious songs. It had taken him a month to stop flinching every time the home team scored.

He would never understand why the team needed music in the locker room as well. Surely five minutes of peace and quiet would do a man good. Had he enjoyed the constant noise during the one semester he'd played intramural college hockey? Ben couldn't remember. He'd only joined the team because his roommate played, and Ben had a crush on him that he was otherwise ill-equipped to handle. His parents had been thrilled by his rare interest in a traditionally masculine pastime. But once he'd managed to score mutual locker room blowjobs, the shine of the sport had worn off, and Ben had happily retired from his hockey career. Even at nineteen, the constant travel, smelly gear, and loud music hadn't been for him.

Phil Easton, on the other hand, eschewed such concerns. When the second intermission of the San Francisco Sea Lions' game against the St. Louis Arches started, he immediately began blasting his playlist over the locker-room Bluetooth speakers. At thirty-four, Easton ranked as the oldest player on the team. The playlist, entitled "Gettin' Pumped," was composed entirely of songs that had been popular during Ben's college years, which meant Easton had been a teenager.

Sometimes, it was just so very hard to respect these people.

Dmitriyev, the starting goalie, ducked into the supply closet for almost the entirety of the intermission, which proved Ben's point. Unfortunately, he'd been around hockey players long enough to have learned the one person on the team you didn't want to have something in common with was the goalie.

At least they were winning tonight, which meant Ben wasn't screwing them over too heavily by being here. Of all the things currently bothering him about this job, the responsibility topped the list as the worst. The team actually listened to him and thought he was doing his best to get them to the playoffs. To be fair, he did listen and tried his best. But how on earth would his best suffice when his credentials comprised an alias, a fake CV, and a made-up letter of recommendation he'd half bribed and half cajoled his college hockey coach into providing? If the Sea Lions got to the playoffs, it would be by virtue of their own talents.

Easton shouted something loud and enthused from his position on the bench. Looking up at him, Ben couldn't help but notice his skintight undergarments clinging to his arms, even with the goofy external skeleton of his chest protector. Add in his tall and lean frame, and if Ben had been in any other venue full of half-dressed, sweaty guys, he knew who he'd be buying a drink, questionable taste in music aside. Sadly, he was in a hockey rink, and he had work to do.

On the other side of the room, Easton hopped down off the bench. He winced as he landed, and sitting next to Ben, Coach Trout's whole body went stiff.

"Easton!" he barked. "That the knee?"

"I'm fine, coach," Easton said.

"You sure?"

"Yep."

The team re-dressed and headed onto the ice for the third period soon after, leaving the locker room blessedly silent for a brief minute before Ben had to go out again and watch more hockey.

"You really think he's fine?" he asked.

Trout snorted. "Fat chance."

Ben raised an eyebrow.

"You know how these young guys are," Trout said. "They keep pushing till they lose it all."

No part of the sentences Trout had just uttered sounded anything like Phil Easton. For one, though younger than both Ben and Trout (an easy feat on a hockey team) Phil hardly counted as young, as evidenced by his taste in music. For another, he was anything but reckless. He saw the physical therapist on staff regularly for his knee, he did a lot of stretching, and Ben had seen the schedule he kept to for weight training. The rigor of Phil's routine outpaced many of the younger team members, solely to keep the muscles in his quads strong enough to stabilize his knee.

All of this impressed Ben, both the dedication and the resulting quads. The physique hockey built was unfortunately exactly Ben's type. If only the sport and the cultures surrounding it weren't mired in relentless homophobia.

But Ben said none of that. Instead, he said, "You'd think they'd listen to us."

Trout snorted again. He clapped Ben on the shoulder as they headed out to the rink.

Progress at last. Trout was a hard nut to crack, mostly because the primary characteristics he displayed on a day-to-day basis (misanthropy and mistrust of everyone under the age of forty) didn't invite friendly overtures. Probably, he had been hoping for the job Ben ended up getting, though he would have been at least as bad at being head coach as he was at being defensive coach. Trout had played a few seasons in the nineties but retired early after a rotator cuff injury, and he appeared to miss the slower pace and higher aggression of his playing career. Ben had invested two months of research into the game, and if he could grasp the concept "speed and finesse good, breaking skulls bad," surely it shouldn't be too much for an actual professional coach. However, Trout's solution to not understanding why skating skills and deft puck handling were more important these days was to work the D-core till they cried every time he got the chance, leading to constant exhaustion and, in Easton's case, chronic knee pain. No GM in their right mind would hire him on as head coach.

Then again, the Sea Lions' GM, Martin Pulvermacher, had hired Ben to solve his coaching problem and had handwaved his shoddy credentials to the press, so sanity had nothing to do with his staffing choices.

Ben had been trying to get Trout to trust him for three months now. Bonding over Trout's lack of respect for his charges counted as progress.

On the ice, a fight broke out. Ben suppressed a groan. Why were hockey games like this? It was Crowler, too, the team captain. He *never* fought. Watching his wildly flailing arms, Ben figured he had good reason to avoid it. "What the—"

"Oh, shit," Edwards, the offensive coach, hissed, as Jaxon Grant and another Arches player joined in.

Easton barreled into the fray. He succeeded in separating Crowler from the man he'd been trying, and failing, to hit. But within seconds, he crashed to the frozen ground, his leg angled all wrong, and when he tried to stand up, it gave way under him.

Ben winced.

At the mouth of the tunnel, Crowler and Grant handed Easton off to Trout, who supported him toward the trainers to evaluate the injury. Ben doubted the news would be good.

He gave them a few minutes, then reshuffled the lines on the ice so someone would be doing Easton's job. When the game resumed play, he followed the others down the tunnel.

Easton sat, propped up on an examination chair, his bare leg stretched out in front of him in a position that made his quads even more impressive. Unfortunately, his wincing ruined the whole tableau.

"Verdict?" Ben asked Trout under his breath.

"ACL," Trout said, not bothering to lower his voice. "Already strained once three years ago. Not sure how bad it is. It's too swollen to tell, but he's not playing the rest of this trip."

Easton glared daggers at Trout, and rightly so. He sounded unbearably smug.

"Guess we'll have to call someone up," Ben said.

"Mm." Trout took his phone out of his pocket. "Lemme check the roster."

In the instant before he pulled out the AHL team roster, Ben caught sight of the page Trout had been on before. Ben didn't know the URL, but he had a distinct feeling he'd only be opening it in an incognito tab when he looked it up later.

It was a shame Easton had gotten hurt, but at least Ben had finally made some progress.

www.ingramcontent.com/pod-product-compliance
Lightning Source LLC
Chambersburg PA
CBHW020650030726
47498CB00002B/441